'Officially a huge fan of Phoebe Luckhurst!' Lucy Vine,
bestselling author of *Hot Mess*

'Loved the concept and characters . . . it's very funny'
Sarra Manning, author of *Rescue Me*

'Beautifully written, warm and fun with a dose of early
noughties nostalgia' Laura Kay, author of *The Split*

'I blasted through this book as it was just so much fun! It made
me laugh out loud many a time and there needs to be more
books in the world that make you smile!' Reader Review *****

'Fresh, funny and with a mischievous edge, *The Lock In* is the
best romcom I've read in ages' Reader Review *****

'A fantastic, hilarious book which brought a real sense of
nostalgia whilst being bang up to date' Reader Review *****

'I honestly cannot recommend this book enough! With
fantastic characters, brilliant pace and a unique plot that will
keep you laughing right up until that final line, this is a must
read debut!' Reader Review *****

'I would recommend this book to anyone wanting to read
a fun romantic comedy that will put a smile on your face!'
Reader Review *****

ABOUT THE AUTHOR

Phoebe Luckhurst was born in London and brought up in Glas-
gow. She is the Features Editor of the *Evening Standard* and
appears regularly on their podcast, *The Leader*. She has written for
the *Guardian*, *Sunday Times Style*, *ELLE*, *ES Magazine*, *Grazia*, the
Telegraph and *Vogue*. She has had the theme tune to *The OC* stuck
in her head since 2003 and once almost spent her student loan
on a micro-pig. She no longer shops online when drunk.

The Lock In

PHOEBE LUCKHURST

PENGUIN BOOKS

PENGUIN BOOKS

UK | USA | Canada | Ireland | Australia
India | New Zealand | South Africa

Penguin Books is part of the Penguin Random House group of companies
whose addresses can be found at global.penguinrandomhouse.com

First published by Michael Joseph, 2021
Published in Penguin Books 2022
001

Typeset by Jouve (UK), Milton Keynes
Printed and bound in Great Britain by Clays Ltd, Elcograf S.p.A.

The authorized representative in the EEA is Penguin Random House Ireland,
Morrison Chambers, 32 Nassau Street, Dublin D02 YH68

A CIP catalogue record for this book is available from the British Library

ISBN: 978-1-405-94952-1

www.greenpenguin.co.uk

To Samuel

Our story will always be my favourite
house-sharing anecdote

1. Ellen

Ellen was a bit rusty on what their tenancy agreement said about flooding the entire ground floor of their house. But she suspected that Elias, the balding, barrel-chested sociopath who owned their property in Lewisham, would have prepared for the eventuality. This would most likely involve damages being pillaged from their security deposit. The prospect of explaining the flooding to him was about as appealing as walking into moving traffic.

There was never any arguing with Elias. True, Ellen had never known a sympathetic London landlord, but Elias was a tyrant. He lacked any empathy or humanity, and overreacted at the slightest provocation. His emails were always abrasive and usually written predominantly in caps lock. Last month, when Ellen's housemate Alexa emailed to ask whether there was a mop in the house, he responded by calling her a 'FREELOADING C**T'. Then there was the Friday evening before a bank holiday weekend, when the dodgy flush had broken on their only loo. When they asked for Elias's help with a handyman he baulked at paying the higher call-out fee and suggested they 'flush it with a bucket until Tuesday'.

He also had a habit of letting himself in without warning, which was, Ellen was fairly sure, a violation of the terms of their lease. They'd hear the grind of his keys in the door and, quick as a flash, assemble in her room (which was technically the living room) for a crisis meeting to determine the party line on when they'd last hoovered the stairs. Elias always found something to complain about, be it the state of the lawn or a lingering smell in the kitchen. (He didn't 'like' Chinese food. On his last visit his eyes were narrowed and searching, as if expecting to find a chow mein sequestered away in a cupboard.) He once called – called! – to warn them that if they didn't polish the kitchen surfaces once a month he'd have 'their bollocks in a vice'. In person, he often eyeballed the docile Jack when he made threats (especially ones about bollocks), fingering his keys. There were two key rings on the chain – a blue bottle opener bearing the name of a casino, and a small plastic busty pin-up girl in a *Baywatch*-red swimsuit.

Ellen had lived at 49 Rokeby Close for three years now, which, she occasionally noted sadly, meant she'd known Elias longer than her longest relationship had lasted.

The three of them did not know what Elias had done to afford this roomy, if rather shabby, house on a nice road in New Cross, south-east London, not to mention his three other properties in the surrounding area. He had something of the used-car salesman about him – it was the brown slip-on shoes and the shiny grey suits, Alexa had once said authoritatively. Google conjured nothing. Sometimes, Elias would bring his lacquered wife, Cynthia, with him on impromptu house inspections and she would stand, wordlessly, drumming her blue shellacked nails along the kitchen counter. Or sit at the MDF table with the wobbly leg, seemingly not listening as he complained that the grass hadn't been mown this spring (the grass was a real fixation; Ellen would never have pegged him for a gardener). On one visit, Cynthia put her iPhone on the table. When the screen lit up Ellen noticed that the background was a picture of a man in Speedos emerging from the sea, Bond-style. The man was not Elias. Cynthia never said a word to any of them, but she had once forwarded them all an email from a community group calling for a boycott of a local primary school which had been teaching its pupils about LGBTQ+ relationships. Ellen had shared the email on Instagram (#tfw your landlord is a homophobe??). Alexa had sent a curt response requesting that Cynthia refrain from sending them 'emails of this nature' in future, Jack and Ellen sitting beside her and nodding wordlessly while she composed the message. Cynthia had replied a few days later, cc'ing them all, stating that while they lived 'under her roof', she would send them whatever emails she wished.

Ellen had woken at 8 a.m. on that April Saturday with the heart-thudding start of a white-wine hangover. For a brief but terrifying moment, her pulse still racing, she barely recognized her own bedroom, until she realized that this was because she had settled – whenever that was – the wrong way around in her bed. Her feet were resting on her pillow and she was, she swiftly ascertained, still wearing her work clothes: a Breton T-shirt under a denim dungaree dress, tights and her left ankle boot. The right one stood smartly in the middle of her bedroom floor, as if waiting to be recommissioned.

Ellen swivelled round so that her head was on the pillow, noting grimly that when she did so her brain felt like it was bouncing off the inside of her skull. Panting slightly, she manoeuvred the left boot off with her right foot, to expose a big toe that waggled from the end of her holey tights. She exhaled deeply as she heard the boot land on the floor, and lay still again.

As she stared at the ceiling, eyes gummy with slept-in mascara, she became aware of a roll-call of further physical complaints. Her mouth was sour, and heartburn roared in her throat. Her muscles were sore, and she had a real bruiser of a headache: a dull, thudding twinge burrowing deep into her skull. Sitting up very slowly and supporting herself gingerly on her elbows, she took a swig from the glass of water next to her bed, which turned out to be a tepid yet potent vodka tonic. Gagging, she spat the liquid back into the glass and wiped her mouth with her hand. She rubbed one eye with a balled fist, and struggled to drag a few of the relevant details from her dehydrated brain. She could remember getting the bus home from work drinks and – ah yes – getting off a stop early to go to the corner shop for a 35cl bottle of vodka. Beside the bed, her laptop lay on the floor, its shell half closed, as if cowering in fear. She edged the lid open with her exposed big toe and jabbed at the trackpad. The screen lit up. It was paused on a YouTube tap-dancing tutorial.

She lay back on the mattress. Her duvet was slumped against the wall alongside her bed, the old clothes that doubled as pyjamas tangled inside. Sighing, she yanked at the pink tracksuit bottoms, her worn grey T-shirt and a pair of odd socks coming with them. Wincing as a bolt of pain coursed through her left temple, she wriggled out of yesterday's work clothes, tossed them off the end of the bed after the boot, and put the pyjamas on. They could definitely do with a wash. As could her hair: its long, dark brown lengths hung in greasy sections.

She started again: her things! She must have had things. Phone? It wasn't on the bedside table, and Ellen was about to panic until she realized it was, in fact, on the floor beside the bed, lying face down but – yes! – completely intact. She jabbed at the side button and the screen lit up: a string of WhatsApps from Kayleigh; an email from a fast-fashion e-tailer whose website she'd sworn never to visit again, advertising a limited-time 'up to 75 per cent off' sale; three responses to her Instagram Story (oh God). She opened the phone's front-facing camera and squinted into it. Mascara crumbled along her eyelids and there was a pustule of a spot erupting on her chin. She pocketed the phone and took another deep sigh.

Water was the answer. Well, it had been about nine hours ago, but better late than never. Using both hands to launch herself from her mattress, she stood up and plotted her route across the disarray of her bedroom. She took a wobbly step, and then – gaining in confidence – another, until she made it to the bedroom door. Ellen opened it and peered into the hallway, testing the house for signs of Alexa or Jack. All was still. Her keys were lying on the first step of the staircase. She padded down the hall, the ache of Friday night in her bones, and walked into the open-plan kitchen and dining room, then stopped suddenly when it dawned on her that her socks were being lapped by a tide of water.

Its source was easily locatable: water was cascading from the cupboard under the sink, making the cheap plastic doors flap wildly. She stood there for a minute, mesmerized by the ebb and flow of the shallow lagoon, before her brain clicked into gear.

'Fuck,' Ellen breathed. The panic started to rise like the

tide of heartburn. It hadn't been like this when she'd got home. It couldn't have been. Unless she'd missed it? Or . . . could she have somehow done this? How could she? She'd only made a vodka tonic. Ellen moved tentatively to the sink, as though the whole thing might blow at any second, her socks now squelching at every step. The tap wasn't open: the water was definitely coming from underneath the sink. She crouched in front of the flapping cupboard doors, then recoiled when one almost banged her on the nose.

She stood up again.

'Fuck fuck fuck fuck fuck,' she moaned. Her voice was higher and more desperate now.

There must be a mains tap somewhere, which would turn off the water at its source, a big switch that would pause the cascade. She crouched closer again in search of one, but all she could discern was the usual tangle of pipes, and a sodden scouring pad at the bottom of the cupboard. She flinched and leaped back as the sink made a low, juddering moan.

A light-bulb moment: the attic. This was where they had unearthed the fuse box, eventually, during a sudden and disorientating blackout. Maybe the switch she needed was there too. Startled by her own quick wit and decisiveness, Ellen turned on her soggy heels, made for the stairs and started running up them, two steps at a time, using the banister to yank herself up.

She paused on the first-floor landing. Jack and Alexa's bedrooms were on the left. The only bathroom was dead ahead of her. Then there was another staircase that twisted back upon itself and ended in the loft. Ellen ran up the uncarpeted staircase into the attic, taking huge gulps of breath. She yanked the door open and took in the scene. Before she could stop herself, she screamed. About a metre or so from the doorway lay a huge, very dead mouse, lying on its back with its paws pointing straight up. She steadied herself and breathed deeply, placing her hand on her chest to slow her hurtling heartbeat, trying to banish the blackness that was seeping into the corner of her eyes.

It was warm in there, and smelled faintly of wood chips and school music cupboards. As her pulse slowed, she peered cautiously into the attic's chaos. She'd only been up here once, and it still had all the ambience of a pound shop on the Old Kent Road: packed to the eaves with plastic crates of DVDs, warped cardboard boxes full of cables, half-full litre bottles of white spirit, and broken dining-room chairs. In one corner, there was an open suitcase of BB guns and next to it a teetering pile of *The Guinness Book of Records*, most of them from the 1990s. She couldn't see anything that might be the mains water switch.

Heart still galloping, Ellen heard a bedroom door open on the landing below, followed by tentative footsteps on the staircase. From the gait, she guessed – correctly, as it turned out – that it was Jack, and rolled her eyes in spite of herself. Jack was not the man you'd pick first in a crisis. Her housemate was about six foot tall and very lanky, with a baby-face and dark hair that was slightly too long. He had the permanent air of an overladen man boarding a train just before it leaves the station and trying to untangle himself from his luggage, carrier bags swinging from every limb. He worked in customer service for a vegetable delivery box start-up, Green Genie, which meant he had access to a bounty of wonky carrots and misshapen strawberries.

Occasionally, he would make them extravagant smoothies that always ended up tasting overwhelmingly of grit.

The footsteps had stopped.

'Hello?' Jack called hesitantly, from below. 'Ellen?'

'I'm up here!'

He didn't move.

She pressed her lips together and resisted the urge to snap. 'Jack, can you come here a second?' she said, civilly. An afterthought. 'Please?'

She heard his footsteps on the stairs again, slow and deliberate. He appeared at last, wearing a pair of blue tracksuit bottoms and a Green Genie T-shirt. The logo was a dancing carrot. He paused on the penultimate stair, watching her warily.

'Sorry, Jack. I didn't mean to wake you. But –'

'You screamed,' he interrupted. When he saw the mouse his eyes widened.

'Yes, sorry, the mouse gave me a fright.' She pointed stupidly at its corpse.

Jack leaned back slightly.

'Sorry – look, ignore the mouse, that's not the real problem. I'm here because of the water – downstairs, the sink – there's water all over the kitchen.' Jack still looked half asleep, and she resisted gripping him by the shoulders. 'Jack. Do you know how we turn the water off?' With a sudden lurch, last night's (cheap) white wine started roaring in her ears. 'It's flooding. Downstairs!'

That did the trick.

'Shit.' He swallowed and frowned. 'Um.'

'I thought maybe the water box might be up here. With the fuse box . . . ?' She paused, hoping that Jack would reveal himself – against type – to be the practical sort. 'Do you have any idea?'

Jack looked stricken. 'No, I don't know how we turn anything off,' he gulped. After a beat, he added, 'Sorry.'

She clenched her left fist hard, and turned back to the chaos of the attic.

'OK, in that case can you just help me look, please? Any box that might . . . control the water.'

'Mm-hmm.' Jack was slowly revving into action.

The two of them stepped over the threshold, past the mouse, with Jack's eyes lingering a second on its rigid body.

'Right. I'll take this side, you take that one.' Ellen shoved Jack gently towards a tangle of golf clubs. He crouched down to get a better look at them. '*Jack!*'

'Sorry, yes! Flooding.' He climbed over the golf clubs and started hunting more purposefully.

The box would be set into a wall, she thought wildly, casting around her own patch. In the corner was a lawn chair, on which rested a half-deflated pool float in the shape of a slice of pizza, and a decommissioned Slush Puppie machine. A sheaf of broken picture frames leaned against the wall. And there was the fuse box, above the frames. Hopefully, the two would be near each other? She stepped over the thicket of junk, clutching the wall for balance, while scanning its surface for another box that might control the water. In spite of the fairly wide skylight set into the ceiling, the chaos created a gloomy pall. She couldn't see anything except the fuse box. Frustration rising like bile, Ellen leaned backwards and called out to Jack.

'Have you found anything yet?' she asked sharply.

Jack was still standing near the golf clubs. 'He's got a SEGA up here,' he said, with some envy, pointing at a grey plastic shell in another corner of the attic.

'Jack!'

Catching her tone, his face dropped, and then – was that a light-bulb moment of his own she was witnessing? – he spoke solemnly. 'We should go and get Alexa.'

Besides being Ellen's best friend of almost a decade, Alexa – bright and considerate, with shoulder-length blonde hair that fell just so – was also the de facto leader of the house. She had three younger siblings, four dogs and three cats, not to mention nearly twenty years' experience handling two parents who could not be in the same room together. Consequently, she was good in a crisis.

'Yes, we should.' Alexa would know what to do. She would also, effortlessly, take charge, relieving Ellen of the burden of doing so. 'I'm going to go get her.' Ellen negotiated her way through the obstacle course of boxes again. 'I'll be two seconds. While I'm down there, can you have a look for the water box, please? It must be here somewhere,' she added, uncertainly.

As Ellen hurtled down the stairs, she recalled an occasion when she had watched with fascination as Jack, slowly and methodically, devoured an entire 300ml tub of crème fraîche after dinner. When she asked him why he'd eaten it, he looked nonplussed and said he'd thought it was a yoghurt. Still, perhaps he'd unearth the right box by mistake, Ellen thought, like that theory about a witless monkey with a typewriter eventually writing the complete works of Shakespeare.

Feeling the tingle of adrenaline in her limbs, Ellen

rapped loudly and insistently on Alexa's door. Alexa, like most people who didn't come home and make themselves a vodka tonic nightcap, probably wouldn't mind being woken up. Ellen didn't think she'd gone out last night – and 8.16 a.m. was fairly late for Alexa. This different approach to things like lie-ins (see also: tidying up) was probably why Alexa was a civil servant and Ellen worked in communications for a CBD tampon company.

There was no answer on her first go. Ellen rapped again, even more insistently. She leaned her head forward, listening for sounds of movement. On the third try, she heard the murmur of voices. Plural?! Last night's white wine quickened her pulse again. She noticed that she was now holding her breath.

'Lex?' she said, cautiously.

Another murmur, and a gruff laugh. Ellen heard the bed creak and footsteps padding across the floor. Alexa opened the door and leaned on the door frame, one slim thigh snaked around the other. Ellen reeled slightly at the sight of this grungy Alexa, in checked pyjama shorts and an unfamiliar baggy black T-shirt. In the doorway, she seemed tiny and Ellen, who was about four inches taller, felt like a hulking giantess. Kohl still ringed Alexa's big blue eyes, and she had a black, chalky stripe down her right cheek. Still, her hair was perfect.

'Hey,' Alexa smiled. She looked sleepy and a little sheepish. 'What's up? I heard someone scream.'

In spite of the urgency of what was going on in the kitchen, Ellen smirked and cocked one eyebrow meaningfully. She couldn't see much, but she could hear the duvet rustling, and the slight murmur of the mattress as someone rolled over. Alexa flashed a glance back into the room and mouthed, 'I'll tell you later.' She looked pleased. Ellen was about to say something, but Alexa pre-empted her. 'What's happened?' she asked again.

Ellen rearranged her face, conscious that, by the grave injustices of sod's law, Elias was probably on his way over for an unauthorized house inspection. She exhaled heavily.

'Sorry, I screamed because I saw a dead mouse – but that's not the major problem –' Ellen placed her fingers on her aching temples. 'The major problem is that the sink in the kitchen has gone mental, and there's water everywhere – and I don't know how to switch it off –' She stared at Alexa, helplessly.

Alexa's eyes widened. 'Wait, what?'

'I don't know what's happened – it wasn't like that when I got in last night – whenever the fuck that was.' A shame-faced grimace. 'Anyway, I was looking for the thing to turn off the water at the mains, and I thought it might be near the fuse box?'

'The stopcock,' Alexa said, authoritatively.

Ellen blinked at this unfamiliar word.

'It's usually under the sink,' Alexa added, with confidence.

'Oh, OK.' She felt slightly reassured. 'Are you sure? I don't know. I thought it might be in the attic.' There was an undignified whine in her voice.

'I doubt it,' Alexa said, briskly. Ellen frowned at this slight but before she could say anything, Alexa had shifted into action mode. 'OK, I'm coming – let me just grab a jumper . . .' Alexa disappeared, and Ellen resisted the urge to peer into her room. Seconds later, she reappeared, pulling her arms through a worn grey zip-up hoodie. 'OK,' she said, calmly. 'Why don't I go look at the kitchen, and you go get Jack from the attic so we can start mopping all the water up?'

Ellen sighed with relief. She had known Alexa would take over. 'Thanks,' she said, rubbing her eye with the base of her palm. 'I'm so hungover,' she added, quietly.

Alexa gave her a complicit look.

Ellen managed another smirk. 'Right, I'll go back upstairs. Jack's rootling around up there and probably shouldn't be left unattended.'

'OK. I'll see you in a minute.'

Her panic quelled, Ellen trotted back up the stairs to the attic, while Alexa descended to the kitchen. Jack was in the middle of the room, leaning over the rubble of an upended Perspex box that contained DVDs and the SEGA. He appeared to be enthralled. Ellen joined him, observing that the collection included the complete boxset of *Sex and the City*. Elias was evidently a man of diverse interests.

'Hi, Jack –' Ellen started.

He looked up sharply. 'Sorry,' he interrupted, slightly startled, putting the DVD down. 'I just stopped for a second.' He added, quickly, 'But I promise I was looking.'

Ellen gave him a hard stare.

He winced.

Despite being fairly hopeless, Jack didn't annoy Alexa as much as he annoyed Ellen. This also annoyed Ellen. While she was sometimes a little short with him, Alexa treated him with the benevolent patience of an experienced primary school teacher. Inevitably, he responded better to this treatment than to her own strangled infuriation. She took a deep breath and tried to summon her reserves of composure. Jack was staring beseechingly at her. She folded her arms and announced, 'Luckily for us, Alexa is fixing it.'

'Oh!' he said brightly, clearly not following. 'Great!' He stood up, abandoning the DVDs, and giving his now-dusty tracksuit bottoms a brush with his palms. He stared expectantly at her.

'She's downstairs,' Ellen supplied. 'Switching the water off.'

Jack nodded enthusiastically.

'So we should go help her.'

'Right.'

'Now?' Ellen jerked her thumb towards the door.

But Jack was already walking slowly towards the skylight set in the ceiling, and opened it. He stuck his head out and then turned back to her. 'It's a really nice day.'

'Right.' Ellen rolled her eyes. While Jack stuck his head out of the window, like a dog in a car, she crouched down, enjoying the periodic reprieve from having to hold herself entirely upright.

'Sorry.' He pulled his head back in. 'I'm coming.' His face brightened. 'Hi, Alexa.'

Ellen turned round. Alexa had appeared in the doorway. She was now wearing slippers, and a downcast expression. Ellen stood up.

'Hey,' Alexa said, quickly. 'So I tried to turn the water off under the sink, but I couldn't twist it. It's really stiff.' She stepped into the room and wrinkled her nose. 'God, look at all this rubbish.' She frowned at a defeated lawnmower, ancient yellowing grass still stuck to its shell. 'Anyway' – she recovered her focus – 'Jack, I was wondering if you could come and help me? I think it might need some muscle.'

Ellen resisted the urge to snort.

'What?' Jack was clearly thinking the same thing as Ellen.

'Could you come and help me turn the stopcock, under the sink?' she repeated, with barely a flicker of impatience. 'It's stuck.'

Ellen was going to add something to emphasize the urgency of the situation when she noticed a lanky man, presumably belonging to Alexa, shuffling through the doorway to join them. He was blinking as though unused to sunlight, and wore a pair of jeans slung low enough to confirm that he wasn't wearing any boxers underneath them. Big bare feet poked out of the bottom of the jeans. He was shirtless – in fact, it seemed quite likely that he owned the T-shirt slung over Alexa's top half – and his chest was lightly hairy. He had the sort of abs that suggested gentle – but not myopic – discipline. Indeed, he was – Ellen observed – extraordinarily good looking: big brown eyes, a shadow of stubble, brown, close-cropped dark hair. He squinted, a lithe forearm thrown across his eyes to shield them from the sun.

Noticing that Ellen was distracted, Alexa turned round. 'Oh, hey –'

Without warning, a gust from the open skylight slammed the door shut.

Ellen jumped, Jack yelped and the stranger turned.

'Hi,' he said, turning back to offer a friendly half-wave. 'I'm Ben.' His voice was slightly higher than Ellen had expected.

Jack and Ellen looked at Alexa. There were pink spots high on her cheekbones, though she looked quite pleased.

'Hey,' Alexa said, stepping towards him. 'Um, I'll be back down in a second, I just need Jack's help with something, so . . .' She trailed off.

Ben appraised her, smiling. 'Yeah, no worries – I just came to see if you have an iPhone charger?'

'Yes, there's one plugged in on my side of the bed,' Alexa said briskly. She was clearly trying to get rid of him.

Ben grinned uncertainly, a little bemused by his reception. 'OK, cool. I'll see you in a second, then.' He turned towards the door.

In the fullness of time, they'd presumably all agree that what happened next wasn't strictly Ben's fault. Ultimately, the door handle could have fallen off in anyone's hand. The door was an unknown quantity: its handle was rarely used. Perhaps, like a faulty escalator or an overburdened heart valve, the door handle was a ticking time bomb, an accident waiting to happen. Indeed, if you were pointing fingers, it was sort of Jack's fault – he'd opened the skylight, which made the door slam shut with such force. (And, to be fair, it was Alexa who had brought home the ham-fisted Adonis in the first place.)

But it didn't really matter whose fault it was, because fall off it did, leaving the door firmly closed, with them all locked inside.

And anyway, Elias would make it everyone's fault when the whole ground floor was underwater and he had to break down a door in order to break all of their necks.

2. Ellen

Ben stared at the handle.

'Oh my God,' Alexa uttered slowly. Her voice was high. 'Have you just locked us in?'

Ben lifted the handle, tentatively. 'I think,' he started, quietly, 'it's possible . . .' He trailed off, abashed, massaging his chin with one hand, the other still clutching the futile handle.

Manoeuvring past Ben, Alexa was at the door now. Slower – always a little slower – Ellen followed her, noticing that Ben smelled of salt and sweat and, very slightly, of something peachy.

She and Ben joined Alexa in a crouch in front of the door. She was examining the abyss where the handle ought to have been. It had left a thick metal pin exposed, which Ben twisted roughly. There was a promising clicking noise and he pressed it again, but this time, the pin gave way and disappeared. They heard the handle on the other side drop to the floor. Ben gave them another guilty look.

The handle's mechanism now truly buggered, Alexa tried reaching through the gap and tugging at the door with her small fingers. When this failed to achieve anything, she shot Ellen a look of concentrated panic.

Ellen's response to this was to stand up – thighs complaining – and to throw her weight at the door. Since it opened inwards, this also had no impact.

Running out of options, Alexa now put her face to the dusty floor in order to peer through the crack underneath the door.

For want of anything better to do, Ellen threw her weight against it again for good measure. She went in a little too hard, and stood back, rubbing her shoulder. She felt heavy with dread.

'This doesn't look good,' Jack whispered.

Ellen glared at him and slumped to the floor.

Alexa joined her, leaning back against the door, her arms crossed over her chest. She was chewing her lip.

Ben was slightly hunched, weighed down by the realization of what he had done – or perhaps he was just aware of the proximity of his head to the ceiling. His hands hung uselessly at his sides.

'Wait, so are we really locked in?' Jack asked, uncertainly, as if hoping he might get a different answer.

Ellen felt the white-wine heartburn rise in her throat again. 'Yes,' she said, from the floor. 'We're locked in, and the kitchen is filling with water – and . . .' It felt like her tongue had swollen to a size that her mouth could no longer support. 'Fuck,' she said, with feeling.

'I'm really sorry,' Ben tried, quietly. 'It just came off in my hand.' He added, hopefully, 'I suppose it must have been busted anyway.'

There was an incredibly awkward silence, during which time Ellen realized that – to add insult to injury – she urgently needed the loo. She scanned the room for items that could be repurposed at humiliating cost, while hoping they wouldn't be in here long enough for it to come to that. The attic ran the length of their house, but was so full it seemed

18

smaller, its eaved ceilings adding to the sense that the walls were closing in around them. Stringy spiderwebs decked the whole room. There was a clearing of ratty, staticky carpet, and a short path from this clearing to the door. There was another short path towards the skylight. The dead mouse remained, lying in state.

'OK, so who's got a phone?' demanded Alexa.

'I do,' Jack said, brightly, producing one and prodding it. 'Oh . . .' He jabbed at it again. 'No signal. I never have any signal upstairs.' He looked stricken.

Ben raised his empty hands. 'Mine's downstairs,' he added sheepishly.

Ellen instinctively patted the side of her upper thigh: phone! She took it out. 'I do, but it's almost dead,' she said, looking at the sad little red battery icon in the corner. 'Three per cent.'

She wished she'd had the presence of mind to plug it in before she passed out. With a twinge of shame, she vaguely remembered spending much of the bus journey home – while she leaned in the area reserved for push-chairs – stalking a girl she went to primary school with on Instagram. Ellen found that she often did this when she was drunk. Joanna Jessop was a doctor and had got married in a frothy ceremony in a converted barn in the Cotswolds last year. But a month later she discovered her new husband was having an affair, and then he'd left her for the other woman. Ellen knew all this because Joanna Jessop had recalled the whole devastating incident in a series of black-and-white pictures of flat whites and roof-top scenes tagged #survivor #reflection #affair #divorce #cryless #smilemore #keepyourheartopen. She liked to return to the sequence often to gather more details. She occasionally stalked the disgraced ex-husband but he was, understandably, less forthcoming on social media. He was very short. It surprised Ellen that he'd convinced not just one but two women to take a chance on him.

'Shit!' Alexa said, enunciating the 't'. 'Mine's downstairs too. Ellen, we need to think fast about how to use yours before your battery dies.'

'Well, I guess we should call your landlord?' Ben said, innocently.

The three tenants shared a glance. It was agreed, word-lessly, that Alexa would field this.

'It's just . . . he'll go ballistic,' she stated, weakly. 'He'll probably try to evict us on the spot –'

'He's fucking deranged,' Ellen interrupted, forcefully. 'If he finds out the kitchen is filling with water, he'll prob-ably drown one of us in there. Add to that the fact we've broken the handle off his precious door, and we're as dead as that mouse . . .'

Ben stared at her.

'Dealing with Elias is a conversation I don't want to have,' Alexa finished, sounding tired.

There was a tense pause.

'OK,' Ben said, finally. 'Landlord is a psycho. Noted.' He was clearly making a strenuous effort to be upbeat. 'Take it you haven't left a spare set of keys with a neigh-bour, or something?'

'We don't really know any of the neighbours,' Ellen said, sulkily.

'I know Mrs Chan,' Jack said, brightly.

'My dad has our only spares,' Alexa remembered,

ignoring Jack. 'He's out near Wimbledon. Although' – she looked at Ellen – 'do you have his new number saved? I only know the office one.' A pause. 'He got a new phone recently,' she added, slightly defensively.

Ellen swiped through her contacts. 'Don't even have his old one,' she said, flatly.

Alexa placed her fingers on her left temple. Her jaw was clenched. 'OK, could we call your mum and dad? They're not *that* far from here, are they?'

'What – to ask them to drive an hour up to London on a rescue mission to break our door down? They don't have any keys.'

Not to mention, they wouldn't do it. Partly, this was because her parents had done the big shop every Saturday morning for twenty-plus years, and would right now be in the car park of a Tesco Megastore, doing their tenth circuit at 6mph waiting for a nana to relinquish her parking space. Nothing would be permitted to interrupt this ritual. Ellen's mother had even been there on the morning her own mother died. Ellen had accompanied her that day and watched as her hands shook – just a little – when she tried to slot the pound coin into the trolley.

Besides the big shop, there was also the fact that her parents thought that moving to the vivid wilds of southeast London was a radical phase – and the sooner Ellen retreated to the muted security of the suburbs, where they lived, the better. Her father's more morbid jokes included emailing her links to articles from newspapers with headlines like LOCAL SAMARITAN MUGGED AT KNIFEPOINT BY TEENAGE GANG LORD or FOUR DEAD IN GRISLY PARK MURDER. Somehow, the fact that she'd managed to get stuck in the attic of the three-bed house she lived in would end up being the fault of London. She really didn't want to give them the ammunition.

'Plus,' Ellen observed, glumly, 'they're miles away.'

Her brother, Tom, would have done it – begrudgingly – except he now lived in Barcelona. She felt, at a stroke, isolated and terrified.

'Well, we have to phone someone,' Alexa said, testily, glancing at Ben. 'Before Ellen's battery runs out. And we can't just sit here, stuck in an attic –'

'While the ground floor fills with water.' Ellen felt responsible for the flood, as she'd had the misfortune to discover it. Not to mention her bedroom was on the same floor as the kitchen. She wondered how long it would take the water to reach her room. She wished she hadn't left her laptop on the floor.

'So, come on, who else can we call?' Alexa asked urgently. She sat hunched, holding on to her knees with her left arm, while she chewed the skin on the knuckles of her right hand.

'What about Soph?' Ellen said, suddenly, her voice higher than she'd expected it to be. 'She's not that far away. Plus she'd probably quite enjoy breaking a window –'

'She's in Dorset this weekend, for Renée's mum's sixtieth,' Alexa interrupted, grimly.

Ellen made a face. At university she'd never have imagined Sophie becoming the sort of person who attended her girlfriend's mother's sixtieth birthday. She had once dropped a lit cigarette into the bin in her room in halls and started a small fire that woke the entire building at 3 a.m. in the depths of exam term.

'We could try . . . the police?' Jack asked, seeking confirmation. None was forthcoming. 'Or would it be the fire brigade?' Ellen noticed his hairy toes poking out of the cuffs of his navy tracksuit bottoms. As if he'd read her mind, he curled them self-consciously.

'It might be a little bit mad to call 999 over this,' Ben pointed out, gently. 'I mean, they probably have more pressing things to do.'

'This is true,' Ellen agreed, begrudgingly. 'But firemen do things like get cats out of trees.'

'I don't think they actually do get cats out of trees,' Alexa observed.

'They got my cousin's head out of the railings when she got it stuck,' Jack said, quietly.

'I don't think we should call the emergency services over this,' Alexa said, finally. 'Not yet, anyway. It feels a little hysterical.' Ellen could see a vein pulsing in her forehead.

'I agree,' said Ben. He crouched down slightly to reach clumsily for Alexa's shoulder. She almost smiled, but the result was rather pained.

Ellen could see Jack concentrating on them both, his mouth slightly open. 'Locksmith!' she said, suddenly. 'Let's call a locksmith.'

'Yes,' Alexa said, urgently. 'Great idea. Google one now.'

Ellen opened her phone again. It had adjusted automatically to preserve what little energy it had left, and the screen was gloomy. As Ellen adjusted the brightness, it went black. Her stomach plummeted. 'Fuck.'

'What?' Alexa said, sharply.

Ellen held it up, her face grim. 'Dead.'

Alexa threw her head back, hands over her ears, and stared at a spot in the eaves. After a few calming breaths, she exhaled loudly and then echoed Ellen. 'Dead. Brilliant.'

'That is not good,' Ben said, stupidly. He lowered himself to the floor.

Noting the mood, Jack padded softly across the room, his face solemn, and joined them all on the floor. They sat in a circle, just to the right of the mouse's corpse. Ellen hoped if they were up here much longer they'd at least move it. She could hear Alexa's breathing, fast and rhythmic.

Eventually, Alexa spoke. 'OK, so Jack's is the only phone, and it has no signal.'

'Or WiFi,' Jack said. 'The signal doesn't seem to stretch up here, either.'

Alexa pursed her lips. 'Right . . .' She paused. 'No signal or WiFi. So we can't contact anyone.'

Ellen felt a sugary nausea in the back of her throat. She was suddenly very conscious of the existence of her brain inside her skull. She had read somewhere that headaches from hangovers were the result of dehydration shrinking your brain. She put her hands on either side of her head to try and stop it shrinking any further. 'What the fuck are we going to do?' she asked bitterly.

Alexa made no response.

Ben raised an index finger. 'We should try shouting out of the window,' he suggested. He sounded pleased with this idea. 'One of your neighbours might hear? Or someone walking past might look up?' He found Alexa's eyes, eager only for her approval.

24

'Yeah,' she replied, evenly. 'We could try that.'

In a shot, Ben clambered to his feet, lanky limbs working in symphony. He virtually leaped the few metres towards the skylight and stuck his head out of the window.

'HELP!' he yelled at the top of his lungs.

Ellen and Alexa both winced at the volume; Jack observed him with detached interest.

'HELLO? CAN ANYBODY HEAR ME?' He paused to draw a bellyful of air. 'WE'RE STUCK! IN THIS ATTIC!' Another gulping breath. '*HEEEEEE EEEEEEELP!*'

Their patch of south-east London remained utterly unmoved. In the distance, Ellen could hear the hubbub of New Cross Road, the occasional honk of a horn or rev of an engine, but nothing human. London suddenly felt more immense and impersonal than ever. She reached for Alexa's hand and squeezed it. Her palm was cool. Alexa squeezed back and gave her a grateful glance.

'CAN ANYBODY HEAR ME?' Ben yelled again. 'SOMEONE?'

He revved up for yet another attempt, but Alexa stopped him. 'Ben?'

He turned.

'I don't think anyone can hear you right now.'

'Except us,' Ellen muttered. His hollering was making her head hurt even more.

'Right.' Ben looked downcast. 'Your street does seem pretty empty.' He lay down on the floor under the skylight, his belly in the shaft of sunshine. He reminded Ellen of a slightly feral cat. 'What time is it?' he asked from the floor.

'Eight thirty-seven,' Jack said, dutifully.

'Pretty early for a Saturday, I guess.' Ben sat up and started shuffling towards them on his bottom, holding his jeans with one hand while keeping his balance with the other arm. When he reached the circle, he shuffled into place next to Alexa. She tucked her hair behind her ears and shot him a shy sideways glance. 'Maybe we should try again in half an hour or so?' he suggested.

'Yeah,' Alexa said, quietly. 'Maybe we give it thirty minutes and then we try again.'

Ellen contemplated this. She suspected that if she were walking down a street on which a shirtless man was hollering from an attic skylight, she would put her head down and speed up. Not to mention the fact that she had never met a single one of her neighbours. Unless you counted the house diagonally opposite, full of mangy Goldsmiths students whom she had met only once, on the Tuesday evening they'd thrown a colossal, foundation-shaking house party and she'd begged them to turn down the bass. They'd laughed and, she suspected, turned the volume up.

'Yeah, maybe,' Ellen echoed, finally, without much enthusiasm. 'I mean, what else are we going to do?' She could feel the breeze from the open skylight. 'I really need the loo,' she moaned, realizing suddenly how true it was.

'God, I feel like hell,' Ben replied. 'I did not need that Negroni nightcap.'

'No,' Alexa said, ruefully. 'I'm definitely feeling it now.' She gave Ben a conspiratorial half-grin.

Ellen looked at her friend with a little surprise. She wondered, for the first time, how Alexa and Ben had ended up together. She was about to make a rather impertinent enquiry, but Jack spoke instead.

'It's weird how the door handle just fell out,' he observed, with the air of someone pointing out that it had started to drizzle but looked like it might stop soon. He had shuffled towards the door and was poking his fingers through the hole where the handle used to be.

'Yep,' Alexa agreed. 'That was certainly unexpected.'

'Do you ever use this place?' Ben asked.

'No, I think I've only been up here once, when the electrics fused,' Alexa replied, quietly.

'I mean it's packed to the rafters with our landlord's old shit,' Ellen said, bluntly. 'So no, we don't tend to curl up here and watch a film together.'

Hurt flashed across Ben's face but he rearranged his expression quickly. 'Right.' He laughed mirthlessly. 'Fair point.'

Ellen felt spiteful. 'I'm Ellen, by the way,' she added, as a peace offering. She stretched out a hand, but then – thinking better of it – turned it into a wonky wave.

'Ben.'

Wait – the penny plummeted very suddenly, hurtling through the whorls of her wine-fogged brain – was this *Hinge* Ben? She smiled neutrally in a way that she hoped disguised that his name meant anything to her.

Alexa had started speaking to Hinge Ben about six weeks ago. After they matched, he had opened their chat by telling her that he used to work at the pizza restaurant where the second picture on her profile was taken – and he didn't want to disappoint her, but all the dough was microwaved from frozen. Alexa had run with it. In the course of their quite extensive messaging, he had proved himself to have an uncommonly good grasp of grammar, not to

27

mention the fact that he had not once used the crying laughing emoji, a quality that made him as rare as a unicorn on the capital's dispiriting millennial dating-app scene.

He was talking again. 'So how do you guys all know each other?'

'Well, we went to university together,' Ellen replied, pointing at Alexa. 'In York. And now we live together. In this attic.'

Gratifyingly, Ben laughed.

Ellen smiled back.

'I wish there was some food up here,' Jack said mournfully, by way of an interruption. 'Hi, by the way,' he said, shyly. 'I'm Jack.'

Ben nodded back warmly. 'Ben.'

Jack offered a half-wave.

'Were you at uni with them too, then?'

'No –' Jack started to explain.

'We got Jack on SpareRoom,' Ellen interrupted, immediately regretting how it had sounded.

Jack had joined the house last September, when their friend Sophie had moved out to live with her girlfriend. He had been, by far, the best of an eccentric bunch of applicants. Their least-favourite had been a thirty-five-year-old actuary who – when asked if he had any questions – had responded, 'What is the policy on group sex?'

'There isn't one,' Alexa had said, firmly.

He'd tried to add them both on Facebook later that evening.

They were both fond of Jack, although sometimes, on evenings when Ellen was alone and heard the front door slam, followed by his hopeful 'Halloo', her heart would sink that she couldn't have a little more time to herself. She'd pause before calling out a subdued 'Hi, Jack' in return. Still, he seemed unfazed by the silences that sometimes fell in the evenings, happy to fill them with humming, or a muttered commentary on the meal he was pulling together. ('Soup? Soup. Bread. And the butter.')

'Yes, they picked me from all the others on the app,' Jack said, quickly. 'I was living with my sister Maisie before, in her house in Earlsfield – after I moved down from Manchester. That's where I'm from.'

'Gotcha,' Ben replied.

Ellen noticed that he was absent-mindedly massaging his left pectoral. She saw that Alexa had noticed this too.

A brief, slightly awkward pause had fallen, in which everyone looked elsewhere, and then smiled when they accidentally caught one another's eyes. When Ellen caught Alexa's, she tried to communicate something about Ben's left pectoral, though she wasn't certain what, and instead ended up sort of winking at her. Alexa frowned slightly. In the sunshine that came from the skylight, Ellen observed a covering of very fine hair on her legs. Alexa definitely hadn't been expecting to see Ben last night.

'This place is messier than my room,' Jack offered, conversationally. 'It's weird, because I don't even have that much stuff.' He looked puzzled. 'It just gets everywhere.'

'So, is that the plan, then?' Ellen asked, ignoring him. 'Wait for half an hour and try shouting again?'

'For now, yes.' Alexa shrugged. 'Let's give it until 9 a.m. You wouldn't ring someone's doorbell before 9 a.m. on a Saturday.'

'I would if it were an emergency,' Ellen said, quickly.

'Well, yelling didn't work a minute ago, did it?' Ben pointed out.

'Let's try in half an hour,' Alexa said, diplomatically.

Ellen shrugged.

There was another silence, slightly less friendly in tone.

After a few minutes, Jack stood up. He stepped purposefully towards the wall of cardboard and started excavating a box. The rest of them watched him dumbly. After some rummaging he turned round, triumphant, holding a large cardboard box that he had managed to free.

'Shall we play a game to pass the time?' he asked, hopefully. He dropped the box in the middle of the clearing, sending a mushroom cloud of dust into the sky. After it settled, Ben, Alexa and Ellen leaned forward to look inside. It was packed with dusty board games. Monopoly, Cluedo, Settlers of Catan, Guess Who?, Snakes & Ladders, Risk. Ellen could not imagine Elias settling down with Cynthia to play a game of Guess Who? and shook her head. She wished her mind would stop drifting towards their tyrannical landlord.

'Look, he's got Risk!' said Jack, with delight.

Even in normal circumstances, Ellen would have been unable to muster much enthusiasm at the idea of playing Risk. Annoyingly, Ben did not agree.

'Great shout,' he said, approvingly. He pulled the game out of the box and rubbed the dust off its surface with his forearm. Ellen noticed that when Ben smiled, it carved a comma-shaped dimple into his right cheek.

She knew, however, with some confidence, that Alexa found board games tedious. On cue, she wrinkled her nose, and Ben hesitated. He put the game on the floor in front of them.

Jack looked at it beseechingly. 'Please?' he said, after a minute.

Alexa's expression softened slightly.

Ellen was having none of it. 'I'd rather sit in silence than play a game,' she said, flatly. She searched Alexa's face for support. Ben was watching Alexa too, and smiling what Ellen assumed he'd describe as his 'winning' smile. Alexa glanced between them, her expression dark and inscrutable. Finally, she shrugged in defeat. 'Alexa, really?' Ellen whined. 'Risk?'

Alexa shrugged again.

Jack had already unfolded the board and was examining each piece individually.

Ellen contemplated sulking, but could see she was beaten. 'Fucking fine, then. But I'm playing for half an hour, max.'

Jack offered her the box. 'You can pick your colour first!'

She glared at him.

3. Alexa

The date had come out of nowhere, really.

On Friday evening, Alexa had made her excuses to opt out of one of work's semi-regular trips to Gordon's Wine Bar. She liked many of her nerdy, earnest and bright colleagues but, aside from academic excellence, work was all they had in common. Plus, there was always an air of self-satisfaction to these Friday nights. Discussing Whitehall proceedings with the superiority of insiders (they were junior civil servants, for God's sake) in a warm, packed basement bar, making noises about the sweaty cheese board they'd inevitably order, honks of laughter over only moderately funny in-jokes, calculating monies owed for rounds on the back of a receipt. One colleague, Stewart – a young fogey who wore mauve corduroy trousers and whose laugh was especially honking – would always email his bank details over minutes after they all parted and went their separate ways. It all made her feel a bit exhausted. She always found herself hoping that their group wouldn't be overheard by someone, and spent much of the time looking over other people's shoulders, brain only half trained on the conversation.

And so, fumbling with her jacket and handbag – leaving her wheezy work computer as it attempted to install some updates – Alexa had made a hollow promise to be there next time. Walking at a trot to Westminster Tube station, she caught the Jubilee line to London Bridge before getting the overground home to New Cross. When she timed every connection perfectly it took about half an hour to get home. This happened a couple of times a week, and it pleased Alexa more than it should have done. By the same token, when the opposite happened and it took over an hour, it made her more furious than she suspected was normal.

Tonight, the journey was neither remarkably quick nor slow, and she felt unmoved, besides a sense of relief, to be close to home as she stepped off the train at New Cross Gate and tapped her card to get through the barriers. She turned left at the station to walk the roughly ten minutes it took to get to 49 Rokeby Close, her handbag – a present from her father when she had got her job – nestled snugly under one arm, a tote bag containing her gym kit bouncing off her hip with every step. She did the route on autopilot, correctly predicting the changes of the traffic lights a beat before everyone else at the crossing. They'd found the house three years ago, after a long summer of ambiguous Gumtree listings and pints in pubs following swift viewings with harried estate agents who all seemed to be called Kenneth. In the end, while they'd all agreed that, yes, it did matter that the third bedroom (Ellen's) was technically the living room and that, yes, the whole place had smelled a little like fried eggs, 49 Rokeby Close was the best they'd seen.

Their house was positioned a few streets away from a busy main road, on a parallel, far quieter row of Victorian terraced houses. It was a smart street, dotted with big oak trees, and only the occasional dismembered bicycle tangled around a lamp post, rusting and useless. Most of the doors were inscrutable: they were painted blue or dark green, though there was the occasional pink or yellow one singing in the mix. A few houses had proper paths, paved with chequerboard tiling, or tiny, well-tended front gardens with huge earthenware pots sitting either side of thick stone doorsteps. But the best clues to the inhabitants inside were collected by careful peeping: all of the houses on the road had front windows that sat almost at street level, and it was possible to peer inside and determine which were owned by someone comparatively rich, and which were occupied by a group like Alexa, Ellen and Jack.

The rich ones had big, modish clocks with white faces and black hands, and large gilt mirrors on the walls that reflected matching sofas and elegant, etiolated house plants. The rest of the houses, on the other hand, had posters tacked up without a frame, IKEA shelving units and an assortment of furniture acquired for free online (though only if you'd gone and collected it). Many of these intended living rooms had been repurposed as bedrooms, like Ellen's. New Cross was a hotchpotch of people living in close proximity, near to both Goldsmiths and Camberwell School of Art, which meant a mixture of students and professors often living on the same street. There were also the families priced out of more expensive homes in Herne Hill or Dulwich – and people in their twenties, who hadn't yet realized they'd been priced out of the property market altogether, and dreamed pointlessly of one day buying one of these homes.

Alexa put her key in their blue door and was, she realized, slightly relieved to find it still double locked. She was home alone. The door swung open with a judder. She flicked the light switch and picked the post off the doormat – a shuffle through the pile confirming it was all addressed to previous tenants, despite the fact they'd been there for three years now – then slung her handbag over the knob on the end of the banister. Ellen's bedroom was to the left of the front door, and beyond the staircase that led up to the first floor was their kitchen, a big room with a large, wobbly table that was the house's only communal space.

Padding into the kitchen now, she opened the door to her food cupboard and – after surveying the sad contents – swiftly closed it again. She added the former tenants' letters to a large, deep bowl that sat at the end of the long kitchen table and contained, among other treasures, a transparent purple lighter, a blister pack of ibuprofen (empty), a takeaway menu for a local kebab shop, a USB cable and about €6 in coins. She pulled out a chair, wincing as she scraped the legs across the kitchen floor, and sat down. She took a deep breath.

Shrugging off her jacket, she pulled out her phone to WhatsApp Ellen. Ellen would – most likely – be out for drinks with her colleagues from The Flowdown. In Alexa's office, everyone was either very earnest or very pompous, and only interested in talking shop. On the other hand, most of Ellen's colleagues were young women about her age (twenty-eight), and she was always texting them about things that had absolutely nothing to do with work. Ellen talked about one girl, Kayleigh, a lot, which made Alexa feel uncharacteristically territorial. When Ellen told a story about something Kayleigh had said or done, Alexa's laughter always sounded – to her own ears, certainly – a little forced. Their office space in Farringdon, which they shared with a bike-repair start-up, Two Wheels Good, sounded fairly riotous, and Friday-evening drinks often ended up in an office party with the bike guys. Ellen had once gone home with a skinny bloke called Lee who ran the Two Wheels Good blog and wrote 800-word tracts about inner tubing. They now had a vaguely flirty but inconsequential relationship that sometimes amounted to a few texts at 3 a.m. on a Saturday (mainly trying to work out if the other one was also 'out').

Sometimes, these office parties ended up in a gay bar on Kingsland Road. Alexa had joined these nights a few times. It made her proud to see how much Ellen was liked by her colleagues – indeed, she was something of a ring-leader – although Alexa always felt her outsider status keenly, needing all the in-jokes explained to her and pan-icking if Ellen left her alone with the group. Still, it was always fun, and definitely more fun than tonight's Plan B – which, as it stood, was to go to the gym.

So Alexa WhatsApped Ellen.

Hey!

What you up to this eve?

Ellen had changed her WhatsApp picture to one of her in a crown, which Alexa recognized from her last birthday party. She smiled, scrolling idly through her WhatsApp inbox while she waited for Ellen to reply, and then noticed – to her surprise – that Ben was typing and stopping and typing and stopping.

This was an unexpected development.

Alexa had reluctantly reconciled herself to the fact that Ben – who had seemed so promising – wasn't going to be a goer, after all. It was a tale as old as time, or at least as old as Tinder – which had, of course, changed the rules of the dat-ing game immeasurably and irreconcilably for their fickle, overstimulated generation. Anyway, after the two of them had matched on Hinge, on a wet Wednesday a few weeks ago, there had been an exchange of hundreds of messages over the course of the next few days, not to mention a first date that had hit all the right clichés: easy conversation; laughter; lingering eyes; knees pressed close under the table; a long, tantalizing kiss outside the pub. There had been three further charming dates (pub, Basquiat exhibition, theatre – she could recall the contours of each one perfectly).

She'd had high hopes for their last date, even though it was to the theatre – his suggestion, which Alexa had fretted about because you couldn't talk much at the theatre. But afterwards, when she'd suggested a drink, he had brushed her off and ended the evening quite abruptly, saying that he needed to get his train. So she didn't get the chance to invite him back to hers – and she'd hoped that might be the night, because it was a Friday and she'd shaved her legs that morning. He didn't text until the morning, and even then it was a rather disinterested message (she'd asked Ellen to read it, and she had agreed sympathetically with Alexa's assessment).

And ever since, he had continued to cool. He took a little longer to reply to her texts, and when he did so, he was less inquisitive, less interested in her. His messages were more perfunctory, less sparkling, not crafted to make her laugh. Crucially, they no longer called for a response, so when she did reply, it made her feel rather foolish.

And so that was almost certainly that, she'd thought. They'd last messaged on Wednesday: she'd sent him a link to an article about a Netflix documentary they'd talked about on their last date – unsubtle, she conceded – and he'd replied a little later, picking the funniest, most obvious line from the article, plus a fire emoji. Alexa couldn't be bothered to reply. She shouldn't have sent the link in the first place. She had spent too much time wondering about Ben: replaying the date in her mind, worrying at it, searching for missed clues. She was talking to someone else now, a guy called Malachi – who did, regrettably, use the crying laughing emoji, but who would do for now.

Alexa stared at the screen. Ben was still typing and stopping. Decisively, Alexa put her phone on the table, face down, then got up and walked across the kitchen to the fridge. In the side door there was half a bottle of white wine, which she was fairly sure was Ellen's (she'd only ever seen Jack drinking beer). Alexa fetched a tumbler from the cupboard and poured herself a generous glass of the Sauvignon Blanc. It didn't smell too much like vinegar; it would do.

She returned to the table and flipped her phone over, jabbing at its homescreen button to see if Ben had bitten the bullet. He had not, but Ellen had replied. She couldn't help but feel slightly disappointed.

Heyyyyyyyy!
We're doing drinks here then pub i think
Is someone at Two Wheels Goods bday
So they have the corporate card
Ding ding dingggg
What you up to?
Wanna join?

Alexa weighed up her options. Maybe she did want to go and meet Ellen. Though she'd made a few of the Kingsland Road nights out with The Flowdown, she'd never been to one of their Friday night office drinks parties. For her, office drinks — like the regular pilgrimages to Gordon's — were to be avoided, except at Christmas, when they all finished early and there was no excuse. Someone would run out for a few bottles of supermarket Prosecco and they'd dole out a small portion in the triangular paper cups from the watercooler while people said how 'nice' it all was.

On the other hand, she'd just got home from town and getting back into Farringdon was a faff for a few drinks; she'd have to change, and it would take forty-five minutes to get there, and maybe they'd be finishing by then. Sometimes, Alexa felt exhausted by the promise of Friday evenings in London: the city's bright lights, modern spires and millions of people offered an odyssey of possibilities, and yet Alexa too often found herself at this kitchen table, staring into the black mirror of her phone screen, wondering what she was doing wrong.

Aware Ellen wouldn't mind either way — it was almost 8 p.m., so she was definitely several drinks in — Alexa's fingers hovered over the keyboard as she considered her response, frustrated by her own indecision. As she held her phone, it vibrated again: Ben.

Got a real hankering for one of those sweet frozen pizza bases

Wait . . . what? She felt faintly panicked. He was typing again. A pizza emoji. He was asking her on a spontaneous date.

She wasn't ready to reply. Closing WhatsApp, a drumming in the pit of her stomach, Alexa opened the Notes function on her phone. She often did this: tested her replies before she committed to sending something. The WhatsApp interface — the blinking cursor, the fact that the other person could see that you were typing — was all very exposing.

OK. First attempt. She tapped fast.

I think we can do better

No! Weird – so weird. Somehow sounded sexual, when the conversation was fundamentally about frozen pizza dough. Try again.

Weird craving to have on a Friday night

Better? Better, but sounded oddly intense, like he had suggested going out on the town to suck people's blood, rather than get a passable pizza.

How the mighty have fallen

Better. Not brilliant, but at least slightly enigmatic, and passed the baton back to him.

She thought for a moment, cocking her head to one side. It would do. Decisively, she opened WhatsApp again, typed out the message, spell-checked it quickly (the shame of a misspelt quip!) and hit send. She put her phone back on the table, feeling a little like she was going to laugh. She took a sip of wine and kicked her shoes off. She picked her phone up again, opened her emails, opened Instagram, did a couple of scrolls and then closed it. Scroll, scroll, scroll.

Another message. That was fast.

Everyone has their vices

She made a face. He was still typing.

So fancy slumming it with me?

She barked a short, nervous laugh.

She reread the messages, chewing her lip, a buzzing in her ears. Wait, so – he was asking her if she wanted to go out for dinner, at the exceptionally average pizza place. Did she? She could feel the slight thrill of the small glass of white wine in her veins; she hadn't eaten since lunchtime and her legs felt light, like they were full of helium. It was just round the corner. And maybe she'd read every-thing wrong, had overthought it. After all, he had just asked her out. And she did like him; she'd been so cross when she thought she'd bungled it. Not cross – despondent. Perhaps this was a second chance?

She tapped out a message, feeling reckless.

The high life is overrated

He was typing again.

Totally

See you and the great unwashed in an hour?

She made another face and sent back the pizza emoji too, feeling suddenly, powerfully shy. Now she had to go on a date: she had to sit opposite him for at least the dur-ation of a pizza – and sparkle. And would it be awkward, after last time? She recalled his face again as they'd parted at the end of an excruciating embrace. She had assumed he'd be going the same way as her (he lived in Peckham and she knew they could both get the 343 bus) and she had been testing what she'd say in her head to get him to stay on until New Cross with her. A 'nightcap' sounded camp and self-conscious (she might as well wink); 'back to mine' was a little clinical. But either way, it hadn't mattered, because he'd pulled away and gone for the train instead, leaving her watching him slope away into the night. On the way home she'd read and reread their past texts for some-thing torturous to do.

Alexa shook her head to clear her thoughts, and drained her wine glass. She jabbed at her phone again. In an hour it would be 9.07 p.m.; she rounded down to 9 p.m., which was quite late for dinner, she thought, catching herself. 'Stop it,' she muttered.

Standing up and slipping her shoes back on, she walked across the kitchen, putting the wine glass on the counter. Noting, with an eye roll, that Jack had left a pot and a shallow bowl covered in cemented-on vegetable soup in the sink, she made her way to her bedroom, collecting her handbag from the banister on the way.

Alexa's bedroom was a neat and ordered version of an IKEA bedroom: its constituent parts were cheap, but the execution was successful in elevating the overall effect. The posters on her wall – a Chagall print, plus another from an exhibition she'd seen at the Musée Rodin with her mother for her last birthday – were presented inside simple black frames. She had two standing lamps – with long, black, elegant necks – in opposing corners of the room, and a chrome Anglepoise imitation on her wooden bedside stool. All her clothes were folded inside a white chest of drawers with black iron handles, or hung in the Elias-issued wardrobe (it was cheap, made of MDF, and Alexa hated how poorly it matched the rest of the furniture). There were two rows of shelves above the bed – where her novels were arranged in perfect height order – a mirror by the wardrobe, and a small wooden desk with yet another lamp (a small orb) and a MacBook Air whose lid was closed. There was a single tall plant, in a black pot, and a large rug with a pattern of black and white chevrons.

Kicking off her shoes, she popped them in the line along the floor where her other pairs were arranged, and opened the wardrobe. Alexa was proud of the fact that she did not dress like a civil servant – specifically, that she did not own a single skirt suit. On her first date with Ben she had worn a black jumpsuit with huge flared legs. He had complimented her on it, and she hadn't known what to do with her face for a minute or so afterwards, not wanting to look too pleased. Swiping through the rails now, she pulled a navy flannel shirt from the wardrobe, and a white polo neck and black jeans from her chest of drawers. Standing in front of the mirror, she tucked and untucked the shirt a few times. She decided on tucking in one side of it, leaving the other free. Sitting on her knees, she squinted in to examine her face. She frowned, prodding at one cheekbone. She went through the improvements she always made to her face: concealer under her eyes and across her brows and nose, more mascara, brushing her eyebrows up, daubing highlighter on her cheekbones and adding kohl to her eyes. She examined her hair, which could have done with a wash. Instead, she pulled half of it above her head, and fastened it with a grip.

8.27 p.m.

It would take her ten minutes to get to the restaurant – five to walk to the bus stop and then five or so minutes on the 171. She rootled around in a basket next to the mirror until she found some red nail varnish and – careful not to drop any on her jeans or shirt – painted her fingernails with two coats, blowing carefully on each finger. Scowling again at her reflection – she looked tired – she reached for her handbag, and started decanting the relevant contents into another, smaller bag: keys, phone, a battered tin of pink Vaseline, wireless earbuds in their little zip-up case. She selected a pair of white trainers from the three she owned. She sat on the bed and stared out of the window at the now-dark street outside. A car revved.

She hoped they'd be able to get a table at Penny's. It would be excruciating to find there was no room for them. Would it be weird to book a table for their impromptu date? In normal circumstances, Alexa would not go out for dinner without booking a table. When people (Ellen) teased her about this, Alexa would play up to it, smiling and shrugging as if to say, 'That's me.' Then she would point out that, this way, they'd definitely get to eat where they wanted to – and that everyone could thank her later. But she did not feel confident enough to pass off this routine with Ben. He didn't know that foresight was one of her winning quirks.

On the other hand, maybe it *was* winning to have booked ahead? She could always be casual about it. Moreover, it was better than the alternative: turning up and finding their last-minute plan foiled, at which point they'd have to walk to a pub – making small talk on the way – and then squeeze in at the bar, pints hovering near their mouths as they misheard each other repeatedly over the boisterous hubbub of the Friday-night throng. Alexa pulled out her phone and googled the restaurant, then tapped the number. It rang five times.

They sounded harried. In the background, Alexa could hear commotion and chatter and someone yelling, 'Aubergine parmigiana!'

'Hi,' she said, firmly, putting in her request for a table.

'One second,' said the voice on the other end of the phone. Alexa could hear more chaos. The person on the other end was speaking to a customer at the till. The noise roared from the phone again – the server was back. 'Um, yeah, that should be fine. What's the name?'

'Brilliant. It's Alexa.'

'Alexa. Right. See you soon.'

It was 8.45 p.m. – time to leave. She took the stairs two

at a time and locked the door behind her. It was cold out now, the sky cloudless. Alexa pulled her cord jacket more tightly around herself, crossed her arms, and set off towards the bus stop, the soles of her trainers smacking hard on the chilly pavement.

The bus was arriving just as she rounded the corner ahead of her stop, and the journey was quick, so she arrived bang on time, as always. Ben was nowhere to be seen, though she didn't mind, as it meant he would not discover that she'd booked the table. Maybe if they got married, she thought amusedly, she could confess this in the wedding speech.

Taking the chair facing the door so that he wouldn't surprise her, she hung her jacket carefully on the back of it. The table was in the middle of the restaurant, sandwiched between two other tables-for-two, both occupied, while waiters weaved balletically through the passages between seats. A procession of scooter drivers snaked outside the shop's front, waiting to be presented with their precious cargo. Alexa rubbed her arms to warm up after the walk, and tried not to watch the entrance. She poured herself a glass of water from the carafe, drained it, and poured another. A sullen, angular waiter, slouching, his eyes peering out from beneath an unkempt fringe, appeared at her left shoulder and she ordered a small glass of Verdicchio (she'd picked the second-cheapest on the menu, her father's voice in her ear). She tucked a strand of hair behind her ear and fiddled with her left earring, comforted by the smoothness of the silver. She took her phone out and then put it away again. Everything she did, she did as though he were already watching.

Inevitably, she was staring at the door when he arrived,

ten minutes late and casually handsome in dark jeans, a grey hoodie and a denim jacket, hair swept from his brow. And she was furious that it looked like she'd been waiting – even though, of course, she was waiting, because he was late. He was intercepted by a waiter but had already spotted her, a broad, open smile on his face.

'Hey!' He pointed towards her and the waiter waved him past.

'Hey!' Alexa wondered whether to stand up, but he was over in two strides and stretching across the table to give her a kiss on the cheek. He smelled of peach and shaving foam, and placed his hand on her back as he leaned in. It was a practised move, and it worked: her stomach swooped. And then he pulled away, shrugged off his denim jacket and slung it across the chair as he sat down, resting both arms on the table, beaming his wide smile.

'Started already, then?' He pointed at her glass of wine, his eyes and mouth teasing.

'You were late,' she said, primly. 'And it's Friday.' She smiled shyly at him through her eyelashes.

'Cheers to that.' He raised his eyebrows at a nearby waiter, who slunk over, gripping a white pad and pen. Pointing at her glass, he asked, 'What you drinking?'

'Oh, um, Verdicchio?'

'That'll do. Shall we get a bottle?'

'Sounds perfect.'

'Bottle of Verdicchio,' repeated the waiter, in a monotone. He sighed and summoned the energy to make eye contact. 'And are you ready to order food?'

Alexa hadn't opened the menu, but Ben looked at her expectantly.

'Are we?'

Anxious not to hold up proceedings, Alexa glanced at the menu on the table in front of her. She barely took the words in.

'I'll have the aubergine parmigiana,' she offered.

''Nduja for me, mate.' A moment of inspiration. 'Oh, and can we share some bocconcini?' Ben looked at Alexa questioningly. She widened her eyes in agreement. 'Cheers.'

The laconic waiter turned on his heel.

'Sorry, did I rush you? I still know the menu here back to front.' He grinned. 'Service has gone way downhill since I left, though.'

'Sure.' Alexa cocked an eyebrow.

He laughed. 'Seriously, I was waiter of the month every month when I worked here.'

She made a sceptical noise.

'Well, I always got the most tips. Same difference.'

She rolled her eyes in amusement. He was watching her face now. She smiled shyly again and wished she'd remembered to brush her teeth.

'So how was your day?' she asked, brightening.

He groaned. 'Long. Work. Boss. Nightmare. You?'

'Oh – fine. I mean, all of the above, but fine.'

They exchanged sympathetic grimaces and then the waiter appeared with the Verdicchio and Ben's glass. With no ceremony, he plonked both on the table and departed.

'Seriously, did something happen between you two before I arrived?'

She giggled.

Ben topped up her wine and then poured his own. He drank a slug of it and smacked his lips. 'Actually, when I worked here, there was this love triangle between the head chef and these two waitresses. He was seeing them both and they found out and confronted him on the lunch shift. I missed it, which was a shame, as apparently one of them threw a bottle of the home-made chilli sauce at his head.' He gestured to the squat, heavy bottle in the middle of the table.

'Oh my God. That could knock you out.'

'She missed.' Ben took another slug of wine. 'Still. Made a dreadful mess.'

Alexa laughed, and he looked gratified. She moved her right hand from where it was clenched on her lap and placed it on the table, within reach of his.

'Bet it's all love triangles and threesomes in the Civil Service,' he said, teasingly.

A mirthless laugh. 'Please.'

Slightly hesitantly, she told him about the Gordon's Wine Bar pilgrimages, feeling rather mean as she exaggerated a few of her colleagues. Still: a reward. He chuckled and held her gaze for so long, she knew she was blushing. And then, in turn, he told her about his colleague Callum who had accidentally sent an email slagging off their boss *to* their boss and had managed – against the odds – to delete it from her computer before she read it. It involved a second colleague acting as a distraction, and a race against the clock.

The bocconcini arrived, delivered entirely without flourish again by their waiter. Alexa speared one with her fork. Ben went in with his fingers.

'Sorry,' he said, through a mouthful of molten cheese. He had a string of mozzarella hanging from the side of his lip. She was about to tell him but he decoded her. 'I have food on my face, don't I?'

'Yeah,' she said, with teasing sympathy.

He wiped his face with a napkin. 'Gone?'

'Gone.'

The pizza arrived too. Ben clocked her empty glass and ordered a second bottle of Verdicchio. She had been hoping he would.

'You don't have to get up early or anything?'

Her stomach pitched again.

'I can confirm I have no early-morning commitments.'

'Excellent.'

Alexa ate her pizza gratefully and, after the first two slices, abandoned her knife and fork. She had been careful to take sips of water in between gulps of wine but she'd had well over half a bottle now, probably more. Her head was the right side of spinning but her lips were loose. She had just finished telling Ben that she had learned about her parents' impending divorce on discovering – aged eleven – that her father was living in the (large) garden shed, and wondered whether this was, in fact, a bit of a buzzkill.

'Whoah,' he said, lowering a half-eaten slice of pizza to his plate in order to give her his undivided attention. 'That must have been pretty bewildering.'

'Well, he spun me some line about it being his office or something. But, obviously, I knew. I mean, it had a bed.'

'Slow down, Sherlock Holmes.' He grinned and picked up his half-eaten slice of pizza again.

She mirrored him, relieved, then refilled both of their water glasses, and took a gulp. She kicked him under the table by mistake, and looked stricken, but he raised his eyebrows and she relaxed again.

'I'm drunk,' Ben pronounced, twenty minutes or so

later, as the waiter cleared their plates. 'But I want another drink.'

'I'm drunk too.' She was; she felt mischievous and spontaneous. They'd been there for almost two hours – and the plan was inevitable, in every shared expression and gesture.

'Are they closing up yet, do you reckon? Or can I get one more?'

She cast around. There were still several other occupied tables, people waving wine glasses and savouring spoonfuls of tiramisu. 'Let's try and get another drink,' she agreed.

'Excellent,' Ben said. He conjured the waiter with a lazy wave. 'Excuse me, are you still serving?'

The teen grunted in assent.

'Can I get a Negroni and –' Ben cocked an eyebrow expectantly at her.

'I'll have the same.'

The waiter slunk towards the bar. The pause seemed to make them both self-conscious, and for a few minutes it was a little stop-start, their conversation punctuated by exchanges of shy twinkles through eyelashes.

Their drinks arrived a few minutes later, with the bill.

'Point taken,' Ben whispered, conspiratorially. He took a sip of his Negroni, shook it so the ice cubes rattled, and smacked his lips. 'This is potent.'

In response she took a sip of her own drink, reeling slightly at the bitterness. Her mind had started to wander ahead, to the next stage of the evening. She hated waking up in strange beds, visiting strange bathrooms and encountering other people's strange housemates. She hated wiping crusty mascara from under her eyes with a waterlogged, balled-up tissue (she knew he lived with three other boys, so there'd be no toiletries to freeload in the bathroom).

And so, when they had split the bill, bid their terse waiter farewell and stepped into the crisp darkness outside – Ben stumbling ever so slightly – she took the initiative.

'So I'm going this way now –' she said, pointing towards the bus stop and looking up to meet his direct gaze. In the low glimmer of the street lights he looked like he was carved from stone.

He stepped towards her. 'Can I come too?'

And then he was so close she could feel the heat from his body. He leaned in, wrapping her in his coat, and he kissed her deeply. When they finished, she peeked up at him with a light grin.

'I suppose so.'

Alexa had been awake for about twenty minutes when Ellen rapped loudly on her door. She always struggled to sleep much past 7.30 a.m., even on Saturdays. When her eyes had opened with a start, it had taken her a few seconds to work out what had happened – and who was lying beside her – though being naked had helped her arrive at the answer fairly quickly. Alexa, as a rule, never slept naked. She'd felt a squirming thrill as the details returned to her in snatches.

Lying very, very still in an effort not to wake Ben, she had moved her left arm – slowly, cautiously – towards the table in order to reach for her phone. She could hear his steady breathing, and realized she was holding her own breath.

She had received six WhatsApps from Ellen: the first

sent at 11.28 p.m, although she hadn't seen any of them. She must have been home with Ben by that point – she couldn't quite get a handle on how the evening had spun out.

Yoooooo

Are you coming to meet us?

Lee is being q weird i think he is avoiding me

Then, from 2 a.m.:

Coming homeeeee

I hope you are up

Bedroom partyyyyyy!!!

She smiled, imagining the scene, rather relieved to have been spared the reality. Ellen had the stamina of an ox.

Concentrating very hard on moving and breathing as little as possible, Alexa checked her emails (mercifully, nothing from work) then Instagram. Ellen had added a picture of herself and Kayleigh to her Story ('Friday in full Flowdown'). Alexa closed Instagram and – out of force of habit – opened a news app, started reading a story about carbon emissions and then closed it again. Remaining very still, she returned her phone to its perch on the wooden bedside stool and snaked her arm back under the duvet. She noted the condom wrapper in her eyeline, and she wrinkled her nose, feeling another squirm of embarrassment and delight.

Closing her eyes for a minute or two, she tested whether she could fall back asleep. No: she was too heightened to the presence of Ben's naked body beside hers, chest rising and falling evenly. She opened her eyes and slid up on to her elbows, observing him, then looked away. It would be very weird if he woke to find her watching him.

Unusually for a Saturday morning – Ellen and Jack were not early risers – there were signs of life in the house.

Alexa could hear footsteps – were they coming from upstairs? – and the low hum of voices. In fact, the footsteps sounded like they were getting closer.

And, suddenly, there was a very loud and very insistent rapping on the door.

She sat up quickly, pulling half of the duvet around her.

'Hmmmm?' Ben said, opening one eye slowly. She tensed, suddenly very conscious of her own nudity.

'Hey,' he said, dopily, a smile playing about his lips. His eyes were half open.

'Hi,' she said, her voice a little gravelly.

'What was that?' His own voice was thick with sleep and partly metabolized wine. 'Man, I feel a bit rough,' he added, with a cough of laughter.

'Oh, must be one of my housemates – at the door.'

Another insistent knock.

'Lex?'

It was Ellen. Alexa was very relieved it wasn't Jack.

Alexa hadn't missed Ellen's smirk when she finally opened the door – not that it had lasted very long, of course. Not once she'd got on to the mini waterfall, and the busted tap downstairs.

So instead of morning sex, maybe, and then brunch, possibly, and chatting in Ellen's room, definitely, Alexa was now, quite possibly, living with the man for the rest of her life. Cloistered in an attic full of *Top Gear* magazines and ventilated by a single window.

4. Jack

Jack didn't know much about Alexa's date – the man who'd locked them in the attic – but he wasn't totally certain about him yet. For a start, he was even worse at Risk than Ellen, who had looked murderous when Jack suggested playing. Ben kept picking up members of his own infantry to fiddle with, and no one could keep track of how he was doing.

Jack hadn't known she was seeing someone; he and Alexa did not have those kinds of conversations, about love lives or dates or boyfriends or girlfriends. It probably would have made Jack feel awkward. Mainly, they talked about the Tesco shop or whether he'd washed up. Still, he liked Alexa. She was smart and neat and always sounded very interested in everything he had to say, even if it was just about the Tesco shop.

He liked Ellen too, even though she was impatient with him, and always went into the bathroom just as he was about to go in. And 49 Rokeby Close was – by far – the best house he'd visited on his SpareRoom hunt. Before, he'd slept on his big sister Maisie's couch in Earlsfield, which was fine, except Trixie the cat kept waking him up by jumping on to his stomach, and Maisie's husband, Rich, kept asking, pointedly, when he was planning on finding 'his own place'.

He'd moved down to London from Manchester after

university, having got the job at Green Genie. He was a customer service rep, or a 'Human Bean', to give himself his official title. Jack hadn't really known which was the best bit of London to live in, but he worked in Bermondsey so he started his search near there. Except everywhere around there was so expensive that Jack thought he'd got the numbers wrong at first. He supposed that only people like his CEO, Bryan, who was thirty-six and ran to the office in trainers that looked like real feet, could afford to live anywhere near Bermondsey. Disheartened, Jack had broadened his search to 'south-east London' and Alexa and Ellen's place had come up. He'd swiped through the pictures and the house had looked huge. He'd read the blurb and then sent a message saying that he, too, liked communal movie nights and getting a bit tipsy in the house, but was also tidy and respectful of others and wasn't the sort of person to throw a mad party on a Wednesday night.

To his delight they'd messaged back and invited him round to view the place and meet them. He'd seen a rival tenant leave the house just as he arrived: a small girl in a beanie hat and a long black coat carrying a large musical instrument on her back (maybe it was a cello?). He'd put his headphones in his rucksack and taken a deep breath before ringing the doorbell. They'd had a nice twenty-minute chat – he'd told them about Green Genie, and his degree (geology), and his friend Johnny who lived down the road in Peckham, and Jack thought it had gone well – they'd both shown him to the door when he left. (Had they done that for the cello girl? He'd been a moment too late to see.) And the next day, Ellen had messaged him to say that if he was still looking for a place, then the room was all his. And so he'd moved in on the Saturday, with his big rucksack full of clothes, a Green Genie tote bag with a few books, and his mum's hand-me-down saucepan and a kettle. It turned out the house already had a kettle.

He'd been there since September, and it was now April, and they hadn't actually had a communal movie night, and the girls tended to have their own plans when it came to drinking. But, still, he liked them both and he liked their life together — even if the house didn't quite feel like his just yet, and Ellen sometimes ate his cereal. And now they were stuck in an attic.

Risk was not going well. It was Jack's turn, and he was being slow. Partly because he was in a muddle about what to do with his artillery, but mainly because he could tell none of the others were concentrating. He sort of wanted someone to suggest they stop playing now. It couldn't be him, because he'd wanted to play in the first place. He had hoped it would distract them until they could try yelling out of the window again, though maybe Monopoly would have made everyone feel more cheerful. Jack never won Monopoly, but he always enjoyed looking at the addresses — more so now that he lived in London. He'd been to all the places in the Manchester Monopoly, but he'd only been to a few of the London locations. He'd never even heard of Marylebone, except for in the board game.

'Do you think the water will just . . . switch itself off eventually?' Ellen said, out of nowhere. 'Maybe there's a mechanism, or something.' She sounded tired, her voice a little far away.

Jack noticed she had a mark on her baggy grey T-shirt. It looked a bit like jam: dark and sticky and bitty.

'Maybe,' said Alexa, dully, turning to look at Ellen, whose gaze was halfway to catatonic now. 'I have no idea.'

'How much water was there?' Jack asked. He wondered, suddenly stricken, if it was his fault. Surely not. He'd come home from the pub with Johnny fairly early and gone straight up to his room.

'A lot,' said Ellen.

Jack made a sympathetic noise. 'I'm hungry,' he added, for a second time that morning, examining the dirt under his nails. The game board was very dusty.

'Me too,' Ellen agreed, glumly.

'Was it under the sink?' Ben asked. Jack noticed that he was clutching his left biceps in his right hand. 'The tap, I mean. If so, I reckon you were in the right place. That's where ours is. The plumber had to switch off the water once when our sink backed up.'

'Yeah, under the sink.' Alexa sounded rather flat.

'Wait, so why did you all end up in here?' Ben asked, still rubbing his biceps. Jack thought Ben sounded like Maisie's husband, Rich, who would ask questions in a way that implied the people he was asking were very silly.

There was a pause.

Alexa breathed in loudly. 'Well, Ellen thought at one point that the mains switch might be up here,' she said, quietly.

Ben screwed up his face. 'Right.' Now he really sounded like Rich.

'I'd tried turning off the water under the sink, but I couldn't turn the tap, so I came up here to get help,' Alexa added.

Ellen swallowed, preparing to take her turn. 'Yeah, it was my idea to come up here to look.' She sounded sheepish; Jack saw Alexa smile at her. 'There was so much water coming out of the sink, and I was panicking . . .' She trailed off.

'It was pretty early,' Alexa said, loyally.

It was Jack's turn. He looked at Ben. 'I heard Ellen scream, so that's why I came up,' he explained.

Ellen pointed at the mouse, stiff with rigor mortis.

Ben grimaced. 'Yes,' he said.

'Maybe we should move it,' Alexa suggested, uncertainly.

Jack noticed she had a black smudge on her cheek, though he decided she might be annoyed if he pointed it out in front of Ben. They all stared at the mouse.

'There's nowhere to put it,' Ellen pointed out after a few moments.

'Yes, but it's creeping me out,' Alexa said, weakly. 'Can we at least give up on Risk?'

'Please,' Ellen said, drily.

Eagerly – and without pausing for Ben's response – Jack started roughly gathering the pieces from the board, tipping all the bits back into the cardboard box. When this was done, he closed the lid and – still seated – tossed the whole thing behind him, somewhere into the chaos of dissembled and discarded objects. The attic reminded Jack of his grandfather's garage: mostly decaying junk, with the occasional unexpected treasure.

Meanwhile, Ben had scrambled to his feet and picked up the mouse by its tail. He grimaced. Jack watched in awed horror as Ben deposited the mouse's corpse to the left of the door. He wiped his hand on his jeans. 'There we go,' he said, grimly.

Jack noticed that Alexa looked a little revolted, but she

rearranged her face into a warm smile as Ben took his seat back in the circle beside her.

'What time is it?' Ben asked.

Jack checked his useless phone. 'Nine-oh-seven, a.m.'

'Right, so shall we try yelling again?'

Ellen looked dubious. 'Do you really think that's going to work?'

Ben looked a little stung.

'Sorry,' Ellen said, quickly. 'It's just . . . well . . . I don't think I'd stop to help if I heard some people shouting from an attic window in New Cross.'

'I would,' Ben insisted.

'*Really?*' Ellen rolled her shoulders slightly, as if squaring up for a fight.

'Definitely, I know if –'

'Hey, wait,' Alexa interrupted, brightly. 'I have an idea.' She narrowed her eyes, testing it. Satisfied, she spoke. 'We should make a sign! And then suspend it from the skylight.'

They all stared at her for a tumbleweed moment.

Eventually, Ellen hazarded a response. 'Saying what?'

'Well . . .' Alexa started, gently, 'I agree that shouting at our neighbours and passers-by might not be the best way to endear us to them.'

Ben shrugged.

'But maybe if we make a sign, then we'll seem less . . . intimidating. And less shouty.'

'But what do we *put* on the sign?' Ellen sounded scornful.

'"HELP"?' Alexa shot back, undeterred.

Jack resisted the urge to laugh. He wasn't sure if it was meant to be funny.

Alexa added, 'Then we could take it in turns to watch

out of the window. So that if anyone spots the sign, then we can shout down to them. And . . . explain the situation in more detail –'

'And scare them off,' Ellen retorted, but she was grinning now. 'Oh fine, of course we'll do it.'

Alexa rolled her eyes.

'It's a good idea,' Ben said, loyally. 'Plus, we aren't busting out of this attic by osmosis.' He stood up and arched his back.

Jack noticed that Ben's head almost nudged the ceiling, and he wondered who was taller.

'We need something to write with,' Ben instructed. 'And on.'

'I think I spotted some paint earlier.' Jack stood and stretched to his full height, sizing Ben up as he did so. There couldn't be more than an inch or so in it. 'Hey, maybe Mrs Chan will see the sign,' he added, quietly. Jack had struck up an unlikely friendship with Mrs Chan, who lived a few doors down, after he took delivery of a parcel for her a few months back. He knew that Ellen and Alexa thought their friendship was strange.

'Exactly,' said Alexa, evenly. 'Or anyone. Where did you see the paint, Jack?'

Jack tried to recall where he'd spotted the tins. 'Near the door, maybe?'

He moved to a pile of boxes near the door frame and started excavating them. He could feel Ellen hovering near his left shoulder. There was one box that appeared to be an unmarked grave for computer parts: hundreds of cables, mouses and keyboards that looked like they'd been decommissioned in the 1980s. Everything was dusty, and there were ancient spiderwebs slung across the devices. Looking at the contents made Jack's eyes feel itchy.

'God, just think of the dead skin cells that must have been in those keyboards,' Ellen muttered.

Jack preferred not to. He opened another box, which appeared to be full of starchy old newspapers. A third contained a pair of children's armbands.

'So creepy,' Ellen intoned, stretching out the 'ee'.

Jack grimaced in agreement, and recalled he'd seen them earlier in his rummage through the attic. Perhaps the box of paint was close? The attic was in such a state of disorder that it was very difficult to remember where anything was. Still, after a little rootling, he disinterred the tins, which were stiff with old paint, from underneath some ratty cloths.

Ellen stepped back.

'Found it!' he called out. 'And I think there are some brushes buried in here too.' With difficulty – and without any assistance from Ellen – he heaved the box out of the pile of chaos. When he turned round, he saw that Ben had his arms wrapped around Alexa's waist. They were facing each other, speaking in low tones. She looked pleased.

'Oh, sorry.' Jack looked at Ellen, who raised her eyebrows. His face felt hot, and the box was – suddenly – very heavy.

'Well done, Jack,' Alexa turned quickly, smoothing her T-shirt.

'Thanks, mate,' Ben said, clapping Jack on the back.

'No worries,' Jack said. Then he added, quietly, 'Mate.'

'Shall we tear up one of the other boxes to use as a sign?' Alexa asked.

Ben pointed to one filled to the brim with crockery and carried it lightly into the centre of the room. Jack struggled over with the box of paint tins and brushes, dropping it with as much elegance as he could muster, emitting a low 'oof' as he did so. He hoped Alexa hadn't heard. Ben and Ellen were removing the crockery, Ellen grimacing as she held a saucer up for inspection.

'This is horrible.'

'Have you taken it all out?' Sometimes Alexa ignored Ellen's jokes. Jack wouldn't dare.

'Yes,' Ellen said, peevishly.

'OK, let's tear into that box to give us a piece of card big enough for a sign.' Alexa was businesslike now.

With a little difficulty, Ben tore a side off the thick cardboard box and presented it to Alexa.

'Thank you.' A grateful smile. 'OK, and now for the paint.'

Jack rushed to remove a tin for her.

'Thanks, Jack. Wait . . . paint doesn't go off, does it?'

'Don't think so?' Ben offered.

'Let's just keep the skylight open,' Alexa said, after a minute's contemplation. 'That way the paint fumes won't get to us.'

'I don't know, I might appreciate the high at this stage,' Ellen said, drily.

Jack laughed on cue. She looked at him gratefully.

'Right, so what are we writing?' Ben asked.

'I say we go with something basic,' Alexa replied. 'Like –'

'Fuck?'

Alexa ignored Ellen again. 'OK, let's say: "SOS, stuck in attic –"'

'"And there's a leak in the kitchen",' Ellen supplied. '"A big one".'

Alexa gingerly opened the paint pot. The insides looked normal: thick and soupy. She dunked one of the hardened brushes into the pot and then pulled it out, paint dripping in a long stream from the end of the brush. The others watched as she started painting their message in long, precise lettering. Even in decades-old paint with hardened paintbrushes, Jack thought that Alexa's handwriting looked like calligraphy. He was glad he hadn't been asked to write the message.

'HELP! We are stuck in the attic. Kitchen is flooded. Please look up!'

She added an arrow pointing upwards on the end, and removed her brush with a flourish.

They all examined Alexa's handiwork.

'Do you think we should add a smiley face, or something?' Ellen asked, after due consideration.

Alexa made a scornful face.

'Yes, I know,' Ellen said, hastily. 'But it might make us seem more personable. Or should we say something like "This is not a joke!!!"?'

'But does that make it sound more like it's a joke?' Ben pointed out.

'I think it makes us sound funny,' Jack tried. 'In a good way,' he added. 'Like we're good people, worth rescuing.'

Alexa cocked her head to one side and dabbed her paintbrush in the pot of paint again. She hovered it over the cardboard, then, after a moment's deliberation, added a message to the bottom of the sign.

This is (sadly) not a joke . . . SOS!

She leaned back, and gave her handiwork a satisfied nod.

Jack agreed that, on the basis of this sign, he'd definitely try to rescue the people stuck in the attic.

'OK, so how are we going to hang it?' Alexa had already moved on. 'There must be something in here we can use?'

Again, Jack got there first: he spotted a long coil of electrical cable nestled near the bottom of some stacked dining-room chairs. He pointed, 'What about that?'

'Perfect.'

Pleased, Jack collected the cable.

Meanwhile, Ben had found a 10kg kettlebell, which he held aloft. With a little effort, he bored a hole in the sign with the handle of one of the paintbrushes, pulled the cable through it, and tied the whole thing to the weight. Jack, Ellen and Alexa followed him to the window as he suspended the sign from the skylight. They watched its jerky passage down the front of the house.

'Do you think the right side is facing out?' Alexa asked, suddenly stricken.

They all contemplated this.

'Well, if it's not, it'll probably sort of spin round,' Ben replied, hesitantly. 'I mean, either way, someone will see it.'

They all stared at the coil hanging from the window. The hustle and bustle of a shared project over, the new calm felt slightly mournful by comparison.

'Well, I guess someone should keep watch,' Alexa said, finally.

'I will!' Jack stepped forward and offered a sort of salute, which he regretted almost instantly. He could tell that Ellen was trying not to laugh.

'Good man,' Ben said.

'Are you sure, Jack?' Alexa asked. 'We'll take it in turns, of course.'

'Yeah. I'll do the next stint.' Ben now had his arm slung casually around Alexa's shoulders.

She looked very small beside him.

'No problem,' Jack said. 'It's nice to get the fresh air anyway.'

'And Jack, remember, if anyone sees the sign, shout down to them.' Alexa looked grave now, and Jack frowned, immediately anxious that he'd do something wrong.

'Thanks, Jack.' Ellen raised her eyebrows. 'We'll be over here, if you . . . need us. Or anything.'

He watched as they shuffled back to the area near the door.

Jack turned and looked out of the window. Rokeby Close was deserted. He leaned out through the skylight as far as he could, but the angle was too tight and he couldn't read the sign dangling from the cord. He'd just have to trust that it was the right way round. In the distance, he could hear a siren yowling.

His phone vibrated and he took it out: he had a Twitter notification. This was unusual. Jack didn't really have many followers – 112, to be precise – although he sometimes helped out with the Green Genie Twitter profile. He'd find memes, or share their song of the week on a Wednesday afternoon, which always had to have a fruit or vegetable theme. (Jack sometimes wondered how long they could carry this joke on, but decided it would be impolitic to point it out to his colleagues.) He liked the social media manager, Deepti, who wore huge pink trainers and sequined leggings that made her look like a mermaid with legs. She had a dachshund, Cody, which she brought to the office. At Christmas she'd dressed Cody up as Santa, with a small hat, white-trimmed cape and little boots on all four paws.

Johnny had tagged him in a meme about Manchester City. Jack smiled, and then realized that the notification was in fact even *more* unusual because he didn't have any signal. It appeared that his phone had finally managed to connect to the WiFi router in Ellen's bedroom, two floors beneath. It was a weak connection – only a bar – but it had been enough for the tweet to come through.

He was about to tell the others about this development, when – with a frown of surprise – he found that he had a different idea entirely. For a few seconds, he ruminated as his idea grew legs, and then, still slightly surprised, Jack opened up the Compose Tweet box and stared at the blinking cursor.

He licked his lips, and with a decisive nod, he started typing.

@jackbarnes93
Sending out an SOS!!!! Stuck in an attic in Rokeby Close, Lewisham, south-east London. Door handle broke off and there's flooding in the kitchen!!! With my housemates (and one of their dates!) #newcross #stuckintheattic

5. Ellen

With Jack by the window, it was difficult not to feel like a third wheel. While Ellen was pretending very hard not to notice, Alexa and Ben kept exchanging what were presumably meaningful glances and whispering to each other. Their hands were on the floor, fingers entangled. Ellen felt a little sullen. Perhaps she'd bring up the dead mouse again.

'So –' she started, not quite knowing where she was going.

Alexa and Ben both looked at her, quizzically.

She recovered. 'Shall we put a bet on how long it takes to get rescued?'

Ben gave a lazy half-smile.

'Loser has to pay for the kitchen to be refitted,' Alexa muttered, darkly.

'Too soon.'

They settled back into a not particularly companionable silence, during which Ellen observed, dully, that in all the time she'd known Alexa, which was about a decade now, and in all the houses they'd shared together (two in York and three in London), Alexa had only brought a few boys home. She wished she could say something to this effect, although she knew Alexa would throttle her. She tried to catch Alexa's eye in order to give her a meaningful look of her own, but Alexa was now totally fixated on Ben.

Ellen frowned.

Ellen and Alexa had their meet-cute in a seminar on

Dream Visions in Medieval Literature during their first week of university. Some stragglers had slunk into the seminar and their tutor – a tall and elegant bespectacled woman in her forties – had accidentally told them to 'shit down'. Ellen had spun round immediately, searching for kinship with one of these strangers. Across the room Alexa's blue eyes had widened, and she bit her lip. Ellen had raised an eyebrow and dared a smile back. After class, Ellen had hung back in order to time her exit with Alexa's. They'd said a shy 'hello' and Alexa had asked Ellen whether she was walking to the library, which she wasn't but pretended she was so that she could spend a little more time in Alexa's orbit. And they'd ended up having tea together in the library cafe, in which they'd mainly talked about their course and which halls they were in, but it was a start. At the end, they'd swapped numbers and Ellen had texted Alexa before the next seminar, asking if she fancied walking there together from town, and they were off.

For the first few months of their acquaintance, Ellen had tiptoed a little around her new friend – an unknown quantity, with her satchel and her frowny resting face. Alexa was unafraid and funny and had a sense of mischief – these were all the things Ellen liked about her straight away – but she was also quite serious and inscrutable. Sometimes, just before they met for a coffee or a walk, Ellen would feel nervous. She'd have date-oriented anxieties, worried their chemistry would be off, that they'd have nothing to talk about, or that she'd say something odd.

Not to mention, the stakes were high. Ellen had been struggling to shake off this girl called Charlotte, who lived next door to her in halls and had suggested they do things like attend a seminar on the Dewey Decimal system together. This made becoming Alexa's friend even more urgent. Charlotte complained a lot, and loudly, about a group of beautiful people who were all from London and lived in their corridor. They sat outside their rooms every evening, eating dinner together and tossing their hair while laughing. The girls sat on the boys' laps – even the ones they weren't going out with – and it was probably very fun if you were involved, but very annoying if you were trying to sleep, or study, or had to climb over them to get to the shared kitchen. And yet, Ellen was certain this group were not the right enemies to make. While she knew it was unkind, she really – powerfully – didn't want Charlotte to be her university friend, the one she saw when they were adults, sharing memories over wine-soaked dinners when they both had jobs (?) and leather wallets. Frankly, one did not reminisce fondly over the Dewey Decimal system.

And so she made befriending Alexa her project, at a cost to most of her university work. They'd walk down cobbled streets, scarves whipping in the wind, and swap histories. Or they'd sit in the front room of a small, crowded tea shop full of students, with copies of *The Canterbury Tales* propped up in front of them. Sometimes they'd sit on a low wall on the main street and watch the world go by together, feeling out the edges of who the other person was.

One evening, after a seminar, when they'd both submitted their essays and a chill sunset stretched across the horizon, Alexa turned to Ellen, her nose a little pink from the cold, shoulders hunched inside her long camel coat.

'Do you want to go for a drink, maybe? We could go to the Eagle – it's just down here.'

'Yes!' Ellen said, practically clutching Alexa's arm with excitement.

They took a small table in one corner of the grand pub, not far from the hulking mahogany bar, near a fire where flames licked and danced. And even though it was chilly and past 5 p.m. in a student town, it stayed pretty quiet in there, and they lingered for hours.

'OK, I've spent all the money I had with me *but* I've got a bottle of wine in my room,' Ellen offered, finally, stifling a hiccup. 'Do you want to come and drink that too?'

'Definitely,' Alexa said.

They swung out of there, warmed from the inside by a bottle of wine, and made their way up to Ellen's room. The beautiful people were in the hall – only a few of them – and one of them said a 'hey' when Alexa and Ellen walked past, which Ellen took as a good sign. They'd never once said 'hey' when she was with Charlotte.

They sat in Ellen's room and demolished the bottle of wine in what seemed like a few swigs, and laughed and rocked backwards and forwards. It was near midnight and there was music playing down the hall and choruses of laughter coming out of every open door. The beautiful people sounded like they were wrestling in the hall. ('Give it back!' giggled one girl, loudly.) Ellen and Alexa decided to go to Kushion, the largest club by the riverside. Ellen took a £20 note, promised to next week's budget, from her drawer – ignoring the fact that she'd regret it when she had to eat pasta pesto for every meal. And on the way out, they caught the end of the beautiful people's party and it turned out they were going to Kushion too. They all started talking total nonsense until Charlotte poked her head out of her door, looking furious. She spotted Ellen, and opened and closed her mouth like a fish, but Ellen walked right past without even saying 'hi'. She felt a little badly about this. But not that badly.

Alexa and Ellen lost the beautiful people in the queue to get into the club, but they stuck together and drank sticky colourful drinks by the bottle and cheap, cheap, nasty tequila at the bar. One shot followed the other, and they said 'I love you!' and admitted how glad they were to have found one another.

They got chips on the way home, and Alexa texted to say she'd got home safely. Ellen omitted to do the same because she'd passed out, fully clothed – including her shoes – and later woke up with the cold chips beside her and her laptop on the floor, which now had angry, colourful lines stretched across the screen.

Alexa texted again.

My. Head. Send help. X

Ellen replied, one eye closed, the other squinting into the dark screen.

Oh jesus. just woke up with shoes still on, chips in the bed and a broken laptop. chaos. can we go get a bloody mary now please?? x

And that was that. They'd been despicable together, and Ellen never again got anxious about seeing Alexa or worried that they'd have nothing to talk about. They were so clearly kindred spirits. Plus, Charlotte never spoke to Ellen ever again, which was a real win.

They were an odd pairing – Ellen loud and chaotic, Alexa quieter and more contained – and always had been, but their relationship worked beautifully. They shared all the important things. They found the same jokes funny and the same people objectionable. They could communicate just with looks and raised eyebrows, and would always tell the other one when an outfit made them look like a rectangle. They had other friends at university – like Sophie – but their relationship existed as a separate, more meaningful entity. They fought with the security of siblings, knowing for certain that they were stuck with each other now.

They lived together first in two shared houses, in York and later in London, initially with strangers, then with Sophie in Camberwell, and latterly, at 49 Rokeby Close. After ten years, it felt extraordinary to think there had ever been a time when they had not known one another, or even slept under the same roof.

Many of their university friends had moved to the city and become unbearable: playing at real adulthood with their couples' dinner parties; competitive WhatsApp messages about long working hours; and a near-uniform uptake of street food and barre classes. This meant that socializing with them was far less fun, because in order to do so, you might have to go to Covent Garden to listen to a long, meandering anecdote about LinkedIn. On the other hand, moving to London had not changed the DNA of Ellen and Alexa's friendship at all. Granted, they had (very different) jobs now, but New Cross was suitably scruffy, bookended as it was by universities. Now, instead of long walks around their small university town, they walked up to the top of Telegraph Hill to admire the spires of the city.

Alexa was still very bright and very good at everything. Sometimes, it was a little difficult to watch her succeed without feeling like a far less evolved version of the same species. But this was nothing new, and Ellen was – mostly – unbothered. Alexa was her best friend, and some people were civil servants who ran the London Marathon in under four hours, while others were the type who occasionally jogged to the corner shop to buy a Ribena Light, and spent their working hours composing emails with the subject line 'Here's #TheFlowdown – £10 off your first box of CBD tampons with the code GETTHEFLOW'. Ellen had worked at The Flowdown for three years now, employed initially as a sort of all-purpose intern – paid, at least – but had worked her way up to Communications Executive, a rather grand title that distracted from the fact she was a team of one and paid very poorly. Still, it was better than her previous job, as a skivvy at a boutique PR firm, where her role had mainly involved booking taxis for women called Lavinia, Davinia or Hum, and returning their dry cleaning, which had been, it seemed, endless. Alexa, meanwhile, had gone straight on to the Civil Service fast stream after university.

It was still silent, apart from the odd sound of a stomach gurgling, and Jack was still standing sentry at the window. Ellen was starting to panic slightly about how much she needed the loo, but didn't feel able to raise this while Ben's arm was wrapped around Alexa, his hand resting on her hip, and hers halfway up one of his thighs. Minutes ago, when he'd thought she wasn't looking, she'd seen him kiss the backs of Alexa's hands lightly; Ellen had watched with almost anthropological interest as Alexa's eyelashes fluttered.

But despite Alexa's obvious delight, Ellen could tell she

was worried about leaving Ellen out — mostly because Alexa kept anxiously checking Ellen's face for tells. Ellen knew she should make an effort. Maybe it would distract her from the throb of her bladder.

'So, where did you two go last night?' she tried, breezily.

'Penny's,' Alexa replied, eagerly.

'I think we had pizza, but mainly we had wine,' Ben said, goofily.

Alexa gave him an indulgent smile. Ah good, a double act.

'I see . . .' A pause. 'I believe that I had no dinner and exclusively wine.' Ellen put her head on her temples to pantomime a headache.

Alexa gave her a sympathetic grimace.

'Where were you?' Ben asked, earning a smile from Ellen for effort.

'We stayed at my office for a while, having drinks, and then went to the pub.' The outline of last night remained a little fuzzy still. 'I invited Alexa to join us but it appears she got a better offer,' she added, with mischievous inspiration.

Alexa pretended to look apologetic, while in fact appearing very pleased with the way the evening had panned out.

Ben grinned. 'Sorry about that.' He clearly wasn't either.

Ellen rolled her eyes good-humouredly and laughed, at which point her bladder throbbed again. She had worked out that if she crossed her legs and squeezed her thighs, then she might buy herself a little time before she inevitably had to relieve herself in the stacks of Elias's junk. But it wasn't going to work for ever.

She was not surprised she was going be the one who broke first. It was a running joke in Ellen's family that she always, always, needed to go to the loo. Throughout her childhood, on any car journey of half an hour or more, she would inevitably find herself leaning forward to stick her head between the driver's and passenger's seats and put in a request for another stop. Her father would jeer, her brother would laugh and her mother would say, exasperatedly, 'Oh, Ellen – didn't you go before we left?'

The worst trips were the long drives to Brittany, where the Fishers rented the same souped-up caravan every summer. On one occasion, nearing the home stretch, her father refused to stop. She had been caught short and had to sit on a picnic blanket for the home stretch to the campsite, near Roscoff. She had been fifteen, which was definitely too old to wet yourself in the car. She had sat there, mouth set in a line, wishing her father would take the corners even faster.

'How was the night, El?' Alexa asked, solicitously.

'Big, I think. I woke up with a shoe on.'

Ben snorted.

'Was Lee around?' Alexa asked, conspiratorial now.

'He was not.'

Alexa had an expression of pleasant interest, though Ellen could see that she was distracted by Ben kissing the skin of her bare shoulder.

Ellen squirmed a little, recrossing her legs in an attempt to postpone the inevitable, and wondered idly whether her parents could have been persuaded to come and rescue her. After some adolescent turbulence, Ellen's relationship with her parents had settled into what was best described as 'fond, mutual irritation', which only occasionally boiled over into a vivid argument. Ellen would make no effort to conceal her eye roll when subjected to one of Linda's meandering anecdotes about the boiler; she was still too quick to take John's characteristic grumpiness personally. But mostly, their interactions were affectionate. Despite their suspicions about London and their utter bemusement at her job – her father couldn't talk about it without going magenta – she was glad to know they were there, at the other end of the phone, or forty minutes or so on the high-speed rail link from Gillingham. It was enormously comforting to think of their lives continuing in her absence: John going to his job as an administrator at Medway Council, Linda still teaching History part-time at a girls' school in the next town.

'It smells really musty in here,' Alexa observed, wrinkling her nose. The attic was heating up like a greenhouse, which seemed to be making all of its assorted contents ripen.

Ellen scrunched her nose up too.

'So this is all your landlord's stuff?' Ben asked. His hand had moved from Alexa's hip and was now lurking near her lower back.

'Yeah,' Alexa replied, and then suddenly giggled.

Ellen assumed Ben's hand had slunk lower. She smirked at Alexa, who flushed. In spite of everything, Ellen was desperate to find out how Alexa and Ben had ended up together last night. She decided to get rid of Ben.

'Hey, Ben?' she asked sweetly.

He looked up.

'Maybe you should go yell out the window again?'

He narrowed his eyes as though she were playing an elaborate practical joke on him.

Alexa twigged it straight away. 'I think Ellen would like a word.'

'Aha,' Ben said. He untangled his fingers from Alexa's and sprang to a standing position. 'I could do with some fresh air, anyway.'

They both watched him lope towards the skylight, making Jack jump.

'That wasn't very subtle,' Alexa observed in a low whisper, with an anxious glance towards the skylight. Her small hand was cupped in front of her mouth, though Ellen could tell she was smiling.

Ellen shuffled round, and indicated that Alexa should do so too, so that their backs were to Ben and Jack. Ellen shot a glance at the boys. Ben was trying to pretend he wasn't watching.

'I know it wasn't my finest.' Ellen shrugged, then tucked a sheet of long, lank brown hair behind her right ear. 'But . . .' She inclined her head towards Ben.

Alexa smirked.

Ellen widened her eyes again, then prodded Alexa's knee with her finger.

'Ow,' Alexa said, hammily.

Ellen prodded her again, and put her own hand over her mouth. 'So?'

Alexa leaned closer to Ellen. 'Well, straight after I texted you last night, Ben texted me –' The words were coming out in a rush. Her breath smelled sharp and artificial, and she still had the smear of kohl on her left cheek.

Ellen rubbed her finger across Alexa's cheek. 'Sorry – you had eyeliner, and it was annoying me.'

'Is it off?'

'Yes. Go on.'

'Well, like I said, he texted, and suggested Penny's.'

Ellen remembered.

'And I knew you were in Farringdon but I couldn't really be arsed to trek back into town . . .' Alexa paused to look apologetic but Ellen shrugged her off, impatient to hear more. 'And I wanted to see him,' she said, more quietly. 'After last time . . . so anyway, we went. And it was fun. Back to how it was on our first few dates. We got quite drunk – very, actually – and the conversation flowed, and then we came back here and –'

'And then he locked us in an attic,' Ellen prompted.

'And then he locked us in an attic.' Alexa laughed, hopelessly.

'This is pretty bad, isn't it?' Ellen looked for reassurance.

Alexa was quiet. 'It's not great,' Alexa agreed, finally.

Another pause.

'But how did it go?' Ellen mouthed, raising an eyebrow.

Alexa was – if not prudish, exactly – uncomfortable with volunteering details. Once, when drunk at their friend Kim's birthday dinner, Alexa had tried to make a principled argument for keeping 'the intimate sacred'. Ellen had heckled her so loudly the whole table had started listening.

On cue now, Alexa squirmed. 'It was really good,' she frowned, embarrassed. Briskly, she added: 'I think I really like him.'

'Yes, we've all noticed the hand holding and lingering glances.'

Alexa flushed, but Ellen could tell she was pleased. 'Sorry. It's definitely a bit weird having Jack watching us.'

'He is the world's most awkward man. There's nothing you can do about that.' She prodded Alexa in the knee. 'It all sounds fun. Definitely worth skipping out on me last night for. Don't overthink it.'

Alexa gave her an anxious look.

'Fine. Do overthink it. In fact, think of it like this: he could be your only chance to have a baby. If we're stuck up here for a decade you might have to bite the bullet. We can raise it together, I'll forgo bearing a child myself. I'm not breeding with Jack.'

'So mean.' But Alexa laughed. Ellen shot a look over her shoulder and observed that both Ben and Jack were pretending not to watch them.

She prodded Alexa again. 'Also, I don't want to alarm you but –'

'What?' she asked, sharply.

'But as well as us being fucking stuck here while the house floods, I am also absolutely desperate for a wee.'

Alexa was relieved enough to laugh again.

Ellen glowered.

'Sorry – um –' she made a hopeless gesture – 'maybe there's a bucket somewhere.' Ellen gave her a hard stare, and she added: 'I can't believe the house is flooding too. This is a nightmare.' Outside in the distance, a lorry sounded a long, mellow note.

Ellen looked heavenwards. 'Don't say it. I might look calm but I am very much not.'

'You don't look that calm.'

'Shut up and help me. I'm serious. I need a wee really badly. I can't hold it much longer. We need to designate a corner as a loo.'

'I mean, I don't think it has to be an entire corner.'

Ellen tried a beseeching look, but it turned into a sort of moaning laugh – which set Alexa off too.

'What is it?' Jack called from the skylight. He sounded a little paranoid.

'Yeah, what are you cackling about?' Ben asked. Unlike Jack, he seemed pleased, clearly assuming (rightly) that he had been the topic of the furtive conversation. He was massaging his pectoral again, the other hand running through his hair.

Alexa and Ellen both stared at him over their shoulders; Ellen resisted the urge to roll her eyes. He stood, silhouetted in the sunlight from the skylight, a grin playing with the corners of his mouth.

'What's so funny?' Jack called out again.

'Yes, do share.' Ben walked towards them, arms crossed, eyebrows raised in challenge.

Alexa looked delighted to have him back.

'What's going on over here?'

'We were just discussing where I could go for a piss, honestly, Ben,' Ellen offered, evenly. 'Any ideas?'

'Gross,' Jack said quietly, wrinkling his nose, and turning back to his post at the skylight.

Ellen made a face at his back. Ben, meanwhile, smirked, settling himself back on the floor beside Alexa, stretched out, thighs almost touching. He was, Ellen could already tell from the glint in his eyes, a worthy opponent.

'Skylight?' he shrugged. 'That's what I'll do when the time comes.'

'I'm not sure you're strong enough to lift me,' Ellen

replied. 'I'm afraid I might have to try that box.' She pointed at the perspex container of Elias's DVDs.

Ben shrugged again. 'As long as you leave it out of sight. And smell.'

'Well, obviously.'

'Off you go then, El.' Alexa said. She was emboldened now, perhaps by Ben's proximity to her thigh. She was playing up for him. It was entertaining to see Alexa act so coquettishly.

Ellen nodded grimly.

'Do you want us to make a noise while you do it?' Jack asked, turning round again. He looked stricken.

'Yes,' Ellen said, after a moment's contemplation. 'I would.'

They were all watching her expectantly. Ellen picked up the box and tipped out the DVDs, in a flourish, in front of the door. Even at a distance, Jack winced as the cascade of plastic boxes landed in a rough pile. Ellen could feel them all watching as she cast her gaze around the room, trying to work out which was the most private spot. There was a full-length mirror standing in one of the corners near the skylight, which she reckoned could function as a screen. It was far from an ideal set-up.

They were still watching her.

She affected bravado. 'Talk among yourselves,' she demanded. Then, more quietly, she added, 'Please.'

Jack sounded a rusty note with his throat.

Gritting her teeth, and trying not to think about how close he would be, she started clambering through the tangle of boxes and dismembered appliances towards the standing mirror. As she approached, she glanced around the room one last time. Jack had dutifully stuck his head back out of the skylight now. Meanwhile, Ben was muttering something into Alexa's ear.

'Guys!'

They all looked at her again.

'Remember to make some noise.'

6. Alexa

'This has sort of happened to me before, you know,' Ben said, a little more loudly, as they both pretended not to be able to hear Ellen from behind the mirror. She had definitely started. Ben's eyes were tired but danced.

'Oh yeah?' Alexa replied. She noticed for the umpteenth time the deep dimple in his chin. It was about the size of the tip of her thumb, and seemed to get deeper when he smiled, which was often.

'Yeah, really.' He was eager to convince her. 'Though strictly, it was a greenhouse, not an attic. My uncle's, in his garden, in Devon. We used to go there all the time when we were small. Anyway, some mechanism in the ancient door broke and Ava – my sister – and I got trapped in there. In the end, my mum had to smash one of the panes, and she yanked the handle open from the outside. I seem to remember we found it rather funny.'

'And was it your fault that time too?' Alexa replied, like quicksilver.

Ben laughed, a high clear note. 'Definitely not. All Ava's.'

Alexa smiled. 'How long were you in there for?'

'An hour or so, I reckon. But I was about eight and Ava would have been six. So to us it probably seemed like for ever.' He smiled at Alexa. 'I remember Ava eating lots of my uncle's tomatoes off the vine. He was furious.'

They could still hear Ellen.

'So you were well taken care of, then.' She tried to ignore the sound. 'Tomatoes on tap.'

'Absolutely. Couldn't have asked for better rations . . .' She sounded like she was stopping. 'How long do you think we've been up here for now?'

Alexa wrung her blank wrist where her watch usually was. 'No idea. It's probably time to take over from Jack, though. He's been there a while.'

'Only fair.' Ben cleared his throat and spoke a little louder. 'Hey? Jack?'

Jack turned, expectantly.

'What time is it, mate?'

Jack consulted his phone, looking anxious. 'Nine thirty-five.'

Alexa smiled encouragingly at him.

'Great. I'll take over in a minute, OK?'

'Oh.' Jack sounded surprised. 'Well, thanks,' he added, after a pause.

'Nine thirty-five.' Ben groaned. 'We should definitely still be asleep.'

'Oh, I don't know,' Alexa said. The way he watched her when she spoke made her feel like she wanted to talk for ever. 'I quite like getting up early on a Saturday. Making the most of the weekend.' Now he was looking at her as though she was mad. 'I'm not very good at lie-ins,' she finished, lamely.

'I am very, very good at lie-ins. Don't worry.' He nudged her, lightly, in the ribs and she felt her whole body buzz. 'I can teach you.'

Ellen was moving around in the corner. It sounded a little like she'd knocked something over. Ben caught her

86

eye and Alexa smiled conspiratorially, then felt instantly disloyal.

'I'm not looking forward to my turn,' Ben said, solemnly.

Alexa was about to laugh when she saw one of Ellen's arms shoot out from behind the standing mirror.

'The good news is, she appears to have finished.'

'Thank God. I was trying really hard to pretend I couldn't hear her.' A smile. The dimple appeared, and the corners of his eyes crinkled too. 'Right, I suppose I should go and relieve Jack of his duties.' He leaned in and kissed her lightly.

'I can come, if you'd like? Although Ellen will be back in a minute.'

'Nah, stay. I can handle it solo.'

He stood up and loped towards the skylight, hoicking his jeans again as he paced the length of the room, slapping Jack on the back, and then squeezing in beside him. They were about the same height, she noted, although Ben was slightly broader, and Jack stood more awkwardly, as if trying to make himself as small as possible. Although the purpose was to relieve Jack of his duties, he seemed reluctant to leave his post.

Ellen had also not returned, although Alexa could see a flash of her pink jogging bottoms through the clutter. She appeared to be sitting down, staring at the wall. This did not bode well. Alexa considered climbing into the scrapheap to find her, but the time out was too appealing. She hadn't had a moment to herself since 9 p.m. last night, and quite a lot had happened since then.

Feeling the first electric flutter of pins and needles,

Alexa shifted until she was sitting with legs outstretched, her back against the door. She closed her eyes for a second, and an image appeared – waking beside Ben, with his arm thrown across her – and she opened her eyes again with a start, as if the others could see what she could.

Of course, this whole predicament was a nightmare. And, strictly, it was Ben's fault. But aside from locking them in, he was doing pretty well: calm, cool, collected. And there were the eye crinkles, and the dimple. Maybe being stuck together wasn't the worst thing.

Perhaps this will be the making of us? she wondered, smiling a little at the thought. She indulged the daydream of herself and Ben as a real couple, no more toing and froing on Hinge, fretting about WhatsApp messages sent or not sent. Alexa had had two serious boyfriends before, though she wasn't sure whether Kai, her secondary-school boyfriend, even properly counted. She'd known him since primary school – he lived in the same village as her, and they'd attended the big school in town together too, getting the same bus to and from school every day. This was about all they'd had in common. After getting together at a sixth-form party, they'd dated for eight months, in which their most meaningful conversations had been about their A Level timetables. She had quietly dumped him in her first week at York, and he still avoided eye contact with her in the pub every Christmas. Their mothers were still in the same book club, so the break-up didn't seem to have come between them.

Then there was Euan, whom she'd started dating in her last year of university, in a relationship that lasted two and a bit years altogether. He'd been the top economist in their year, had gone to one of those schools whose names people knew and whose alumni still talked about them a decade later, and he had a chorus of female friends whom he'd met as a teenager, all of whom were cloyingly nice to Alexa. Until he'd decided the best move for his career (as a management consultant) was to move to Singapore. They had tried a long-distance relationship for a couple of months, but the distance had been too great, and the time difference too topsy-turvy. After the second month, they both stopped talking about Alexa visiting. And then, after three, they both agreed – sadly – that they couldn't carry on this way indefinitely. She'd cried most nights for a month, moped for another and then got over it. That had been about four years ago. Every so often he popped up on her Facebook. He had a new girlfriend, Venetia, who worked for a bank out there and was beautiful in an unexciting sort of way (hair, nails, expensive jeans). On social media, they would regularly 'check-in' on extravagant mini-breaks. 'You can never have too much of Paris – unless you are a credit card' read one recent post, showing the two of them grinning near the Musée d'Orsay. Six months ago, he'd added her on LinkedIn. In his profile picture he looked handsome in a slick, groomed sort of way, his wide smile slightly vacant. Still, she'd accepted the request.

Undeniably, Ben would be an upgrade. Euan was impressive in many ways but Alexa found herself agreeing with Ellen's verdict that he was 'pretty bland' (she had politely waited a full week after the break-up before offering this assessment.)

She was getting ahead of herself. She still barely knew

Ben, of course. A few dates, one night, some social media sleuthing, which hadn't revealed much. She knew that he'd studied Social Anthropology at Bristol, worked at a housing charity, lived up the road in Peckham and liked Dulwich Hamlet FC. He had a private and manicured Facebook account that had the hallmarks of a post-university purge (the only reference to university at all, in fact, was that he had graduated from one), and a Twitter account he hadn't used for almost a year. This was generally used to retweet left-leaning housing think tanks. His last post on Instagram was a group picture from a friend's wedding last July, captioned: 'They went to the chapel.'

Ellen had snorted when Alexa admitted that she'd also stalked his profile page on his office website ('Have you asked for references as well?').

Ben is the junior communications associate at Make A House A Home. He likes football, cycling and his mum; he dislikes olives, green tea and structural inequality. He lived in Berlin for six months, five years ago. His ultimate ambition is to keep getting this anecdote into almost every conversation he has with anyone.

It was sweet of him to mention his mum, she had thought. The 'structural inequality' line was like admitting in a job interview that one of your flaws was 'being too much of a perfectionist', but it was a work profile and in a clumsy way, she supposed, he was showing that he had a conscience. Mercifully, they had not discussed structural inequality on any of their dates.

She could hear Jack and Ben now from the window.

'When I get the choice, I usually pick butternut squash,' Jack was saying. He must have been talking about his own job.

'Yeah, it's good in a curry,' Ben replied, kindly.

Ellen, on the other hand, had not returned from the corner, and appeared to still be staring at the wall.

Steeling herself, Alexa called out, 'El? Are you OK?'

There was a pause. The boys both turned to look at her and she shook her head, mystified.

After a second, Ellen replied. 'I'm fine!'

Her voice was strangled, and contained a discernible note of panic.

Alexa sighed.

She resolved to go over in a second. But first, she permitted herself one last silly daydream: introducing Ben to her parents.

Separately, of course. As far as Alexa knew, Marcus and Elizabeth hadn't been in the same room since she was fourteen, and then it was by mistake; an absent-minded mutual friend had invited them both to the same summer party. Her father had been the one to leave. Unfortunately, social sacrifices rather came with the territory when you had gambled away £30,000 of the family's savings playing high-stakes online poker (it was 2003, and he'd been an early adopter). Elizabeth had found out in the normal, awful way; he'd forgotten to close down his AOL account one evening. When she'd slunk off to play solitaire on the Apple Mac in the large garden shed that doubled as his home office, the mishap had been writ large on the screen. Unfortunately, Alexa had been unable to repress the memory of her mother going for her father with her big handbag, shouting that he was a 'parasite'. Alexa remembered wishing that, aged eleven, she didn't already know what that word meant.

Alexa wasn't certain they'd been happy before – until they became unhappy, she hadn't had much cause to think about it. Shortly after, her father had moved first into the office/ shed – it had a daybed, which soon became his only bed – and later into a series of flats in south-west London. Alexa, always a rather self-possessed child, did not tell anyone at school this. Around this time she developed a tendency to chew her knuckles until they were red and chapped, until one day, her mother spotted this and – aghast – insisted that she wear gloves all day and all night until the skin grew back. Alexa learned her lesson, namely that it was easier for all involved if she did not give any outward indication of inner turmoil.

Plus, she was lucky. Not much else changed, really. Her mother kept the house in Sussex, most of the furniture – and custody of Alexa and her three younger siblings, Nina and the twins, Jacob and Lucy. Her father was, as it had turned out, an average poker player but a very good partner in a law firm, and therefore didn't struggle much for money. In the holidays, the four of them would shuttle between the country and whichever flat he was living in at the time. There were invariably only two bedrooms in the place, so it would be a squeeze. Jacob and Lucy would get the bed, with Nina on the bedroom floor and Alexa usually on the sofa in the living room. ('Sorry, kiddo, I keep meaning to upgrade to a pull-out sofa!' her father would chuckle, every single time Alexa placed her pillow on one end of his regular sofa and prepared to bed down for the evening.) Meanwhile, her mother continued her job as an editor at a publishing house, working three days a week up in town, and the other two at the house, which meant that sometimes she could pick them up from school.

Jacob and Lucy were six years younger than Alexa and currently occupied a shared world of theatre and student parties in Edinburgh, but they WhatsApped often. They were too young to remember the tumult of the divorce in any meaningful detail. For them, life had always involved shuttling between two homes and pretending, diplomatically, to one parent that the other didn't make their fish fingers the way they liked them.

But Nina – Alexa's junior by only two years – had been there for all the rows subsequent to the big one. The two of them would sit at the top of the stairs and listen as Elizabeth delivered her acid assessments of Marcus's failings, and then watch as he shuffled out to the shed again, sending his shadow up the garden path until Elizabeth slammed the back door and the garden was cast into darkness. They'd exchange worried glances and, sometimes, share a bed.

The two remained telepathically close, even though Nina was currently living in Lisbon, working as a copy editor for a start-up. Alexa missed her. They spoke most evenings, and usually for an hour on Sunday. In fact, Ellen reminded her of Nina, which she suspected was what had drawn her to Ellen that first day at York. Both women were clever and loyal and dramatic and extroverted. There was space in her life for the two of them.

With the exception of the handbag episode, their mother was always very composed. She wore glasses that rested on her nose, long navy shift dresses and was always holding a manuscript, or a large glass of wine. She loved parties and gossip, and often worried that Alexa wasn't having enough fun in London. Alexa tried not to be annoyed that her mother often signed off calls by urging her to do 'something wild' that evening. Naturally, Elizabeth adored Ellen.

Alexa and her mother had a standing arrangement: lunch, every month, in which Alexa was obliged to tell her mother everything that had happened in the last four weeks. It always took place on a Saturday, and her mother always picked the restaurant – usually somewhere new, or under-the-radar, or both. Alexa tried not to take it personally that her mother was more plugged into London's zeitgeist than she was.

The last lunch had taken place about three weeks ago, in Soho, at a small, unobtrusive Spanish place on the corner of Poland Street and D'Arblay Street. It was so unobtrusive, in fact, that Alexa had walked past it three times before finding it. When she did, she spotted her mother sitting on a stool in the window, laughing.

'You could have called me instead of letting me walk past,' Alexa said, crossly, allowing the waiter to take her coat.

Her mother had already ordered wine. 'I'm sorry, darling. It was just too funny.'

'Clearly.' Alexa clambered on to the high stool. Her mother was four inches taller than her.

'Right –' Elizabeth had already ordered olives, and was

gnawing the flesh off one now – 'this one has to be quick, I have to be back in the office in an hour or so. Marketing meeting.' She dropped the stone into an earthenware bowl between them. 'So, let's start with your love life.'

Alexa had been on two dates with Ben at this point. She recalled the first kiss outside the pub.

'This bit will be quick too – there is no love life. Work's busy, though.'

Her mother frowned, fondly. 'Oh, Alexa, I do hope you're having enough fun.'

Already.

'Fun doesn't have to mean boys, Mum.'

Elizabeth had tutted and taken another olive.

Alexa smiled at the memory now. She knew her mother would be delighted by Ben. Marcus would, she imagined, be charmingly disinterested in him. Her father rarely called, though always professed to be delighted to hear her voice when she rang him. Despite living only a Tube journey away, she did not see him regularly, and suspected that he was currently in the midst of a full-throttle mid-life crisis. He had bought a motorbike and had taken to wearing full leathers in all situations (except, of course, in the office). Still, he'd been useful when they'd had to fight an old landlord to get their deposit back in full.

Alexa had shaken off the pins and needles. She'd left Ellen in freefall long enough. Though as she stood up, Jack shuffled over. He curled his toes by way of a greeting.

'How did it go, Jack?'

'Didn't see anyone,' he replied. He seemed a little distracted.

'That's not good.'

'No.' Jack looked mournful, then brightened. 'Ben waggled the sign a few times, though. And I think he's going to shout again soon.'

'Good.' She sounded like her mother. 'I'm going to go —'

Jack nodded solemnly, and she started to wend her way through the stacks. It was no easy feat; there was a hairy moment when Alexa almost lost a slipper inside a box that turned out to be unstable footing. After a minute or so, she found Ellen, buried in the middle of all this junk, wild-eyed. She could not see whatever Ellen had repurposed as a toilet.

'It's there,' Ellen muttered, reading her mind, pointing to a perspex box about a metre further in, balanced between the wall and what looked like a folded-up table-tennis table.

'What's up?' she asked, gently, manoeuvring herself into a crouching position until she was at Ellen's level, only wincing slightly as her knees clicked. She kept her voice low.

'OK, so I'm slightly freaking out,' Ellen said, also in a low voice. Her eyes were darting from side to side.

'Wait, why?' Alexa noticed she was a little clammy.

'I can't stop thinking about last night,' Ellen said, with a low moan. 'I keep remembering all this . . . awful stuff.'

Alexa scrunched her face into a frown, mystified. 'What happened last night?'

Ellen was taking shallow breaths. 'OK, so I said this stupid, *stupid* thing to Felicia, because I was drunk.' Her face fell at the memory.

Felicia was Ellen's boss, whom she had nicknamed the 'Grand High Witch'. Alexa was going to offer something weakly reassuring, but Ellen was off again.

'Also, I think Lee is ignoring me and I don't understand why. And I can't remember whether I took my work laptop home and I'm suddenly really worried I left it on the night bus.' Ellen was clenching and unclenching her fingers. 'Also, it is really, really hot in here.' She appeared to be at risk of hyperventilating.

'El, shh. Deep breaths.' Alexa moved to tuck Ellen's hair behind her ears, but she flinched, and Alexa raised her hand in surrender. She needed to tread carefully. Ellen was beginning to spiral, and it was best to see the danger off at the pass, but one wrong move and this could go on for hours. 'OK,' she said, decisively, 'this is a spiral. Listen to me. We are stuck in an attic. We have plenty of other things to worry about right now. You simply must not think about Felicia, or Lee, or your work laptop.'

Alexa took Ellen's chin in her palm. This time, Ellen didn't flinch.

'It is all going to be OK in the end. I promise. You have not done anything wrong.'

Ellen looked unconvinced. Alexa proceeded gingerly.

'Maybe you should come out of this corner for a bit and sit back down with me. Over there?'

Ellen shook her head, firmly.

Alexa stifled a sigh and put on a gentler, more beseeching voice. 'Come on. Please. I don't want you sitting here alone. Next to your own urine.'

A small, small smile.

'Let's get some fresh air – it's probably about time one of us took our turn by the window. We could do it together?'

Ellen smiled, barely. 'Fine,' she said, eventually. 'I'll

come, if you'll hold my hand.' Quickly, she added, 'I didn't wee on it.'

Alexa looked at her best friend. Her long brown hair was lank, and there was a spot threatening to erupt on her chin.

'Yes, of course I will. You idiot.'

7. Ellen

As Ellen had hovered over the Perspex box with all the elegance of a barnyard animal, she'd acknowledged that the morning really was not going according to plan.

Especially since she was fairly certain she had weed on her tracksuit bottoms. A glance between her legs confirmed the worst: there was a not inconsiderable wet patch. She hoicked them them up – while trying to remain low to the ground, in case Ben or Jack spotted her bare bottom. Fully decent, she grimaced as she examined the patch in more detail. It was definitely big enough and wet enough to be noticeable to the others. She padded at it desperately with her T-shirt, then observed that this would create an additional problem.

Could she . . . blow on it to dry it? No, it seemed that her spine definitely did not bend that far. She threw her hand out as she almost lost her balance, clutching the side of a mini-stepladder for safety. Perhaps, if she waited it out for a few minutes, it would dry, she thought, listlessly.

Still, she had to move the box – partly because it smelled, and partly because the liquid was a rather alarming orange colour, which was also making her anxious. She crouched up again, grasping the box – only just – in one hand, and narrowly avoiding thwacking her head against the sloping ceiling, which knocked her over again. After recovering, she balanced the offending item on a cardboard box a metre or so away, and then, hesitating for a second, returned to the same spot. She didn't feel like rejoining the group yet. She stared at the wall.

She could hear Alexa and Ben talking in low voices to one another. She rolled her eyes. While she was delighted for Alexa that her date with Ben had gone so well, she was still furious that he had imprisoned them in an attic on a Saturday morning, and she was not yet quite certain that he had paid his penance for doing so. A sigh. She glanced behind her left shoulder to see Jack, who was leaning on the skylight, his face still gormless in this (almost) profile. She returned to the wall and closed her eyes, steeling herself. She sensed a tailspin coming on.

Even on a good day, her hangovers usually involved shame and anxiety, as her misdeeds and mishaps returned in a torrent. This was not a good day. And right now, an alarm bell was ringing. A Felicia-shaped alarm bell. Ellen had a very bad feeling about her boss. Specifically, she had a very bad feeling about a conversation with her boss that had taken place over Friday-evening drinks in the small kitchen of the office building they shared with Two Wheels Good.

Of course. There Ellen was, holding court, swilling the wine in her tumbler, necking satisfied slugs in between pronouncements. 'Thing is' – she was saying to her boss, eyes trained, as they always were, on one of her impossibly dark, manicured eyebrows – 'honestly, I've never even used one.' Another satisfied slug. 'A Flowdown tampon, I mean.' At this point she had laughed – for far, far too long – while her boss had stared at her, impassive. Eventually, after what was surely an eternity, Ellen had stopped laughing.

'I see.' And there was the face – Felicia looked like she'd been poisoned. A sniff. 'Please excuse me for a second.'

Ellen remembered the sound of her spiky heels retreating and felt sick with horror.

Granted, discussing female hygiene products at Friday night drinks rather came with the territory when you worked at a CBD tampon start-up. But Ellen had to wonder what had possessed her to make such a damning admission to the company's CEO, a former Goldman Sachs banker, who had started the company from her kitchen table while on maternity leave with her second child, and who was a woman unburdened by anything approaching a sense of humour. Ellen and Kayleigh had nicknamed Felicia the Grand High Witch, partly because she had dark hair and wore pointy patent boots and fitted black dresses with full skirts that fell to just below the knee; but partly because she was wicked. She was rude and demanding and unforgiving. She would also send incoherent emails at all hours: sentences that finished halfway through a word; references to conversations she'd had in her mind, rather than in her office, as stated; messages setting expectations that were excessive, considering the meagre sums she paid her staff.

If an employee offered an idea she liked, she would pause for a second, process it and then, seconds later, parrot it back to them as though she herself had come up with it. And she never said please, thank you or sorry. Despite hiring each and every member of The Flowdown's staff, she could not – or rather, would not – remember a single one of her employees' names. When she wanted you she would stare at you, call you by whichever name came to her, and expect you to twig that it was you who she required. Often, she'd also click her fingers.

The worst moment of the week was on Friday morning, when Felicia presided over a meeting that was billed as an 'informal catch-up', but was in fact an opportunity for Felicia to list the things that were making her unhappy, which were usually numerous and highly personal. Yesterday had been particularly gruelling. Felicia had already taken her seat at the top of the long, bleached wooden table when the others arrived. She was wearing an unseasonal black cape dress that made her look even more like a witch than usual. Eventually, she spoke crisply into the hush.

'Houston, we have a problem.'

The women and their single male co-worker, Martin, all stared at her, uncertain whether or not to breathe. One of the interns, who had been standing up at the back of the room, slid quietly to the floor.

'Girls' – Felicia always referred to them collectively as girls – 'tomorrow afternoon is the Live Well Festival. The Flowdown has its very own stand.' She announced this grandly. Ellen failed to see how taking a small, fold-up table at a free event inside a London department store was an honour, but she had long ago accepted that she and Felicia rarely saw eye to eye on anything.

Felicia continued, imperiously. 'This is a big deal for the brand, and' – she inhaled, sitting up straighter in her chair – 'for me personally, as a businesswoman.' She paused to cast a glance around the room, one eyebrow raised. 'And yet, as of this morning, not a single one of you has volunteered to join me at The Flowdown's stand this weekend.' She stopped speaking, allowing the immensity of this wrong to sink in. Her face was set in a bitter scowl.

In response, there was a sticky silence during which most people looked at the table, willing this section of their lives to be over. The only sound was Felicia drumming her talons on the long table.

'Well?' she demanded, sharply, after a few moments.

On cue, Ellen's phone, which was sitting face up on the table, lit up. She leaned forward slightly in her chair in order to read the WhatsApp message. She knew it would be Kayleigh.

felicia hun i'd rather volunteer to have a cervical smear broadcast on live television than spend my sat afternoon with you

Ellen smirked at the exact moment Felicia looked at her, which was an unfortunate coincidence, to say the least.

'Oh, I'm sorry,' Felicia spat, sarcastically, 'have I interrupted?'

Ellen quailed. She could kill Kayleigh, who – she knew, without looking – was loving this.

'No, Felicia –' Ellen started. She could feel her colleagues' eyes on her. They'd be sympathetic afterwards, but right now, there'd be a thrill in the spectacle of Felicia closing in on her prey. Ellen understood: she always felt the same way. 'Sorry, I was just thinking. Of something else. Something entirely and totally unconnected. Just a funny thing . . . that came to me,' she added. 'Just there. At that exact moment.'

Too much?

Felicia raised an eyebrow again. 'Right.'

A long pause, in which Ellen's ears rang with shame.

'How convenient.' Felicia licked her lips. 'Still, while

I've got you . . .' She paused here. 'Eleanor' – a satisfied smirk – 'can you tell me why, exactly, you haven't volunteered?'

Ellen opened her mouth, hoping an excuse would manifest itself. 'I have something on . . .' she said, certain she sounded unconvincing. 'In the daytime. On Saturday. A family thing,' she added, in a rush of inspiration. 'It's a private thing. I would rather not say. It's personal.'

Felicia arched one micro-bladed eyebrow. 'Of course,' she said, coolly.

Ellen struggled to brazen out the eye contact.

'I do hope it's nothing serious.'

Ellen put on a grave face. 'Thank you.' She hung her head, expression downcast, and hoped again she wasn't overdoing it.

After a pause, Felicia snapped a finger at the intern sitting on the floor.

'Abha, you'll come. Right, girls, what's next?'

At least she'd remembered Abha's name, Ellen thought.

After the meeting, Kayleigh apologized. 'Your face, though. It was really funny.'

Ellen tried sulking but was helpless in the face of Kayleigh's impression of her. They giggled. As Felicia stalked past, skirts swooshing, Ellen heard her tutting. She had forgotten laughing was frowned upon.

Despite showing little more than utter contempt for most of the people she had employed, Felicia would occasionally stick around for Friday-evening drinks, as she'd done yesterday. Ellen assumed she had seen this suggested in some zeitgeisty Silicon Valley executive handbook. Felicia's presence disturbed the natural order of things, and

Ellen usually became very self-conscious about how she was standing, and whether or not her voice was too loud. Last night, though, it seemed that Ellen had drunk enough to overcome this shyness. Her body seized with shame at the recollection. Felicia had an elephant's memory; Ellen would be punished.

Drinking with your colleagues was dangerous, when would she learn? Ellen had heard plenty of her friends' horror stories from Friday evenings that had gone awry: boasting about recreational drug use in front of senior managers; ill-placed seductions. Once, Sophie had clambered on top of a table at a leaving do, gesticulating with a bottle of (house) Sauvignon Blanc as she did an impression of the boss, who had – inevitably – just walked into the snug where they'd reserved a table. When she was made aware of this, she promptly fell off the table. It was 7 p.m.; she was in a taxi by 7.30 p.m. (and throwing up in the loo at 49 Rokeby Close by 8 p.m.).

Ellen's colleagues were mainly women in their twenties – aside from Martin, who worked on the tech side and whose ears went very red when Felicia asked him to redesign a banner on the homepage which directed users to a promotional deal on The Flowdown's prestige, super-absorbent tampon. Felicia had sat at his shoulder all morning, rewriting the words countless times, while he tried to pretend he didn't care that everyone else in the office was laughing at him. Still, the fact that the office was staffed mainly by Ellen's peers did, at least, mean there were fewer opportunities for career-ending humiliation. The millennials shared plenty – from hangovers to dates to nights out that sometimes ended only hours before their alarms squawked and they all struggled back into the office to wrestle with the coffee machine. Ellen, particularly, was an oversharer. Kayleigh – who was both the company's graphic designer and the younger crowd's de facto leader – was virtually impossible to embarrass. On mornings after nights before, she'd gather the millennials around and, hand on hip, toss her long blonde hair back and start on the graphic details of her latest outlandish misbehaviour.

Ellen shifted her weight now, nudging the ancient mirror, which let out a low moan, and placed her fingers on the side of her neck, feeling for her pulse. She did this often when she was anxious. There was something else from last night eating away at her: Ellen was fairly sure that Lee, from Two Wheels Good, was ignoring her. It bothered her because she'd thought they had quite a nice, non-committal flirty thing going: a stirring distraction that also worked as a mutually beneficial arrangement.

She was confused by her attraction to Lee, as he was, by many of her usual yardsticks, very unsuitable. He was very slight and not especially tall, and sometimes wore what looked like a pair of hiking boots to work. Probably because he was also outdoorsy (which was usually another of Ellen's red lines). In the course of their relatively recent Facebook friendship, it appeared he had already cycled from London to Brighton, gone camping near Fort William, and sailed down the Thames in a small craft that doubled as a tent. From what she could see, all of his friends were men. Three of them were called Adam. All of them wore fleeces.

And yet, he was also sweet, funnier than his earnest Two Wheels Good persona suggested, and had seduced her on three separate occasions, including one encounter – their latest – which had taken place in the third-floor unisex loo. Ellen knew this was a little cheap (Alexa's cheeks had flushed when Ellen had confessed). Still, sometimes she grinned when she passed the third floor in the lift. She'd had to physically restrain Kayleigh when she admitted it, her friend had been so keen to share this bombshell with the rest of the office.

After each occasion there had been plenty of messages, mostly non-committal but intriguing enough to warrant some of Ellen's attention. But last night, when Lee and the rest of the Two Wheels Good lot had come up to The Flowdown's floor to extend the use of their company card at the pub, he had stayed close to the door, not quite meeting her eye. He'd come to The Fox on the Hill, but left fairly early and without speaking to her, sticking instead to the side of one of his colleagues, a taciturn UX engineer called Bill, who rode a unicycle in the atrium (she'd made a joke about two wheels being 'bad', but he hadn't got it). She'd spent most of the evening trying to catch Lee's eye while pretending she wasn't, and feeling acutely conscious, always, of exactly where he was in the room. When he left, she'd been disappointed.

She was getting cramp in her legs now. More half-memories surfaced: she remembered getting on the night bus, and stumbling slightly in her ankle boots, some blokes at the back jeering at her. She hadn't known where to sit so she'd stood at the front of the bus, in the section reserved for buggies and wheelchairs, feeling exposed, the whole journey home. She shook her head to try and knock these tormenting thoughts from it, and then determined that, in fact, she needed Alexa. She hoped she'd come for her soon.

Ellen wouldn't tell her about the wet patch, though. Maybe she could cover it with her hand.

'See? Fresh air is better, isn't it?' Alexa closed her eyes.

They were hanging out of the skylight, with Rokeby Close in all its deserted glory below them. Ben was lounging on the floor near their feet, grinning lopsidedly. Jack kept taking his phone out, then looking disappointed, and putting it back in his pocket again.

Ellen scowled and spoke in a childish sing-song. 'Yes, Alexa, I agree that fresh air is better than sitting in a corner near a box I pissed in.'

Alexa gave her a look.

'Sorry.' Ellen nudged her. 'It's quite weird how deserted our street is,' she added. 'Is it always this deserted?'

'It *is* Saturday morning.' Alexa shrugged. 'Also, I guess it's not really on the way to anywhere.'

'I think my street would probably be the same,' Ben said, conversationally.

'Should we try yelling again?' Ellen asked Alexa. 'It might make us feel better.'

Alexa looked unconvinced.

Ellen could tell that Alexa really did not want to yell out of the window in front of Ben. She would consider this behaviour to be uncouth and demeaning. However, Ellen was fairly keen for this nightmare to be over. Alexa would have to suck it up, frankly.

'We haven't done it for a while. And someone might hear us,' Ellen cajoled. 'And I am really very keen to be out of here.'

'Well. Obviously, I am too.'

Ellen leaned further out of the window, took a deep breath, and then let loose.

'HEEEEEEEEEEELLLLLOOOOOOOOOOO OOOOOOO. CAN ANYONE HEAR ME?'

Alexa had her palms pressed over her ears.

Ellen turned to Ben and Jack. 'How was that?'

'Ten out of ten for effort,' Ben said. He mimed applause.

Ellen turned back to the open skylight. She took another gulp of air.

'HEEEEELLLLOOOOOOOOO. WE'RE STUU UUUUUUUUUUUUUUUUUCK.'

Alexa had her palms pressed tightly over her ears again. She removed them and leaned further out of the window. Alexa was a lot shorter than Ellen. She jumped, trying to see a little further. Ellen noticed that when she did this, Ben's face softened.

Ellen turned round to face both Jack and Ben properly. 'I hate to break it to you all, but I really don't have a lot of faith in this plan.' Remembering her predicament, she hovered her hand in front of the offending patch of her tracksuit bottoms and lowered herself to the floor, narrowly avoiding sitting on Jack's left foot. 'Sorry, Jack.'

'No worries,' he shrugged. He curled his big toe. He was being very quiet, even for him.

Defeated, Alexa also joined her on the floor, crosslegged. She sat very close to Ben.

'Also, I think I'm very dehydrated,' Ellen continued. 'I don't want to put too fine a point on it, but my wee was very orange.'

'Ellen,' Alexa cautioned. '*Please.*'

Ellen was suitably chastened.

Ben massaged his chin, looking careworn. 'I will agree that my hangover is starting to really hurt.'

'I wish I'd had more sleep,' said Alexa, who promptly flushed at the implications of what she'd said. Ellen swallowed a laugh.

Ben leaned in and wrapped an arm, casually, around her inner thigh. Alexa smiled gratefully.

Ellen cleared her throat for ceremony. 'This morning, I took a swig of what I believed to be water, but it turned out to be vodka.'

The others made sympathetic noises. There was a pause.

'I did that once,' said Jack, conversationally. 'But I thought it was beer, and it was actually someone's urine.'

'Oh my God!' said Alexa and Ellen, almost in horrified unison.

Ben looked appalled.

'Festival,' Jack said, shrugging.

The others made understanding noises. There was a subsequent pause, as they all tried not to imagine this scene, before Ellen spoke again.

'I can't believe not a single one of us has a working phone.' She scowled.

'I thought I did for a second,' Jack replied mournfully. 'I connected briefly to the WiFi. But it's gone again.'

'Really?' Alexa said, sharply.

'Yeah,' Jack said. 'Sorry, I forgot to say.'

Ellen glanced at Alexa, who was definitely trying not to look frustrated by this news.

Jack continued. 'It happened when I was by the window, a little while ago. I got a Twitter notification.' He looked at his phone. 'But it's gone and it hasn't come back,' he said, sadly. 'I keep checking.'

'Move closer to the window, then,' Alexa commanded. 'You might get it again.'

Ellen gestured to Jack to swap places with her. She shuffled around on her bum, still careful to keep her hand in front of the damp patch. When she'd last taken a peek at it, it was still visible enough to warrant her concealment.

'What now?' Jack asked Alexa, anxious for instruction.

'Maybe you should try hanging out of the window again?' Ellen suggested, dubiously.

Jack looked at Alexa.

'He can't just hang out of the window all day, watching for WiFi,' Ben pointed out.

Jack now glanced uncertainly between him and Alexa. Ben's arm was still looped around Alexa's thigh.

'No,' Alexa said, finally. 'He can't.' She sniffed. 'But if we could get WiFi, we could try calling someone on WhatsApp.'

'True,' Ben said, shooting a sympathetic look at Jack.

Ellen turned on what she hoped was a beseeching expression. 'Go on, Jack. See if you can find it again.'

Jack shrugged. 'OK.' He stood up, all limbs and toes. 'It's nice to get some fresh air.' He leaned out. 'Hey, I see someone.'

'Shout!' Ellen instructed him.

'Hello?' Jack said, at the volume someone might answer a phone call.

'Jack, *I* can barely hear you.' Ellen scrambled to her feet. She squeezed in beside Jack – up this close, he smelled like he needed a shower, though she supposed she did too – and leaned out of the window. Alexa and Ben fitted in behind them, so that the four of them were all packed into the window frame. Ellen spotted the pedestrian in question: a woman of indeterminate though possibly fairly advanced age, who was moving at a shuffling pace and dragging a small, neat shopping trolley behind her. She had her back to them and was already walking away from their house.

'Shit, she's getting away.' Ellen took a deep breath and placed her hands on both sides of her mouth in order to amplify her voice and show Jack how it was done. 'HEY! EXCUSE ME!'

There was a tense pause, in which the woman did not look up but continued to make steady progress down the street.

'HELLLOOOOOOOOOOOOOO?' Ben shouted, from behind Ellen's right ear.

She winced. Then she filled her lungs again. 'EXCUSE ME . . . MADAM?'

Behind her, she heard Ben suppress a snort.

'MADAM, CAN YOU HEAR ME?'

Jack's breath was ragged. The woman was still shuffling. She was definitely getting away, albeit slowly.

Ellen tried one more time. 'PLEASE?'

'Give it up,' Ben said. 'We've lost her.'

'Maybe she was wearing AirPods,' Ellen supplied.

'El, she was like seventy,' Alexa said, but she sounded amused. She and Ben had stepped away from the window and were now a few paces back, towards the middle of the room.

'Well, good to see our plan is foolproof,' Ellen said,

ducking into the room herself, Jack at her shoulder. She sat back down on the floor, beside Alexa and Ben. They were entwined once more. Alexa looked very pleased, in spite of this latest setback.

Jack tried to sit down too.

'Wait, no!' Alexa raised a hand. 'Jack, can you please stay by the window a little longer and see if you get the WiFi back?'

'Oh, of course,' he spluttered. 'Sorry. I forgot the plan.'

'It's not really a plan,' Ellen said.

He looked confused.

'Can you maybe just wave your phone around for a few minutes and see if you get any WiFi, though. Or signal,' she added. She could feel Ben's gaze. 'Please?'

Dutifully, Jack returned to the skylight and stuck his phone at arm's length out of the window and waved it around. After he'd done this for a few seconds, he brought it back in to look at the screen, tutted exaggeratedly, and stuck it back out again. After observing a few cycles of this, Ellen could no longer bear to watch. She turned to Alexa and Ben and dropped her voice to a whisper.

'Imagine if he accidentally throws it out of the window.'

8. Jack

The fourth time he waggled his phone out of the window, pointing it towards the ground this time instead of up at the sky, Jack's phone vibrated and he almost dropped it in surprise.

He pulled his arm in and was about to tell the others when he noticed it was a Twitter notification. Which was unusual, as it would make it the second tweet he'd received that morning. He tapped the blue notification. It started loading very, very slowly. Panicking that he'd lost the connection already, he stuck his arm back out of the window, trying to point it at the ground again like last time, and then stuck his head further out so he could see the screen a little better. It was still loading very slowly.

After several slow breaths – Jack willing the page on as it buffered – it got there. He blinked fast in surprise. His tweet about being stuck in the attic in New Cross had got 257 likes. Which wasn't really very many when you considered how many people there were in the world – or rather, how many there were on Twitter. But considering the most likes Jack had ever got before was seven (he'd pointed out an inconsistency in an old *Simpsons* episode), it was a lot. From the state of his mentions, it looked like he'd had a few replies too.

Some of them sounded promising.

@rockyb1999
Where in #newcross are you mate

@littlewandering
I'm on trafalgar drive – where u based #newcross #southeast #LDN

Others, he conceded, sounded less promising.

@RVQ88
This sounds like a punchline to a joke

@thegooner87
HAAAHAA!!!

And he was particularly excited about this one, which was from a woman who had lots of followers. Jack clicked on her profile. She was a columnist for a newspaper.

@SteffyWrites
South London network assemble! Anyone in the New Cross area and willing to help this bloke out?!

Jack marvelled for a second that his words were being seen by this woman, whose bio said that she had once been nominated for an award. He'd never had anyone like that interact with any of his tweets before –

And then he couldn't see any more replies, because his phone had lost the connection again, so it was only showing him what had been downloaded before it dropped off. He refreshed the screen, holding the phone out of the window, with one eye on the top-right corner, watching for the WiFi, and considered this development.

He'd hoped for a response or two, of course – that had been the point. But he was surprised the message was doing quite so well. It had been an experiment, more than anything.

The screen still wouldn't load, but he continued staring at it anyway. In spite of everything, it made him feel a little special. Obviously, none of the people who had responded had actually offered to do anything to help. But it was still exciting. Plus, they only needed one helpful person, really. Just a single person to see Jack's tweet and offer to come to Rokeby Close and rescue them. He wondered if Alexa might tell him off for putting their address on the internet. But he hadn't put the number, just the street they were on. And he really wanted them to escape before the whole ground floor was flooded. Jack had started to really worry about the flood. He wondered if his shoes were ruined. He'd left them by the front door, and he didn't have a second pair.

The WiFi still hadn't come back, and his arms were starting to ache a little from being held out at full stretch. His phone had 40 per cent battery. He chewed his lip. Perhaps he should stick it on airplane mode for a little while to preserve the power. Soon it would be someone else's turn to hang out of the window. He turned and stared at the others. They were sitting in the middle of the room, Alexa and Ben sort of cuddling, and Ellen close by. They were quiet.

He couldn't tell if it was awkward.

Jack had decided he liked Alexa's sort-of-boyfriend, Ben, whom she had met on Hinge (Ben had told him, with a grin). Granted, he hadn't been much use at Risk. And he'd locked them in the attic. But Ben had kept him company at the window, which was kind. And their conversation had been alright, really; they'd talked about football a bit, which was easy enough, and which pubs they'd been to around here, and his job. And around Ben, Alexa seemed softer too – smiling, rather than stiff – although it was strange to watch her tucked under Ben's arm, in her pyjamas. Jack had never seen Alexa act like this before.

He glanced at his phone again. Still not connected. He folded his arms, and decided he wouldn't mention any of this to the others just yet. It would be better to see if anything concrete came of it, any proper offer of rescue, before he let them see the whole thread. That way, they didn't need to know he'd put their address on the internet.

'Any luck, Jacko?' Ellen demanded from the middle of the room.

He shook his head sadly. 'No. Sorry.'

'When we get out of here, we should change internet provider,' Ellen said, sniffily.

'Is it OK if one of you takes over here for a bit? So I can sit down? ' Jack asked.

'Yes, of course, Jack,' Alexa said, kindly. 'One of us can switch with you.'

Still, no one moved. Alexa remained curled under Ben's arm. Ellen was picking at a stain on the carpet. It looked a little like hardened paint.

Jack lowered himself to the floor. He swiped at his phone and put it on to airplane mode. He'd go to the window again in a little while and see whether he could find enough WiFi to check the Twitter thread. He crossed his legs and smiled shyly at the others. 'We could play another game?'

'I wonder how flooded the kitchen is now,' Ellen said, ignoring him.

'Let's not think about it,' Alexa replied, a little irritably. Jack noticed she was fiddling with her earring. 'Someone should really go to the window – we don't want to miss anyone passing by.' They all exchanged nods and glances, although still no one moved.

After a minute or so, Ellen spoke. 'OK, fine. I have a game.' She looked a little mischievous.

Alexa, Ben and Jack watched her, Alexa rather wearily.

Certain she had command of her audience, Ellen began. 'Would you rather have your thumbs replaced with your big toes . . . or have your pinkie fingers replaced with your pinkie toes?'

'Pinkie fingers, pinkie toes,' Alexa replied, without pause. 'Obviously.'

Ellen grinned at her. 'Obviously.'

Jack smiled, hesitantly. The girls played this game a lot. They were really good at it: they were so fast at deciding. It always took Jack ages to work out the answer to his question.

Alexa was going. 'OK. Would you rather never know what your real name is' – Ellen was listening intently – 'or never know what you really look like?'

Ellen considered this. 'Name,' she said, after a few beats. 'Because I can just get everyone to call me by another name.'

'Yeah,' Alexa agreed. 'Me too.'

'OK.' Jack sensed Ellen had already prepared this one. 'Would you rather find out you're adopted or find out one of your parents has a secret family?'

'That's dark.' Alexa screwed up her face.

'Pinkie toes were dark,' Ellen protested, grinning.

Jack was concentrating on Alexa. He definitely didn't know what he'd say to this one.

'I think secret family. Because although that would be awful, I think I'd feel less confused. Just.'

'Yeah, I think that's right.'

'Ask me one,' Ben commanded. He was animated now, and sitting up a little straighter.

Jack sensed he liked this game. Probably more than Risk.

Ellen gestured to Alexa.

'OK . . .' Alexa paused and narrowed her eyes. She thought about it for a few seconds. 'Would you rather,' she began, 'be trapped with ten thousand spiders for ten minutes, or . . .' a pause, 'have to eat ten spiders in ten minutes?'

'And they're alive,' Ellen added, quickly.

She and Alexa exchanged a mischievous look.

Ben made a shuddering noise. 'I actually really hate spiders.' He looked at Alexa. 'Have I already told you that?'

She shook her head and made an innocent face.

'Ugh. OK.'

'Come on,' Ellen hurried him. 'Think fast.'

'Ummmm, probably be trapped with the spiders.' He cocked his head to the side, testing his decision. 'Yeah. I reckon I could kill some of them.'

Alexa grinned. 'Good answer.'

'Right, my turn,' Ben said. He looked at Jack. 'Would you rather drink Ellen's urine from that box over there, or have to wee in a box for the rest of your life?' He added, 'Just wee.'

Jack blanched. Ellen and Alexa made identical disgusted faces.

'Ew, Ben.' Alexa prodded him in the side. 'That's gross.'

Ben shrugged, grinning.

Jack wasn't sure how to answer. They were watching him. 'Um . . .'

'Poor Jack,' Alexa said. She was looking at him sympathetically.

He felt like they were teasing him a little. 'OK . . .' He swallowed. 'I choose the box. Because I can always pour it away.'

'True.' Ben winked.

Jack felt relieved that he'd got away with it. There was a silence. He hoped that he wouldn't have to come up with one. He could never think of anything clever. Usually, Ellen told him his ones didn't really work.

'I wish you hadn't mentioned that box. I'm worried I have to go for another wee,' Ellen said, miserably.

'Already?' Alexa asked, disbelievingly. 'Your bladder really is tiny.'

Ben laughed.

'Yes, already.' She looked accusingly at Ben, as if he were responsible for her predicament, then turned back to Alexa. 'And you already know my bladder is tiny.'

Jack bit his lip and gave Ellen a sympathetic look.

Alexa, meanwhile, smiled mischievously. 'Sometimes, she needs to go to the bathroom three times in the night.'

'Yes, and you know it makes me worry every day that I have developed diabetes,' Ellen moaned.

Ben laughed again.

Ellen didn't get up, though she shuffled around a little.

Ben's hand was lingering on Alexa's lower back now. Jack felt a little awkward around this new, demonstrative Alexa. Still, she seemed happy. Though she had a nice smile and always looked very clean, Jack could not imagine going out with Alexa. She had a job he didn't entirely understand, and in the evenings she would often sit at the kitchen table with thick piles of paper, wearing her glasses and sometimes making marks in pen. Jack would tiptoe around, terrified that he was disturbing her. Sometimes, she ran to work, which was really rather far (Jack had looked it up on Google Maps when she told him). Her room looked like no one lived there. When she cooked, everything was arranged symmetrically on the plate.

Jack hadn't had much luck dating in London. He'd tried, sort of. One evening in the kitchen, about two months ago, Ellen had declared it was time to set up a Hinge profile for him. He'd been telling them both, shyly, about his ex-girlfriend, Niamh, whom he'd dated for five months at university. She had been in the year above and they'd met when Jack had gone along to the university's swing dance club. He wouldn't usually do anything like that, but he'd seen the flyer in his third week and he'd remembered that university was supposed to be about trying new things. And he hadn't tried anything new at that point. Because he was from Manchester, he was still living at home, still waking up in the same childhood bedroom that he'd slept in his whole life, walls plastered with his Man City posters, the drawers under his desk still full of his sixth-form folders. Anyway, at the swing dance night, he'd been paired up with Niamh, who was also new, and they'd had fun and then he'd gone back the next week to see her. And then a month later he'd asked her out for a drink. They'd started going out, and he stopped going to swing dance club, which was a huge relief, as he was awful at it.

But she'd broken up with him in the middle of his second term. 'I'm not sure this is working,' she'd said, making it sound final, and he couldn't really argue with that, even though he'd thought it had been working fine. He hadn't had a proper girlfriend since then. He didn't always mind, but it would be nice to have someone to do things with. And so he'd mentioned that to Ellen and Alexa, hence the decision to put him on Hinge.

'It's sort of awful,' Ellen said, authoritatively. 'But everyone's on it, so you have to join too . . .' She paused. Jack had been looking a little apprehensive, so she added, 'Well, it's not *always* awful.'

'I've definitely had a few good dates,' Alexa said, encouragingly.

So they set up his profile, both of the girls scrolling through his Facebook page for photos.

'This is a good one,' Ellen said, selecting a picture of Jack at his graduation ball.

Jack had felt uncomfortable that evening. He'd worn a rented suit, which had added to the sense that he wasn't himself but, in fact, a different man altogether. Still, Ellen said he looked 'dashing'. The second picture was one of him holding a tankard of beer up beside his head, to show how large it was. Jack thought he had a goofy face in this image, but Alexa said it was 'sweet'. The third picture was him with his friend Patrick. 'But you look better than him, so it's OK,' Ellen said. Jack couldn't help feeling a little pleased, but also guilty. He liked Patrick.

Jack let Ellen and Alexa fill in all the answers to the silly questions, watching as they built a version of him to share with the world. They were down at one end of the kitchen table, heads together, with Jack's phone. He was at the other end of the table, palms a little sweaty. When they showed him the results, Jack didn't really recognize himself.

What I'm looking for
The love of my life. Failing that, some solid 7/10 dates.

Dating me is like
Finding £20 in an old jacket.

Let's debate this topic
Mayonnaise: what's the point?

Typical Sunday
Hangover pizza.

A shower thought I had recently
Do crabs have toes?

'But I don't take showers,' Jack said, literally. 'I always take baths. And I don't really understand the one about finding £20.'

'It doesn't matter that you don't take showers,' Alexa said, kindly, before handing his phone back to him. 'You're allowed a bit of creative licence.'

'And the thing about the £20 is meant to be funny,' Ellen said, firmly. 'It's great when you find £20 you didn't remember was there. Dating you is like that feeling, all the time.'

'Exactly. It's perfect,' Alexa said, as if the matter was closed.

'OK,' Jack said, though he wasn't sure. He thought he sounded like someone he wouldn't want to be friends with.

Still, that was that: he'd joined the world of online dating. Jack liked that it was easy: he'd open the app and there would be pretty girls on the screen. Jack said yes to everybody, because he felt mean saying no, though the girls Jack liked the look of best were the ones who looked like Annie.

Annie was his friend Johnny's girlfriend. She had really long, shiny dark hair and she always wore the same trainers: white ones with really thick soles. She had four earrings in each ear, and a nose ring, and she worked all day in a little studio where she made these tiny white pots with black polka dots on them. Once he and Johnny had gone to meet her at her studio, which she shared with all these other people who wore dungarees and colourful scarves in their hair. Annie had white residue from the clay smeared all over her face, and she showed Jack this long, skinny pot she was making; it was a vase for her friend's birthday. She had gone to the pub with the white on her face, even though Johnny had laughed at her and told her she looked like a painter and decorator. She drank pints of cider, smoked roll-ups and lived in Deptford in a property guardianship that was an old school. None of the residents had their own rooms, they just had bits of tarpaulin dividing up one big room. They had a big sheet in the kitchen with a rota for doing the cooking. Everyone was a vegan. Jack didn't think he'd have liked living there, but Annie said it was really fun – and she only paid £300 a month, which was really good for London.

Once, Jack had gone to a party there with Johnny and had eaten a hash brownie and started feeling rather peculiar, like his lungs were breathing inside out. He'd been walking around the party, lights strobing a little, but then – by a stroke of luck – he'd seen Annie. He'd told her what had happened. He'd laughed, although he was also scared of the way it felt, as if his brain was rolling like a tide, but Annie had grabbed his hand, led him outside to the small stone wall that ran through the old schoolyard, and sat there outside with him for an hour. She'd rolled him cigarettes and told him all about the people she lived with. Some of them were in a poly couple, which meant – or so it appeared to Jack – that they had relationships with several people, both men and women, at the same time. Annie said the noise didn't really bother her that much – plus, when they were having a proper sex party she just arranged to stay round Johnny's. Jack had looked at her, wide-eyed, when she'd told him this, and she'd laughed. 'I thought you were from Manchester? Aren't you meant to be cool?' Listening to Annie had calmed him down, and after a while his brain had stopped doing backflips.

Anyway, Annie was going out with Johnny. But at least Jack got to spend a lot of time with her. He liked how easy it was to talk to her. He found he wasn't very good at sending messages on Hinge to the other girls. He usually felt stupid and couldn't think of anything to say beyond, 'Hi!' Or sometimes, 'How was your day?' He hadn't gone on any dates yet, and he hadn't opened the app in weeks.

Still, Ben and Alexa had found each other. And it looked like it was going well. Ben had just placed a kiss on the back of Alexa's arm. Maybe Jack should start using Hinge again. The last message he'd had was from a girl called Hanna, who liked gin. This, from what Jack could understand, seemed to be an important part of her personality. She worked in food PR, though Jack wasn't really sure what that meant. They'd exchanged a few messages but it had fallen silent since then. Perhaps he'd send another one.

He took out his phone now, then remembered it was on airplane mode and he wouldn't have any signal here anyway. Still, it reminded him that he wanted to check if the Twitter thread had any more likes, so he swiped it off airplane mode and stood up.

The others regarded him, lazily.

'Just want to get some fresh air.'

'What, again?' Ellen asked, but he ignored her.

9. Ellen

Ellen watched Jack retreat to the window again, shoulders sloping, and reflected that, although they all coexisted in the same skinny terraced house day after day, she, Alexa and Jack did not often spend long periods of time in each other's company. This was probably the first morning they'd whiled away together since the day Jack had moved in. She and Alexa had taken him for brunch to say welcome, and they'd talked a lot and he'd dribbled baked beans down his T-shirt. On weekday evenings, they'd often collide in the kitchen in the evening for about twenty minutes but everyone would be cooking separately, jostling elbows and bending over each other's pots on the hobs in order to stir their own supper. Then there'd be some chatter, but that was mainly her and Alexa talking, while Jack bent low over his soup bowl and slurped. He ate a lot of tinned soup, they'd noted, always served in the same deep white bowl (Ellen was certain that it was, strictly, a salad dish). Jack would balance a slice of white bread on the side, spread with a layer of margarine (never butter), and blow slowly on spoonful after spoonful of soup, slurping each one down noisily.

This ritual completed, he'd usually go back upstairs to his bedroom, leaving his pan in the sink, which Alexa would invariably wash up while Ellen rootled in the cupboard for something else to eat. She wondered whether

Jack was happy in London. Apart from his friend Johnny and the people he worked with, she wasn't sure who he spent time with. She felt mean about Risk now.

Granted, if Alexa was working late, or was at the gym, Ellen and Jack would catch up over dinner, although Ellen wasn't sure how much Jack got out of her stories about Felicia's various crimes.

'And apparently she wants a "core team" of us working over the May bank holiday,' Ellen had exclaimed one day last week, as Jack stirred his soup at the stove. 'I mean' – putting her fork down in order to gesticulate – '*who* is shopping for CBD tampons over a bank holiday weekend?'

'Yeah,' Jack had replied, with feeling, after a pause to check Ellen was finished telling her story. 'That's definitely weird.'

'I think she's a sociopath. We did a test for her online and she hit all the markers.' She sighed. 'How's your job going?'

Another pause.

'Oh, it's OK.' He'd turned off the stove and transferred the soup to his bowl. 'I don't really like it when I have to answer the phone.'

Ellen had made a sympathetic noise through a mouthful of whatever she was eating.

'It's fine when I get to do it over the messaging service.' Jack had walked to the table to sit down. 'Speak to the customers, I mean. But I hate having to use the phone.'

Eventually, these conversations would peter out amicably, and they'd finish up and then retreat to their own bedrooms. She hadn't been inside Jack's since Sophie moved out – only stood on the threshold. She remembered lots and lots of odd socks.

Partly, she supposed, the problem was that they didn't

have a living room. What should be the communal space was in fact Ellen's bedroom, where Alexa and Ellen would often watch television in the evenings and on weekends. It was always untidy in there but, as a result, more relaxing than Alexa's room. It looked on to the street, so Ellen invariably had the curtains drawn, even in broad daylight. She had squeezed a small sofa in there, where the two of them would sit, with the laptop resting on a borrowed kitchen chair, stationed in the middle of the room, while they took it in turns to rest their feet on Ellen's knock-off Eames armchair. She had bought it on eBay, thrilling at the maturity of her purchase (furniture!), until it arrived and it was cat-sized. Alexa had laughed – it *was* very funny – then sympathized that it was easy to forget to read the measurements. Ellen did not mention that she actually had read the measurements. She now used it as a footstool and a talking point for visitors to her room.

But they never invited Jack to watch TV with them, and he never asked. They must have been to the pub together once or twice, surely? But at the weekends, she and Alexa often had some sort of social commitment with one of their university friends. Maybe they should ask Jack to the pub more often, she thought, guiltily.

It was really heating up in the attic now. The April sun was beating down on the slate roof and making the whole place feel like a dusty greenhouse, or a zealous garden shed with a space heater. Ellen felt dopey and stupid; her eyes heavy, as if drooping down her face because of the heat. But besides the occasional gurgle of someone's stomach, or the sound of a siren from New Cross Road in the distance, all was quiet again.

Ellen sniffed and then felt a rush of hot shame; she could smell herself ripening in the heat. She thought back to her last shower and noted, with chagrin, that it had been on Thursday morning. Standing under the trickle of their shower would feel like the ultimate luxury right now. Or a bath! Lying back in the tub and closing her eyes while she washed off all the dirt and indignity of last night. She shuffled on her bum until she was a few inches outside the circle, hoping that none of the others were offended by her personal musk.

She glanced at Jack again. He was still hanging out of the window. His grey tracksuit bottoms were baggy and, she assumed, had not been washed since he became a tenant at Rokeby Close. While Ellen's hygiene was her own ongoing personal battle, Jack too had unorthodox habits. He kept all of his laundry in a bin bag, and the first time he had used the washing machine in the kitchen, Alexa had caught him just in time, before he used washing-up liquid ('I thought it was the same,' he said, shrugging). He appeared to keep only a single toiletry item (a 2-in-1 supermarket shampoo and conditioner) in the bathroom, and while she assumed he must have changed his toothbrush – he'd lived there almost eight months – did he really buy the same one, over and over again? It was certainly always the same colour.

However, it was his aversion to the shower that fascinated Ellen the most: indeed, she didn't believe she'd ever known him to take one. Instead he always, *always* took baths; usually fairly long ones, even in the morning before work. On weekday mornings, Alexa – who had to be in the office at 8.30 a.m. – had always risen, washed and left the

132

house before Ellen or Jack were awake (no matter where she'd been the night before). This left the two more slovenly members of the household to engage in an unspoken competition to get into the bathroom first.

When Jack had first moved in, he had always managed to get in there five to ten minutes before Ellen did. She'd go up to the first floor, see the door locked and think *surely, that can't be him running . . . a bath?* She hadn't believed it, the first three or four mornings. But that was precisely what he was doing: he'd run one, and then he'd sit and swill in it for twenty minutes – twenty minutes when Ellen would have to sit, stewing with frustration, on the stairs until he'd come out, a little pink, fully dressed (including his shoes?!) and say, 'Halloo'. The bathroom mirror would be all steamed up, and there was – invariably – no hot water.

After two weeks of this, Ellen had WhatsApped Alexa from the stairs, as she waited for the bathroom to be free.

Omg he has done it again
He's having a fucking bath!
I am sat here on the stairs waiting to get into shower
HAS HE NEVER HAD HOUSEMATES BEFORE???
HE CANT JUST HAVE A MORNING BATH
Also tbf it is creepy af

Alexa had replied later that morning.

Sorry was in meetings
I mean you can't stop him having a bath
Agree is q weird
Maybe just set your alarm five mins earlier??

After a further week, Ellen had given up and set her alarm ten minutes earlier. As soon as she left the bathroom and was halfway down the stairs, she could hear Jack shuffle in and lock the door. She knew this was unkind, but she'd kept being late for work. As punishment one morning, Felicia had made Ellen stand outside Farringdon Tube station and hand out free tampons to harried passers-by. This was a role usually reserved for the intern.

'I swear I can still smell the mouse,' Alexa blurted now, wrinkling her nose.

'I might go join Jack at the window,' Ellen replied, with a sigh. 'I could also do with some fresh air.'

Alexa yawned in response. Ben was massaging his pec yet again – with the arm that wasn't cradling Alexa – squeezing and releasing it absent-mindedly. Ellen supposed it was a very good pec. She'd leave them to it.

'Hi, Jack.' Ellen announced her arrival, and stuck her head out of the window beside his.

He looked startled, and shoved his phone into his pocket.

'Any luck with the signal?'

'Oh . . . um . . . no.'

'Oh, well. At least it's a beautiful spring day to be stuck indoors.'

'I'm meant to be going to the pub with Johnny,' he said mournfully. 'To the Elephant. The outdoor bit.'

'Hey, it's only early still,' Ellen said, comfortingly. She had no idea what time it was. 'You might still make it.'

Jack looked rather dubious. 'Do you think we'll get out of here soon?'

Ellen shrugged. 'Right now, it doesn't look good, does it?'

Jack shook his head, thoughtfully. After a second, he

stole a furtive look at Ben and Alexa. 'Hey, is that Alexa's boyfriend?'

'Hmm, sort of. They've been on some dates.'

'He's nice.'

'Yeah.' Ellen realized she hadn't really tried to speak to Ben properly yet. She was starting to feel guilty about that too, when she noticed something. 'Hey, a person.' She pointed at a man coming out of the house opposite.

He looked like he was in his mid-thirties, was wearing trainers, black trousers and a light jacket, and he was leading a toddler by the hand down the garden path. The toddler, in turn, was dragging a tiny tricycle.

Ellen wasted no time. Bracing herself, with both hands on the edge of the skylight, she took a huge gulp of air and bellowed into the street's hush.

'HELLOOOOOOOOOOOOO?'

Jack stepped back slightly.

'EXCUUUUUUUSE ME?'

The man had reached the end of his path by now, but he looked up and down the street, seeking the owner of the voice.

'*Yes!*' Ellen said to Jack. She cupped her hand around her mouth and shouted, 'UP HEEEEEEEERREE!!!'

The man looked in the wrong direction again a few times and then, finally, found Ellen. He threw his palm over his eyes to protect them from the sun.

This was her chance. Her legs felt light.

'SORRY FOR SHOUTING AT YOU,' she continued, shouting at him. She could feel Jack watching her, and Ben and Alexa scrambling to their feet behind them. 'IT'S JUST THAT WE'RE LOCKED IN THIS ATTIC AND

ALSO THE KITCHEN IS FLOODING.' She took a deep breath to recover and arranged her face into what she hoped was a non-threatening smile that still emphasized the urgency of their situation.

Though perhaps she should have taken things a little slower: kitchen and attic in the same sentence was quite a bombshell, and the man looked hesitant. In spite of everything, Ellen felt vindicated. This *was* an unlikely plan: obviously, people didn't want to be bogged down in other people's business.

Ben and Alexa had joined them in the window frame now, Alexa virtually standing on Ellen's foot in her eagerness to catch a glimpse of their neighbour. He was still staring up at them. The housemates held their breath.

But then – joy! – the man picked up his toddler, glanced both ways across the street, and crossed the road towards them. Midway across the road, the toddler dropped the tricycle and the man stooped to pick it up.

Ellen turned to Alexa, who raised her eyebrows in encouragement.

The man made it to the pavement at the end of the path leading up to their front door, and shouted up to them, still squinting into the sun.

'SORRY, CAN YOU REPEAT THAT?' he called.

Now he was closer to them, she swore she could make out his designer stubble. The toddler was wriggling in his arms. Alexa was jostling at Ellen's shoulder now and, without needing to be asked, Jack stepped back in order to let Alexa take his place nearer the window.

'HELLO!' Alexa took over. 'SORRY TO HAVE

BOTHERED YOU.' Her voice was more self-contained than Ellen's, though it appeared to be travelling.

The man was still looking up at them, frowning a little.

'IT'S JUST THAT WE'VE MANAGED TO GET STUCK IN OUR ATTIC. THE HANDLE FELL OFF THE DOOR,' Alexa continued.

'AND THE KITCHEN IS ALSO FLOODING – SORRY – WHICH IS VERY BAD LUCK.' Ellen felt it was important to emphasize the kitchen situation too.

'OH DEAR . . .' the man replied slowly, after a moment's hesitation. He sounded a little overwhelmed. 'OK.'

He didn't say anything else.

'WE WERE WONDERING IF BY ANY CHANCE YOU MIGHT BE ABLE TO CALL A LOCKSMITH FOR US?' Alexa looked anxious. 'WHO MIGHT BE ABLE TO GET INTO THE HOUSE AND THEN GET US OUT OF HERE.'

'THEN WE CAN SORT THE WATER OUR-SELVES,' Ellen shouted. She realized she was shouting very slowly, as if trying to make herself understood in a foreign country. 'WE MADE A SIGN,' she added, stupidly, waggling the cord.

The man glanced at the sign. He appeared unmoved. Still, he released his squirming charge, who sat clumsily on the tricycle and started pedalling up the path, and then took his phone out of his pocket, which suggested action. After another few beats, in which he was clearly deciding whether he could be bothered to help, he called out, finally.

'I SUPPOSE I COULD DO THAT FOR YOU.'

Ellen thought he had a slight accent, perhaps French, but it was hard to tell when he was yelling.

'*Yessss,*' she heard Ben mutter behind her.

'THANK YOU,' she replied quickly, before he could change his mind. 'IT'S JUST WE DON'T HAVE OUR PHONES BECAUSE WE DIDN'T MEAN TO GET STUCK UP HERE,' she added.

After another beat, the man crouched down to say something they couldn't hear to the toddler, who didn't seem to respond. Ellen realized she was now holding her breath.

'What's he doing?' asked Ben, stretching over Alexa's head.

The man stood up again and shouted up to the attic. 'GIVE ME A FEW MINUTES TO GO GIVE HIM BACK TO HIS MUM.' He scooped his little boy off the seat of his tricycle. On cue, the child wailed. They all watched as the man picked up the tricycle and – again, glancing both ways – prepared to cross the road. He turned. 'I'LL BE BACK IN A MINUTE.' He walked across the road and then remembered something. He turned again. 'WHAT'S YOUR NAME?'

'ELLEN,' she shouted back. 'FISHER,' she added, for propriety.

He did an awkward thumbs-up in response, then walked back up the path to his own home, the child thrashing in his arms. He placed the tricycle beside the front doorstep and – after a little difficulty juggling both toddler and keys – opened his front door. The pair disappeared.

There was a brief silence as they all stared at the impassive door.

'Do you think he's coming back?' Jack asked, eventually.

'I'm not certain,' Ellen admitted. 'He didn't sound very enthusiastic.'

'I think he will,' Alexa said, though her brow was furrowed. 'He seems like a nice man.'

'You just think that because he's got a small child,' Ellen said.

'He'll come back,' Ben said, confidently. He stepped back from the skylight and stretched his arms behind his back. 'He'll be calling a locksmith or something right now.' Clearly satisfied with his reading of the situation, he turned and sat back in the centre of the room.

The housemates remained at the window, watching the door opposite.

A good ten minutes or so must have passed. At first, Ellen, Alexa and Jack exchanged a series of increasingly anxious glances. Occasionally, someone muttered something that was intended to be reassuring, but had the opposite effect. Slowly, anxiety gave way to tension and Ellen found she could no longer look at either of them, let alone speak. In the distance, she could hear a car revving, but she couldn't tell if it was on their street or an adjacent one.

She'd been about to say something terse about giving up when the man reappeared at his door with his son. She felt Alexa stiffen. This time, the child was attached by reins and no longer had the tricycle. The man was holding his phone. He led the boy across the road again and resumed his position at the end of the path.

'HELLO.' He sounded strangely formal. The child was looking up at them too now.

'HI!' Ellen replied, hopefully.

Behind her, Jack did a wave, although Ellen wasn't certain the man could see it.

'OK, SO THERE'S A LOCKSMITH ON THE WAY,' he said, evenly. Ellen opened her mouth to respond but he added, quickly and loudly, 'BUT IT'LL BE A FEW HOURS. THEY'RE PRETTY BUSY TODAY.'

Her heart sank, but she pretended it hadn't. 'NO WORRIES, THANKS,' she hollered out of the window.

'YES, THANK YOU SO MUCH,' Alexa shouted. 'THAT'S SO KIND.'

'SORRY WE YELLED AT YOU OUT OF THE WINDOW,' Ellen added. She did another of her most winning smiles.

'ANY PROBLEMS AND THEY'VE GOT MY NUMBER,' he added, simply.

'GREAT!' Ellen shouted. She did her own thumbs-up.

This earned a smile. 'I'M GOING OUT WITH HIM NOW FOR HALF AN HOUR' – he pointed at the toddler – 'BUT THEN I'LL BE ACROSS THE ROAD.'

'THANK YOU SO MUCH!!' Alexa cried.

The man nodded awkwardly at them in farewell and then said something to his son. The two of them started toddling up the street, with Jack, Ellen and Alexa watching their retreating backs.

'Success?' Ben called from the middle of the room.

'Success!' Alexa said. She sounded exhilarated.

Ellen watched her return to the floor beside Ben, who grinned at her. They kissed lightly: a victory peck.

Ellen breathed out at last. 'God, I can't believe that worked.'

'Oh, ye of little faith,' Alexa shot back.

'And now we wait, I guess?' Ben said.

'Couple of hours,' Alexa replied, apologetically.

Ben shrugged. 'Better late than never.'

Ellen agreed. Still, she felt deflated. A few hours was a long time to stagnate in this attic replaying the misdeeds of last night. Her hangover reasserted itself, as did her bladder; she slumped down on the floor beside Ben and Alexa to deliver the dispiriting news in a whine. 'I think I'm going to have to use the box again.'

'Go, then, and stop talking about it,' Alexa retorted.

Ellen hesitated while she worked out whether she could be bothered to get offended about Alexa's tone. She decided she could not. 'OK,' she said. 'Wish me luck.'

'Good luck,' Alexa said, evenly.

Ben raised his eyebrows.

Ellen grimaced at her friend, then started to pick her way through the muddle and clutter yet again, aiming for the corner where she'd relieved herself last time. She accepted, miserably, that she would almost certainly have to make this pilgrimage a third time, if the neighbour was right about the locksmith taking hours. Navigating a sticky situation between an inscrutable cardboard box and a blue IKEA bag containing three sets of menacing garden secateurs, she reflected that certain of the objects around her were starting to feel like acquaintances. The lawnmower, for example, looked like it was grinning.

The act itself was just as dispiriting on the second go, though at least she didn't get any wee on her joggers this time. When she returned, Alexa and Ben tried to act like they hadn't been snogging, while Jack remained at the window. Alexa looked up as she approached.

Ellen jerked her thumb towards Jack. 'Scared him off, did you?'

Alexa looked scandalized, and then a little shamefaced. 'Are you alright, Jack?' she called out, ignoring Ellen. 'Why don't you come sit with us for a bit?'

'Oh, er, I will.' He sounded very distracted. 'Just give me a minute.'

Ellen and Alexa exchanged a mystified look.

'OK,' Alexa said, after a pause. 'We'll be here.'

Ellen gave her a sarky look. 'Where else would we be?'

10. Jack

He'd felt his phone buzz again while he'd been hovering near the window as the girls spoke to the man across the road, but now that Jack tapped the Twitter notification, it wouldn't load properly.

Trying not to let the frustration get to him, he hung a little way out of the skylight again, phone in his outstretched arm, and watched the screen carefully. Nothing. He waggled it towards the ground. Nothing. He wondered if there was a way he could balance it in the window frame so that he didn't have to hold it. But when he tried this, it fell on to the floor beneath the skylight. He bent down to retrieve it.

'What are you *doing* over there, Jack?' Ellen called out.

'Just dropped my phone,' he mumbled.

He crouched down and prodded at the screen. Still nothing. Determined not to give up, he crawled forward slightly, into the space between the skylight and the wall, one of the only sections of the whole attic – besides where Ben, Alexa and Ellen were sitting – that wasn't full of Elias's old things. He wondered if that would take him closer to the signal.

Still nothing.

He was desperate to know how many replies he'd received to his tweet; it felt like being instructed not to blink. It was all he could think about. Especially since he'd just had a new idea. He'd tapped it out on his Notes app while Ellen was in the corner again.

Housemate is having to go to the toilet in a box #newcross #stuckintheattic

Crouching over his phone, Jack read and reread it. He liked it. It was definitely funnier than the first messages. He wondered if Ellen would mind him sharing it, but no one would know it was her, he reasoned. And she hadn't seemed to mind too much when Alexa had made fun of her. Plus, perhaps more people would want to help them if they found out that their only toilet was a box. It did make their situation sound rather desperate. Of course, now they had the neighbour who had called the locksmith — but Jack thought they should probably have a backup plan. Maybe the locksmith would forget and wouldn't come, after all. Plus, he had felt that exhilarating rush when he'd realized that all these strangers he'd never met, and probably would never meet, were reading his tweets. He wanted to feel it again.

He was thinking about this — about all the people in the world who'd seen his tweet — when the WiFi reappeared. He jumped to his feet and banged the back of his head on the base of the skylight.

'Ow,' he moaned.

'Oh, Jack,' he heard Alexa say as Ben made to get up.

As he was rubbing the back of his head, his phone buzzed again. 'Oh no, no, I'm fine, don't come over,' he said, quickly.

Ben stopped in his tracks, uncertainly. Jack tried his best to look totally fine, despite the throb in his skull. It did the trick: Ben backed away and sat back down again.

'I'll be back over in a second,' Jack added, more casually this time. 'Just want to make the most of the sunshine.'

He could feel them all staring at him, so he turned round again.

It was a Twitter notification. Heart pounding, he tapped, and it took him straight to his mentions. The tweet now had 697 likes, and his notifications were chaos; it was hard to keep up with all the names of people tapping the heart button. The little red notification bubble at the bottom of the screen couldn't keep up either. He noticed his hands were shaking a little. Before he did anything else, he pulled up the Notes app, copied the tweet about Ellen, and hit send in a rush of conviction. She probably wouldn't ever see it. Ellen didn't follow Jack on Twitter, though he followed her. Her profile picture was one of her holding two spoons over her eyeballs and gurning, and she posted lots of polls about which takeaway she should get to 'satisfy her hangover'.

Quickly, Jack scanned the notifications, with one eye half trained on the WiFi, expecting it to vanish at any second. People *did* think he was funny! Lots of them had said so.

@namesbond
Hah mate this is classic

@long_tall_sally
Omg!!!! Too funny @BBCRadio1 have you seen this ???

@fun_phil01
looooooooool mate bet she won't like you putting this up

He screenshotted the responses, so that he could look at them when the connection dropped off. He kept scrolling.

As he did so, a WhatsApp from his mum came through. He tapped it unthinkingly, and his phone left Twitter, but when it tried to land on WhatsApp he just got a spinning wheel at the top of the screen and he couldn't see his mum's latest message. He must have lost the connection again. He tried to return to Twitter, but when he'd refreshed, the app didn't load anything properly. He breathed a sigh of frustration. He waved his phone around again a few times, but nothing happened. He felt furious with his mum for texting, and then guilty that he felt so cross. He pocketed his phone again and turned round to face the others.

They had definitely been watching him.

'Are you sure you're OK, Jack?' Ellen sounded like she was talking to a small child.

He felt a little annoyed. 'Yes,' he said shortly. 'I'm fine.'

'OK.' She raised her hands in surrender. 'As you were.'

He had been about to go back over to sit with the others, but now felt like he couldn't, because he'd been snappy with Ellen. Instead, he turned back round and looked out of the window. He took his phone out again. It had 33 per cent battery. He put it back in his pocket and decided to try and go for ten minutes without checking it. In the background, he heard the others talking about the locksmith and trying to predict how long it would take for them to arrive.

A woman was walking down Rokeby Close with a dog. It was small and it waddled, as if its legs were too short for its body. He wondered if he was still supposed to be shouting, or whether they'd given up on that plan now that the man said he had contacted the locksmith. Either way, Jack felt bashful, and the woman was too far away. He swallowed, feeling a little guilty.

He thought of the beer garden at the Elephant, where he was supposed to be going later. There was no particular occasion – Johnny had just suggested it because, apparently, it had some good craft beers on tap. Jack went along with a lot of what Johnny suggested. He seemed to know how to do London better than Jack did. In fact, it had been Johnny who had suggested Jack join him in London in the first place. They'd been at university together, but Johnny had moved down straight afterwards, and he said it was amazing: so many pubs and people. And Johnny was getting really into climbing at this indoor climbing wall. And then he had forwarded him this email from their university – Jack got the emails too but he never bothered to open them – and Johnny had said, look, they've got a job with this start-up in London. The founder had gone to Manchester too. And Johnny had said, 'Apply and come live down here, mate.'

Jack had applied, in the end – on a whim, really, never expecting it to go anywhere – and then he'd been asked for an interview and then he'd got the job. His mum had narrowed her eyes at first when she saw the contract and that his job title was 'Human Bean', but Jack said he was fairly certain that was just how the company did things, little jokes like that. And she'd been satisfied and said it was good for him, to get out and live on his own. She had called Maisie, who said Jack could stay with her for a bit until he got on his feet.

Jack had never really had a specific job in mind. Other people at university had seemed to really know what they wanted. Law, or a master's degree, or to work in sustainability or have a job in publishing. A girl he had talked to at a party once had really wanted to be an actuary. Jack had googled it afterwards and it still hadn't made much sense to him. But he'd just gone back home and then got the job at the garden centre. He knew that he wouldn't work at the garden centre for ever, obviously, but bumbling along hadn't really bothered him. And his mum didn't mind, unlike other people's parents, who did seem to really mind. Jack didn't know what his dad would think, as he'd left Jack's mum when Jack was four and Maisie nine. He didn't mind – his mum was brilliant, and his dad wasn't, so he knew which one he'd rather had stuck around, though this news sometimes seemed to make other people sad on his behalf, and Jack wouldn't know what to say.

Anyway, he'd been pleased when he got the job at Green Genie. Jack had told Johnny straight away, and he'd been delighted. He handed in his notice at the garden centre – they were sorry to see him go, they said – but Jack was excited. It felt like he was going on an adventure. He went to the bus station near the Arndale with his rucksack and bin bag of extra things, as well as the packed lunch his mum had made him. He got on the coach and watched his city slip away as they got on to the motorway, following the big blue signs to London. He remembered when he turned up in Victoria Station in the early evening, on the Saturday night before he started his job, and he tried to work out how to get on the Underground to go to his sister's house. He'd seen a group of people his age near the station, spilling out of a pub on to the road, holding their pints and laughing and smoking, and he'd thought, hey, this could be fun.

And so far, it had been fun. He liked the house. Johnny was quite busy, because he had Annie, but Jack still saw him a fair bit, and it was good that he lived nearby. And he did like the pubs and the climbing wall. And when the weather got better, Jack was going to get a bike and start cycling to work. And work was OK. He liked having somewhere to go every weekday morning, and all the free fruit and vegetables. He enjoyed having money go into his bank account every month. It wasn't a lot of money – some people in London must have a lot of money, a dizzying amount of money, in order to live in the big houses near the office in Bermondsey – but he liked feeling like he was making his own way. On payday, on the last Friday of the month, he would always go to the pub with his colleagues, and he felt happy when he thought of those numbers in the bank and that he could have a third pint if he wanted to.

Plus, they got free lunch most days. Sometimes, Jack would go downstairs with Flora to collect the crates from the man with the van. Flora was helping out on the social team, with Deepti, and Jack would talk to her a bit about her work. Flora had just graduated and was living back in her parents' house in somewhere called Angel, which was in north London ('Angel of the north,' Jack had said, though he didn't think Flora had got it) and so it didn't matter that she wasn't getting paid. That was how Jack had started helping with the memes, every so often – he and Flora would message each other funny things all day and sometimes she'd put them on the Green Genie Facebook or Instagram accounts.

He wasn't lonely, not really, though sometimes when he thought about how big London was and how he didn't really know many people here, it made him feel a little bit dizzy. He liked commuting to work, feeling like he was part of the city's rhythm. He liked the tribalism too: rolling his eyes when the Tube was delayed; those moments of fleeting kinship with others on the platform when the announcer made a bad joke over the tannoy. But when he realized how few people knew him here, then it was easy to feel a bit like he didn't exist. He had his sister but she was miles away, and they didn't really have the sort of relationship where they went to the pub or did things like that. And Jack wasn't sure if Alexa or Ellen would notice if he didn't come home one night. They'd just assume he was at a friend's house, or somewhere else, maybe at a party. And Johnny probably thought that Jack had lots of other friends, like Johnny did now – people he'd met at work, and mates of Annie's.

Still, whenever Jack's mum called to say hi, he'd always tell her he was having a great time, and give her a story about the climbing wall or what he'd been doing at work or how he'd gone to a really nice pub. He wouldn't want her to think he wasn't having a really great time in London.

He knew she enjoyed telling her friends about how he was living and working down south – just like his sister. Two grown-up children settled in London! He knew she liked that, even though she missed him and she always told him so before they hung up.

11. Ellen

'What do you do, Ben?' Ellen asked, suddenly.

She knew this made her sound a little like she was Alexa's maiden aunt. Still, it was a question – and it was the question you asked, even though she knew the answer, because she'd heard all about him from Alexa.

'I work for a social housing charity in Peckham,' he said.

'Cool.'

'How about you?' he said. He teasingly kissed the back of Alexa's neck and she turned, delighted.

'I work at an organic tampon company. Doing their blog and Twitter and stuff. You could say . . .' She paused, to give the requisite oomph to a line she had delivered many times before. 'I am the voice of the UK's leading brand of CBD-infused tampons.'

He raised his eyebrows. He appeared underwhelmed.

'It's a talking point,' she added, although it hadn't seemed to inspire conversation in Ben. She groped for her script. 'And where are you from?'

'Peckham,' he supplied, '. . . well, not originally. I grew up somewhere called Gillingham and then I went to uni in Bristol. But now I'm in Peckham. Near Queens Road?'

Ellen sat up straighter. 'Gillingham, in Kent?'

'What? Oh, Gillingham, yeah. In Kent.'

'That's where I'm from!'

She reeled. No one was ever from Gillingham – in fact,

she hadn't met anyone from there since she'd left home for university. It was a standard-issue British town, with little to recommend it, as far as Ellen was concerned, other than a high-speed rail link that took you away from the place.

Ben laughed, incredulously. 'What? Which school did you go to?'

'Rainham Girls?'

'Ha. I went to Rainham Boys!'

'Oh my God.'

Ellen hadn't spoken to anyone from Rainham Boys since she was eighteen. The school's name conjured memories of sticky snogs on the dance floor at one of the three Wetherspoons on the High Street. All three had dance floors of varying sizes, and on Saturday nights all the underage pupils from the sixth forms of the three local schools (Rainham Girls, Rainham Boys and the mixed school, St James's) had tried their luck. First with the intimidatingly wide bouncers who straddled the doors, and then with each other on the dance floors.

'Wait, so what year did you finish school?'

'In 2009?' he replied.

'Same! We must have been in the same year!'

'This is a very weird coincidence,' Alexa said, brightly.

'OK, so we have definitely been in the same room before.' Ben was animated now. He shuffled slightly, so he could get a better look at Ellen.

She noticed he had very long eyelashes.

'We must have been . . . we must know so many people in common! I'm trying to remember who I knew properly who went to Rainham Girls –'

'Surely Joanna Jessop,' Ellen supplied, quickly.

'Oh my God!' Ben gazed at her, his face solemn. 'JJ.'

Ben's tone communicated, at a stroke, that he too had been following on Facebook the dramatic events of Joanna Jessop's divorce and return from 'the brink'. Guilty laughter.

'She went out with one of my friends for about three months when we were fourteen. I remember going to a gathering at her house and she was wearing a pink feather boa and matching cowboy hat.'

Ellen could see it. In fact, she was fairly sure that JJ had worn a feather boa to their leavers' dance.

'Is she the one you always show me on Instagram?' Alexa asked.

'Yeah,' Ellen said, shortly. 'My mum tells me she's bought a lovely two-bed near the new station,' she added, rolling her eyes. 'I'm sure we'll see some panoramas on Facebook in no time.'

Ben snorted. 'Did you know Sarah Bletchley?'

'God, I have not thought about Sarah Bletchley in *years*.'

Sarah Bletchley was the clichéd mean girl of Rainham Girls: boobs by the age of eleven, long blonde hair, lip gloss, pink bras under white school shirts with one too many buttons undone. Her father worked in the City and they had a big mock-Tudor house and a Maserati in the driveway. Ellen remembered the time she had tackled Sarah Bletchley at hockey and been told in the changing rooms after the match that her father would sue her. Even as a twelve-year-old, Ellen had known this was an absurd thing to say.

'I had such a thing for her, obviously.' Ben rolled his

eyes to mark the inevitability of such a statement. 'We texted for a month and I thought I was in with a chance. And
then I went to the Regal one Saturday and she was there
getting off with Harry Grahams.'

'Obviously, I fancied Harry Grahams,' Ellen replied,
guiltily. 'Although, Jesus – how the mighty have fallen.
Last time I checked, his Facebook profile picture was
his car.'

'He was such a fucker.' Ben shook his head. 'Proper,
brutish bullying. I remember him making another bloke
move schools after he stuffed him inside a wheelie bin just
outside the school gates.'

Alexa laughed brightly, then stopped when she realized
this was not a joke.

'Christ,' Ellen exhaled. 'I had terrible taste in men. Wait,
so where exactly did you live?'

'Gunwharf Close – Mum and Dad are still there. My
younger brother was at Rainham too – Oliver?'

Ellen shook her head.

'Fair enough, he was a maths prodigy and didn't do a lot
of socializing. My sister went to St James's – Ava Kenny?'

'Hmm, doesn't ring a bell,' she mused. 'But my brother
Tom was at St James's. Maybe they knew each other. Is she
older or younger?'

'Younger – by two years.'

'Ah, same as Tom! They were probably in the same
year too.'

Jack had shuffled over and joined them all on the floor
again, offering a muttered hello. Alexa smiled at him,
though Ellen appraised him rather coolly, not forgetting
that he'd snapped at her earlier.

'Wait, wait, wait . . . so . . .' Ben leaned forward. 'Were you at Amber Outhwaite's party?'

Ellen's eyes widened. 'God, yes!' She recalled the whole evening with awful clarity. All the mums had talked about Amber Outhwaite's party for weeks afterwards – as had the attendees. It was one of the first parties in Year 13, a few weeks after the school term had started. Amber's father, like Sarah Bletchley's, was something monstrously wealthy in the City. There was a cluster of them in that part of the south-east: flash and showy; houses dressed up to the nines, with extravagances like swimming pools, jacuzzis and wet rooms and, in the case of Amber's, a hedge maze and four tennis courts. The Outhwaites were a family of three.

Amber – in contrast to her manor house – had always been fairly quiet and a bit mousy. If you ended up sitting next to her on the bus to or from school, she'd want to talk to you about how many free periods you had on your time-table this term, her eyes wide, blinking fast, leaning in a little too close. But something seemed to happen to her the summer before starting Year 13 – Ellen could remember Kate, her best friend, remarking on it on their first day back. Amber had come in all done up: lots of make-up and big hair, and she'd made a beeline for Sarah Bletchley in the dining hall where Bletchley and her coven sat at lunchtime. Whatever Amber had said, she'd been allowed to sit down with the rest of them. And about three weeks later, Amber made an event on Facebook: she was having a party, and it was 'BYOB bitchezzz'. Ellen wondered if Sarah Bletchley had had something to do with the party, specifically the wording of that invitation.

If she had, Sarah owed Amber more than an apology. Because the event had been listed as a public event on Facebook, which meant that anyone with an account could find it and come along – and come along they did. By midnight, there were about 500 people stuffing fag butts in the jacuzzi's water jets, tearing branches from the hedge maze and vomiting in the swimming pool. Amber was blind drunk, stumbling around her own house, telling people that it was 'cool' because her parents were away for their anniversary weekend and not back until Sunday evening. Until James Kingston had smashed up the master bedroom's en-suite and started wearing the broken toilet seat around his neck: a trophy for a thug. A short while later, the police turned up – one or two vans; a neighbour had called them – and shut the party down.

Amber missed a week of school and when she came back, the make-up and the hair and the 'bitchezzz' attitude had disappeared again, and she was plain and mousy once more. She no longer got the bus but was driven to school by her very blonde mother. The story had made the local paper.

'I think that party ruined Amber Outhwaite's life,' Ellen said. 'It was so awful.'

'My main memory from that evening was walking into the kitchen and finding a group of lads I'd never seen before dropping plates on to the kitchen floor.' Ben's eyes were wide. 'Then one of them started using a chopping board like a sort of cricket bat and getting another to bowl crockery at him so he could smash things into pieces in mid-air. I ended up half running home as soon as the police arrived.'

'Yeah, I think I made a pretty quick exit at that point.' She remembered running away, ballet flats flapping, clutching Kate's arm, the fleet of police cars in the driveway, Amber Outhwaite crying rivers of eyeliner. 'My parents were horrified. They refused to leave my brother and me alone in the house again until we were in our twenties.'

'God, that poor girl,' Alexa whispered.

'Once, I went to a party and someone ate a goldfish,' Jack said, solemnly.

They all looked at him.

'It was in a bowl in the living room,' Jack explained. 'And then this guy got really stoned and ate it.'

'That's disgusting,' Ellen said, flatly. 'Poor goldfish.'

Jack blanched and Ben gamely changed the subject.

'So, who else do we know in common?' he wrapped an arm around Alexa's waist absent-mindedly and she smiled.

He looked mischievous. 'Who did you go out with?'

Ellen laughed. 'Oh God, no one really. I spent a lot of time having intense chats with boys on MSN Messenger and worrying I was actually chatting with Sarah Bletchley in disguise. And trying to snog people down the Regal, obviously.'

'Trust me – Sarah Bletchley wasn't eloquent enough to trick anyone into thinking she was their boyfriend on MSN,' Ben snorted. 'I used to speak to her on there a bit – before she betrayed me with Harry Grahams – and she *really* didn't have a lot to say. Atrocious spelling too.'

Ellen was about to launch into her Sarah Bletchley anecdote about the hockey pitch and the suing threat, and how Sarah used to torture this substitute Geography teacher – she'd once made her cry by saying her trousers made her look like a virgin (the ultimate Sarah Bletchley insult) – when Alexa suddenly froze.

'Wait, is that someone calling your name?' she asked.

They all held their breath for a second.

Ellen could hear what Alexa had heard: her own name, coming faintly from the street. 'It must be the neighbour,' she said, scrambling to a standing position. As she did so, she noticed that the damp patch on her jogging bottoms had finally dried. She walked the few paces to the skylight and stuck her head out of the window to see the man from across the street, who was standing on the pavement outside their house.

'HI!' she shouted back. 'YOU CALLED?'

'AH, YES – THERE YOU ARE.' He was holding the toddler again, and shifted him from one hip to the other. 'JUST WANTED TO SAY I'M BACK.'

'GREAT!' Ellen yelled, with a little more enthusiasm than the situation required.

'SO I'LL LET YOU KNOW WHEN I HEAR ANYTHING FROM THE LOCKSMITH.'

So it was not news of their imminent rescue.

'GREAT!!' she repeated, disguising her disappointment. 'THANKS SO MUCH!!'

The man gave a half-wave of farewell. She watched him cross the road – always careful – and then walk up the path to his own house. A woman opened the door as he approached and crouched down, arms outstretched. He deposited the toddler on the ground. Ellen watched as the boy ran towards his mother. The family closed the door.

Ellen returned to the fold. They all looked at her with commiseration.

'He was just letting us know that he's back from his walk. And that he'll let us know when he hears from the locksmith.'

'We heard,' Alexa said, glumly. 'I'd hoped he was going to tell us rescue was imminent.'

'Yeah.' Ellen shrugged and crossed her legs.

Ben kissed Alexa lightly again, which seemed to cheer her up slightly.

'I can't believe the plan actually worked,' Ellen offered, after a moment of silence. 'I owe you all an apology.' She picked at a loose thread on her tracksuit bottoms. She couldn't wait to have a shower.

'Let's not speak too soon,' Alexa cautioned.

'Home stretch, guys,' Ben said, confidently. He drew a circle on Alexa's thigh with his finger. 'OK, so. Where were we?'

12. Alexa

Alexa wasn't put out by Ben and Ellen's unexpected connection, per se. But it was making her feel a little left out.

'Did you ever go to Pulse?' Ellen was asking Ben. 'It had that bouncer with the serious anger-management issues.'

On cue, a conspiratorial chuckle.

Alexa looked at Jack for some solidarity, but he appeared to be swiping through the photos on his phone. She could hear the pipes hissing from somewhere inside the walls, and wondered again about the water cascading from the sink downstairs. Outside a horn blared in the distance. The wider world felt like an unknown quantity right now — as though almost anything could be happening.

'Thommo?' Ben was saying now. 'Oh, yeah. He's still there — the sociopathic bastard. In fact, we ended up there at some point last Christmas. It's as shit as it always was, but they've erected this sort of cage in the middle of the dance floor and people can get inside it and dance. Dreadful.' He shook his head in pantomime disgust.

Disappointingly, Ben had untangled himself from her — blaming cramp — and was now sitting stretched out along the floor, resting on one arm. Still, with the other hand, he was regularly squeezing her thigh.

'I cannot believe you went back to Pulse that recently,' Ellen laughed in disbelief. 'I haven't been since I was about eighteen.'

'We actually found it a little bit too bleak in there, last time. It wasn't worth it for the nostalgia. We finished in the Regal in the end, which is also cheap and nasty, but a little less volatile.'

'Yes, Linda says that end of the High Street is a bit dodgy these days . . .' A pause. 'My mum,' Ellen added for Ben's benefit.

'I love Linda,' Alexa enthused, seeing an opening.

'Yes, and she prefers you to me.' Ellen rolled her eyes exaggeratedly.

Alexa had been to visit Gillingham a few times when they were both at university and she had instantly loved Linda and John, who were warm and funny and formed a sort of double act that was fluent but not practised. Alexa envied this enormously, as she could not remember a time when her own parents had been any sort of double act. She could see why Ellen had turned out the way she had: warm, silly, funny. Alexa had envied Ellen, too, for growing up in a town where she could get night buses home instead of relying on the services of a single taxi. In rural Sussex, there were no clubs for Alexa to sneak into. She went to the pub all the time, but the owner was her neighbour and knew exactly how old she was. She always let Alexa have a shandy, but the granting of permission – and the fact her mother was usually there too, in the corner, with her glasses pushed down her nose – had rather taken the rebellion out of the whole ritual.

'Oh, oh, oh –' Ben sat up quickly and ran a hand through his hair. 'Did you know Chris Barclay?'

Ellen looked a little abashed. 'Not properly, but I definitely used to talk to him on MSN. Or tried to. Sometimes it was like getting blood out of a stone. I used to spend ages talking to guys from Rainham and St James's on MSN – these meaningless conversations about coursework that I dreamed might blossom into true love.' Ellen made a face.

'I'd use the family computer in the living room and get really angry with my mum when she wandered past and read out something I'd just said to some girl I'd never met but had decided I really fancied.'

'Oh but those were the most intense ones,' Ellen said, sounding – Alexa noted – very intense. 'The ones where you didn't even know their real name but in your head you were already planning how to lose your virginity to them on the dance floor at Pulse.' She added, a little more breezily, 'Oh, and remember all those statuses you'd do' – she screwed up her face at the thought – 'song lyrics to show you were really deep and meaningful? I remember putting up a Kooks lyric and virtually thinking I was Nietzsche.'

Alexa had to laugh at that one.

'I definitely used to do the thing where you'd type your status in a mixture of caps and small letters.' Ben mimed typing on a keyboard with two fingers.

'So much.' She smirked. 'What was your name?' She paused, for dramatic flourish. 'I was miss_BehaviourX91. *That* was the hotmail address I put on my UCAS application.'

Alexa scrunched up her face. 'Ellen, that is *dreadful.*'

Ellen rolled her eyes in agreement.

'Mine was jackthelad93.' Jack sounded solemn.

'Standard.' A guilty grin danced about Ben's mouth. 'I don't know if I can tell you mine. It's too embarrassing.'

'Oh, come on,' said Ellen. 'Maybe I'll remember speaking

to you. Or maybe one of my friends had a long and passionate virtual relationship with you.'

He looked to Alexa, his expression like that of a child who's been caught out in a far-fetched lie.

With effort, she affected lightness. 'Go on – spill.' She smiled, archly.

He returned an appraising look, one eyebrow cocked, and then turned to face Ellen and Jack.

'OK, bear in mind I also applied to university with this name. I'm shocked they let me in.' Another glance at Alexa. 'Don't judge me – I was an awkward teenager.'

'OK, I promise I won't judge you.' She was pleased to be included. 'Too harshly.'

'OK –' Ben started. 'I can't believe I'm going to admit to this.' He cleared his throat, hamming it up. 'Rainham_romeo1991,' he said, slowly, dramatically. A pause. 'In lots of ways I think it's the underscore that's the worst part.'

'That is even worse than Ellen's,' Alexa confirmed, haughtily.

He gave her a begging look, playing up to it.

'Wait . . . hang on.' Ellen's voice had dropped several degrees.

Alexa and Ben both turned to look at her.

She was alert, her mouth pursed. 'You're telling me *you* were rainham_romeo1991?'

'I know.' Ben shook his head. 'Just dreadful, I –'

'No,' Ellen interrupted, louder and more distinctly this time. 'I mean – *you* were rainham_romeo1991?'

This time, Alexa noticed the emphasis. Ben did too.

'Yeah,' he said. He sounded a little hesitant. 'That's what I said. Why?'

Alexa noticed that the colour had risen in Ellen's cheekbones.

'We used to talk on MSN,' she said, quietly. She was staring straight at Ben, eyes slightly narrowed. After a second, she added, almost to herself. 'Of course. *Benjamin.*'

'What?' Ben said, disbelievingly. 'Did we?'

'Every night.' Ellen's voice was subdued, but she was still focused on Ben's face. 'Don't you remember?'

'What?' Ben laughed, uncertainly, and then stopped abruptly when he saw Ellen's expression. He looked at Alexa for support, but she was watching Ellen closely. Her hackles had risen and her face was set.

Alexa's thrum of foreboding ramped up several decibels.

'We did!' Ellen sounded urgent, her hands clenched on her lap. 'I remember it so clearly – I have such a good memory for things like this . . .' She waited for someone to challenge her, then continued in a near growl. 'We used to talk every single evening – I would log on after dinner, and we would talk for hours and hours.'

'No.' He had tensed slightly, and his cheeks were a little flushed. 'I don't remember that at all.'

Alexa opened her mouth as if to speak, but thought better of it and closed it again.

'I don't believe you,' Ellen said, flatly. 'I don't believe you don't remember.'

Ben searched Alexa's face, as if for help.

'I-I'm sorry' – he stuttered, bravado gone – 'I don't remember you at all. Miss_Behaviour . . . I don't remember. Maybe you have me mixed up with someone else?'

'No way. I know it was' – she paused to do air

quotes – '"rainham_romeo1991" I used to speak to.' She stuck her chest out, revving up for a theatrical reveal. 'So that would sort of make you a piece of shit.'

'What?!' Ben laughed, disbelievingly.

He cast around now, looking at Alexa and Jack, hoping for backup. Alexa gave him a shifty stare, her mind immobilized. Jack, meanwhile, didn't move his eyes from the floor.

'What do you mean?' he urged again. He was rooted to the spot. 'Sorry, but this is all really weirding me out now.' Ben looked hunted.

Alexa tried to help. 'El, what are you –?' she started, in a tone just above a whisper.

'OK, *rainham_romeo1991*,' Ellen interrupted, with emphasis. 'I'll remind you of the gory details.' She drew in a breath. 'Jesus,' she exhaled loudly, gazing heavenwards. Then she laughed, a bitter bark. 'I've been waiting for this moment since I was seventeen.'

13. Ellen

Ellen examined herself in the full-length mirror, tugging down the hem of her dark blue ruffled miniskirt. She re-arranged the wide black, fake patent leather belt around her waist, and undid another button on her off-white blouse, then did it back up again. She made a face.

'I'm not sure about this,' she said to Kate. 'Does it look weird with tights?'

'It looks great,' Kate said, impatiently, not looking up from the smaller mirror on her chest of drawers, where she was putting the finishing touches to her fake eyelashes. Satisfied, she pouted at herself in the mirror, cocking her head from one side to the other, and then turned to Ellen. 'Have you got the hair glitter?'

Ellen cast around and spotted it in front of her own mirror. She picked it up and passed it to Kate.

'Thanks, babe.'

Ellen returned to the mirror. She brushed her side fringe from her eyes and strained to look behind her, try-ing to work out what exactly the miniskirt was doing back there.

'Does it make my bum look really square?'

'Elly, you look great.' Kate stood up and smoothed her tight dress, which reached about a quarter of the way down her thighs. It had capped sleeves and a loud, geometric print in shades of pink and orange. She shrugged into a lace waistcoat. 'Too much?' she asked Ellen.

'Too much.'

Kate shrugged it off again. 'Heels or no heels?' she asked, crouching down to peer into the bottom rack of her teeming wardrobe.

'Oh, don't wear heels,' Ellen moaned. 'You take ages to walk down the street. And it's, like, a twenty-minute walk.'

'Fine,' Kate said, protesting. 'Chill out. Have you made the drinks yet?'

Ellen shook her head and Kate tutted at her. She moved to the desk, where – beside Kate's laptop and her A Level English folder – were a bottle of squash, a 35 cl bottle of Glen's vodka, purchased from the one Costcutter on the high street that didn't ID them, and two glasses.

Kate poured a slug of squash into both tumblers and held them out. 'Go to the bathroom, and top these up with a little water. Only a little.'

Ellen obliged, returning thirty seconds later, handing one back to Kate.

She scrutinized it, took a swig from the glass and then – with a practised air – topped it up to the rim with the vodka. 'Give me yours.'

Ellen passed it to her.

Kate gave it the same treatment. Then she held her glass out to clink Ellen's. 'Saturday night.' She took a swig and grimaced. 'Ugh.' She swallowed. 'Let's leave in forty minutes.'

Ellen took a more conservative sip of the concoction, though it still burned the back of her throat. It tasted like fermented glue. Kate had started to bob to the Flo Rida song that was playing from the tinny speakers on her laptop. Ellen laughed and nudged her gently, then moved to the desk to sit at the laptop. She took another swig of the drink. It tasted less noxious this time.

She opened Facebook, logged Kate out and logged herself in. She scrolled down the homepage for a minute and then went back up to the top, to the status box.

What's on your mind?

She watched the cursor blink. Her current status was her BBM pin. She tapped into the box.

soooooooo drunk right now.

She would be soon. She drained her glass.

'That's better,' Kate said, bobbing towards her. 'Another?'

The vodka had gone straight to Ellen's head. 'Definitely.'

Four vodka squashes later, and they were verging on hysterical – and ready to sneak past Kate's parents' room, her father's snores reverberating around the hallway, making sure not to wake the dog on their way out. Tonight the plan was Pulse, if they could get in, and the Regal if they couldn't. They basically always got into the Regal.

'Shit, have you got the digital camera?' Kate asked, in a hoarse whisper, as soon as she'd closed her front door. Her parents' room looked on to the street, which was deserted and dark, though punctuated by pools of warm light from the street lamps that snaked down the long, curved road.

Ellen unzipped her tiny bag and riffled through it. Lipstick, purse, BlackBerry, ten-pack of cigarettes, camera.

'Got it.'

'Phew,' Kate said, linking Ellen's arm. 'Fuck, it's freezing — let's walk fast.' Neither of them wore a coat, in order to avoid having to buy cloakroom tickets with money that could be better spent on shots. It was a rule that the cloakroom was never worth it, but shots always were. They set off at a trot, the vodka warming their veins, though occasionally making one or both of them veer off the kerb.

The queue snaked down the road and Ellen was anxious, but tonight was one of the alchemical nights when they got into Pulse. The key, Kate whispered as they approached the fleet of brawny bouncers, was to pout and stick your boobs out. Ellen didn't think she'd done it right, but while she was still trying to work it out, the brawniest one grunted something about 'having a good night' and Kate was tugging on her arm before he could reconsider.

They could taste the smoke machines as soon as they walked into the club, and feel the bass in their feet. Pulse was basically two big rooms, both with sticky bars and white pleather couches bordering square dance floors, each illuminated by strobing lights. The soundtrack in both rooms was the Top 40, occasionally remixed with an R 'n' B beat.

Ellen cupped her hands and spoke into Kate's ear. 'Bar?'

Kate hooked Ellen's arm again and took the lead. As they forced their way through the crowd, trying not to touch too many sweaty backs in polo shirts, Ellen spotted Harry Grahams and a couple of the other Rainham boys sitting on one of the banquettes. They were all holding bottles of beer. Harry was smirking while another boy whom Ellen didn't recognize shouted something into his ear. She nudged Kate, who whipped round and then nudged her back. At the bar, they ordered two Malibu Cokes and then weaved their way into a spot on the dance floor where they knew that Harry and his group would be able to see them.

As the Malibu and Coke hit her empty stomach, it suddenly struck Ellen that she was an exceptionally good dancer. As was Kate, who was currently rubbing her hands up and down her own thighs in time to the beat. Ellen loved this song. She loved every single one of the songs.

'Shall we get a shot!' Kate squealed into her ear, her breath hot, after fifteen or so minutes of dancing.

'YES! MY ROUND!' Ellen screamed back, brandishing the fiver her mother had given her for pizza before she left the house.

Ellen elbowed her way back towards the bar, leaving Kate gyrating on the dance floor. A man was leaning in to try and talk to her, but Kate was oblivious, lost in her own movement.

Ellen squeezed into the bar, her elbows slipping on the wet counter. She tried to get the attention of the bar staff, but they seemed to be working according to their own internal system, and Ellen was far down the list. She clung on to the fiver, watching as they squeezed shots of vodka into glasses and then fired Coke out of the gun. And then she noticed Harry Grahams was standing beside her, with a boy she was pretty sure was called Scott on his other side.

'Hey,' she slurred, without thinking.

They appraised her, looking blank.

'Ellen,' she reminded them, although she wasn't certain they'd ever got as far as being properly introduced. 'I go to Rainham,' she added, then put her hand over her mouth, remembering that she was very much here under false, under-age pretences.

'Right,' Harry grunted.

He was quite sweaty, but Ellen decided this was attractive. Scott grinned and made a sort of salute with two of his fingers.

'So, what can I get you?' she winked.

They looked at each other, then shrugged.

'I'm alright, thanks,' Harry replied. He jerked his thumb back towards his group at the banquette. One of them – possibly Craig Gordon – appeared to have passed out. He was slumped sideways, head lolling. 'We're getting a round in anyway.'

'Oh, go on, do a shot with me!' Ellen said. She waved the fiver even more vigorously over the bar, earning a glare from the best-looking bartender. 'We can do Sambucas!'

'Nah, I'm alright, thanks.' Harry turned back to Scott, who was whispering something in his ear.

'So, do you guys come here often?' Ellen batted her damp fringe from her eyes.

Harry nodded, but didn't look at her.

'We love it here,' she said, with the air of a regular. 'The music is *so* good.'

He looked like he might have been about to reply when the female bartender swooped in to serve him and he leaned across the bar to grunt, 'Five pints of Stella.'

Ellen watched, mouth slightly open, as the woman poured five sloppy pints, arms moving in all directions. Harry paid for the drinks and he and Scott started to pick them up.

'Want some help?' Ellen asked, eagerly. It was worth losing her place in the queue to talk to Harry Grahams.

'Nah.' Harry managed to pick up all five. Without a backward glance, he stepped away from the bar, the throng parting slightly as he did so.

Scott smirked and gave her that salute again. In the time that she was gaping at them, open-mouthed, a woman stepped in beside Ellen and got served immediately.

She couldn't remember getting home when she woke up in Kate's double bed the next day. There was a glass of water beside her, and a washing-up bowl that Ellen was relieved to see she hadn't made use of. She didn't feel too bad. Kate was sleeping beside her. She was still wearing her fake eyelashes, and it looked like she had a spider resting on each eyelid.

Propping herself up on her elbows, Ellen reached for the glass of water and took a grateful gulp. Thankfully, she could see her bag on the floor, and she swung her legs out of the bed and crawled towards it, to retrieve her Black-Berry and her camera. Her mum had texted, asking when she was coming home. There were no other messages. Dispirited, Ellen locked the phone and put it back in the bag. She returned with the camera to the bed, and started to swipe backwards through all the photos from last night.

Luckily, filling in the blanks of Ellen's memory wouldn't be too hard: they appeared to have taken more than a hundred photos. Most of them were of Ellen and Kate posing on the dance floor. There were a few from the bathroom, and several that featured a girl whom Ellen swore she had never met before. Still, in one of the pictures she had her arm around the girl, whose fake tan had seemed to protect her from the spectral effect usually delivered by Ellen's 4x optical zoom. There were also a number of pictures from the centre of the roundabout on the A road, which had clearly been taken at the end of the night. In several of them, Ellen was holding a traffic cone.

The camera bleeped every time she scrolled through the photos.

Eventually, the bleeps stirred Kate, who turned on her side to face Ellen. 'Hi,' she said, one eye still closed. 'How are *you* feeling?'

Ellen spent most of the rest of the day at Kate's, doing an edit of last night's pictures to upload to a new album on Facebook ('ellen and kate go 2 pulse . . . AGAIN'), while eating stacks of toast and Nutella. It turned out they had actually spoken to the Rainham boys for a few minutes.

'Shit, was I really weird?' Ellen moaned.

'No, you were fine,' Kate said, impatiently. 'You were drunk, in a club, under-age. They thought we were really cool.'

Ellen wasn't certain she believed that, but decided she didn't want to know any further details.

At 6 p.m., she conjured the energy to go home. She walked the fifteen minutes from Kate's house to get the bus from the station next to the NCP car park. There was scant shelter, and it was raining. Ellen knew the timetable intimately: the next bus wasn't coming for another fifteen minutes, and of the two that served Ellen's house, it was the least direct. She sat down in the plastic seats by the bus stop, pulling her hoodie up around her ears. She considered smoking one of the remaining cigarettes in her ten-pack to pass the time, but didn't want John and Linda to smell it on her. She picked listlessly at a ladder in her tights.

Eventually, five minutes later than billed, the bus arrived.

She paid the £1.20 fare and made her way up to the top deck, sitting at the front of the bus, the perfect vantage point for watching it wend its way past new builds, tattier terraces and an eclectic high street. At this time on a Sunday evening, she had the place to herself. The journey took twenty minutes, and when she let herself in with her set of keys, her mother's head appeared instantly in the doorway of the kitchen. She was wearing an apron and her house shoes. Ellen could hear the sound of the kitchen television, which was tuned to something terrestrial and Sunday evening.

'I thought we'd seen the last of you,' her mother teased. 'Did you have a nice time with Kate?'

'Yeah,' Ellen grunted, kicking her ballet pumps off and leaving them on the rack by the front door. Her mother's head disappeared and Ellen followed her into the kitchen, going straight for the fridge. She opened it, scowled at the contents and then closed it again. 'What are we having for dinner?'

'Fishcakes,' her mother replied. 'With cauliflower cheese and green beans.'

Ellen opened the fridge again. She took out a chocolate mousse.

'Ellen, don't ruin your dinner.'

'I won't.'

Her mother tutted. 'It'll only be ten minutes.'

Ellen grunted again, and worked on excavating the chocolate mousse with a teaspoon.

Her brother wandered into the kitchen. He was in his pyjamas. 'You look terrible,' he said, sitting down opposite Ellen at the kitchen table.

'Tom, don't say that to your sister,' their mother called out, reprovingly.

Ellen shrugged. 'I'm really hungover,' she said to her brother, in a low voice. 'Got into Pulse last night,' she added, in a whisper now so that her mother wouldn't over-hear. Linda would definitely not approve of her evening at Pulse.

'Good for you,' Tom said, at a regular volume. 'Isn't it shit there?'

'No,' Ellen said, defensively. 'It's, like, the best place to go out round here.'

Tom sniggered. 'Yeah, I mean, doesn't say much, does it?'

Ellen made a face at him.

'Tom, Ellen, can you set the table, please?'

They stood up, sighing, and shuffled over to the cutlery drawer. Tom took the knives.

Ellen tried to snatch them out of his hands. 'I want to do the knives.'

Tom stared at her. 'You're an insane person.'

Ellen was about to say something but her mother spoke sharply.

'Stop it. Both of you.'

They set the table in silence. Their father drifted in from the kitchen, holding a newspaper. He lowered himself into his usual seat, without stopping reading whatever had interested him. Ellen and Tom glared at each other.

Their mother put plates in front of them. 'John?' she said, irritably.

'Ah, sorry, love.' He tossed the newspaper on to the cabinet behind him.

Dinner was eaten almost in silence by both Ellen and Tom, while their parents chuntered on to one another about the rain, the boiler doing that thing again, and an injustice against Nana Margaret that involved a parking ticket.

'How was your sleepover, love?' John asked, serving himself some more cauliflower cheese.

Ellen winced at the babyish term. 'Yeah, it was fun, thanks.' She pushed her plate away from her, eyeing the door. 'Can I be excused, please?' Her mother opened her mouth as if to protest, and Ellen added, 'I've got coursework.'

Ellen had an offer of a place at York to study English, and knew by now that 'coursework' was the secret pass-word for getting out of dinner early. When she'd told her parents about the offer, Linda had teased Ellen about studying a language she already spoke fluently, before giv-ing her daughter a quick squeeze and promising she'd make something special for dinner. John hadn't said very much, which was a sign he was pleased. Ellen had picked York because it looked old – and it was also very far away from Gillingham.

Her mother relented, lips pursed, as Ellen sidled out of the kitchen and took the stairs two at a time. She shut her bedroom door, walked to her desk and opened her laptop.

Now it was time for the other, virtual – and somehow realer and more vivid – part of her life to begin: MSN Messenger. Ellen signed in as miss_BehaviourX91 and then signed out again instantly, and then signed in again, and then signed out again. This was what she did every school night – and had done for the last two years – in the hope that one or several of the specific targets of her attention-seeking would notice her. It worked about 30 per cent of the time, but Ellen was an optimist.

A message appeared: Nathan. He was in her year at Rainham Boys and was, indeed, one of the specific targets of her attention. He was alright looking, and alright – though not the best – at football. As a result, Ellen reckoned she might have a chance.

nathan_harris_chelseaFC: *hi*
miss_BehaviourX91: *hi*
nathan_harris_chelseaFC: *heard u were at pulse last nite*

Who had he 'heard' it from? Ellen felt suddenly panicked. Maybe she had done something really awful last night and Kate hadn't felt able to tell her.

miss_BehaviourX91: *yeah with my friend kate*
miss_BehaviourX91: *such a gd nite*
nathan_harris_chelseaFC: *ye i was gonna go but got 2 drunk at amars lol*

Amar was another boy on her list.

miss_BehaviourX91: *oh kl*
miss_BehaviourX91: *did he have an empty*
nathan_harris_chelseaFC: *ye we recked the place lol*

This did not sound that funny. Ellen remembered Amber Outhwaite's party.

miss_BehaviourX91: *omg*

nathan_harris_chelseaFC: *ye his parents are gunna hit the roof*

miss_BehaviourX91: *lol*

nathan_harris_chelseaFC: *u gunna go out nxt wknd*

She inhaled sharply. Maybe he was trying to engineer a meeting.

miss_BehaviourX91: *yeah def*

miss_BehaviourX91: *lol*

nathan_harris_chelseaFC: *kl*

Maybe not. He didn't say anything else. For a while, she stared at the blinking cursor, and then minimized the chat screen. Only 13 of 157 contacts were online, and Nathan was the only one on her target list. Ellen sighed and signed out. Not a successful evening. Still, at least news of her and Kate's night out at Pulse had travelled around the Rainham Boys network, although she could not shake the pervasive anxiety that this must mean she'd disgraced herself in some way. Either way, she would bring it up with Kate tomorrow. She retrieved the camera and flopped on to the bed. Maybe she'd take Nathan off her mental target list.

For most of sixth form, Ellen's approach to MSN was scattergun. She would be speaking to a roster of maybe four or five Rainham or St James's boys at any one time. Their MSN names were passed around her girls' school like a swot's pot of Tippex. Sometimes, Ellen knew the boy in question in real life; usually, she hadn't met him. She preferred it that way. This allowed her to create a story around the person at the other end of her stuttering broadband connection.

Of course, there were stories. When girls offered up MSN names, they'd also offer up titbits. 'He asks you to talk dirty,' the legend would run. 'He comes on too strong,' the warning would go. 'He'll ask you to meet up and then he won't turn up,' was a forlorn, well-worn story. Ellen had never had a dramatic tale to tell. Often, boys would disappear without warning, only to pop up again about a month later, without an explanation. But there were always other boys to talk to.

The intimacy of these relationships varied wildly. With some people, you never really got beyond A Level subjects and wildly exaggerated stories about nights at the Regal. With others, it would simply be a matter of days before you were talking about your 'type' and what you looked for in a relationship. Ellen had never actually had one, obviously, but she had plenty of specifications and knew exactly what she was looking for. Blond and tall – Ellen was five foot eight, and self-conscious about it – but also cerebral, literary and – ideally, though not necessarily – 'a bit troubled'. As she attended a suburban comprehensive, this meant perhaps someone with divorced parents (separated would do), or who had been caught smoking in Rainham Boys' school uniform and subjected to three weeks of after-school detentions.

On Monday afternoon, she and Kate were hiding out in the sixth-form centre during a free period. They were sitting on a pair of elderly chairs near the single PC. Ellen's chair had a large tear and she was absent-mindedly pulling its cotton-wool guts out. They were alone, apart from Holly Stanley, who was at the computer, staring at the screen, her beautiful head resting on a slender wrist. Holly Stanley was the chicest girl in sixth form. She needed no make-up, and wore a Ramones T-shirt under her school shirt. She was long and slender, had once been 'scouted' outside the big Topshop on Oxford Circus and had gone up to London to do a test shoot in Soho.

'I've taken Nathan Harris off the list,' Ellen said, absent-mindedly.

Kate was familiar with the list. 'Oh yeah,' she said, putting on lipgloss in a compact mirror. 'Why?'

'Well, you know I had high hopes for him,' Ellen said, regretfully. 'But he's got no chat. And his grammar's terrible.'

'Your standards are too high,' Kate snorted. She puckered her lips and stared at Ellen. 'It's MSN. It's not about grammar.'

'Yeah, but he's also really boring,' Ellen protested. 'If he had great chat but bad grammar, I wouldn't mind.'

Kate raised her eyebrows. Ellen shrugged and returned to pulling the cotton wool out of the chair.

'I've got a name,' Holly said, conversationally.

Ellen looked up in surprise, as if uncertain that it was Holly who had spoken. Kate also stared at Holly, her newly glossy lips slightly parted. Holly didn't seem particularly phased by their nonplussed reaction.

'If you want someone a bit clever,' she said, turning back to the PC. 'Well, I've got someone you can have, if you like.' She tapped a key on the keyboard, hard. 'Or whatever.'

Kate was still staring at Ellen, who gathered her wits and senses.

'Um . . .' Ellen started. 'Yeah . . . um, I mean, if you don't mind? That'd be . . .' She paused, and then leaned in. 'I mean, what's he like?'

Holly did not react. She pressed another key.

Ellen looked at Kate. Kate widened her eyes and shrugged. Perhaps Holly hadn't heard her.

'Yeah,' came Holly's reply, eventually. She tapped another key, hard, then slowly turned towards Ellen and Kate. 'So,' she cocked an eyebrow.

Ellen observed that Holly's skin appeared celestial in the glow of the sixth-form centre's strip lighting.

'He's smart. Likes books. Goes to Rainham. Doesn't just want to chat about the size of your tits.' She tucked her hair behind her ear. 'I mean. No offence if that's your thing.'

Ellen felt that it was very, *very* important that Holly Stanley should know that chatting about the size of her, Ellen's, tits was very, *very* much not her thing. She also knew it was important to sound as casual as Holly Stanley did.

'Yeah, no, not really my vibe,' she said, as casually as possible. Kate was still staring at her. Ellen's face felt warm.

Holly Stanley appraised Ellen for a few seconds. Her eyes were unusually pale.

Then she spoke again. 'Cool.' She shrugged her shoulders, almost imperceptibly. 'I'll give you his name.'

Holly reached into her school bag, a black tote bag marked with the logo of what Ellen assumed was a band, or possibly a political movement, to pull out an A4 sketchpad and a pencil. She held it between an elegant thumb and forefinger, and wrote down a name.

Ellen and Kate held their breath for the duration.

'Here . . .' She passed it over. 'I used to chat to him a lot last year, but it sort of fizzled out. I know the name's a bit' – she made a face, screwing up those exquisite features – 'but I think you'll like him. He's got good chat.'

Ellen paused for a moment to savour the flattery of Holly Stanley thinking that she would like someone Holly thought was cool. 'Thanks,' she said. 'That's really nice of you.'

Holly shrugged and stood up to her full, extraordinary height. She slung the tote over her shoulder.

'Bye,' Kate said.

Holly didn't look back.

'Well, that was weird.' Ellen examined the piece of paper.

'Um, so weird,' Kate agreed. She blew a bubble with her gum. 'So, are you going to add him, then? Can I add him too?'

'Rainham_romeo1991,' Ellen read. She contemplated it, cocking her head to one side, making a slight grimace. 'I suppose it's not the worst I've heard.' She looked at Kate. 'No, you cannot add him! You have Ryan.'

Kate spent most of her weekday evenings chatting to Ryan, a guy two years above them from Rainham Boys who now worked as a bartender at the gastropub near the station. It wasn't one of Ellen and Kate's regular haunts, mainly because it was favoured by parents from their school celebrating anniversaries and birthdays or just escaping their taciturn teenage charges. Occasionally, though, Kate and Ellen would risk it – on a Thursday afternoon, when they had a free period. They'd change into their civvies in the loos, which were straight on the left as you went in, and then they'd go to the bar and sit on the high stools. Kate would chat to Ryan while they both sipped an illegal vodka cranberry. In person, Ryan had dimples and close-cropped, yet strangely greasy, curls and was almost bashful. Online, he asked Kate to tell him – in detail – what she'd like to do to him.

That evening, Ellen went up to her bedroom after dinner. She sat down at her desk, then opened her laptop, waited for it to creak to life – whirring like a propeller – and signed into MSN. Then she added him as a contact. Ellen was blasé about this stage; certainly, she would agonize about conversations and pauses, and the wait when someone would type for ages but no message would appear. But she didn't mind adding strangers. Everyone knew that the girls swapped the boys' names on MSN. It didn't mean anything to add someone. What mattered was what happened next.

Fleetingly, she worried that Holly Stanley was playing an extravagant joke on her. Perhaps rainham_romeo1991 was, in fact, Holly herself, or one of her forgettable friends. This was rumoured to have happened to a girl in the year above, Alison Kay. A group of St James's girls had done it as revenge, to get back at Alison for chatting to one of their ex-boyfriends. Apparently, they'd tricked her into talking dirty and then printed out the conversation and posted it to Alison's home.

Still, while Ellen conceded that she did not know Holly Stanley at all, it seemed fairly unlikely that she would be trying to blackmail her, or deceive her for sport. Ellen had never wronged Holly, and vindictiveness for vindictiveness's sake seemed way too pedestrian for her. Also, Ellen supposed that Holly probably had other things to do on a weekday evening. Like throw paint at a canvas in the studio she imagined the Stanleys had in their three-bed maisonette, or stare into a mirror at her own face. Holly was probably happy to relinquish a contact because she was sort of over MSN. Maybe she had a boyfriend in a band, or one who attended an art school.

Fear dispatched, Ellen settled into the evening's normal pattern. She surveyed her contacts landscape. She googled a few of the song lyrics she didn't recognize. She changed her own status to a Mystery Jets lyric. Shortly after, one of her regulars, chrisdbarclay_90, popped up. It was always gratifying to see how easily teenage boys responded to basic triggers.

chrisdbarclay_90: *hey*
chrisdbarclay_90: *how u*

It would take barely any time to type 'how *are* you?' Ellen thought. She and Chris (whom she had, in fact, met in real life) had started talking on MSN about two months ago, after meeting at the Regal. It had been a near-perfect evening: she and Kate had got in without being ID'd and when they got to the bar, they'd spotted a whole group of Rainham Boys, but not a single gaggle of Rainham or St James's Girls. Ellen and Kate knew the boys were from Rainham because she recognized one or two of them from the bus home. Within about ten minutes, she and Kate had been invited to join their group and Ellen had spoken to Chris for a while. She'd actually fancied his friend more, but they'd swapped MSN names because everyone always did. The next day – a Sunday evening – he'd added her, and they'd been talking most evenings since, seemingly out of habit.

Out of habit, she responded.

miss_BehaviourX91: *hey*
miss_BehaviourX91: *i'm good*
miss_BehaviourX91: *how are you?*

She might as well set an example.

chrisdbarclay_90: *yeah good we won at football*
miss_BehaviourX91: *oh nice*
miss_BehaviourX91: *well done*
miss_BehaviourX91: *what was the score?*

Conversationally, this was rather scraping the barrel.

chrisdbarclay_90: *3 nil to us*
chrisdbarclay_90: *i didnt score but assisted on the second one which matty scored*

Ellen didn't know who Matty was.

miss_BehaviourX91: *amazing!*
miss_BehaviourX91: *well done*

Possibly a bit much. As he had just explained, he hadn't actually scored himself.

chrisdbarclay_90: *yeah really happy*

chrisdbarclay_90: *all the lads are gunna celebrate this weeknd at regal prob*

chrisdbarclay_90: *gunna go 2 sams first he has an empty*

Maybe he would invite her to the parent-free drinks party.

chrisdbarclay_90: *gunna be sik*

Or not.

miss_BehaviourX91: *nice one*

miss_BehaviourX91: *haven't been to an empty in a while*

Shit, did this sound like she was angling for an invite? Say something else!

miss_BehaviourX91: *me and my friend kate are probably going to go to pulse*

Saved.

chrisdbarclay_90: *kool*

chrisdbarclay_90: *will u get fukd*

chrisdbarclay_90: *weve got 4 cans each for sams*

chrisdbarclay_90: *gonna be so wasted*

This wasn't worth the effort. Ellen minimized the window and scrolled through the rest of her contacts: owen_willett69 was online. Last week, they'd had a rather intense conversation about her dream first date, which had logged off promisingly.

owen_willett69: *mebbe your dream will come tru one day ;)*

They hadn't spoken since.

Ellen noticed that rainham_romeo1991 was online. Perhaps she should log out and log back in again? She was mulling it over when two things happened simultaneously: chrisdbarclay_90 sent her a 'nudge', shaking her screen, and rainham_romeo1991 took the initiative.

rainham_romeo1991: *hello*

Ellen's heart drummed.

miss_BehaviourX91: *hi*

A few seconds passed. Too nonchalant?

rainham_romeo1991: *so, been doing this long?*

Ellen barked a high, nervous laugh. From downstairs she could hear the blare of the television. Parked cars nestled under the street lights on her quiet road. There was no one outside – it was March, and the weather morose and drizzly – although most of the houses in the cul-de-sac were illuminated as her neighbours went about the small, comforting rituals of their weekday evenings.

Ellen started typing.

miss_BehaviourX91: *what, propositioning strangers on the internet?*

miss_BehaviourX91: *oh, a few months, i suppose*

A pause. Was that a weird thing to say?

rainham_romeo1991: *i suppose there's a thrill in the fact that you could in fact be a middle-aged man . . .*

That was definitely a weird thing to say. But it was also quite funny. Perhaps Holly Stanley had actually meant 'this boy is weird, and you are weird so you will get on'. Still, it was better than Chris's conversation and spelling.

miss_BehaviourX91: *that's definitely what my parents think msn is*
rainham_romeo1991: *ha mine too*
rainham_romeo1991: *i think they hope i'm up here doing bbc bitesize worksheets or something . . .*
miss_BehaviourX91: *mine think coursework*
rainham_romeo1991: *ha. standard*

He was typing again.

rainham_romeo1991: *it is a strange thing though, isn't it?*
rainham_romeo1991: *the idea that we all just start having these long and intense chats with people we don't really know*
rainham_romeo1991: *sorry, am getting philosophical*

Say something smart! Say something smart!

miss_BehaviourX91: *yes these long conversations with people you wouldn't know if you walked past them on the street*

Was that smart? Or was she literally just echoing back exactly what he'd just said to her?

rainham_romeo1991: *TOTALLY*

Well, it seemed to go down well.
He was typing.

rainham_romeo1991: *well, we're here now*
rainham_romeo1991: *shall we agree that it's weird and get on with it?*
miss_BehaviourX91: *seems like a sensible approach*
rainham_romeo1991: *what kind of music are you into?*

This question used to catch Ellen off guard. The pressure of answering invariably wiped her mind blank. So, as a memory aid, she had written down a few palatable favourites on a Post-It note, stuck on the wall above her laptop.

Music: Fleet Foxes, MGMT, Mystery Jets,
Radiohead, Bloc Party

Television: Skins, South Park, Family Guy,
The O.C.

Books: 1984, The Catcher in the Rye, The Great
Gatsby, The Stranger

Ellen dutifully typed out her list of approved bands.

miss_BehaviourX91: *mainly fleet foxes, mgmt, mystery jets, radiohead, bloc party*

miss_BehaviourX91: *how about you?*

rainham_romeo1991: *i like older stuff, mainly*

rainham_romeo1991: *rolling stones, hendrix, pink floyd, fleetwood mac, the doors, the ramones*

rainham_romeo1991: *that sort of thing*

He was so cool.

rainham_romeo1991: *i feel like the 70s is the decade i would most like to have lived in*

miss_BehaviourX91: *yeah*

Ellen did not know much about the seventies. Mainly, the decade she wanted to live in was the next one, when she would be an adult and didn't live at home with her parents and younger brother. Think of something funny, she thought, desperately.

miss_BehaviourX91: *i'm wearing my flares right now*

Oh God, where had that come from? Was it too flip? Maybe he would think she was taking the piss? He was typing.

rainham_romeo1991: *ha. yes*

rainham_romeo1991: *you are talking my language*

Fine. She swallowed. She seemed to have got away with it.

rainham_romeo1991: *so do you go into london a lot?*

Real answer: no.

miss_BehaviourX91: *yeah all the time*
miss_BehaviourX91: *i go to victoria mainly*

The cheap train went into Victoria. On the few school trips Rainham Girls had been on, they'd gone via Victoria.

rainham_romeo1991: *cool*
rainham_romeo1991: *yeah i go to victoria and i love going into oxford circus*
rainham_romeo1991: *i love the buzz of the city*
rainham_romeo1991: *feel like real life doesn't really happen in the suburbs*

Ellen's heart fluttered. They were kindred spirits.

14. Ellen

'We soon settled into a routine, where we'd talk every night for hours.' Her throat was dry and it was giving her voice a slightly strangled quality. 'All pathetic teenage things, really, about which bands we liked, and how we wanted to move to New York, and how no one understood us. But with most of the boys I was talking to on MSN, it was all stupid stuff about how many beers they'd drunk that weekend, or how many goals they'd set up at football, so this definitely felt more meaningful.'

She stole a glance at Ben, hoping for a squirming flicker of recognition, but his face was set in affected concentration. Still, he and Alexa now sat a chilly few centimetres apart. Jack, who sat cross-legged beside her, still had his mouth open a touch.

She continued. 'It's worth pointing out at this time that I'd never had a boyfriend before. Or anything close to one. Not that . . .' a pause, '*Benjamin* was my boyfriend, exactly – we hadn't said all that to each other. But with the others it always petered out after a few weeks, so to have someone who wanted to talk to me every single evening was a novelty.'

She was surprised at how much colour and detail was returning from the dim recesses of her mind. She could see herself at that desk chair, hoodie pulled on over her school uniform, face uplit by the blue light of the screen, heart fluttering and stomach swooping.

'Oh, so sometimes my dad' – she decided not to refer to him as John – 'would turn the broadband off because he was going to bed and I'd be logged out all of a sudden, and I'd sprint downstairs and switch it back on, panicking all that time that . . .' another pause, '*Benjamin* would think I'd just logged off without saying goodnight and that we'd never speak again.'

At this point, Ben did look like he was about to say something, but then seemed to think better of it, and instead he frowned. Alexa, meanwhile, was sitting very still, except for her left hand, which she was using to thumb the hoop pushed through her left earlobe. Her face was inscrutable.

Ellen looked away. She had started all this without thinking about how Alexa would feel, and now felt a wobble of guilt somewhere deep in her gut. She'd been so stunned by the shocking coincidence – finding out that Ben was Benjamin – that she had lashed out, unthinkingly. But she couldn't stop now. And surely Alexa deserved to know.

'Anyway, it must have gone on for months. I know it was spring term when it started, because we chatted all Easter holidays. And it definitely went on until the summer, because we talked all the way through A Levels.' She remembered spending the evening before her French A level exam with a textbook propped up on the keyboard, unable to resist his siren call even for one evening.

'And I obviously started listening to all this music he liked' – she rolled her eyes – 'like the Rolling Stones, blah blah blah . . .' She paused, and fixed Ben with a hard stare. 'Ringing any bells?'

Ben hadn't been expecting to be called on so directly.

He looked terrified, and managed only a strangled 'ah' noise. Beside him, Alexa squirmed. Her eyes were big, and Ellen noticed, for the first time, how tired she looked.

'Whatever,' Ellen continued. 'Anyway. At some point, it stopped being just this intense conversation and started being – well, more like heading for boyfriend and girlfriend territory.'

Ben looked agitated.

Good.

15. Ellen

May 2009

rainham_romeo1991: *i've been thinking about relationships a lot recently*

Ellen's skin buzzed. She watched him typing. He stopped. Typed again. Still typing.

rainham_romeo1991: *it must be amazing to find someone you feel a real connection with i guess*
rainham_romeo1991: *do you know what i mean?*

Ellen's breath caught in her throat.

miss_BehaviourX91: *yeah, definitely*
rainham_romeo1991: *have you had a boyfriend before?*

Ellen pursed her lips and tapped the side of the laptop as she weighed up the answer to this question. She wasn't sure whether she should tell the truth, but something made her want to be honest with him. Finally, she typed.

miss_BehaviourX91: *no, i haven't*
miss_BehaviourX91: *i mean, not a serious one*
rainham_romeo1991: *yeah me neither*

rainham_romeo1991: *a girlfriend i mean. haha*

She typed it before she got too scared to say it.

miss_BehaviourX91: *do you have a type?*
rainham_romeo1991: *i guess you could say that*
miss_BehaviourX91: *?*
rainham_romeo1991: *anyway. i should probably go to bed*

She sighed in exasperation.

miss_BehaviourX91: *yeah*
miss_BehaviourX91: *me too*
miss_BehaviourX91: *french speaking tomorrow*

Maybe that would keep him online for another minute or two.

rainham_romeo1991: *good night x*

Nope.

miss_BehaviourX91: *bye x*

She put her hand to her throat to feel her pulse, which fluttered under the skin. This was surely the biggest milestone they'd reached since he'd started leaving a kiss at the end of his messages. They'd discussed relationships! Ellen set herself to appear offline in order to read back through their entire conversation from that evening, to try and work out if she'd missed anything else worth noting. She did this most

nights, unless it had been an unusually short correspondence. She liked to imagine him doing so too, sitting in his
bedroom reviewing her replies for the same clues she sought.
His likes and dislikes, things she could bend herself towards
or away from, and significances she might have missed.

She returned to the top of the conversation, noting
with delight that they'd spoken for almost two and a half
hours. Topics they had discussed included: Mick Jagger
(Ellen had started doing her research during free periods
when she should have been doing her coursework); *Animal Farm* (which had replaced Orwell's *1984* on Ellen's
prepared list of palatable books); their respective relationships with their parents (parents fundamentally lacked
empathy); their hopes and dreams for university (finding
people who were more like them); New York (they both
wanted to live there one day). She'd talked a little about
Kate, but he rarely mentioned his friends. She could never
work out if this meant he was actually quite unpopular –
but she really wasn't sure she cared.

Ellen was now at the stage where she spent most of her
waking hours thinking about him. Their conversations were
chaste, but they thrilled her. When something remarkable
happened at school, she spent a lot of time imagining how
she would explain it to him, smiling as she scripted the story
in her mind. She also spent a lot of time peering at his small
profile picture, trying to see more clearly what he looked
like. She was desperate for them to swap numbers so they
could text, but didn't want to be the one to suggest it.

Kate had teased her about him. 'He doesn't sound like
anyone we know,' she'd said, cocking her head on its side.
'Are you sure he's not, like, a teacher or something?'

Ellen had shrieked.

Kate had added, 'You never know. I think Holly Stanley is secretly a bit wild.'

Ellen had laughed, but afterwards had stopped sharing so much with Kate. She was too protective of the conversations.

Ellen closed her laptop now. She could hear her mother and father in the midst of their nightly wind-down rituals. It sounded like her father was bolting the front door, and her mother was switching off the lamps in the hallway and turning on the landing light up to Tom's attic bedroom. Her eyes felt dry. She changed from her school uniform and into her pyjamas, then shuffled into the family bathroom across the hall. In the mirror, as she brushed her teeth, she imagined things she could or should have said: 'I know my type is you.' She virtually squealed at the thought.

'Ellen, is that you in there?'

She spat toothpaste into the sink and scowled in the mirror. 'Yes, Mum. Am I not allowed to use the bathroom now?'

She could hear her mother sigh through the door. 'I was just going to say there's a spare hand-soap out here. Can you pop it in the bathroom when you're done?'

'Yes.' She felt mean. 'Night, Mum.'

'Night, love.'

It was May when it happened: the biggest moment of Ellen's life to date.

Downstairs, she could hear the hubbub of Linda and John chattering over the television. She picked at a spot on her forehead, worrying at it with the tips of her thumb and forefinger. She knew when she looked in the mirror it would look terrible, but she couldn't help it. It was just past 7 p.m., and she was waiting for him to sign in. After what felt like for ever, but was probably only three minutes, he appeared.

miss_BehaviourX91: *hi*
rainham_romeo1991: *hey*
rainham_romeo1991: *good day?*
miss_BehaviourX91: *so-so*
miss_BehaviourX91: *how about you?*
rainham_romeo1991: *it was ok. 6/10*
miss_BehaviourX91: *haha*
miss_BehaviourX91: *i'd give mine 7, but only because i had three free periods*
rainham_romeo1991: *jealous*

She watched the screen.

rainham_romeo1991: *ok*
rainham_romeo1991: *admission time*

There was a long, long pause in which Ellen wondered if her stomach could actually fall out of the soles of her feet.

rainham_romeo1991: *i've got feelings for you*

Her stomach threatened to plummet to her feet again. She read and reread the message and then, before thinking, tapped out a response in kind.

miss_BehaviourX91: *i have feelings for you too*

As soon as she'd sent it she screamed and jumped back from her desk, knocking the desk chair backwards. She stood in the middle of the room with her hands over her mouth, panting slightly. She had never sent a message this monumental before.

As she contemplated this, her mother interrupted her.

'Ellen?' Linda called sharply, from downstairs. 'What was that noise? What are you doing up there?'

'Nothing, Mum!' she snarled. 'The chair just fell over.'

She heard her mother grumble from the foot of the stairs. 'Well, stop mucking about. You'll bring the ceiling in the living room down.'

Ellen didn't say anything in response but returned the chair to its position in front of the desk, closing her eyes until she'd lowered herself into it. When she opened them, she could see he had replied. Her eyes blurred. She rubbed them.

rainham_romeo1991: *I just feel like you're the only person in my life i can talk properly to*

rainham_romeo1991: *which is weird because we've never actually met.*

rainham_romeo1991: *do you know what i mean?*

She was still breathing heavily. Feeling rash, she replied.

miss_BehaviourX91: *totally*

miss_BehaviourX91: *it's so easy to share so many of my thoughts with you in a way i don't have with any of my friends*

rainham_romeo1991: *exactly. i feel like with you i am my realest self*

rainham_romeo1991: *i don't know what happens next. i don't know what i mean to do with this admission*

rainham_romeo1991: *i just knew i had to tell you*

rainham_romeo1991: *i hope that's ok*

miss_BehaviourX91: *i'm really glad you did*

Again, he was typing.

rainham_romeo1991: *i'm really glad you feel the same way x*

Wait, was he signing off? Should she sign off too?

miss_BehaviourX91: *yeah x*

Oh wait, no, he was still typing.

rainham_romeo1991: *so. more news. i've been writing you something*

rainham_romeo1991: *it's not ready yet*

rainham_romeo1991: *but it will be soon. and when it is i'd like to send it to you. if that's ok*

Writing something? But they were already writing things to one another, every evening. Maybe it was . . . a poem. Or a song?

miss_BehaviourX91: *i'd love that*

rainham_romeo1991: *you don't have to answer. but obviously i'd love it if you did*

OK, so it was unlikely to be a love poem. Or a song. Ellen swallowed her disappointment He was typing again.

rainham_romeo1991: *it will be ready probably on sunday*

Her ears felt hot.

miss_BehaviourX91: *i can't wait to read it*
rainham_romeo1991: *good*

Ellen sat at the computer, watching the cursor flash. She chewed her lip. He was typing again.

rainham_romeo1991: *on that note, m'lady, i may retire*
rainham_romeo1991: *bonne nuit x*
miss_BehaviourX91: *sleep well x*

'Sleep well' had felt really risqué when Ellen first used it, mainly as it had referenced – however obliquely – the idea of being in a bed. Now she used it as her preferred sign-off. He had started using French after she'd mentioned the annual family holidays in Brittany. She'd told him about her first cigarette too, shared on last summer's trip with a friend she'd picked up there. Though not the part where she was sick afterwards.

That Friday evening and the rest of the weekend passed as normal – which was to say that she spent most of it obsessively thinking about him and what could possibly be coming. On Saturday, she went to sleep over at Kate's. It was a week until allowance day, and neither of them had any money to try going out, so they spent the evening watching films in the snug and eating bowls of Crunchy Nut Cornflakes. Ellen felt weird not telling Kate about the conversation, but she also didn't want to tell her, in case her friend said something that might ruin it.

On Sunday morning, they woke up and Ellen had made her excuses a little earlier than usual.

'Wait, do you not fancy Lakefield or something?' Kate asked, not looking at her. She was still in her pyjamas but was painting her nails with something glittery, splashing polish all over the top of her scuffed, white wooden dresser.

'But we don't have any money,' Ellen pointed out.

Kate made a face. 'True. But I'm sure my dad will give us some for a Frappuccino or something.' Kate dabbed paint on her right pinkie. 'Shit,' she added, as she spilled some more on the dresser. She looked up. 'Please, Elly. I can't sit here all day, my mum is driving me mad. We don't have to go round the shops.'

Ellen deliberated. It would be the evening before they spoke. Neither of them was ever online during the day.

'Oh, fine,' she relented, smiling. 'But you have to buy me a Frappuccino. *And* get my bus fare.'

'Deal,' Kate grinned. 'Can we just wait for my nails to dry and then we'll walk to the bus stop?'

'Yeah, of course.' Ellen was sitting on Kate's bed, one leg curled, one leg outstretched. She leaned back against the wall, and watched as Kate blew on every nail in turn, twice.

Ellen spent longer in town than she'd intended to. Once they were there, Kate – of course – managed to persuade her into a few of the shops, linking Ellen's arm and steering her through the doors. It was a warm and sunny day, and Ellen was overdressed in grey skinny jeans and black pleather jacket. Up and down the grey high street, women walked in floaty kaftans and flip-flops, unearthed that weekend from the loft. Yesterday had been sunny too, and much of the flesh on display was pink and slightly shiny.

When Ellen finally arrived home, she dealt a few monosyllabic pleasantries to her parents and mooched on the sofa, flicking through the music channels, to kill the time before dinner. By 6 p.m., she felt like she was about to sit an exam, her stomach flipping, her pulse fluttering in her throat.

After dinner, she went up to her room and lowered herself into her desk's swivel chair. She wrapped herself in the felt blanket that lived on the back of the chair. She logged into MSN Messenger. It was almost 7 p.m. Would he be online already, waiting for her? Her stomach flipped again.

She jumped: owen_willett69 had sent her a message.

owen_willett69: *hey how u*

She ignored it. She set her status to a Stones lyric. There was such a thrill in setting a public status intended only for him to read. Ellen paid a lot of attention to his statuses, which he changed less regularly than she did. This made decoding each one even more of a treat.

He was online. 7.04 p.m.

She waited for him to say hello. Usually, she wouldn't mind initiating, but this evening, it felt important – symbolic – that he be the person to say something first.

Minutes inched past – she watched the clock in the

bottom-right-hand corner of her screen mark the passing of each one. Why wasn't he saying anything? She stared as the clock clicked to 7.05, 7.06, 7.07 p.m., then made a pointless bargain with herself: if she left the room to go to the bathroom, by the time she came back, he'd have messaged.

Unusually, she took her time washing her hands, staring at her face in the mirror. She made a face at the Ellen staring back, gurning to try and expend the energy pulsing in her temples. When she returned, the MSN toolbar at the bottom of the screen was flashing. She willed it not to be owen_willett69 or one of his ilk.

It was him.

rainham_romeo1991: *good evening*

Her fingers felt all tingly. What if he hadn't meant it? Maybe he'd changed his mind? She wondered if she should say something or play it safe. She always preferred to play it safe.

miss_BehaviourX91: *hey*
rainham_romeo1991: *good weekend?*

This was very normal.

miss_BehaviourX91: *yeah it was nice, if fairly uneventful*
miss_BehaviourX91: *how was yours?*
rainham_romeo1991: *honestly, i spent a lot of it waiting for this moment*

Her heart roared in her ears.

miss_BehaviourX91: *me too*

miss_BehaviourX91: *i couldn't really think about anything else*

rainham_romeo1991: *good*

rainham_romeo1991: *i'm going to send you something*

miss_BehaviourX91: *ok*

With the stroke of a key, a long, long message appeared on her screen. It was written in the style of a letter.

Dear E,

Over the past months I have developed strong feelings for you, and I think you feel the same way.

I used to speak to loads of girls on here but I didn't really feel like I connected with many of them; none of them saw the world in the same way that we do. I feel like we are unique and have a similar outlook on life, one that is so different from so many of our peers. We both know that there is more to our existentialism than life in these streets. Sometimes when I am on the bus home, I think that you must be out there too — maybe even on this bus — and I feel a sense of peace.

I do not know what will happen next for us. I feel like in order for us to take things to the next level we should meet up in person, but I also don't want us to ruin whatever fragile and beautiful thing we have made. But I want to find a way for us to take this relationship on to new heights as you have become such a central part of my life.

x

Ellen's eyes leaped over the sentences, so that she read everything in a jumble and had to keep going back and rereading everything a second and then a third time. As the message became a coherent whole at last, she squirmed a little: she had not expected anything so effusive. She closed her eyes for a second, trying not to imagine what Kate would think if she could read this. Kate did not have much of a sense of romance.

Still, ignoring the words themselves – the *execution* of his love letter – the meaning was everything she could possibly have wanted. He wanted their 'relationship' to reach 'new heights'. He was calling it a 'relationship'! Surely, this meant that they must meet. She wondered what she'd wear.

Another message was flashing in the toolbar at the bottom of the screen.

rainham_romeo1991: *i don't want or expect a reply tonight. or necessarily at all*
rainham_romeo1991: *but i feel like this letter expresses some of the way i feel about you*
rainham_romeo1991: *anyway i'm going to go now, i think*
rainham_romeo1991: *let's speak tomorrow x*

Before Ellen could type a word, he'd signed out.
She stared dumbly at the screen.

16. Alexa

Alexa had the foreboding sense that Ellen's big reveal approached. She was correct.

'And so, one Sunday, I got this letter . . .' Ellen paused. She pressed her lips together. 'It was very intense. Sort of like it was written by an algorithm to make a teenage girl lose her mind.' She let the line land.

Alexa almost laughed, in spite of herself. Ellen was, as ever, very good at this. Trying not to turn her head, she glanced up at Ben through her eyelashes. He was self-absorbed, frowning now, and felt very distant from her. Ellen had rather punctured the mood.

She was continuing now. 'Anyway, I had spent seventeen years waiting for someone to write something like this to me.' She sighed, dramatically. 'And then less than a week later, he went totally silent on me . . .' A calculated pause. 'He ghosted me. And we never spoke again.'

Ellen crossed her arms, resting her case.

Alexa inhaled deeply. She had been expecting that. She hung her head and stole a sideways glance at Ben. He and Jack were both staring at Ellen dumbly. As the seconds ticked by, there was a ring of anti-climax in the air.

'Well?' Ellen said, impatiently. She rounded on Ben, wild-eyed. 'What do you have to say to all that?'

'Um . . .' he started, eventually, before trailing off. He

squared his shoulders and sat up a little straighter and took a deep breath before he continued. 'I mean, that wasn't me.' His voice was steady.

'It was,' Ellen flashed back. Her cheeks were a little pink.

'It wasn't,' Ben replied. He sounded apologetic now, though the expression in his eyes was rather hard. He shook his head. 'It really wasn't,' he repeated. 'No way. I never had an MSN girlfriend who –'

'It was you!' Ellen interrupted. She laughed, disbelievingly. 'Rainham_romeo1991, that was you! That was your name, we've already established that.'

There was a pause.

'You did say it was your name,' Alexa agreed, quietly.

'Yeah, no, of course.' He looked at Alexa, his hands raised in surrender. His eyes were dark and deep. 'It was definitely my awful screen name. There's no doubt about that . . .' He paused. 'But I definitely didn't have an MSN relationship with someone for months. I'd remember that. And I never wrote a letter like that. I'd remember that too.' He found Alexa's eyes again.

She offered him a weak smile, aware that Ellen was watching them both.

'Maybe someone else had the same name?' Jack tried, slowly.

'I doubt it,' Ellen said, sharply.

'Maybe you . . . maybe you got it mixed up?' Jack said. His voice sounded slightly muffled, as though he was speaking into his chest.

Ellen shook her head, her expression flat.

Ben sat up. His hand brushed Alexa's as he rearranged

his legs. 'Look, I'm sorry, but I'd remember if I'd . . . I'm sure I would . . .' He trailed off, thinking. He tried a half-smile. 'Hey, maybe we spoke at some point, and that's why you remember the name?'

Ellen scowled.

He shrugged again. 'I'm sorry, but it had to have been someone else. You must have got that bit mixed up.' He tried another hopeful half-smile. 'I mean, it was a long time ago. A really long time ago.'

Alexa was watching Ben carefully. His face was open, unguarded.

Ellen shook her head. 'No way. I remember the name so well. I was absolutely heartbroken. Not to mention humiliated that I'd been dumped by some boy on the internet –' She broke off, wrong-footed.

'Oh, Ellen,' Alexa said, her voice sounding strangled. She felt wretched and disoriented; the walls of the attic seemed more oppressive than ever. Throughout the story, she'd stolen glances at Ben's handsome face, trying to read it for telltale signs, but spotted none. Was Ellen wrong? Alexa felt a curdling in the pit of her stomach.

Ben was breathing deeply through his nose. 'Look, Ellen, this guy sounds like a shit,' he said, quickly. He sounded sympathetic still, if ever so slightly impatient. 'But look, I promise, it wasn't me. It can't have been.' He shrugged again. 'Really – none of this rings a bell, not even slightly.' He turned to Alexa. 'It wasn't me,' he said, flatly.

Alexa wished he hadn't repeated himself for her bene-fit. She felt exposed, knowing Ellen was rooted to the spot, watching them both.

Jack, meanwhile, was staring at the floor. Outside, a van started reversing noisily.

'Seriously,' Ben said, a defensive edge creeping into his voice. 'I don't really know what else to say.'

There was a long pause. The beeping from the reversing van finally stopped.

'Sorry?' he added, hopelessly.

Alexa wondered dully if everyone else could hear her pulse thudding in her ears. Ben cleared his throat as though he was about to say something else, then seemed to think better of it. He didn't look guilty, she thought, though he seemed very uncomfortable. Alexa observed Ellen. She was now staring out of the skylight, towards freedom. Her arms were folded firmly across her chest. She still looked a little flushed.

Undeniably, with Ellen's stories, it was occasionally difficult to find the boundary where truth and exaggeration met. Something would happen – on the way to the pub, or to someone's birthday party – they'd arrive and she would listen to Ellen plumping up a detail here, tossing a line in there, playing the room for laughs. In Ellen's telling, everything became a little more vivid, a little more extraordinary.

Everything was always broadly true, of course. Ellen just had the storyteller's facility for colour and narrative and exaggeration. Most of the time, Alexa would play the willing accomplice, laughing in all the right places, adding affirmative statements, though on a very few occasions, when things had got a bit out of hand, Alexa would offer some renunciation ('It wasn't as bad as *that*!'). And Ellen would shake her head, grinning, refusing to be called out.

'It absolutely was,' she'd say. Case closed – and what a thrilling case it invariably had been.

So perhaps Ellen was hamming things up for dramatic effect. Perhaps they had messaged for a month, rather than four; maybe she was overstating the intensity of the connection. Plus, these things were – obviously – subjective, and teenagers are intense and melodramatic. Alexa suspected Ellen had probably been an especially intense and melodramatic teenager.

Still, Alexa snatched a glance at Ellen now. She had no doubt at all that Ellen had had this experience with *someone*. Alexa believed there had been a boy – a virtual boy – and that he'd ghosted Ellen. It was cruel. She tried to imagine Ben sitting behind a keyboard, writing all those meaningful things – to Ellen, her Ellen! – and then one day deciding to just stop. If it had been him, she couldn't bear it.

Admittedly, she didn't know him very well. But she couldn't imagine it. Ben was kind. She recalled last night. He had been charming and engaging and engaged; a perfect date. There had been the previous awkwardness – the theatre lobby and the cooling off. But that didn't mean anything, really. And he was so certain it wasn't him.

It was possible – surely it was – that Ellen had misremembered the details. She could have mixed Ben up with someone else, misremembered the name of the real teenage villain. This could all be an unfortunate and emotional misunderstanding.

Alexa needed to say something. She opened her mouth, her brain in slow pursuit. 'Um?' she said, hopefully. 'OK. I think –' They were all watching her now. 'I think that was a lot of information . . .' She left the thought hanging.

Ben laughed a wry laugh. 'No shit.'

Ellen looked at him again, indignant. 'Yes, well,' she stated, firmly, 'it all . . . it was a bit of a shock.' She raised her eyes heavenwards, and Alexa wondered, in horror, if she was about to cry. Mercifully not – when she returned her gaze to Ben, it was steady. 'You could just say sorry, you know.' She sounded prim, not at all like herself.

Ben pressed his hands to his temples. 'I did! And anyway, it wasn't me!' he protested. 'Really, truly. You must –'

'Holly Stanley,' Ellen interrupted. 'Do you remember speaking to her?'

Ben looked stumped. 'No? I don't know?'

Ellen muttered, 'Liar –'

'Maybe we should forget about it?' Jack interrupted. He sounded hesitant. Even he couldn't have thought that was going to work.

Ellen stared at him. 'Um, wow. Thanks, Jack.'

He looked anguished. 'I didn't m-mean –' he stuttered. 'I just meant that maybe, since Ben has said sorry, then maybe you could forgive him.'

Alexa smiled weakly at Jack.

'Not that I should have to say sorry,' Ben muttered. He looked at Alexa again, searching for – expecting – her to back him up.

She returned an expression of what she hoped he would read as sympathy. She could feel Ellen was eyeballing them again.

'Look,' Ellen sighed, 'I'm really not trying to make it awkward for you.' She gestured towards Ben and Alexa, who was about to say something, but Ellen wasn't finished.

'But also it was a really shitty thing to do, and I never thought I'd meet the person who –'

'You haven't!' Ben laughed with frustration. 'Ellen –'

She rolled her eyes in retort.

Alexa knew this was not the right tack. Ellen was uncommonly sensitive. She perceived slights at many turns and still remembered them, in high definition, years later.

'Maybe we could agree to disagree?' Jack asked, desperately, after a few seconds.

'OK –' Alexa raised one hand.

They all looked at her.

That was all she had. There was an unnerving silence.

Ben snaked his arm from the floor in order to give Alexa's knee a tentative squeeze. Alexa willed him to stop, knowing that it would trigger something.

On cue, Ellen exhaled impatiently. 'I think I need a time out.' She stood up, her eyes darting into the corners of the attic.

They all watched her, Alexa with her heart in her throat. There was something slightly excruciating about trying to flounce off when there was nowhere to flounce to; after some deliberation, Ellen started in the direction of the toilet corner. Unfortunately, in order to get there she had to navigate the thicket of junk, cutting a clumsy figure as she clambered through the heaving canvas bags and warped cardboard boxes. She sat down in front of the full-length mirror, still half visible. She was facing a wall.

Alexa could feel that Ben wanted to say something to her. She tried to ignore it and took a deep breath. She knew what she had to do. 'Wait, Ellen –' she commanded. She stood up. 'I'm . . . I'm coming.' Finally, she dared to look at Ben.

He looked rather hurt and seemed to have deflated slightly; his shoulders were rounded and his arms hung at his sides.

'Alexa? Do you want me to come?' What this situation did not need was Jack.

She replied with a look, which he understood.

Taking a deep breath, she followed Ellen's path. As she did so, she knocked a hat stand. She glanced back at the boys again. Jack watched her with big eyes, but Ben was now looking at the floor. Turning again, she picked her way carefully through the attic's stacks.

Ellen looked up as Alexa approached. She said nothing, but wriggled along to make a little room for her to sit down. Alexa wrinkled her nose – she could smell the contents of the Perspex box – and then sat down, her back to the boys. The attic's acoustics were unfamiliar, but she knew their voices would carry from down here. She snaked an arm around Ellen's shoulders, but her friend remained stiff. Alexa withdrew her arm and placed it in her lap, feeling uncommonly clumsy.

'Hey,' she mouthed, trying a smile.

Ellen glanced sideways at her. She looked a little abashed. 'Sorry,' she mouthed. 'About all that.' She continued, softly, 'I just . . . I can't believe –'

Alexa gave her a wan smile. She could see Ellen relaxing slightly. From metres away, they heard Jack clear his throat.

'What are you thinking?' Ellen asked, after a minute.

Alexa looked at her, hard. 'Well,' she muttered, finally. 'I'm thinking that Rainham Romeo was a dick.'

She'd hoped this might conjure a smile, but Ellen was impassive. She continued carefully.

'It could have been Ben,' she started, slowly. 'You clearly knew each other – well, almost – at school.' She swallowed. She could feel how much Ellen was concentrating on what she said next; her breaths were stuttering and shallow. Alexa continued. 'In which case, it could be that he doesn't remember.' Alexa felt Ellen gently flinch. She added, quickly, 'He seems genuinely bewildered, though that's not conclusive either way.' She hesitated. 'There is also a chance' – yet another pause, this was delicate – 'that you could have . . . have got him mixed up. With someone else.' Alexa had been staring dead ahead as she spoke, but now turned to meet Ellen's eyes.

Ellen avoided hers, instead casting a fierce glance at the ceiling, as though she was trying to recall a fact she'd once known. After a second, she shook her head, defeated.

'That name, though,' she muttered. With this conversation taking place just above a whisper, it was not clear if this was to herself, or to Alexa. 'I just remember it so well.' She shook her head, and in doing so seemed to find a little conviction. 'Plus, really, what are the chances? Same town, same schools, we know so many people in common. You heard us, before it all started.'

'Well . . . 'Alexa began slowly, quietly. 'It could have been him and he's lying.' She wasn't sure if she believed that or not.

'He doesn't seem like he's lying,' Ellen admitted, reluctantly. She looked at Alexa. 'Though' – the merest of teasing smiles – 'he could be a sociopath.'

Alexa tried a pained smile in return.

They sat, cross-legged, knees nudging, for a few minutes. Alexa could hear Ellen's breaths rise and fall. She thought of Ben, metres away. She really hoped he wasn't lying.

'It *was* horrible,' Ellen whispered, into the silence. 'At the time,' she added. 'Not to mention really embarrassing.' Her eyes were downcast. She was fiddling with a loose thread on her jogging bottoms. 'I have to say, it is very weird that you've ended up . . .' She found herself searching for the right word. 'With him.'

Alexa felt her stomach plunge. After a second, she spoke. 'We're not . . . we're not, like, going out.' Her voice sounded thicker than usual.

Ellen gave her a 'yeah, right' look.

Alexa wasn't really sure what to say in response to that, so she said nothing. They both sat very, very still. Alexa imagined she was making her body as small as possible. When she tired of shrinking herself to nothing, she tried speaking again.

'Obviously, if it was him –' she started and then abruptly stopped. No, she still wasn't sure where she was going.

She knew Ellen wouldn't let that one drop: she was staring at her, hard.

Alexa tried again. 'Obviously, if it was him, then –'

'Then what?' Ellen snapped. 'You're still going to see him, anyway, aren't you?'

Alexa felt a little roar of indignation. 'Well, yes,' she shot back. 'I really like him. But I really care about you and –'

Ellen groaned. 'Don't be so condescending.'

'I'm not being condescending –'

'You are, you're over here pretending to check I'm OK but you're really just checking it's still OK for you to go out with him.'

That stung.

'That's not fair, that's not what I'm doing.'

Ellen snorted.

Alexa felt her temper bubble.

'That is definitely what you're doing –' Ellen started, accusingly.

'You didn't even go out with him!' Alexa said, incredulously. She was sure the boys could hear them now. 'You never even met! And it was, like, ten years ago!'

'Oh, what, so "get over it"?'

'I mean, just an idea!'

Ellen shook her head, squared her shoulders and stood up as best she could under the steeply sloping ceiling. For the second time, she attempted to flounce out of a very restricted space. She appeared to be making her way to the skylight.

Alexa turned back round and fixed the wall with a murderous glare.

17. Jack

After they watched Ellen rocket off to the window and hang out of it, there was a silence. Ben gave Jack a dark look, and Jack wondered if Ben was about to try and speak to him about all this and hoped he wouldn't. Sadly, he was out of luck. He was often out of luck.

'It just doesn't add up –' Ben started, in a low voice.

Jack considered that perhaps he was speaking to himself, until Ben found his eyes with an urgent stare.

'I swear I'd remember if I'd had this . . . *passionate* relationship with a girl from another school, right? I don't even remember being on MSN that much.' Ben sounded rather hurt.

'But that *was* your name,' Jack said after a second or so, also in a low voice.

Ben looked a little taken aback.

'Your MSN name – the Romeo name.'

'Well,' Ben admitted, a little defensively. 'Yeah, it was.' He ran one hand through his hair, wearily. 'But I honestly don't remember any of the rest of it.'

Jack shrugged. 'Maybe it's a mistake.'

Ben shrugged too. He looked downcast. There was a silence during which Jack tried to ensure he didn't breathe too loudly. Perhaps what Ben needed was a distraction.

'So . . . mate' – no matter which way Jack said it, it never came out quite right – 'what's your job?' He'd overheard the answer to this already, but could pretend he hadn't.

Ben looked up at him and almost smiled. 'I work for a charity.' He was picking violently at a stain on his jeans.

'Sometimes Green Genie gives spare food to charity,' Jack said, cheerfully.

'What's that?' Ben sounded rather unenthusiastic.

'My job. At Green Genie. We're a company that delivers organic vegetables. In boxes.' He'd told Ben all about this at the window before, but he must have forgotten.

'Oh, yeah, you said.' Ben massaged his chin. He looked preoccupied. 'I've seen the adverts on the Tube.'

'Right,' Jack said, brightly. That was right. He'd been excited the first time he'd seen a Green Genie advert on a Tube carriage. He'd taken a picture of it to show his mum and Maisie, although at the last moment someone had half walked into the frame to cling on to the pole that ran above it. He'd felt awkward taking another one, in case they'd thought he was trying to take a picture of them. So he'd sent the one that had their head in it, slightly obscuring the Green Genie logo of the dancing carrot. Still, his mum had been impressed and had sent back emojis: the arm flexing and a carrot. His mum was funny with emojis.

'I work in customer services, but I occasionally help on the social media,' Jack rambled on. 'Doing the Twitter and stuff.'

'Nice,' Ben smiled a little sadly. 'That sounds fun.'

A breeze came through the skylight again; goosebumps stood up on Jack's arms. He wanted to say something else that would get Ben talking. 'God, I miss beer gardens,' he tried.

Ben gazed at him curiously for a beat or so. Eventually, he laughed. 'It's, like, eleven o'clock in the morning.'

'Oh, yeah,' Jack said. He'd rather lost track of how long they'd been in there. He was desperate to go to the window and try and pick up the WiFi connection again. His phone felt like a little voice in his ear. But now Ellen was at the window. And Jack wasn't sure that Ellen would want to talk to him all that much.

'I didn't go on MSN very often,' Jack tried again. 'When I was at school, I mean. I didn't use it much.'

'It was a big thing at our school,' Ben replied, quietly. He offered a tired smile.

Jack had talked to a few girls from his class, and from the other school near his. There had never been a girl-friend, exactly, but he'd chatted to girls – about teachers and school and football, which Jack liked, though not quite as much as everyone else in Manchester did.

'Are you hungry?' he asked. 'I'm quite hungry.'

They were still muttering.

'Starving, mate,' Ben replied. He rubbed his hand through his hair. 'I'm absolutely starving.' He stretched. 'Here' – he beckoned Jack closer, keeping his voice low – 'do you think I should go talk to Alexa?'

Jack felt a prickle of anxiety.

He decided to say something non-committal. 'Hmm.' He nodded.

Ben looked at him in confusion. 'What do you think? I mean, that' – he pointed at Ellen – 'didn't exactly sound good.'

Jack observed Ellen's back. She was standing with one leg wrapped around the other, and was slumped forward out of the window. In turn, he peered into the clutter. He could just about see Alexa's small blonde head. She was staring at a wall. He felt sorry for Ellen, but he also felt sorry for Alexa. Actually, he mainly felt sorry for Ben, not just because he looked really sad but because he didn't have a T-shirt.

Jack wasn't sure if he was supposed to be cross with Ben, but that didn't seem entirely fair.

'I didn't mean to upset her,' Ben was saying now. 'Ellen, I mean . . .'

Jack gave him a shy smile. He knew that was true. 'Maybe they'll make up soon.' He added, with conviction, 'After all, they're best friends.'

This didn't seem to make Ben feel any better. He looked a little agitated, in fact.

'Right. Best friends.'

'Are you and Alexa –?' Jack stopped.

'We've been on a few dates.'

Jack felt awkward suddenly. He hoped Alexa wouldn't be angry that he was asking Ben about her. He also wondered if she'd be more, or less, angry than Ellen about the peeing-in-a-box tweet. He shook his head.

Ben looked quizzical.

'Sorry,' Jack said. 'Just hungry.' He added, in a whisper, 'So, will you see her again?'

'Well, it rather depends on what happens here, doesn't it?'

Jack could see that.

'I'd like to,' Ben added. 'A lot.'

'Alexa is great,' Jack said. His eyes lit up. 'She's so smart.'

Ben smiled wanly.

'But Ellen is great too,' Jack added, quickly. 'She's so

funny.' He looked up suddenly. Ellen hadn't turned round, although he sort of wanted her to hear this bit. 'I've never really met anyone like either of them before.'

Ben softened. 'Yeah? Brilliant.' He cleared his throat. Jack looked at him expectantly, and Ben gave him an awkward smile. 'Be a great time for that locksmith to turn up, eh?'

Amidst all of this, Jack had slightly forgotten that they were, technically, going to be rescued at some point. 'Yeah.' He thought about the Twitter thread again. 'Um . . . I think I might get some fresh air, actually.' He pointed towards the skylight. 'And maybe,' he swallowed, 'see how Ellen is doing?'

'Good plan.'

Jack stood up. Alexa was still staring at the wall, her slight shoulders hunched. She looked very small, buried there, in amongst all the boxes. Jack walked towards Ellen, who started, nervously. When she saw it was Jack, she relaxed and looked away again.

He waved limply at her.

'Hey, Jack.' Although she wouldn't look at him, she budged up a little in order to make some space for him to squeeze into the window frame beside her.

He joined her. 'Have you seen the man again?' he asked, conversationally.

Ellen didn't reply for a few seconds. 'No,' she said, finally. 'But I haven't really been concentrating.'

'No, of course,' Jack said, in an understanding voice. He patted Ellen gingerly on the shoulder.

As he did so, his phone vibrated in his pocket and he felt a thrill in his stomach. He glanced at Ellen quickly to see if she'd noticed, but she appeared to be staring into the middle distance, lost in thought. From up here you could see across the Thames all the way to the shiny, modern monuments of the City, and Ellen's eyes seemed to be fixed on these gleaming spires. Jack wondered if he could get his phone out without her noticing. He was anxious that the connection might drop off again before he could see what the notification was.

'Did you hear any of that?' Ellen asked, finally. She still didn't look at him.

'Oh . . . no.' Jack added, 'Not really.'

'Good.'

A bird landed on the roof a few metres away. Jack eyed it warily. After a few seconds, it leaped back off again.

'Are you OK?' he asked, finally, awkwardly. He knew he probably should have asked that before.

'Been better.'

'Right. No, of course.'

The phone! It vibrated again!

It was in the pocket beside Ellen. Trying not to jolt her, he snaked his right arm behind his back in order to reach into his left pocket and remove it. Success – he palmed it into the right pocket. Ellen gave no indication that she was paying any attention to him. Testing this theory, he removed it from his pocket.

She didn't flinch.

It was Twitter! Tilting the screen away from Ellen, and with one eye on the right-hand corner – the WiFi was there! – he tapped the icon. He felt dizzy. He had 100+ notifications – so many that the app had given up count-ing. The tweet about Ellen had been liked more than 1,500 times – 1,500! A comedian with 12,000 followers had DM'd him a thumbs-up.

Palms a little clammy – this was so exciting! – he scanned through his mentions to see who was replying. There were now so many people interacting it was a bit hard to see the individual replies.

@witnessthefitnesss
name and shame!!!

@old_vic67
*how disgusting!!! hope she clears up after herself young women
   today . . . from vic*

@SteffyWrites
We need to help these kids. For the good of hygiene

@Juice4U
Get 10% off ALL slimming juices with my CODE SLIM 10

He didn't really get that last one. But he noticed that a singer in a band he liked, who had more than 70,000 followers, had retweeted him, which might explain why so many people had seen it and liked it. He was screenshotting a few of the best responses when Ellen spoke.

'What time is it?' she asked quietly.

He almost jumped. 'Oh . . . um . . .' He recovered. 'Eleven twenty-three.'

Ellen moaned. 'I can't even bear to imagine what the kitchen looks like right now.'

Jack chewed his lip. He couldn't really imagine it, but it made him feel unsettled.

He returned to his phone, but the WiFi had already dropped. Still, that had been brilliant! He couldn't believe that real famous people had seen the thread! Not to mention it was funny! Everyone was saying so, with their own tweets and their likes and their retweets. The journalist woman, Steffy, she loved it. It still felt strange that they all knew about it – and Alexa and Ellen and Ben didn't, but now didn't seem like the time to explain to the others.

He tapped the Twitter icon again. His phone was trying valiantly to connect when Ellen shifted her weight forward to lean further out of the skylight, and Jack's heart leapt into his mouth. He didn't think she was paying attention to him, but to test the theory, he sniffed loudly. Ellen continued to stare across the vista of rooftops and satellite dishes and chimney stacks into the middle distance beyond. Ben was still sitting with his back to the window, broad shoulders sloping.

Jack was staring nervously at Ellen's profile again when, with the power of a vision, he had another idea. The story about Ellen and Ben – that would probably do well too. People had cared about them being locked in the attic, after all, and this was much more exciting. Well, not exciting, exactly. More of a strange coincidence. But it was definitely the sort of thing Jack saw on the internet all the time: people live-tweeting something extraordinary that was happening to them. And the others wouldn't see it until they got out of the attic – at which point they wouldn't mind as much, probably.

In fact, the more Jack considered it, the more it seemed sensible that he should share it.

He glanced at the top-right corner of his screen,

keeping one careful eye on Ellen. He had a bar of WiFi! This meant that everything would load slowly. But it was enough for him to tap out a tweet and hit Share.

@jackbarnes93

wow NEWS FLASH: housemate has found out that our other house-mate's Hinge date is actually her MSN boyfriend from when they were at school #newcross #stuckintheattic

It was buffering, so it would take a few minutes. But it would send in the end. He could feel it.

18. Ellen

After he'd dropped the letter, he signed out and left her reeling, and it took Ellen a good fifteen minutes of reading and screaming silently into her pillow before she gathered her senses in order to type her own reply.

Dear Benjamin,

I agree utterly with everything you have written. In the course of our correspondence, I too have developed strong feelings for you. Sometimes, all this barely feels real and I have to remind myself that you do really exist.

Like you, I struggled for so long to connect on here — it feels like a lot of the boys I spoke to weren't really on the same level as me. They are immature. Not like you, though. I definitely agree that we see the world in the same way. I like to think of you, out there somewhere, looking at the things that I look at. It feels weird that we must be so close sometimes and not know it.

I agree about meeting. I feel like it would be a really special step for our relationship. I also want to find a way for us to take this relationship on and to grow closer.

E x

She spent the whole day at school on Monday thinking about it. It was the last week before study leave began, and she was supposed to be using this time to make the most of her harried teachers' attention, but the day passed in a blur of daydreams and anticipation. When the bell finally rang, she snuck to the bus stop without texting Kate, who'd definitely have wanted to go to Starbucks.

Dinner was an ordeal – her mother had made bolognese, and the sound of John's slurping made Ellen clench her fists under the table – but her mother clearly blamed her taciturn presence on the stress of exams, and kindly told her she could get down from the table without helping to clear up.

Ellen grunted her thanks and galloped up the stairs to rouse her laptop.

Mercifully, he signed in only a few minutes after she did. She sent her reply straight away, breathing fast as she read her letter again on the screen, imagining him reading it at home in his own room.

rainham_romeo1991: *wow*
rainham_romeo1991: *thank you so much for writing this and sending it to me*
miss_BehaviourX91: *thank you for yours*

She could feel her pulse in her ears. Her face was flushed.

miss_BehaviourX91: *i feel like i can remember every word*
rainham_romeo1991: *i just can't believe how much we agree on everything*

rainham_romeo1991: *it's so rare and unique*
rainham_romeo1991: *i've never had this with anyone before*
miss_BehaviourX91: *definitely*

He typed and then stopped. She watched her cursor, gnawing on her thumbnail, and considered what to say next. She started typing.

miss_BehaviourX91: *so i was thinking*
miss_BehaviourX91: *maybe we should meet up*

She leaned back and watched the message box, chewing the nail of her thumb. He was typing.

rainham_romeo1991: *definitely*
rainham_romeo1991: *i've also been thinking that*
miss_BehaviourX91: *great*
rainham_romeo1991: *maybe we could do it this weekend?*
rainham_romeo1991: *if that works for you*
miss_BehaviourX91: *definitely*
rainham_romeo1991: *we could go for a walk maybe*
rainham_romeo1991: *it would be nice to be somewhere where we wouldn't be distracted by other people*
rainham_romeo1991: *from school or something*

She wondered if this was the most romantic thing that had ever happened to her.

miss_BehaviourX91: *i'd love that*
rainham_romeo1991: *ok great*

rainham_romeo1991: *let's work out the time and place this week*

miss_BehaviourX91: *perfect*

On Thursday evening, she dispatched her dinner at lightning speed, as usual, and scaled the stairs two at a time. It was almost 7 p.m., and tonight they had agreed they would set the time and place for their first meeting that weekend. Ellen threw her blazer on to her bed and slammed her bedroom door shut in a fluent, practised movement, ignoring her mother's reproachful cry from downstairs, then prodded the button that brought her laptop to life. She logged in on the stroke of seven exactly and waited expectantly, her eyes trained on her MSN contacts list, so she'd see him as soon as he logged in.

And this was how she sat all evening, alert, wired, hardly blinking – or so it seemed – as she watched the screen. She rubbed at the worn spot on the carpet underneath her desk with her foot, watching for his name to appear. She ignored Owen Willett, who had opened with something about a house party she hadn't been invited to that upcoming weekend. As the minutes ticked past, and she grew more agitated, she tried to quell the rising panic by running through possible reasons for his absence. A football match that had overrun, maybe, or an argument with his parents? Maybe he was ill, or someone in his family was ill? There would be an explanation.

Not that evening: he didn't appear at all in the end.

She sat in place for four hours, until past 11 p.m., shoulders hunched around her ears, jaw clenched so hard she developed a headache. Her eyes were dry, her pulse racing.

But finally, she got into bed, turned off the light and stared at the ceiling, the occasional slant of light racing from wall to wall as a car drove past. She tried to quell the interior klaxon that blared 'ALL IS NOT WELL.'

There would be an explanation.

But whichever way she squared it, she couldn't come up with an excuse to logically explain what happened next, which was a long, yawning stretch of absolutely nothing.

He didn't appear online ever again.

She had no other way to reach him. And so, for want of any closure, in the weeks and months to come, numb and disbelieving, she read and reread what now would go down as their last messages to one another.

rainham_romeo1991: *it's mad. how we think the absolute same about everything*
   miss_BehaviourX91: *i know*
   rainham_romeo1991: *two halves of one whole*
   miss_BehaviourX91: *that's exactly how i feel*
   rainham_romeo1991: *good*
   rainham_romeo1991: *right, m'lady. i must to bed*
   rainham_romeo1991: *adieu, until tomorrow x*
   miss_BehaviourX91: *bonne nuit x*

And that was the end of that one.

Those days and weeks afterwards were miserable. Having to tell Kate the whole sorry – tragic, really – story one afternoon, as they sat in the changing rooms near the PE hall, under the broken pegs, a bin full of musty, suppurating spare gym kit in the corner. They often sat there – despite the odour – as it was empty (Rainham Girls had a reputation for having the sorriest netball team in the Kent and Sussex area), remote and indoors, and therefore weatherproof.

It was the not knowing, of course. For the first week after he went AWOL she remained hopeful, believing – naively – that he could still come back with some fantastical but entirely legitimate excuse. ('My entire family was kidnapped and held in an underground bunker and I've only just managed to dig us out using a ladle.') On the bus home that Friday, she even desperately scanned a local newspaper for any deaths or disappearances of boys called Benjamin around her age. But as the days passed, she gave up on even the most outlandish of excuses.

The chasm he'd left invited her to fill in the gaps. Was it something I said? she wondered, endlessly. It must have been – because he didn't know what she looked like, beyond a small avatar on a screen. And they'd never met, so it couldn't have been something she'd done. And so she obsessed every night, replaying every conversation they'd ever had.

It cast a shadow over the rest of that final summer term – and the summer beyond. She felt detached, a beat behind everyone else. She was also mortified. She'd been dumped by a boy from the internet – her first and only approximation of a boyfriend.

For much of the summer, the prospect of university in September felt shapeless. Ellen had no idea if her exams had gone well. But they were done, and the die was cast, and now she'd play the waiting game until she found out whether she'd be going to York. Her family were going to France the day after she got her results, and, daily, her mother would make impertinent enquiries about whether or not her 'cossie' still fitted.

She still went on MSN, though less frequently. She'd have half-hearted conversations with the same old cast of people, and it would be distracting if a little unfulfilling, like eating junk food when you really craved a proper sit-down meal. Still, she had vague designs on losing her virginity that summer, and needs must, even if it all made you feel rather cold. She spent a bit of time talking to a guy called Charlie Seeley – or slayer_chucks90 – whom she did know in real life. They went on a few dates, one of which culminated in him fingering her at a screening of *The Hangover* at the Odeon in Gravesend.

It sort of fizzled out when she got her results, which were exactly what she needed to get into York, and at that point she realized she'd been holding her breath for months. They texted a few times – Charlie prematurely wished her 'happy 18th' the day before her actual birthday – but the texts cost a lot and Ellen would rather use them on Kate, detailing the mundane humiliations of her family summer holiday to Brittany.

Linda made a friend called Kerry, and the two of them would appear at the bar each evening, order glasses of *vin blanc* in parodically bad French. Meanwhile, John refused to wear any suntan lotion at all, despite being beetroot-coloured after his first day on the beach, and Ellen found it painful to look at him. He also insisted on walking around the site with his shirt entirely unbuttoned. Occasionally, she did imagine that she was writing her texts to Benjamin instead of Kate – though, some days, she realized she hadn't thought about him at all.

Her eighteenth birthday passed without incident. There was a special breakfast of croissants and coffee. Her haul of presents included an Argos saucepan, a student cook-book and a pair of bed socks. They went to the beach and persevered with badminton, even as the clouds threatened, then went for an unceremonious *steak frites* before return-ing to the beach, where they all cooperated in an unspoken agreement not to mention the quite brutal easterly wind, until it blew Linda's umbrella out of the sand, almost hit a German family, and they had to apologize. They hurried off the beach, Ellen and Tom trying hard not to laugh.

Linda had sourced a birthday cake for dinner, so they shared a bottle of wine, and then Tom and Ellen had a drink in the bar, which was fun until Linda and Kerry turned up.

The next day, Ellen woke up, feeling dispirited that she hadn't even managed to get drunk on her eighteenth birth-day. And that was that: she was an adult. After texting Kate a blow-by-blow account of the dreariness, her best friend promised her a proper night out when she got back to Gillingham.

Shots then Pulse then puke then home!!

There were worse nights, certainly.

And as was inevitable, she thought of Benjamin more and more rarely. Now she fantasized about confronting him, rather than getting him back. When the family returned after their holiday, she avoided MSN in favour of nights with Kate, who had quit her job at the old man's pub and was now working at TK Maxx. Realizing they only had a few weeks left, they reminisced about their schooldays and eyed up the future. University was coming, though Kate had decided she didn't want to go up to Leeds after all, so was taking another year to work things out.

On the morning of Ellen's departure, Kate turned up on the doorstep, of course, wearing her glasses, which she never usually wore in public. Her eyes looked small and watery. Ellen said goodbye and Kate made her promise not to turn into a nerd. And then Ellen climbed into the car with Linda (John was staying at home – there was football on) and sat in the passenger seat, knees almost up around her ears. They'd packed the rest of the car with her entire room, including the saucepan and the cookbook and the bed socks. Her mother chattered and Ellen responded to every third request, while she watched the cul-de-sacs slide past.

She was leaving a blank place and gaining a blank slate.

19. Alexa

She and Ellen had bickered countless times, of course. They had sat beside each other sulking, on trains and on sofas, and on walks home from the Tube, during silent breakfasts where the air was loaded with grievances and swallowed asides. And there were little things that annoyed each one about the other. For example, Alexa always, inwardly, rolled her eyes every time Ellen told someone about her job at The Flowdown and reeled off the same six or so jokes ('I'm such a fanny', 'It's a place for twats who like talking about vaginas').

But while Ellen's grudges were legion, and mythical, she was usually more lenient with Alexa. As a result, they'd only ever fought properly once. It had been over Linda and John. This was at university – their third year, maybe – and Ellen had made a cruel, snide remark about her parents, who had been enthusing about a new Bella Italia on the high street near them, and Alexa had snapped at her.

'You're so rude about your parents,' she'd said, acidly.

Ellen had been taken aback, and – instantly – furious. 'They're my parents, and I can say what I want about them,' she'd retorted, babyishly.

And then, suddenly, they'd been off, the argument building to a crescendo, clichés being brandished on both sides, Alexa calling Ellen a brat and Ellen retorting that, just because her parents loved her, it didn't mean she had to be nice about them all the time. Then Alexa – it had definitely been her – had grabbed her scarf and her black felt coat and said something like, 'Look, I'm sorry but I just can't listen to this', and then she'd stormed out of the coffee shop near the faculty, where they always sat in between lectures. She recalled the crisp peal of the bell above the door, when it opened, inviting the chill air in.

They hadn't spoken for two whole days, and then Alexa had finally relented and sent a text. She remembered now the craft that had gone into it, the forty-eight hours of precision and redrafting and inserting and deleting commas.

Hey. Sorry – I overreacted. I'm just sensitive because my parents despise each other and haven't been in the same room in a decade. I shouldn't have got so cross. I'm sorry. Will you forgive me? Also, do tell Linda Bella Italia isn't a patch on PizzaExpress. X

Ellen had replied instantly.

hey I'm sorry too i was insensitive and dumb. you can borrow linda and john whenever (srsly). can we be friends again plz. coffee? now?? xx

Alexa had been watching her phone when the text arrived. She fumbled the slide mechanism in her haste to read it. Relieved, she had replied immediately.

Yes! Copper Kettle? I'll get us a sofa. X

Yayyyy!!!! Let me find some pants and i'll be on my way xx can we get a cake??

When Ellen arrived they had hugged, and Alexa had felt comforted by the warmth of her. For the previous forty-eight hours, it had been like she didn't exist.

'I couldn't find any pants so I'm wearing bikini bottoms,' Ellen had admitted when they separated. 'It's quite nice, actually.'

Alexa sighed now at the memory, and then fretted that one of the others might have heard. A spider was picking its way across an ancient newspaper nearby, and she watched it for a few seconds as her temper subsided. She could hear the occasional murmur of Jack and Ellen's conversation from the open window, though couldn't tell what they were saying to each other. She didn't dare steal a peek at Ben. She still felt too irritated by everything.

She knew it was beneath them to fight over a boy, and she knew – realistically – that she wouldn't pick Ben over her best friend. Still, she hated that it was being presented as a choice. She wished, suddenly, that she could speak to her sister, Nina, about this. If only there was a way they could tell for sure whether it was Ben who had ghosted Ellen – although if it was, she reflected, that definitely wouldn't help matters.

She regretted snapping. She should have been more sympathetic. Sometimes it just happened: a chink in her armour, a temporary loss of control, like that row in the cafe. They joked about it now – it was one of their riffs – but she remembered how adrift she'd felt for the two days she and Ellen hadn't spoken. Alexa chewed the skin on her thumb knuckle. She knew she needed to apologize. It wouldn't solve anything, but she needed to show Ellen she was on her side. She tried not to think of Ben and his dimple.

Her legs were aching, anyway. She stood up, remaining in a crouch in order to avoid knocking her head on the ceiling. She could feel Ben watching her. Jack and Ellen didn't turn round. She picked her way cautiously through the chaos, aiming for them. Now Jack turned. He looked a little relieved and automatically stepped out of the way.

'Hey.' She sounded more confident than she felt.

Ellen was inscrutable.

'I can . . . I'll go –' Jack offered, clumsily. He pointed towards Ben, though remained hovering at the window.

Alexa still couldn't look at Ben, in case it challenged her resolve. She nodded kindly at Jack. 'Thanks, Jack.'

He gave her a nod in return and shuffled towards Ben's spot on the floor.

'Hey,' she tried again, in a whisper, after a few seconds.

'Hello,' Ellen muttered, shortly. She wasn't going to make this easy.

'Um, I'm –' Deep breath. 'El?'

'What?' Ellen replied, quietly.

Alexa took another steadying breath. 'Look, I'm sorry.'

Ellen remained still.

Alexa added, 'I'm on your side.' Her voice was trembling on the edge of a plea now.

'Really?' Ellen sounded flat and unconvinced.

'Yes, really. I am.'

'Right.'

'Really,' she added again, with feeling. 'I'm really sorry. I didn't mean to be a cow about it, and I know it must have been really upsetting, and just because it happened a decade ago, that doesn't mean it doesn't matter, and of course I was upset, because I like him, but I like you more, obviously.' She said this all in a rushed mutter before she paused. 'And, well' – she steeled herself – 'I get that it would be weird if I went out with him.' She could feel that Ellen was tense. 'So I . . . I won't. If you don't want me to.' Alexa hoped that the boys hadn't heard any of that, but she didn't dare check if they had.

'I mean it would be more than a bit weird.'

'Yes.'

'I'd have to see him all the time.'

'Yes . . .' She stared into the distance now, like Ellen. 'I guess you would. Quite a lot, anyway.'

There was a long, uncomfortable pause, in which Alexa assumed they were both imagining a version of the same stock scene. Ben and Ellen in the kitchen of Rokeby Close – in this version it was not flooded – trying to have a cordial conversation, while Alexa played harried diplomat. She linked arms with Ellen, whose face softened slightly.

'I know you really like him.' Her voice was rather bloodless.

'Yes.' Alexa's skin prickled. 'But you're obviously more important.'

Ellen laughed, mirthlessly. 'Sure.' She unlinked her arm.

'Don't be like that,' Alexa said, hurt. 'You know you are.'

Ellen had the good grace to look a little abashed. 'Sorry,' she said, finally.

There was another silence.

Alexa watched as a woman climbed out of a car a little way up the street. She was struggling with armfuls of supermarket carrier bags. Inevitably, she dropped one. Alexa heard a smash – a wine bottle had come a cropper. Eventually, Ellen sighed heavily. She was now resting her cheek on her hand and inclined her face a little closer to Alexa's so that they were almost making eye contact.

'It *was* a long time ago,' Ellen muttered, finally, gruffly. She stopped.

This was delicate and unexpected. Alexa willed her on.

'I'm not saying I don't think it was him. Because it was.

I'm not mad.' Ellen was gracious in neither defeat nor victory.

Alexa replied, gently, 'I don't think you're mad.'

'OK.' Ellen seemed satisfied. She inclined her face a little closer to Alexa's. 'Well, that's good. Because I'm not.' She muttered, 'He's just forgotten all about my humiliation.'

Alexa's chest tightened. 'It's such a weird coincidence,' she managed, finally.

'Yes. I didn't think we had similar taste in men at all.'

'No,' Alexa said. She tried a smile.

'I don't . . .' Ellen paused, shifting her weight on to the other foot. 'I don't really know what to say.' An embittered, self-conscious laugh.

Alexa watched her, carefully.

'I guess, I give you my blessing?' Ellen rolled her eyes at her own theatrics, but they were smiling now. 'Will that do?'

'Yes. Thank you,' Alexa said, instantly hating how formal she sounded. 'But also . . . I mean, it's only been a few dates. We aren't exactly getting married.' She laughed and then added, honestly, 'Until last night he wasn't even that interested in me.'

'Well. He's got form,' Ellen shot back, but Alexa could tell she was mostly joking.

She smiled back, hoping to give power to their fragile new truce. A silence fell, which had a slightly prickly quality. She kept stealing sideways glances at Ellen, whose eyes were glassy and inscrutable.

Eventually, Alexa risked it. 'Should we, maybe, go back over?' She gestured behind her with her right thumb. 'When you're ready,' she added, quickly.

Ellen sighed. 'Yes. I suppose.' She didn't move. 'You go first. You're allowed to go and speak to him.'

Alexa looked a little hesitant. She did want this, a few seconds with him to explain. 'Are you sure?' she said.

'Yeah, of course,' Ellen urged. 'You'll have to get rid of Jack, though.'

'Yes.' A knowing look.

'I'll happily take him for a few minutes while you kiss and make up.'

Alexa gave her a look. 'Oh, shut up,' she added, affecting lightness, then worried instantly about how it had come out.

But Ellen hadn't flinched, and she returned Alexa's small, grateful smile as she squeezed her shoulder, trying to invest the gesture with meaning.

Feeling at least a little better, Alexa walked back into the middle of the room.

Jack peeked over his shoulder as he heard her approaching footsteps.

'Hey.' Her voice sounded high and reedy. 'Jack, could you . . . ?'

'Oh.' He looked stricken. 'Yes, do you want me to – ?' He pointed at the corner where Alexa and Ellen had had their argument.

'No, Jack,' Alexa replied, gently. 'You can go to the window.'

20. Jack

'Oh, it's you again,' Ellen said when he arrived, but he was fairly sure she was joking.

She was resting both arms on the skylight's frame. There wasn't much room for Jack.

He stood back slightly. 'Hello.'

'Left them to it, then.'

'Yes.'

'When the hell is that fucking locksmith going to come?' She rested her chin on her hands now, head still cocked away from him.

He took out his phone. There it was: Twitter. He cupped the phone carefully, angling the screen far from Ellen, but the connection was slow. He was desperate just to stand and watch the screen until it reconnected, to confirm that the previous tweet had sent – but he didn't want to look suspicious. Plus, he remembered Ellen had said something to him.

'Yeah. It seems weird it's taking so long.'

'Have you got any signal yet?'

'Oh. No.' Then he added, quickly, 'That's why I keep checking my phone.'

'Right.' She glanced at him, but she seemed to have bought it. She asked, 'What time is it now?'

He checked his phone. 'Twelve-oh-eight.'

Ellen sighed. 'Maybe everyone in south London really has locked themselves out today. Or in an attic.'

'Yeah.'

Twitter was still buffering wheezily. With some difficulty, he put his phone back in his pocket. He strained slightly to see if he could hear Alexa or Ben talking, but he couldn't.

'So' – wondering how to phrase it – 'are you and Alexa OK again?'

Ellen lifted her head from her chin and turned to look at him. 'Yeah.' She sounded a little unconvincing.

'Oh, good . . .' Jack paused. 'So, does that mean that Alexa and Ben – ?'

Ellen shrugged. 'I think that's probably what they're chatting about.'

'Should we give them a few minutes?'

'Yeah. Let's give them a few minutes.'

For some time, they both stood at the window in fairly comfortable silence. After a while, Jack couldn't tell if they'd left Alexa and Ben to talk for three minutes or thirty. He took out his phone. It had been seven. He couldn't resist: he tried opening Twitter again.

It had loaded! Jack gasped, in spite of himself, but passed it off as a deep breath. It appeared @SteffyWrites had shared the latest tweet too, adding that she 'REALLY wanted to be a fly on the wall in that house'. Jack's ears went pink. It was doing well: 1,356 likes and 323 retweets, which wasn't bad for under an hour. A few people had quote-tweeted it with a crying laughing emoji, an 'OMG', an 'OMFG' or a 'loooooooool'.

@fulhamFC_boi

We need more

'Hey, look – our friend's coming out of his house.' Ellen nudged him, urgently.

He stuffed his phone back in his pocket. She was right. The neighbour was alone, this time, dressed in gym clothes and wheeling a bike. Jack was wondering if he'd look towards the attic, when the man waved up at them.

'HI, GUYS!' he shouted.

'HI!' Ellen shouted back.

Jack did a wave.

'STILL HAVEN'T HEARD FROM THE LOCK-SMITH, I'M AFRAID.'

'Fuck,' Ellen muttered. She shot Jack a dark look, then rearranged her face. 'OH, NO WORRIES AT ALL,' she shouted back to the neighbour. 'WE CAN WAIT.'

Jack frowned at her.

'GREAT. I'M GOING TO THE GYM BUT HE HAS MY HOME NUMBER SO MY WIFE WILL PICK IT UP.'

'GREAT!'

He did another wave and then climbed on to his bike. They watched him cycle up the street.

'Fuck's sake,' Ellen muttered. 'Did he call the most

useless locksmith in London? The kitchen is going to be ruined. We're so screwed on the security deposit.' Her eyes were glassy. 'Imagine us explaining this to Elias.'

Jack shared her horror. All day, he had been concentrating very hard on not thinking about Elias. The Twitter thread was now more important than ever, he realized. Surreptitiously, he sneaked another look at his phone.

The first tweet had more than 7,000 likes now – 7,000!

@carmelwafer

whats happening now we need updates

But as he contemplated another response, he realized he'd lost the connection again. He felt a stab of frustration.

'Right, they've had enough time,' Ellen said, decisively. 'I'm bored of hanging out of this window. I want to sit down.'

Jack said something non-committal. He wanted to stay by the window with his phone. Still, he could see that Ben and Alexa had their heads quite close together, which seemed like a good sign.

Ellen started to march towards them. 'Coming?' she demanded.

'Um . . .' Jack took a step forward, then stopped. Perhaps he could stay here and be sort of half in the conversation. They didn't really need him, anyway.

As Ellen got closer, Ben and Alexa looked up.

'Hey,' Alexa said, warmly.

Ben looked wary.

'Hi,' Ellen said, stopping in front of them. She was scrunching her toes up.

'Hi,' Jack called, brightly, from the window. That would do it.

'Any update?' Alexa asked.

'Oh, we saw the guy from the house opposite,' Ellen replied. 'But we're not getting anywhere. He hasn't heard from the locksmith in a while.'

'Eek,' Alexa said. After a second, she suggested, 'Sit down?'

Jack watched as Ellen lowered herself to the floor.

For a moment or so, no one said anything. Alexa looked like she was about to, when Ellen started up again. She was quiet, and her bravado at the window was gone; Jack felt a little apprehensive.

'So, I've had a think,' Ellen said haltingly, addressing Ben. 'And a conversation. With Alexa. Anyway. Look. I don't know. I remember what I remember.' She saw Ben open his mouth to say something, but she continued, heedless. 'And look, you remember what you remember. Which is different to what I remember. But anyway. That's not — anyway, it's fine. It was all just this teenage thing and . . . well, I should be done with it. Over it all. That's the real . . . that's what should . . . should happen. So you know.' She stopped, squirming.

Jack had not expected this.

Ben clearly hadn't either. He seemed to reel slightly, before offering a weak, 'Thanks . . . thank you.' He cleared his throat.

Jack noticed that Alexa had reached for Ellen's hand.

Ben started speaking again. 'Um.' A hard swallow. 'Look, I'm . . . I'm sorry all that happened. And I feel . . . it's horrible. But also, I remembered' — his voice strengthened – 'well, one thing came to me while you two were talking. In the corner . . .' A pause. 'I was just telling Alexa, actually.'

Jack noticed she looked a little uncomfortable at this.

'Well, it's just that in our last year of school, I had this girlfriend. Imogen. Like a real girlfriend.' He added, quickly, 'No offence. But it's just that, well, timings-wise, I just don't think it makes sense. Because we were together from sixth form until the end of my first term at Bristol. So I don't think I'd have been talking to another girl on MSN, you see,' he said, finally.

Jack wondered why Ben hadn't mentioned Imogen sooner.

'A girlfriend,' Ellen said, eventually. 'Right.' Her voice was even, but she was chewing her thumbnail.

'Yeah, we were serious for quite a bit. So, I'm not sure, but look, as I said before, maybe we chatted at some point? I mean, we clearly almost knew each other,' Ben added, quickly. 'We were in the same town, going to the same pubs, the same parties. We know so many people in common . . .' He trailed off, shrugging. 'Maybe the timeline is a bit off or . . . I'm sorry, I mean it's obviously weird that I've turned up here with Alexa and . . .' He trailed off again and stared at his feet.

'It's definitely weird,' Alexa said, quietly. 'But –'

'Look,' Ellen interrupted. 'Thanks for all that. Especially the bit about how you had a "real" girlfriend instead.'

This seemed to wind them all for a second.

Jack realized he'd half-closed one of his eyes. When he opened them both properly, Ellen was speaking again.

'Sorry' – she made an uncomfortable face – 'ignore me. Look, what I mean is maybe we could just, not . . . not talk about it any more.' She said this last part in a rush. 'Any of it. The MSN or the girlfriend or any of it. I know it's my fault for starting it, but I don't want to do the "he said, she said" any more.' She sat up a little straighter and locked Ben in her sights.

Alexa was hunched, her arms folded across her chest.

Jack took a small step backwards, towards the window.

'Right,' Ben said, eventually, with feeling. 'I agree. To drop the whole thing, I mean.' He made a circle with his finger on Alexa's thigh. 'Thank you – really.'

'Not at all,' Ellen replied, primly. 'I'm glad we've cleared things up.' She did not sound glad, or as if she believed much had been cleared up.

'Yes,' Alexa tried. 'I'm glad too.' She also sounded unconvinced.

'Great!' Jack called from the window.

Ellen scowled at him. Perhaps that had been a little too loud.

For a minute, the three of them sat wordlessly. Alexa looked like she wanted to say something, but in the end it was Ellen who did, and Jack held his breath.

'Just promise me you won't go cold on her again, Ben, and we'll be OK.' Ellen sounded a little shrill, but raised an eyebrow cockily. 'Otherwise, I really will have good reason to hold a grudge.'

A cloud passed across Ben's face. He removed his arm from around Alexa's shoulders in order to get a better look at her. 'Huh?'

Alexa's eyes were wide. She looked horrified. 'I mean like when you ditched her by the side of a road. After the theatre.' Ellen laughed, but stopped abruptly when she caught Alexa's expression.

'I didn't "ditch her by the side of a road".' Ben repeated, slowly.

'Um.' Ellen bit her lip. 'Right. No. Of course you didn't.' Ben was leaning away from Alexa, who had flushed a deep red. Jack curled his toes and willed Ellen to stop.

She continued. 'I just mean that after you had that date, you stopped texting her, and so we both thought that maybe you were dicking her around –'

Alexa finally managed to interject. 'Ellen's just confused, I think –' she started, hurriedly.

'Remember?' She stared at Ellen hard. 'Ben didn't dump me, we went out last night?'

'Completely,' Ellen said, solemnly. It sounded like she'd stopped, until she hadn't. 'I just meant he'd stopped texting you for a bit, so you were surprised when he texted you last night. Like it wasn't a planned thing, it was all very last-minute, right?'

'Ellen?' Alexa sounded incredulous.

Ben looked like someone was playing a coordinated, elaborate practical joke on him. 'Um, OK –' he ventured, coolly.

'No, it's OK – I mean, you'd just got a bit commitment phobic, right?' Ellen continued. 'We've all been there –'

'Ellen, shut up,' Alexa interrupted.

'Sorry, of course,' Ellen said. 'Shutting up.' A pause. 'Again. Maybe just forget what I said.'

Ben put his face in his hands.

Jack was quite glad he'd stayed at the window now.

Ellen opened her mouth again, but this time Jack caught her. He frowned and shook his head, imperceptibly. She closed her mouth again. He was surprised that had worked.

21. Alexa

Ellen opened her mouth again, and Alexa felt the dull despair of the inevitable.

Instead, Ellen whispered, 'Oh, shit.' It appeared that she had realized, at last, what she'd done.

In response, Alexa clenched her jaw tighter.

Ben remained tensed and silent.

For a few seconds, Ellen was still too, until she started jerking her head in Alexa's direction.

Alexa glanced up, before she could catch herself.

'S-O-R-R-Y,' Ellen mouthed, her face stretched in horror.

Alexa turned to stare out of the window by way of response, and started working on excavating a hangnail on her thumb. If she worked hard, she'd probably draw blood before long. There was a good, chilly metre between her and Ben now. He felt even further away.

'Well, I hope the locksmith rescues us soon,' Ellen stated, uncertainly, into the silence. She added, unable to stop herself, 'It's definitely feeling a bit *Lord of the Flies* in here.'

Ben gave a hollow laugh.

Clearly emboldened by his response, Ellen hazarded another comment. 'Maybe we could do some yoga to pass the time?' she said, affecting brightness.

No one said anything. Alexa decided to not even dignify

this with a glance Ellen-wards. Instead, she concentrated as hard as she could on staying calm.

To think they'd been just about to put the stupid awkwardness of the MSN business behind them! This was classic Ellen: reckless self-sabotage that managed to take another person down as collateral damage, a freight train careering off its rails.

And yet, Ellen's clumsy cruelty had also triggered Alexa's unease. She frowned. Was she being silly, placing so much stock in Ben? He'd definitely been cooling on her, and she didn't really know what had changed between their penultimate date and the one last night. She felt disconcerted.

She shook her head. No, last night's date had been different. A turning point. Sometimes, things just took a little while to get started, she tried to reassure herself. She'd be able to convince him it was all stupid, wouldn't she? As soon as they got out of this attic, she'd be able to speak to him – alone – and explain that it was just a silly thing that Ellen had said and hadn't understood.

It really was very warm now. The pipes ticked and hummed: Alexa assumed that their unpredictable heating had clicked on. Despite appeals to Elias, the radiators would click on in June and then refuse to warm up in December. Subtly, she felt under her armpits – disguising the action as hugging herself. They were damp. She could feel the sweat beading her forehead. She must smell dreadful, she thought, in horror. She'd last showered yesterday morning, and since then she'd completed two commutes, a date to a pizza place, rolled around on someone else's body and slept beside them.

Ellen was trying again. 'How long can humans go without food?' she asked, quietly.

'A lot longer than we've gone,' Alexa replied, testily.

'What about water?'

'A lot longer than we've gone.' She wasn't sure, but she thought Ben might have snorted at that. She felt a tiny bit better.

'I wonder if anyone's ever died of boredom.'

Alexa rolled her eyes. 'Who knows?'

'It *is* weird how long the locksmith is taking,' Ben said, quietly. 'Right?'

'Yeah.' Alexa leaped at the chance to speak to him. 'But I guess we don't really know exactly what was arranged with that neighbour.'

Ben made a nod of agreement. It was a start.

'Maybe I should just climb on to the roof?' he suggested. 'I'm sure I could shimmy down a drainpipe and break in the front door –'

'I don't think that's safe,' Alexa interrupted, alarmed.

'Well, you could tie the cord around my waist, or something?' He looked at the skylight.

'I don't think we should send anyone out on to the roof just yet,' Alexa said.

He shrugged, but at least he'd looked at her. She held his eyes for a second, trying to communicate an apology for the whole horrid misunderstanding. It felt a little like he'd softened, but she couldn't tell if this was just wishful thinking on her part.

'Jack's being a bit weird, isn't he?' Ellen whispered. 'He keeps sneaking off over there –'

'I think he was giving us space,' Ben pointed out, jumping in. 'After your attempts at further sabotage.'

Alexa looked at him sharply, but he had the ghost of a smile. Her stomach loosened its anxious clenching slightly.

Ellen opened her mouth indignantly, then also clocked that this might just be the start of a reconciliation.

'Right. Yeah. Um . . . I just . . .' Ellen floundered.

'Can we not?' Ben said, sharply. 'Please.'

Ellen closed her mouth and resumed looking at the floor.

Alexa tensed again. Ben rubbed the inside of her wrist with his thumb and then found her eyes for a second. His expression was unreadable.

22. Jack

THERE'S NO PLACE LIKE HOME!

SOUTH LONDONER STUCK IN OWN ATTIC GOES VIRAL

What would you do if you found yourself trapped in an attic? Shout for help? Try to climb out of the window? Or tweet about it?

For south Londoner Jack Barnes, 28, the answer was to get straight on social media. And his hilarious Twitter thread has gone viral – thanks in part to some serious drama.

Barnes and his housemates found themselves trapped in the top floor of their home on Rokeby Close in Lewisham this morning when the door handle broke off. To make matters worse, the kitchen was also flooding. The quick-thinking Barnes decided to share the news with his 112 followers, in an appeal for help.

@jackbarnes93

Sending out an SOS!!!! Stuck in an attic in Rokeby Close, Lewisham, south-east London. Door handle broke off and there's flooding in the kitchen!!! With my housemates (and one of their dates!) #newcross #stuckintheattic

Instantly, the thread went viral, with offers of assistance. Meanwhile, things were becoming desperate.

@jackbarnes93

*Housemate is having to go to the toilet in a box #newcross
#stuckintheattic*

But things took a turn for the dramatic when Barnes revealed that
not only were they stuck up there, but his housemates had learned
about an awkward coincidence.

@jackbarnes93

*wow NEWS FLASH: housemate has found out that our other house-
mate's Hinge date is actually her MSN boyfriend from when they
were at school #newcross #stuckintheattic*

Jack closed the article, which had been posted on the
website of a newspaper that he picked up on the Tube
sometimes, without reading the rest of it. It was making
him feel a bit dizzy. Things had got a little out of hand.

Still, the good news was that it looked like – maybe,
possibly – they might be about to be rescued. Among the
other responses, Jack had also been tweeted by Lewisham
Fire Brigade. They had a station just down the road.

@LondonFireBrigadeLewisham

Hi Jack. Looks like you're in a bit of a pickle! Can we help? Ken

@jackbarnes93

Hi Ken yes we are stuck ! but when we called no one could help. Jack

@LondonFireBrigadeLewisham

OK Jack, no worries. What is your address? Ken

@jackbarnes93

Hi Ken we are at 49 Rokeby Close. Jack

. *Great, thank you, Jack. We will be there as soon as we can. Ken*

Hi Ken oh great thank you!!!! Jack

After this exchange, Ken had sent Jack a DM promising they would 'dispatch a truck as soon as we can' and to 'hang in there'.

Jack reckoned you could probably rely on firemen more than you could on locksmiths.

The other good news was that the WiFi had held strong for a good fifteen minutes now – long enough for Jack to also clock that one of his tweets had been liked by someone from a reality-TV show that Jack had never watched but which he knew his sister Maisie liked. And the reality-TV person had loads of Twitter followers, which might have explained why his own mentions were going so mad. Before the connection dropped again, he saw that hundreds of new people were popping up and retweeting and favouriting and following him. He was up to almost 323 followers now! And Jack had also received a DM from someone at BBC London called Simran.

Simran said he was a senior producer and that his programme would love to send someone round to interview Jack on camera once he was out of the attic. Would that be OK? And could he keep them posted on how he was getting on?

Jack supposed so, although if they sent someone to interview him about the Twitter thread, then the others would definitely know what else he'd been tweeting about in the attic. Still, he figured they probably wouldn't mind, seeing as he was about to rescue them. He felt another surge of pride. He did wonder whether any of his bosses at Green Genie would have seen the article, or the tweets. The messages didn't seem very like him. Viral! He really hoped that, at the very least, Deepti and Flora had seen it.

Jack hadn't replied to Simran yet. It would be pretty exciting to be on the BBC, although he wished he was wearing some socks so no one could see his feet. Still, he was sure they could avoid showing his hairy toes on the television.

It was time, he decided, steeling himself. He was going to tell the others all about the firemen. He'd tell them about the Twitter thread, gloss over the details, and then they'd be out before he had to answer too many awkward questions about exactly what had happened. It was a foolproof plan. Jack stood up a little straighter, pleased with himself, and proceeded towards the group. He couldn't quite believe it would be him – not Alexa – who saved them from the attic.

'There you are,' Ellen said quietly, as he approached.

'Yes. Here I am.'

Ellen gave him a bit of a weird look.

He sat down and cleared his throat at them in greeting. It seemed a little less hostile over here now. He hoped they'd made up in his absence.

Ben rubbed his eyes. 'I'm so thirsty.'

'Me too,' said Alexa.

'Me three,' said Ellen. 'I don't know if I mentioned recently but my wee was very orange –'

'You did,' Ben said, grimly.

'Well, I can't believe none of you have had to go to the loo.' She added, 'Also, it is *very* hot in here.'

Jack was very relieved he hadn't had to use the box. Ellen was right, though, it was hot. There was a fly zooming around the open skylight in the ceiling. Jack watched it for a few loops. It kept missing the way out.

'Mind over matter,' Ben muttered.

Alexa laughed quite loudly. It wasn't that funny.

This seemed like an opening. He could say, 'Don't worry, soon you'll be able to use the real loo!' He was practising this in his head, until he realized the moment had passed, because Ellen was talking about something else.

'What's the first thing you'll do when you get out of here?'

'Probably go and see how bad the kitchen is,' Alexa muttered, drily.

'Point taken.'

Jack frowned. What if Elias had seen the article? Or the Twitter thread? He wasn't sure if Elias would remember his name, because he'd only moved into the house in September and they hadn't met that many times. But the article mentioned their address. And at least one of his tweets mentioned the name of their road – Rokeby Close. Maybe Elias would see it and explode because Jack had made his house the centre of a news story – not to mention the fact they'd flooded it. And then they'd all have to go and live somewhere else. He supposed that maybe he could go and live with Annie in the old school in Deptford, which always seemed to have space for one more. Although he wasn't a vegan, and the toilet wasn't very nice. Besides, he wanted to stay living in Rokeby Close.

He squirmed. Perhaps he should take the tweets down? The firemen were coming now, and they had the address anyway. But if he took them down, then it was less likely that someone at Green Genie would see the thread. Maybe Jack could email the website of the newspaper and ask them to take the article down? But he sort of wanted Johnny to see it – perhaps with the picture that Mia had taken of him at the festival. And Annie – Jack would love Annie to see the article.

He shook his head. He'd go ahead with telling the others. They'd be delighted. They could deal with Elias when they had to. Or rather, he hoped Alexa would.

'Um, guys,' he started, conversationally, as Ben stood up and walked to the window. 'So, this thing –'

'Hey!' Ben turned sharply, interrupting him. 'There's a fire engine coming up your street.'

'Wait, what?' Alexa jumped to her feet and crossed the room. She stood beside Ben, leaning on tiptoes to peer out of the window. 'Do you think it's for us?'

'Why would it be?' But Ellen had also sprung to her feet and marched across the room in a few paces. 'Come on, Jack,' she urged.

Jack rolled his eyes. Of course, after all that, he wouldn't even get to be the one to tell them.

23. Alexa

They were all crowded together, hanging out of the window now, watching the fire engine motoring up their street. Rokeby Close was a long road, and number 49 was in the very middle. There were a few trees lining the pavements – big, ancient, lumbering things with thick papery trunks – urban oaks, peeling and unhealthy. The fire engine looked comically large for their street, the cars lining the road like toys.

'Wait, is it stopping here?' Ellen was leaning so far out of the skylight that her voice sounded far away. 'Is it coming for us?'

Ben was doing the same. 'I don't know,' he replied. 'But it's certainly coming this way.' He took a deep breath, and cupped his mouth. 'HEY! UP HERE!'

Alexa couldn't fit into the frame, so tried instead to wave at the fire engine over their shoulders.

'Oh my God, it is,' Ellen said. 'It's stopping right outside the house.' It parked up and three firemen tumbled from the truck, dressed in T-shirts and fireproof trousers and, of course, the familiar sunshine-yellow helmets. One of them slapped the other on the shoulder. They closed the doors of the fire truck. The third fireman was carrying what looked like an axe. Alexa felt a powerful rush of relief.

Jack started to say something. 'Yes, well, I've sort of been expecting them –'

But before he could go any further, Ben interrupted. 'HEY!' he hollered again, at the top of his voice. 'WE'RE UP HERE!!'

Alexa looked at Jack, quizzically. He appeared to quail a little under her scrutiny and, instead of finishing what he had to say, concerned himself with peering out of the window at the fire engine too.

The firemen had clocked the four of them.

One of them gave the housemates a wave. 'WE'LL BE WITH YOU IN A SECOND!'

'THANKS!' Ellen shouted. 'Look at them,' she breathed.

They watched as two of the men paused on the front path. Suddenly, there was a loud crack that they could all hear from the top floor.

'Oh my God. The front door,' Ellen moaned. 'They must have smashed the front door down. We are definitely not getting the security deposit back now.'

'Yes, but we're also being rescued,' Ben pointed out. 'How else were they going to get in – wait for the locksmith, who's never coming?' He stepped back from the skylight. 'Christ, imagine being so stacked that you could smash a door down with your shoulder.' He appraised his own biceps.

They did not have time to imagine this as, almost immediately, they heard the stomping of heavy boots on the main staircase, and then the narrower stairs that led up to the attic itself.

'Hello?' called out a cheerful voice. 'We're here from the London Fire Brigade. Lewisham lot. Heard you guys were in a spot of bother.' A pause. 'We're here to rescue you.'

'In here!' Ben, Ellen and Alexa called out in eager

unison. Alexa could not help noticing that Jack was now regarding the door as though it was about to blow.

'Right, guys,' said the voice from the other side of the door.

Ben moved towards it.

'We're going to have to knock this door down to get you out of there. So can you all please make sure to stand well back? Wouldn't want to hit one of you, or we'd probably have to get an ambulance here too, eh?'

None of them replied, although Ben stepped back a few paces again.

'We're well back from the door,' Alexa shouted. Her voice sounded reedy.

There was the loud crack of wood splitting again and the blade of an axe appeared in the door. Through this crack, they could make out a yellow helmet. There was a second crack as the axe swung again, this time taking most of the door with it. The firemen wrestled with what was left of the door and then, having dismantled it, two of them ducked slightly in order to step through the large hole they'd created.

With two burly men in the room, the place suddenly felt even smaller. The taller one took off his helmet and held it under his arm. The firemen paused for a few beats as they took in the scene around them. Alexa suddenly felt like Jack's cousin, who'd got their head stuck in the railings. She hoped that no one at work would ever, ever find out about this.

'Hello,' said the smaller fireman, who was still pretty tall. He also removed his helmet in order to rest it under his arm.

'Bit of a predicament you've found yourselves in, eh?' said the first one, with a grin. He had long eyelashes and a superhero's jaw.

'And it looks like one of you didn't make it,' added the second fireman, pointing at the dead mouse. Alexa had forgotten about him. 'Poor thing,' he added.

The four of them stared at their two rescuers. As they gaped, a third fireman appeared and climbed through the splinters of the door, taking up position beside his buddies.

'Hello,' he said, waving. He faltered as he noticed the strange atmosphere.

'We're just doing introductions,' said the first fireman, clearly enjoying the moment.

Alexa's brain felt swamped, as if she were trying to drag speech and thoughts from the very bottom of some ocean. She was missing something, and she had a feeling it had something to do with Jack.

The firemen smiled back, good-natured in the face of the housemates' stupefied silence.

Eventually, the first one spoke again. 'So, first of all, which one of you is Jack from Twitter?' He beamed at them.

They all swung round to stare at Jack. He was a little pink.

Jack did a half-wave. 'Hullo,' he said, quietly.

'Nice to meet you, sir.' The first fireman waved at Jack. 'Quite the morning you've had then, eh?' He turned to the others. 'We've been following the whole story, along with the rest of the world.' He gestured to his colleagues, then added, with a bright smile, 'Sorry we took a little while — hit some traffic on the A1.'

'Wait, *what?*' Alexa said, more loudly. 'Jack, what about Twitter?'

'Jack's Twitter thread made it sound like you were in quite a lot of trouble,' said the third fireman, speaking slowly, as though waiting for them to catch up with the joke. He was the stockiest, and possibly the most handsome, of the three. 'Stuck up here, with a leak – and a bit of a domestic brewing. So we got here as soon as we could.'

'Jack, what the fuck is going on?' Ellen asked, slowly turning to look at him.

Alexa frowned. 'Your phone doesn't even work up here . . .'

Jack cleared his throat, and then cleared it again. He was definitely stalling. He said in a small voice, 'Well, the thing is . . .' He paused. 'I suppose it sort of did work, in the end.'

Alexa let this sink in.

Jack was quick to continue. 'But it was only WiFi, and it was very patchy. It came and went a lot, and I could only really get it near the window . . .' He trailed off, lamely.

She stared at him. His cheeks were blazing and he seemed to have shrunk a few inches.

'But why didn't you tell us?' she asked, disbelievingly. 'Even if the signal was rubbish, we could have used it to get out of here hours ago.'

This observation hung in the air, before a sticky silence settled, in which they all stared at Jack, who seemed to be registering the enormity of this reality.

Alexa noticed the firemen exchanging worried glances.

'Well, um, yes, but w-we're getting out of here now,' Jack stuttered, finally. 'Thanks to me.'

Alexa continued to stare at him in astonishment, trying to get her thoughts in order. 'OK, but what did it even *say* –'

But at that point, Ellen interrupted. 'Wait, fuck – sorry, first – downstairs, there was loads of water. Is it OK?' She glanced at the now open door, fearfully, as if expecting the water to be lapping at the door of the attic. 'The tap – or the sink, or something – all over the kitchen, there was water everywhere this morning, that's why we ended up here. We were trying to turn the mains off, but then the door – the handle broke – and now –' These half-details cascaded from Ellen's mouth in a rush.

'Ah, yeah, we knew about that from the thread,' said the second fireman.

Alexa frowned at Jack again.

'Don't worry – I've just turned off the water at the mains,' said the third fireman, reassuringly. 'At first glance, it looks like something might be wrong with your pressurized water hose.'

Ellen looked aghast.

'Easily fixable, though, if you get a plumber in,' he added, kindly. 'Your kitchen is in a bit of a bad way, but the hall has held up OK. Might just need recarpeting.'

'And your door will need a new lock,' said the second firemen, quickly. 'Afraid we had to force it.' He raised his hands in surrender. 'Didn't use the axe on it, though, like we did with this one. So should be easy to sort quickly,' he added, in the straightforward tone of a man for whom knocking up a drywall or fixing a busted front door was no bother.

'Fuck,' Ellen said, with the intensity of a tenant for whom a security deposit was a serious bother.

'So, how did it happen?' asked the first fireman, his tone that of the pleasant air of a man asking how the weather had been on your holiday. 'How did you get stuck up here?'

'The door handle fell off,' Ellen said, quietly. She pointed at the discarded pieces on the floor.

'So, Jack, is that what the thread said?' Alexa asked him, urgently. She was determined to get to the bottom of this. 'Just about the flood?'

'Yeah' – Ellen was concentrating now too – 'why would tweets about our kitchen flooding go *viral*?' She added, meanly, 'You don't even have any followers.'

There was an awkward pause.

Jack opened his mouth and then closed it again. He looked indignant, but also a little like he wished he could disappear.

Alexa continued to give him a hard stare.

Eventually, Ben broke the stalemate. 'Shall we perhaps get out of this attic, then?' he said, haltingly. 'Not to put too fine a point on it, but I'm absolutely bursting for a piss.'

It suddenly seemed to occur to them all, afresh, that they were still standing in the attic.

'Yes,' Ellen said, with feeling. 'Please let's get out of here.'

There was a moment of silly English politeness as no one wanted to appear rude by going first. Then Ellen muttered, 'After you,' and the firemen climbed out through the door frame. The last one picked up the mouse gingerly by the tail as he left and carried it out of the room. He was followed by Ellen, then Ben and then Jack – who, Alexa noted, got his T-shirt caught on a sliver of wood.

'One minute,' she said, quietly. 'Just going to close the skylight.'

Alexa took a little time over it, relishing the fleeting moment of solitude. Then, grasping the side of what looked like a bed headboard for balance, she climbed out of Elias's chaos for the last time, holding the box of urine at arm's length.

She carried the smelly liquid downstairs and disposed of it in the bathroom, leaving the perspex box in the bath to be (thoroughly) washed out. She locked the door and used the toilet – closing her eyes in relief that she was free and hadn't had to use the box – and then washed her hands. She gulped some water from the tap, gratefully.

When she unlocked and opened the bathroom door, she heard the din of voices from downstairs and – she winced – some splashing. Down the hall, her bedroom door was open. She peered inside.

The curtains were still pulled and the duvet was balled in the centre of the mattress, sheets a little rumpled. She resisted the urge to hide from the world. Instead, she walked downstairs to join the others, her feet squelching as she reached the hall.

24. Ellen

'Jesus, fuck,' Ellen said, in blasphemous horror, rolling up her jogging bottoms to her thighs as though she were paddling in the sea. It was dreadful, surreal. The security deposit had definitely drowned somewhere in this mess.

One of the firemen looked a little agitated.

'He'll evict us,' Ellen blurted, with a rush in her gut and her throat.

'Look at that bag.' Ben, whose jeans were also pulled up around his knees, was pointing at the back door, where a sodden tote bag was plastered against the glass.

'How do we get rid of the water?' Ellen breathed. The horror felt like bile in her throat.

The firemen exchanged glances.

'We can hose the worst of it out,' the very tall fireman began. 'You'll need to get it wet vacuumed after that, I reckon.' Then he added, cautiously, professionally, 'Are you the homeowner?'

Ellen looked at him. 'Do I look like a homeowner?' With one hand, she gestured with a flourish at her pink tracksuit bottoms. The water was cold, and she had goosebumps. 'Obviously, we rent this place. Hence the fears of eviction.'

'Righto,' replied the fireman, brightening at the opportunity to get procedural. 'Well, in that case, you should probably get in touch with the landlord – explain what's happened here. His insurance should cover most of it . . . it's not your fault.'

'Isn't it?' asked Ellen, quickly. They surely wouldn't get off that lightly. 'Trust me, the landlord will find a way to make it our fault.'

Alexa had appeared behind her.

'Well, for all he knows, we weren't in when it happened,' she said, in a half-whisper. 'And the attic door could have happened on another occasion –' She came to an abrupt halt, realizing the enormity of what they needed to explain away. 'I guess the main thing is, the whole house isn't ruined.'

It was definitely a bit ruined, but Ellen looked at Alexa gratefully. Alexa appeared to avoid her eye, although perhaps she was just looking at the cupboards flapping and the shelves swilling with dirty water. The sensible firemen might have made it all sound so easy: landlord, insurance, liberation from blame. But Ellen couldn't really imagine Elias buying that this hadn't been their fault. On one of his most recent impromptu house inspections, the man had blamed Ellen for the fact that someone was parked in front of their house so he couldn't park there himself. She wondered if there would be an indelible tide mark across everything, grime licking at their home for ever.

As if on cue, someone rapped on their open front door.

Ellen, Jack and Alexa froze.

'Hello!' said a man, brightly. A stranger appeared in the kitchen doorway, wearing a North Face windbreaker, jeans and brown shoes. His hair did not appear to move when he did. He grimaced slightly when he shifted his weight and heard the squelch of his brown lace-ups on the now dark brown carpet, but he recovered quickly, his grin wide and toothy. Ellen noticed he was holding a microphone, and from his vantage point in the dim hall, he seemed delighted to see the firemen. Behind him, hovering on the threshold, a more cautious interloper was supporting a television camera on his shoulder.

'Hello! I'm Tim Thompson, and I'm a correspondent at BBC London,' he announced brightly to the room, the line sounding trilling and fluent.

Ellen heard Jack say, 'Ah.' She turned to stare at him. He hadn't rolled his navy tracksuit bottoms up, but had simply waded in. They were now ballooning around him. He looked like a very dour clown.

'Wow, it's a bit soggy in here, eh?' Tim pointed out, still smiling toothily. 'Right. Which one of you is Jack?'

'Him,' Ben said, quickly indicating Jack. He seemed relieved that this, at least, was the right answer.

'Hello, Jack!' Tim said, about to step forward, before thinking better of it. Instead, he extended a hand tentatively – Jack was still halfway across the room in his ballooning sweatpants – and then retracted it again.

'Hello,' Jack muttered, finally, from somewhere inside his neck.

'I think my producer Simran mentioned we were coming?'

'Um, yes. I hadn't actually replied to his message, I don't think?'

'Not to worry, I found you! And you're out already! That was quick, eh?'

Ellen glared at him.

'Anyway, I'd love just a few minutes of your time to talk about your escape from the attic and the Twitter thread and' – Tim put on a flourish here – 'your new viral fame!'

Everyone stared at Jack, who was trying very hard to appear at ease.

'Jack,' Alexa said, commandingly. 'Now that we are free, will you please tell us what precisely is going on? What did your Twitter thread say? Why did it go *viral*? And why is there a man from the BBC in our kitchen?' She crossed her arms.

Alexa had said it better than she could, but Ellen felt impelled to add something for good measure. 'Yeah, spill,' she said, threateningly.

Jack now looked like a man cornered. His shoulders were slumped, his head bowed, and his clothes looked baggier than they had in the attic. He put his hand on the back of his neck and peered up at them all through his eyelashes.

'We're waiting,' Alexa added, coldly.

Realizing he couldn't put this off any longer, he took a very deep breath. 'Well, as you know, I helped to get us out,' he said, quietly. 'It was my Twitter thread that found its way to these guys.'

'Yes, I think we'd all sort of got there already,' Ellen said, drily. 'Perhaps you could enlighten us as to what precisely the Twitter thread said that seems to have got the press interested.'

'And stop stalling,' Alexa directed.

Jack opened his mouth and closed it and – in a moment of rashness – Ellen made to sprint towards him to grab the phone from his hand. Except they were both wading through water, so instead of sprinting, she started floundering. He was about two metres away. Time seemed to stand still as she stepped, comically slowly, towards him. He moved backwards in slow motion, his trousers distended and flapping.

Ellen reached him, and held out her hand.

After a pause, he surrendered the phone.

'What's your code?'

'123456,' Jack said, quietly.

'Are you joking?' She tapped it in. He was not joking.

'That's not a very secure code,' Ben pointed out.

'Maybe we should stop worrying about Jack's code and see what the Twitter thread is all about?' Alexa sounded tetchy.

Ellen found the Twitter icon. He had a hundred plus notifications – the little bubble had given up telling him precisely how many. She tapped it and opened his account. She went straight to his page and read the tweets.

It was as she had suspected. Jack had been detailing the humiliations of the last few hours: her and Ben's MSN relationship and the arguments, and even the weeing in the box. The tweets had been liked and retweeted by tens of thousands of people now. Thank God he hadn't used her name.

'El, what do the tweets say?' Alexa asked. She sounded terrified.

'Everything,' Ellen said, grimly. 'About us being in the attic and the MSN drama and me pissing in a box.'

'Jack?' Alexa sounded hurt. 'Why would you do that?'

Ellen handed the phone back to him. She felt exposed, furious, uncomfortable.

'Hope Elias doesn't see that, or we're screwed,' she said, coldly. She couldn't look at him. 'If he knows that we locked ourselves in the attic, then there's no getting away with anything.' She wished toothy Tim weren't here to witness this.

'Sorry,' Jack said, limply. He was staring at his submerged feet. 'I was only trying to help . . .' A pause. 'And I did, in the end. I got us out.'

'Yeah, but you also humiliated me on the internet,' Ellen said, brusquely.

'Why didn't you say something?' Alexa asked. 'We could have all done the thread together.'

'Well, it probably wouldn't have got as many retweets, without him sharing all the intimate personal details.' Ellen bit her lip. She couldn't believe meek Jack had done something so underhand. She wanted to shake him.

'I'm sorry,' he said, miserably. 'I thought you'd be pleased.'

Alexa made an infuriated noise. 'Obviously, we're glad you got us out.'

He glanced at her, hopefully, but she remained stony-faced.

Ellen narrowed her eyes.

The awkward silence was broken by the sound of one of the firemen, who was sploshing down the few steps to the dining area to save the tote bag. Having done so, he placed it gently on the side of the table, which was marooned in the centre of the flood like an island. He looked up, as if to say something, before thinking better of it and sploshing back up the stairs to join his buddies.

'Shall we go prep the hoses and see if we can get some of this water extracted?' asked the stocky fireman.

His colleagues nodded and squeezed past Tim, who seemed rather awed to be in their company. The cameraman also hopped out of the way. They all listened to the sound of the men's footsteps squelching in the hall. Jack was very pink.

'Well, er, thanks for rescuing us, mate,' Ben said into the silence. 'I might, um' – he looked at Alexa, meaningfully – 'maybe, go home?'

'Yes, um, your stuff's upstairs, I think. Do you want to . . . ?' She trailed off, pointing at the door.

They both edged past Tim, Alexa apologizing as she did so. Ellen was still watching Jack. He was staring at the water.

'Well!' said Tim. 'Jack, do you have time just to do a quick interview, outside?' He stepped marginally closer, so he could catch a better look at Jack. 'You could get changed, maybe?' he added, spotting Jack's tracksuit bottoms. 'Or not – we'll be shooting from the waist up anyway, so it doesn't really matter about' – he paused for a second, to work out how to phrase it delicately – 'your trousers.'

Tim looked at Ellen. 'Hey, we could get you on too! You could give *your* side of all this?' He cocked an eyebrow.

'No way,' Ellen snapped. This day had got worse in ways she had never imagined. 'I'm going to my room. Or whatever's left of it.'

She started wading her way back across the kitchen, and squelched down the hall, one of the legs of her tracksuit slipping down her thigh with each wet step.

Ellen pushed the door and stood on the threshold of her bedroom. The curtains were still drawn roughly. She flicked on the light switch beside the door and noticed that the water had reached her room, though only barely. It had seeped through from the damp hallway and formed an uneven oval patch that stretched from her bedroom door towards the middle of the room. Luckily, it hadn't caught anything important in its path: a beach towel, a copy of a freesheet newspaper dated from September the previous year, a pair of knickers. Her bedroom felt unfamiliar, like she had returned to it after a long time abroad. It certainly had the air of someone who had left in a hurry.

She squelched over the damp patch towards her bed and lay like a starfish for a few minutes before realizing that the creeping chill from her feet was not death's cold embrace but, in fact, her wet socks. Perhaps death would be more welcome than the Elias tirade that must, surely, be coming. Ellen yanked herself up, wincing as she pulled off one sock and then the other. She balled them and flung the pair towards the damp threshold of the room, then collapsed backwards again. She felt exhausted, her bones aching. It was the hangover, but also the weight of all the different ways she'd fucked up that day. She stared, without seeing, at a patch of peeling plaster in the centre of the ceiling, near the naked bulb hanging from its flex, closing her eyes periodically to bring them back into focus.

Her bedroom door was ajar, and from the front doorstep she could hear Tim twittering and Jack's indistinct responses. As she stared at the door, willing it to close, she heard footsteps on the stairs to the first floor: Ben and Alexa. She sat up – her stomach muscles protesting – and cocked her head to one side, trying to listen to them over the inane din of Tim and Jack.

'. . . text you,' Ben possibly said, although it could have been something else ('Bless you'? 'Atishoo'?).

She thought she heard Alexa murmur something back, though at the same time, Tim started telling Jack to stand a little closer – 'I don't bite!' – and then there were more footsteps and the front door slammed with a thunderous clap. Ellen held her breath. Was Alexa still in the corridor? Or was that the creak of her footfall on the stairs? As she wondered, there was a smart rap on her bedroom door. In response, Ellen flopped backwards on the bed.

'Ellen?' Alexa called out, uncertainly. 'Can I come in?'

'Yeah.' Her nerves jangled.

Ellen sat up as Alexa opened the door. She had changed into black leggings and a black sweatshirt, and had swept her hair into a bun on the top of her head. She had her trainers on. Alexa stepped over the wet patch in one stride and stood in the middle of the floor, left hand massaging her right shoulder.

'Hey,' she said, quietly, taking another careful step, then stopped smartly.

'Your room's OK, then?' Standing in the centre of its chaos, she looked petite and ordered.

'Yeah,' Ellen replied. 'I mean, it's a mess but . . .' She didn't finish. An apology was overdue, though she didn't know where to begin.

'Ben's gone,' Alexa said, more quietly.

Ellen swallowed.

'And Jack is still with the interviewer outside.'

'Hmm,' Ellen started. 'Yes. I'm fairly furious about all of that, actually.'

'Me too,' Alexa agreed. She moved cautiously towards the edge of the bed, and sat on the end, crossing one Lycra'd thigh over the other. She started fidgeting with the bedspread. 'I can't believe he did it all in secret. I didn't have a clue that's what he was up to that entire time.'

'No. Although, I suppose we were a bit distracted.'

There was a long, loaded pause.

'I'm sorry,' Ellen said, finally. 'About what I said to Ben. It was thoughtless and silly.'

Alexa had stopped fidgeting and was sitting very still now.

'I lashed out. I was still angry, I think.'

Alexa looked rather sad.

Ellen moved closer to her and grabbed her hand. 'Look' – she squeezed Alexa's cool palm now – 'I'm really, really sorry. I didn't mean to say it. In my head it sounded a little more funny and a little less spiteful. But it was horrible. I'm really sorry.'

They heard the squelch of footsteps down the hall, then the sound of the busted front door opening and closing.

Ellen held her breath.

'I know you didn't mean it,' Alexa said, finally. She was very still and tense, but when she spoke again, she sounded more like herself. 'Really. It's all fine. What's done is done. And he gave me a kiss when he left, so there's that.'

'I think he really likes you,' Ellen said, in a small voice.

'Maybe,' Alexa said. 'Anyway,' her voice was businesslike now, 'I don't think we can stay here until the ground floor has dried out. I'll email Elias in a minute and tell him what happened. With a few details omitted, obviously. Might not bother telling him about the damage to either door for now, and I think if we just foot the locksmith's bill ourselves, then we can avoid him finding out about the front door. We can pay to get the attic door fixed ourselves, I guess? And then I suppose I'm going to have to go and stay at my dad's.' She rolled her eyes. 'I'm sure Jack can stay at his sister's. Do you reckon you could stay at Kayleigh's, or something? I'd invite you to stay at Dad's but I think it would be a bit of a squeeze,' she added, awkwardly.

Ellen stared back at her. She couldn't work out if Alexa was still cross. She didn't think so. But it still bothered her that they'd now be separated for weeks, giving Ellen no chance to gradually make amends.

'Oh God, of course – don't worry,' Ellen replied, hastily. 'Yeah, I'll just text Kay. There's always room on her uncomfortable sofa bed for one more.'

'Someone will need to wait in for the locksmith. We need to get the front door fixed before we can leave the house. Otherwise, someone might steal everything we own.'

'Yes. Which would clearly be a tragedy.' Ellen gestured to a bag stuffed full of The Flowdown leaflets that she was supposed to have stuffed through doors in south-east London a few weekends ago. Instead, she'd gone to the pub and left a pile in the ladies. 'I can do it – wait in for the locksmith. I'll just go to Kayleigh's a bit later. No problem.'

'Brilliant,' Alexa replied, politely. 'Thank you.'

'No worries.' Ellen attempted a joke, 'About time I did something useful today.'

Alexa smiled. A small smile, but a start.

25. Ellen

Lee Two Wheels Good
Hey, sorry I left quite early yest
Had to get up for cycling
How was the rest of your night

Ellen
Got drunk, got home, got more drunk, got locked in an attic

Kayleigh
Oh my godddddddddd
What even happened last night
Have just ordered McDonalds straight to bed
Only ronald can save me now

Ellen
OK Kay
So I have had. Quite. A. Morning.
Appreciate is now like 2pm
Anyway, bit complicated to explain but any chance I can come stay at yours???
Long story short our house is flooded

Kayleigh
Wait rewind wtf flooded??
But yeah babe no problem
Just get an uber here we can watch a film in bed
I'll save u a mcnugget (i got 40 don't judge me)

Ellen

OK amazing THANK YOU

Just gonna get some stuff together and have to wait for a locksmith

But then will get in an Uber

What's your address again

?

Kayleigh

17 morgan street e3

Plz bring me a diet coke when you come i finished my milkshake

Linda

Just checking you're still free on 23 August for Auntie Nora's garden party? She'd love to see you. Dad and I will be setting off from home about lunchtime, so could give you a lift. Drive takes about 45 minutes – traffic permitting. Love Mum x

PS are you still a vegetarian? Will have to let Nora know.

Ellen locked her phone, turned it over on the bedside table and left it to charge. It was April and Ellen had absolutely no idea whether she was free in August. Moreover, she had been vegetarian for about three weeks when she was fourteen. She rolled on to her side and lay curled up, her mind blank. The hangover that had ebbed all day – such a long, merciless day – licked at her insides again. She hoped that Alexa really had forgiven her.

She heard the front door bang again. She rolled her eyes, and groaned. Before she could get up, there was another knock on the door.

'Yes,' she called out, tersely, hoping it wasn't one of the firemen, then propped herself up on her elbows so she could see the door.

Jack pushed it open, slowly. He was hugging himself, his teeth chattering slightly. His trousers were still sopping wet and his feet were still bare, hairy toes wiggling on the carpet. 'Hi,' he said, softly.

Ellen extended an arm to reluctantly welcome him into her bedroom.

Jack darted into her room, glancing furtively behind him as he entered. He closed the door. He was breathing as though he'd just finished a jog around the block.

She sat up properly, crossed her arms and raised an eyebrow. This better be good.

'Um – OK,' Jack started, unpromisingly. He caught her expression and seemed to steel himself. 'Look, Ellen, I'm sorry about the Twitter thing. I didn't' – he took a deep breath – 'it sort of got a bit out of hand. I mean, no one usually cares about my Twitter.' He glanced at her, hazarding a small smile, which Ellen, in spite of herself, returned. 'But at first, I just hoped it would maybe help to get us out of the attic. And then, well, when people started liking it . . . and then more people saw it and then . . . well. I liked it, I suppose.' He glanced up again. 'Everyone thought I was funny and . . .' He trailed off.

Ellen watched him, hopping from one foot to the other, damp still spreading up his thighs. She exhaled through her nose and rolled her eyes.

He looked anguished.

'Oh, for God's sake, Jack – it's fine,' she said, suddenly utterly over the whole thing. 'Look, you got us out, didn't you? In the end.'

Jack smiled uncertainly, as though he was still waiting for a blow to land.

'I mean, I'd have preferred you didn't broadcast the painful details of my personal life to a large audience. And you could have told us you had signal and saved us a few hours of misery.'

Jack looked terrified.

She continued, 'But to be honest, I can't be arsed to have a fight with anyone else today.' She sighed. 'So. There you have it. My forgiveness.'

Jack still looked rather anguished. 'I saw Ben leave when I was doing my . . . interview.' He said the last part virtually in a whisper.

'Yeah, he's left,' Ellen said, flatly. 'We'll have to, as well, I think. Alexa is going to email Elias and tell him what happened – sort of – and then I think we'll all have to stay somewhere else.'

Noticing Jack's stricken face, she added, 'Just for a bit. Provided he doesn't evict us, I'm sure we can all move back in.' She wasn't actually sure, but it seemed easier to pretend.

'I guess I'll go call Maisie,' he said, resignedly. 'I can probably go stay with her for a bit.'

'Cool,' Ellen said, wearily.

There was a pained silence; she could tell Jack was trying to conjure the words to say something reassuring. She noticed his toes were curling again.

'Um, Ellen, I do think – well.' He looked at her properly, emboldened. 'I believe your story. About Ben. I think it was him. The guy who –'

'Thanks, Jack,' she interrupted. She wanted him to stop, though she wasn't sure why. She sighed. 'It doesn't really matter. But thanks.'

Jack nodded. He stood awkwardly for another minute,

before Ellen pointed limply towards her bedroom door and Jack took her clumsy cue to leave.

Once she could hear his footsteps on the stairs to the first floor, Ellen jabbed at her phone again.

Alexa had already sent Elias an email, cc'ing them all in.

From: alexa_ingram@gmail.com
To: elias@southeast_homes.com
CC: jackbarnes@greengenie.london; ellenfisher@gmail.com
Subject: 49 Rokeby Close

Dear Elias,

I hope you are well.

I'm sorry to disturb you on a Saturday with unfortunate news: there has been a flood at 49 Rokeby Close. I'm afraid the kitchen is submerged. We were all out when it happened.

We have got rid of the worst of the water, but the pipe and the hall carpet will need professional attention. Please contact me at your earliest convenience to arrange a time for all of this to happen.

In the meantime, we have all made arrangements to stay elsewhere.

My sincerest apologies,
Alexa

Ellen was glad Alexa hadn't mentioned the mutilated attic door too. Still, she felt sick at the thought of Elias reading it. She buried her head in the duvet to block the world out.

26

BBC London Evening News bulletin

TIM THOMPSON: *[Holding a microphone]* I'm standing here with Jack Barnes, who – along with his housemates and a special guest – has just been rescued from the attic of his home in New Cross! *[Turns to Jack, grinning]* So, how're you feeling now, Jack?

JACK BARNES: *[Casts a nervous look at the camera]* Um, yeah – good, thank you.

TIM: *[Turning back to camera]* For those who haven't followed this story – a quick recap! This morning, at around 8 a.m., Jack and his housemates found themselves *trapped in the attic* of their three-storey house on Rokeby Close in New Cross, after the door handle *fell off.* *[Pause for effect]* After a locksmith failed to appear, Jack decided to take matters into his own hands and start a Twitter thread about their misadventures that went viral. Finally, the good guys at Lewisham Fire Station saw the thread and came to rescue them from the attic!

[Tim turns to Jack, and positions the big microphone under his chin. Jack glances down at it, then at the camera, then at the floor.]

TIM: Jack, how did it feel to be rescued in such dramatic circumstances?

JACK: *[Slightly more animated]* Um, yeah . . . well . . . yeah, it feels pretty great to be out. It was really hot in the attic.

TIM: And how did it feel when your Twitter thread started going viral?

JACK: Well, it was a bit of a surprise really – I didn't . . . *[Trails off, with inaudible muttering]*

TIM: But now, Jack, there's a bit more to this story than just you and your housemates getting stuck in the attic, isn't there? Can you tell us a bit *more [knowing glance to camera]* about what was in the Twitter thread that made it go viral?

JACK: Um, well, you see, I don't know if I can really explain – it's not really fair – I didn't . . . *[Trails off, with inaudible muttering]*

TIM: *[With the air of a slick professional who will not let the evident discomfort of his interviewee stop him from barrelling right on]* Well, as it happened, it was a bit of a soap opera. I believe you should be able to see some of the tweets on your screen right now.

[Item cuts to screenshots of Jack's tweets.]

TIM: So, as you can see, it sounds like it was quite the drama up there for a time! Jack, when you started sharing the intimate details of your housemates' lives online, did you think that it would get so much attention?

[Jack looks off camera, as though he has spotted a predator approaching at speed.]

TIM: Quite the drama, eh, Jack? But what we really want to know is, have the housemates kissed and made up?

[Jack looks at the floor.]

JACK: Um, I can't really say much about that, except that . . . *[a pause as he looks up and straight into the camera]* I'm sorry to Ellen if I made her embarrassed about anything. I didn't –

TIM: *[Interrupting]* Oh dear, it certainly sounds – dramatic! And any words for the hero firemen who rescued you and your housemates and *[grins to camera, crescendoing to a big moment]* their date?

[Jack shakes his head. He is looking at his shoes again.]

TIM: Righto. I'm afraid that's all we have time for, I think – but thanks for sharing your extraordinary story with us. Aakash, it's back to you in the studio.

27. Ben

Ben had returned home to little fanfare. He supposed that none of his housemates had thought it particularly strange he hadn't come home last night. He'd said on the Whats-App group that he was going on a last-minute date, and when he'd left the house, he'd rather hoped that he wouldn't be returning at all that evening. His three housemates were out now, though the debris of a cooked breakfast littered the kitchen: a frying pan slick with bacon grease; a pot encrusted with dried baked beans in the sink; a stack of dry toast on a plate in the middle of the table. He picked up a slice and turned on his heel, chewing on the cold bread as he climbed two flights of stairs to the second floor, to his own attic bedroom. He sat on the end of his bed, still wearing his jacket and shoes.

The events of the past sixteen hours presented themselves in random vignettes. Alexa, with a Negroni in hand, across the table at Penny's. Jack peering at him kindly. Ellen scrutinizing him, without any kindness. Alexa's bedroom, grappling with each other's clothes, a little self-consciously. Ellen accusing him of dumping Alexa. Three firemen breaking down the door of the attic. Hollering out of the attic window. The door handle coming clean off in his hand.

Another image presented itself: saying goodbye to Alexa in the hallway of 49 Rokeby Close, the busted front door open and swinging gently in the breeze.

'Well, that was quite a date,' Alexa had said, lightly. Now that they were no longer sitting on the floor of an attic but stood opposite one another in the hallway, he noticed again how small she was. Her eyes were searching, hopeful.

'Yeah – have to say, I didn't expect any of this when I messaged you last night,' Ben had replied, with a shy grin. 'Still, all's well that ends well, eh?' He hadn't been quite sure what he meant by that.

'Yes,' Alexa had said carefully. 'Well, I hope so.'

Ben had shifted his weight on the hallway carpet, his foot making a squelching sound.

'Look,' she'd added, squirming, 'I'm sorry about the thing . . . about what Ellen said. I think things got a bit . . . confused.' She had shaken her head and switched tone. 'Anyway. I had fun. Except for the bit where you locked us in an attic and Jack had to sacrifice us all to the internet in order to set us free.'

Ben had laughed heartily at this. He liked how quick she was.

'Yeah. Thank God for Jack's instinct for social media, eh?'

'He definitely got lucky.'

A pause, and then Ben had gone for a kiss. It had been short and chaste, but it had happened. Afterwards, they'd had an only slightly awkward hug.

'I'll text you,' Ben had said, as he pulled away.

'Right,' Alexa had replied, brightly.

Ben had decided he'd walk home. It would only take about half an hour and he had spent five hours sitting under those oppressive eaves. He could do with a reminder that the sky was, in fact, limitless. On a sunny spring

Saturday, south-east London was thronged with people: at the cluster of cafes around Queen's Road, twenty-somethings nursed coffees, though some had already started on pints. Harried mothers corralled children down the road, towards the big Morrisons. As he rounded Rye Lane, he narrowly avoided being knocked over by two boys riding a single Boris bike, one perched in the basket, his knees around his ears. The boys laughed as he leaped out of the way. By the time he'd made it to his front door, there was a light sweat on his forehead.

Ben shook his head to return himself to the moment. He shrugged off his jacket and unlaced his shoes. He would text Alexa, he decided. He really wanted to. He'd been delighted about last night – their date, what happened afterwards. Even the attic hadn't been so bad – he'd enjoyed sitting beside her, watching her movements, trying to read her mind – until everything had started to go wrong.

Ellen. Her accusation that he'd been ghosting Alexa had struck a nerve, it was true. Ben had been dithering about Alexa – before last night, anyway. He hadn't been sure what he wanted. Ellen's remarks had made him feel exposed. And he'd been worn out by the ordeal of the other accusations, the ones about MSN. Ben hadn't expected to have to fight on another front. But he would text Alexa and try to put things right. He'd ask her out again. He really hoped she'd say yes. Despite that clumsy kiss in the hallway.

But Ellen's story. He didn't understand any of it. She was so certain that he was *that* person. And certainly, he almost could have been. There was no doubt that their lives had run in near tandem: they knew all the same people, had been to all those same parties. It was a small place. And she had recognized his MSN name immediately. So *why* didn't he remember her? Could he really not remember this whole section of his life? A disturbing thought. Ben supposed there must be huge swathes of time that he couldn't remember, but the idea that he could simply erase something that had been so momentous to another person did not sit well with him. Not to mention the fact that if he had done it, it would have been an unkind thing to do. Could that be why he couldn't remember any of it?

But it simply didn't make sense. He had been going out with Imogen for the period Ellen referred to. He wouldn't have two-timed her with some girl from the internet. He remembered – cringing slightly – how loopy he'd been about her: their saccharine nicknames and text message after text message in which they'd make rote statements of mutual adoration.

Ben reached behind him. His laptop was on the bed. He opened its shell and booted the thing into life. He'd closed it on some long-read about artificial intelligence that he had no intention of finishing; he opened a new tab and pulled up Facebook. He found her without difficulty: Imogen Berry. Friends since January 2009. Her profile picture was her and a man he presumed was her current boyfriend. In fact, it seemed he was her fiancé. As Ben scrolled down her page he found a post from February: 'He liked it so he put a ring on it.' Lots of people from school had added likes and hearts and congratulations.

He went into her photo albums. He knew the one he was looking for: she'd made it after they'd gone on a day trip up to London. He wondered if she would have deleted it, but no, it was still there: *he* was still there, so skinny, with his floppy fringe in his eyes, and his big brown loafers that he'd hoped would help them get into pubs in the capital (they hadn't). The album was dated April 2009, which – he reckoned – would have been the same time as he was supposed to be involved with Ellen. He remembered that day in London quite well, considering it was a decade or so ago. They'd gone for lunch at a PizzaExpress near Victoria Station. There was a picture of Imogen smiling, holding a glass of Coke, a straw between pouting lips. Ben could not imagine taking Alexa on that sort of date. He was fairly sure that after PizzaExpress they'd gone to Oxford Street so that Imogen could go shopping. And then they'd tried unsuccessfully to get into a series of pubs near there, before getting the train back home.

He closed the laptop's lid. He stared at the wall again for a few minutes, until he thought he could hear his housemates downstairs. He heaved himself up from the bed, shuffled to the door and opened it. There was a distant clatter of pans in the sink. He took the two flights of stairs at pace. He craved some uncomplicated conversation.

'Alright,' he said, as he wandered into the kitchen.

Max and his boyfriend, Matteo, were sitting at the kitchen table, Matteo eating a bag of Nik Naks. Pete was at the sink, scrubbing at the baked-bean-encrusted pan.

'Aha, Casanova returns,' Matteo said, raising an eyebrow.

'Ha,' Ben replied, flushing slightly with his own success, in spite of everything.

'So?' Pete asked, without looking up from the sink. 'Good date, then?'

'Well, in a manner of speaking, yes.'

They all waited, expectantly.

'Date was great,' Ben continued. He walked to the table and joined Max and Matteo, who offered him a Nik Nak, which he gratefully accepted. 'Yeah, date was great, and so was the bit afterwards.' He caught Max's eye; he was grinning. 'In fact, it was all great until I accidentally got us all locked in the attic for, like, five hours.'

Matteo started laughing, disbelievingly.

'Wait – what?' Pete put the pan down. 'You pervert.'

'Not like that,' Ben said, exasperated. Pete found suggestiveness in everything. He filled them all in on the day's dramatic events.

As Ben had hoped, they all fell about laughing.

'The fire brigade?' Pete asked. 'Like you're a cat up a tree.'

'Yeah, a truck, busted the front door down, smashed the attic door with an axe . . . the full service. Kind of exciting, if it wasn't also pretty embarrassing.'

Max laughed.

'They definitely had better things to do. Imagine a house burned down because they were up there rescuing you!'

'Thanks, Pete.' Ben slapped his friend on the shoulder.

'At least you're out, eh?' Matteo picked up the Nik Naks again and burrowed in for the remaining few.

'Yeah.' Ben decided he wouldn't – couldn't – tell them about 'rainham_romeo1991'.

'You going to see her again, then?' Max asked. He slung his arm around Matteo's shoulders. 'The date, I mean.'

'Alexa,' Ben supplied.

'Yeah, Alexa. Are you going to see her again?'

'I want to.' Ben shrugged.

'Nice,' Matteo said, approvingly.

There was a companionable silence. Pete had returned to scrubbing the saucepan, banging the rim off the inside of the sink.

Ben winced. 'Right, I need a shower. What are you guys up to for the rest of the day?'

'Me and Matteo are going to watch the football,' Max said.

'Might go for a walk,' Pete suggested. 'Up Telegraph Hill.'

'I could be up for that,' Ben said. 'Can we take some beers?'

'Definitely.'

'Cool. See you in a bit, then.'

He went back upstairs and straight into the bathroom on the first floor. It had not been cleaned in some time. There were loo roll tubes littering the floor, blobs of toothpaste in the sink, and the corner of the shower was sprouting blooms of black mould. Nostalgically, Ben remembered the cleanliness of Alexa's bathroom. He turned on the water, climbed into the shower, and – after trial and error – worked out which of the four shampoo bottles on the floor of the shower actually contained any liquid. Once his body was clean, he gave his teeth a good scrub with what he hoped was his own toothbrush, and climbed the stairs to his bedroom. He was still deep in thought.

He sat back down on the end of his bed, towel around his waist. He picked up a tennis ball that was sitting on his floor and started bouncing it idly. It still didn't add up.

His sister! Maybe Ava would be able to shed some light on it. He and Ava had always been close – they were only two years apart in age. In fact, it was through Ava that he had met Imogen – they'd both been at St James's together. He WhatsApped her.

Hi Aves, how are you?

He put his phone down on the bed and started hunting for some clothes. His drawers were fairly barren – second-tier T-shirts and his more ancient boxer shorts. After some consideration, he pulled on a blue tee from Bristol Fresher's Week 2009, and a set of boxers with a hole in the waistband. He remembered his jeans were still in the bathroom. He nipped down, grabbed them and climbed into them on the landing, before running up the stairs back to his bedroom.

He prodded at his phone. Ava had responded.

Hi brother!

Been up all night

Ben laughed. Ava was lots of fun. He responded.

Big one eh

She replied.

Rozina's bday got a tiny bit out of hand

I'm at some house in Homerton now

Need to make a move soon

How are you?

He remembered the task at hand.

Had a really weird night myself

Well day actually

Will tell you more when i next see you

Is a bit of a long story

Anyway what I need to know right now is dyu remember me ever having an MSN girlfriend I spoke to loads in 2009?

Ava started typing, then stopped. Ben watched the screen. She started again.

You are really messing with my fragile mind this morning
No I do not remember much of 2009

Ben replied quickly.

Well obv neither do i

She was still typing.

But no I do not remember your MSN girlfriend you weirdo

Ben smiled.

Point taken

She was still typing.

I remember Oli being on MSN more than you tbf
Coz he'd be on the computer in the living room and I could never get on it coz he was chirpsing some girl unsuccessfully

He laughed again.

Hahaha!
Poor Ol

Thanks
Now go home and go to sleep you lunatic
Let's get a drink soon

Ava sent a crystal ball emoji back.

Ben searched for Oli's name in WhatsApp. He hadn't spoken to his younger brother over text since February. Gallingly, Oliver was now doing a PhD at Oxford, after three years and a master's at UCL.

Hey Ol!
How's Ox?
Hope all going well
Wanted to ask you a question – can you give me a ring later?
Nothing serious just long story

He closed his phone and dropped it on the bed. He wondered what Alexa was doing now: whether she'd already left the house for her dad's place in Wimbledon.

Ben decided it was too early to text her. He'd do it when he got back from his walk.

Right now, he needed food. He stuffed his phone into his back pocket and then skipped down the stairs, to find Pete at the kitchen table.

'Hi,' Pete said, looking up from a copy of the *Guardian*.

'Just going to have some toast and then I'm ready when you are, mate,' Ben replied.

'We're out of bread,' Pete said, without looking up.

There was nothing like a stomp up a very steep hill to blow the cobwebs away – or rather, to help Ben forget that for a large part of today, he had been imprisoned inside the same four walls, with limited prospects of escape. When he and Pete returned, their ears a little pink – it had been blustery at the top of Telegraph Hill – Ben felt restored, if also knackered. He took the stairs back up to his room at a plod and lay down on top of his double bed.

He was dimly aware that his room was chaos. Laundry tumbled from a basket in the corner. On his desk were piles of thumbed magazines and pamphlets from exhibitions; a tangle of cables and USB sticks; balled-up socks, some paired, some not. On the floor were more clothes – plenty of sports kit, which might explain the slightly musty smell – plus a pair of football boots, crusted with mud and blades of mulchy grass, and lots of books. He closed his eyes to shut it all out.

He'd told Pete the full story, in the end, because he was still rather distracted by it all. After a few minutes of laughter – 'Sorry, mate, it's too funny!' – Pete had agreed it was an extraordinary coincidence and sympathized with

Ben's (growing) concern that he might, indeed, have simply forgotten several months of his life. Noticing that his friend had grown rather melancholy, Pete had geed Ben up by asking about Alexa.

'You like her, though?' he'd asked, gruffly. Pete didn't really do feelings.

Ben had duly muttered his own awkward reply.

'Yeah, I do. She's really quick. And kind of high-powered at work, I think.' He'd added, more loudly, 'Plus, she's really fit.'

Pete had raised his eyebrows, appreciatively. 'Sounds good, man. Sounds good.' A pause. 'So, what will you do about the housemate? Is it going to be a problem?'

Ben had paused. A group of teenagers were daring each other to run at full pelt down the hill until they all, inevitably, fell over like dominos.

'I dunno. Should try and put it behind us, I guess. But I still want to know what really happened, you know?' He had looked at Pete, who shrugged. 'Because then, if she's got the wrong guy –'

'– she owes you an apology.'

'Right. But then if it was me – well, then I can apologize sincerely. And then hopefully that'll be enough.' A heavy sigh. 'I don't know. Going to have to do some detective work.'

Pete had slapped him on the back by way of sympathy.

Ben sat up now. He glanced at his watch: it was almost 6 p.m. He could definitely text Alexa now. He squeezed his phone out of his jeans pocket, and noticed that Oli had replied to his message.

Hi Ben. All good in Oxford, thank you – how is London? Yes – of course, I will ring you this week if that is OK? Love, Oli x

Ben smiled. Oli had not yet mastered the fluency of WhatsApp. It reminded Ben of texting their mother.

Yeah mate, just ring me sometime this week

Around every evening

Now: Alexa. Ben looked at his message thread with her. Their texts from last night seemed like they belonged to two entirely different people.

He scrolled back down to the end of their messages and tapped out a text.

Well that was an absolutely mad morning eh

Satisfied, he hit send, then flopped backwards on to the bed. Maybe he'd order a pizza.

28. Alexa

From: elias@southeast_homes.com
To: alexa_ingram@gmail.com
CC: jackbarnes@greengenie.london; ellenfisher@gmail.com
Subject: Re: 49 Rokeby Close

ALEXANDRA

What do you MEAN that there has been a FLOOD at 49
Rokeby Road?
   If you have BROKEN a PIPE you will PAY for the PIPE and
another thing the KITCHEN was put in in the last FIVE years
and the fixtures and fittings are expensive please see the
inventory for more INFORMATION.
   PLEASE can you respond to this email ASAP as possible
ALEXANDRA I need to know more about the FLOOD
   THIS IS SERIOUS!!!!!!!!!!!

Elias
PS also the carpets are custom MADE

It took Alexa a few reads of this email to confirm that it
was something she did not wish to deal with 'ASAP as possible'. Also, the carpets were absolutely not custom made.

She would not respond herself but would, instead, wave
the email in front of her father, who was at least – for all
his many other faults – a senior partner in a London law

firm. Perhaps he could cross-reference it with their tenancy agreement, and help her draft something official. Elias would, surely, be chastened by a formal-sounding notice from someone with an email signature reading Hunter, Dacre & McCarthy, Alexa thought, hopefully.

She glanced up at the electronic board on the platform at New Cross. Noting her train wasn't due for seventeen minutes, she lowered herself on to one of the cold metal benches along the concourse. For a Saturday afternoon, the platform at New Cross Gate station was fairly quiet, and only a few other passengers were scattered around. Cantankerous clouds stretched over the huge Sainsbury's megastore next door. Hoping she wouldn't be observed, Alexa opened her phone camera, turned it to selfie mode and squinted into the screen. She grimaced at the face in the camera, wishing she didn't look so washed out. As she was squinting into her screen, it lit up: Dad. She closed the camera and opened the text.

Can't wait to see you, love — will be out all afternoon but back by the evening. Let's open a bottle of red!!! Xxx

Thank goodness she had keys to her father's flat. In her bag, besides the keys, she had a spare set of gym kit, PJs, her make-up and a few changes of work clothes. She wasn't sure how long she'd be exiled from Rokeby Close.

She leaned back in the cold chair, the memory of the morning gnawed at her. She and Ben had parted sweetly but a little awkwardly; she couldn't help imagining the morning that should have been: saying goodbye with a proper kiss, after coffee. Perhaps they might even have gone for brunch at the small cafe with the sticky tables, exorbitant prices and staff who wore tiny beanies on their heads and always forgot your order the first time around. Or perhaps, Alexa reflected evenly, it might still have been awkward. Perhaps he might have shuffled out early that morning, without so much as a backward glance. Eight minutes now. She did really hope he'd text. She really, really hoped Ellen hadn't ruined everything. As she was settling into this anxiety, a pre-prepared announcement rang out from loudspeakers and Alexa glowered at the interruption.

And then there was Elias! She worried their landlord would charge them thousands of pounds to fix the house. Alexa supposed she should text the others to tell them not to panic about the email – she knew Ellen would, right now, be panicking – and that she was planning to enlist her father's help to sort things out. She hunted through WhatsApp to find the underused house group – '49 Rokeby', it was called, with house and sunshine emojis.

The last message had been sent on a Saturday in early March. (Alexa had been wondering if anyone had heard the doorbell ring that morning as she'd been expecting a parcel and the app had told her an abortive delivery had been attempted. There had been no answer.) She started tapping out a message.

Hey guys

She paused, without hitting send, watching the cursor flash, then started typing again.

Just to say ignore the response from Elias for now. I am going to get my dad on the case and get him to help draft a message back. I'll dig the tenancy agreement out of my emails. So basically don't panic. I'll keep you both posted. Hope you both have somewhere to stay!! Speak soon X

She sent it, then put her phone back in the zip pocket of her jacket. Five minutes until the train. She leaned back on the metal chair and watched a pigeon tack unevenly down the platform.

She spent the evening folded into her father's sofa – he was not yet back, though she'd opened a red from the rack anyway, feeling a little decadent, confirming first via a quick google that it was a satisfyingly expensive one. She picked up the remote and flicked unenthusiastically through the TV channels, barely concentrating. Every few minutes she picked up her phone, prodded the button, and then put it down again.

Her father's flat was a two-bedroom property inside a new build – and she'd lost count of how many of these he'd moved into since the divorce. He would up sticks on the slightest pretence: a pipe he swore whistled at dawn; a neighbour whose voice carried; a sticky latch on a balcony door. As always, this latest model was populated with furniture that she recognized from the house in Sussex – like the large mahogany coffee table that didn't really go with the grey corner sofa (new) that she was sitting on. There was some evidence of her father's fairly new girlfriend Priya around the place – Clinique in the bathroom cabinet, an elegant linen robe on the back of the door – but it didn't look like she'd moved in just yet. A stack of magazines on the coffee table confirmed that, besides motorcycles, her father had enthusiastically taken to the sort of grunting, alpha exercise that several of the other male junior civil servants in her department also enjoyed.

Restless, Alexa picked up her phone again and started:

there was a WhatsApp from Ben. She set her wine glass down carefully, and muted the television. She scrunched her toes – snug in their bed socks – and released them again before she opened the message.

Well that was an absolutely mad morning eh

A nervous bark. She was, at least, not (yet) being ghosted.

Throwing custom and caution to the wind, she started typing back in the box immediately, not drafting and redrafting in her Notes. Her father's cat, Bumble – a fluffy, spoiled madam with hair that shed everywhere – sashayed into the living room and leaped on to the sofa, stretching out, her claws catching on the sofa's expensive grey expanse. She typed, nudging the cat gently with her foot.

Yes, certainly not what I expected . . .

Alexa hit send. He appeared online; the ticks went blue almost instantaneously. He was typing.

How's the house now?

Alexa sat up slightly, alert despite the soporific effect of the wine. Bumble protested at this sudden movement by digging her claws into the sofa. Alexa replied.

Ha

Last thing I saw, the firemen were scooping water out with a bucket

AND our sociopathic landlord has sent a sociopathic email which I sort of can't be bothered to deal with rn

In the meantime we've all taken shelter elsewhere

I'm at my dad's in Wimbledon

She added an eye-roll emoji for good measure. He was typing again.

Oh man, what a pain

Still at least we're not still in the attic aka prison

Celebrated my freedom by going for a walk up Telegraph Hill with my housemate

She smiled, and typed out a response.

I miss south-east London already

My dad's cat rules the roost here

Meanwhile, he was expected home hours ago and is yet to appear . . .

He is such a teenager

She was gratified by his response.

Haha!

You should meet mine

That hung there for a second. She waited, hoping he'd fill the silence. He was typing.

So do you fancy a drink this week?

Could do somewhere central if you're staying in Wimbledon

She was touched he had remembered her location, despite the fact she'd mentioned it only a few minutes ago.

Yeah – sounds good!

Ugh, exclamation mark. He was typing.

Weds?

Would Wednesday work? Usually she only sanctioned school-night drinking on a Thursday. She rolled her eyes at herself. Of course it worked.

Perfect

I finish work at about 6.30 near Westminster

Where's good for you?

She watched him type, then stop. She held her breath and closed WhatsApp impulsively. Seconds later, a response popped up.

Soho?

Could go to the John Snow

Alexa saw it in her mind's eye immediately, on the corners of Lexington and Broadwick Streets. She remembered standing on the cobbles there with Ellen one summer afternoon, in the thoroughfare of a swelling crowd, moving aside every few seconds to let yet another sweaty body past.

Perfect

7pm?

He replied.

Perf x

OK gotta go, my housemate has people round and I haven't been very sociable

But I'll see you Weds

Was this an excuse? She supposed it didn't matter. She replied, a little giddy.

See you then

I'll return to fighting the cat for the sofa x

He signed off.

Haha x

Alexa reread the exchange a couple of times to confirm its existence. Satisfied, she placed the phone back on the mahogany table. As if sensitive that her good name was being taken in vain, Bumble had hopped off the sofa and flounced out of the living room, tail sashaying with each step. She had been sitting on the remote. Alexa picked it up, unmuted the volume and committed to a show about a group of privileged teenagers on New York's Upper East Side. At university, she and Ellen had watched this show religiously, despite both professing to powerfully hate its unrealistic plot.

Alexa wondered what Ellen and Kayleigh were doing

right now. She thought of them together, perhaps tucked up on a sofa, sharing a bottle of wine. The second evening in a row they'd spent together. Alexa picked up her phone yet again and scrolled to their WhatsApp messages. There was nothing since the very early hours of that morning, those WhatsApp messages sent when Ellen was drunk and on her way home from her night out; an entirely different time.

She typed.

Hey, how's Kayleigh's?

Dad obviously hasn't got home yet

Such a teenager

Alexa paused.

Also Ben texted

So that's fun

She put her phone down and returned to the television.

By the time she got into bed, her father was still not home, so she'd made the bed with crisp clean linens herself. Ellen had read her message but not yet responded, and Alexa felt a little slighted. If anyone should be playing distant it was her! Frowning, Alexa stared at her own message a few times, then turned her phone on to Do Not Disturb and closed the door firmly. She remembered from last time that it had a habit of creaking open in the night. Twigging that she'd been exiled from the room, Bumble started scratching at the door.

She spent the week wishing that she'd packed some better clothes in her grab bag. And so inevitably, on Wednesday lunchtime, flushed and flustered, she legged it to Piccadilly Circus – hopping on the Bakerloo line for two stops – in

order to do a swift recce of the shops there. It was driz-
zling and they were packed with browsers and window
shoppers who were taking shelter from the rain; she
grabbed a sleek one-shouldered black top from a shelf
and, without trying it on, paid the £38 for it. She could
wear it with the black trousers she had on already, and she
had a pair of white trainers in her bag. The top wasn't
worth the money – nor was she certain she liked it – but it
would do, and it was better than her work shirt, which was
expensive but, she feared, frumpy.

She clock-watched for much of the afternoon, the minutes ticking past in the bottom-right-hand corner of her
ancient desktop. Mid-afternoon, a colleague had to speak
twice in order to rouse her from her trance. Flustered, she
resolved to concentrate properly for the rest of the afternoon. He was just a boy, after all.

Finally, at about 4ish, he had messaged to reconfirm.

Hey!

How's your week?

Still on for 7 tonight?

She replied, gratefully.

Hey!

Week slow and tedious . . .

Hope yours is better

Yes!

John Snow still work?

He responded immediately.

Works for me!

He hadn't forgotten or changed his mind.

She replied.

See you tonight x

He replied with a single kiss.

She left work earlier than usual, at around 6.20 p.m. Although Alexa's contracted hours were 8.30 a.m. to 6.30 p.m., she had somewhere to be – and she supposed ten minutes was nothing, really. Still, she'd scuttled out of there quickly, just in case someone spotted her. She stopped off at the loos on the floor below, to switch into her trainers and new top (she winced as she looked in the mirror) and to fix her make-up (more eyeliner, she decided), before setting up the street towards Westminster Tube station at a trot. She would go to Bond Street and walk: the whole journey should only take about twenty-five minutes – she'd cross-checked on both Google Maps and Citymapper – but she was still anxious about being late.

In fact, of course, she was early – only by five minutes or so, but enough to see that the pub was teeming: every table was occupied, and packs of braying post-work people were standing on the pavement, holding pint glasses and lit cigarettes, and jackets slung over their arms. The clouds had parted and sunshine warmed the pavements. Still, her heart sank. She could not concentrate on Ben while she worried whether the person to her left was going to upend their pint down the side of her arm.

Right on cue, someone jostled her and she whipped round, stricken. But it was Ben, and she quickly rearranged her face into what she hoped was casual enthusiasm. His hair was tossed off his face and engineered – subtly – in place with a lick of something. He smelled newly showered. She wished she'd splashed some perfume on during the walk between Bond Street and the pub. Self-consciously, she smoothed her hair.

'Hey,' he said casually, going in for a single kiss on the cheek.

Uncertain, Alexa almost tried for a second kiss but styled it out.

He gave her a twinkling grin.

'Looks like the pub is packed.' She rolled her eyes. 'But we can stand outside, or . . .' She trailed off.

'Ah yes,' Ben said, lightly. 'Seems like some other people had the same idea as us. Who'd have thought that Wednesday-evening-Soho-pub was such a crowd-pleaser.'

Alexa relaxed. She had an idea.

'Shall we try somewhere else nearby?' he suggested, stepping into the road. 'I think there's a Red Lion or something down here.'

'We could.' She stepped after him and gazed into his face, finding it warm and open. 'Or' – she pointed a finger – 'different idea. We could get a few drinks and go and sit in Soho Square?'

'Gins in tins,' he said, after a moment's consideration. 'I like it.'

He took her hand and she squeezed it, emboldened.

They were about ten minutes away and they still had to wend their way through Soho's narrow, congested streets – a tale of two Londons with their split bin bags and puddles of urine pooling outside restaurants where a starter cost £20. It was hard to have a meaningful conversation while they navigated this hurly burly, though they chattered away easily about nothing much in particular. Ben led, clasping her hand tightly and turning regularly, as if to check she hadn't been swallowed by Soho's maw.

He stopped at the first available newsagent's, and insisted

on buying the drinks (two Tyskies for him, two slimline gin and tonics for her – and an extra pink gin to share, he'd declared, twinkling – and Alexa felt a little self-conscious). Ben presented the drinks at the till with a flourish, and the man rang them up wordlessly, with his eyes trained on a football match playing on a small, wonky telly in the corner (the colours were all wrong and, every few seconds, rainbow-coloured lines would stretch across the screen). Ben grabbed her hand again when they left the shop, the blue plastic bag swinging on his other arm.

Soho Square was busy too – and there were more pigeons in residence than Alexa would have liked – but it was warm enough and this was definitely, definitely better than stomping through the streets trying to find somewhere with a seat. They sat down – he crossed-legged, facing her, knees touching hers – after making an exhibition of checking the ground carefully for cigarette butts (or worse). He handed her a gin in a tin and opened his own Tyskie, inclining the can towards hers in cheers. She took a sip: sugary and fizzy and a touch chemical.

'Shall we?' she asked, mischievously.

'Oh, go on, then.' He gave her a cocky grin. 'Let's do it. The debrief.'

'Well' – she laughed again – 'I'm not totally certain how to begin –'

'Well, it wasn't exactly how I imagined that morning going,' Ben interrupted, but warmly. There was a pause; his expression hardened slightly. 'But look, well, I feel like . . . I feel like a lot of things were said that were maybe said because of the stress of the . . . situation –'

'I don't know, Ellen is often quite highly strung,' Alexa

interjected, feeling a little mean and disloyal, but also gratified when Ben laughed.

He took a big swig of his beer. 'Maybe,' he said, looking more solemn again. 'But I understand. I mean, she thinks I'm this' – he grasped for the word – '*villain* from her past. And we were stuck in an attic. Until Jack, the unlikely hero of the hour, busted us out of there.' He frowned. 'Have you spoken to Ellen?'

Ellen had replied to Alexa's WhatsApp on Sunday evening – though not until about twenty-four hours after Alexa had sent it. She'd been relieved to see her name appear.

All good here – just at Kayleigh's
And oh yaaaaaay
I'm very glad my foot in mouth moment hasn't ruined everything

To the end of this message, Ellen had added the emoji of the monkey with its face in its hands. It was one of her favourites. She sent one more message.

And hope your dad's is cosy and he's not driving you too mad xx

Alexa had replied immediately.

Oh, he is!
Motorbike this, motorbike that
Miss you x

She had added a pink emoji heart for good measure. Ellen had responded in kind. Since then, they'd reverted to their usual din of messages. Ellen had messaged about an hour before her date.

GOOD LUCK on your HOT DATE
(Not that you need it)
(Because i won't be there so will run smoothly)
Love and miss you xx
PS call me tomorrow at lunch maybe?

She'd replied right away.

Eeek thank you

She'd adding a blushing emoji.

Yes I definitely will

Love and miss you too xx

'We've spoken plenty,' she reassured Ben now.

He still looked worried.

'Honestly, we're all good, really. We always are. I think she just found the whole day a bit overwhelming . . .' Alexa wasn't quite sure how to address what had happened between Ellen and Ben.

'I'm completely stumped by it all,' Ben said, carefully, reading her mind. 'I hope I wasn't too harsh on her. I just didn't really understand what on earth was going on.' He added, 'Still don't, really.' He unfolded his leg and winced. 'Sorry. Old football injury.'

Alexa smirked and raised her eyebrows.

After a beat, he continued. 'Anyway. I'm so sure it wasn't me, but she's so sure it was and . . . I don't know?' He looked mystified.

Alexa watched him here, as she'd watched him in the attic, looking for any tells that would suggest he was lying. But he was holding her gaze, and looked troubled. She believed him.

He went on. 'I texted my sister to ask her if she could remember anything, but no leads there.' Ben's eyes were wide and searching. 'It's such a weird, unsolved mystery.'

Alexa frowned. 'I think Ellen's also weirded out that she might be misremembering things,' she tried.

'Oh, definitely.' Ben shook his head. 'It's totally disorienting. But I don't want you both to fall out over it.'

'We really haven't,' Alexa said, warmly. 'It's OK.' She placed her hand on his, and he turned and squeezed hers gratefully. 'Honestly. Don't worry.'

Ben didn't look totally convinced but seemed to conclude that, for now, this reassurance would do. 'Right' – Ben rubbed his palms together, ran a hand through his hair – 'now that's dealt with, sort of, can we please briefly discuss Jack.' His eyes danced.

Alexa laughed, guiltily.

'Oh, Jack,' she added, fondly. She tipped a measure of gin and tonic into her mouth. 'I can't believe he didn't think to tell us he had signal that whole time . . .' She paused. 'In fact – what am I saying? – of course I can. I doubt he'd notice if someone set fire to his shoes.'

Ben cackled. 'To be fair to him, we gave him plenty to tweet about. No wonder he didn't think about anything else.'

'True. Very true.' Another guilty laugh. 'But still. I would never have expected it from him. In a way, I'm very impressed.'

'It was quite a rescue.' Ben smiled at the memory. 'Where's he hiding out now?'

'His sister's, I think? Who lives not all that far from my dad's place – in Earlsfield.'

'Nice bloke, Jack.' Ben added, 'Totally crackers. But he's very nice.'

'That's about the measure of Jack. Ellen's least favourite thing about him is the fact he exclusively takes baths. Never showers. Even before work. He always takes a bath.'

Ben looked politely baffled. 'That is very unusual.'

'Yes,' Alexa replied. 'It definitely is.' She paused, and then rashly started, 'About the other thing Ellen said –'

Ben squeezed her palm again, to interject. 'Look, I'm really sorry about all that. She made me feel a bit exposed and . . . obviously, we'd been on a few dates and everything, but that was the first time I'd stayed –'

'It's fine.' She felt shy now.

'But,' he began, in a lower voice, so low that she had to lean in slightly to hear him, 'I'd really love to see where all this could go.' He was watching her through his eyelashes. 'If you'd like to.'

Her stomach swooped. 'I'd like to, too,' she said. Worrying it was inadequate, she added, 'Very much.'

And then he leaned in, and closed the gap between them. And after a bit of that, they sat beside each other like any other young couple in the April sunshine of Soho Square.

29. Jack

It was now Saturday, a full week since he had moved out of Rokeby Close, and Jack was slumped on the sofa in front of the 55-inch wall-mounted LCD television that Rich spoke about often.

On this sofa was where Jack had spent most of the day. He was hungover. Last night he'd stayed at the Green Genie offices until almost 11 p.m., and now his head ached and his limbs felt slightly hollow. He had eaten a lot of toast and a big bag of Monster Munch, and drunk two cans of Coca-Cola. Rich had gone to the shop to buy the crisps and the Coke. He had seemed to find the novelty of Jack's hangover quite amusing.

Still, Rich's good mood had proven to be short-lived, and Jack had spent the afternoon feeling like a bit of a bother. Rich and Maisie were going to a friend's house for a dinner party and as they'd bustled around, getting ready, he had heard them arguing about whether to take red or white wine, and whether to take an Uber or get the bus from the end of their road. In the end, Rich had won both arguments (red, Uber). As they left, Maisie had promised they wouldn't be back too late, which made Jack feel like a baby. He'd heard Rich telling Maisie to hurry up and then they'd been out of the door, arguing in the hallway.

He closed his eyes, glad of the peace. Last night had got rather out of hand. They'd been celebrating. It had been quite a big week, for Jack, actually. Bigger than usual, definitely. It was weird, he thought. He'd waited so long for things to ever happen to him.

Jack didn't know what to expect as he sat down on the District line train heading east on the Monday morning after his liberation from the attic. He supposed that some people from work might have seen the thread. But he was confused about how he felt. Part of him wanted everyone to know. But he was also nervous in case there was a big fuss and people crowded around his desk to ask him all about it.

When he arrived, just before 9 a.m., the building was almost empty. He had forgotten how long to leave to get from Maisie's in Earlsfield to the Green Genie offices in Bermondsey, so had arrived far earlier than usual. The office took up the entire second floor of a co-working space inside an old warehouse. The atrium was cavernous and a long fish tank stretched across one wall of it. Jack had nicknamed one of the fish Chips, like his deceased childhood goldfish.

He walked to his desk and put his jacket over his chair, stuffed his rucksack under the desk and turned his office MacBook on. Once it had started purring, he walked over to the kitchen to make a cup of tea, saying a shy hello to Petroc, the burly head of UX design, who was drinking a can of Red Bull while his porridge rotated slowly in the microwave. Jack could hear it bubbling.

'Hi, Petroc,' Jack tried.

Petroc grunted in response.

'Good weekend?' Jack asked.

Petroc grunted in response, though this time the sound was slightly more melodic, which Jack took as an affirmative.

'Cool,' Jack replied.

He took his mug from one of the cupboards and made a tea. Petroc removed his porridge from the microwave, barely wincing as he touched the hot ceramic bowl. He walked back to his desk, which was near Jack's in the middle of the office, and started shovelling steaming spoonfuls into his mouth, eyes fixed on his screen. Jack had to assume that Petroc had not seen the Twitter thread, or any of the articles, or watched the (very short) news segment that Jack had appeared on.

Over the next half-hour, other members of the Green Genie team arrived. Many came on bikes, which they parked in the racks near the door, removing packed lunches from their panniers. Jack's boss, Bryan, arrived on foot: as was customary, he had run to work.

'Morning, Genies!' Bryan boomed as he opened the glass door of the second floor. 'Ready for another incredible week?' He bent over to massage his calf. 'All-hands at 10.30 a.m.' Bryan removed his shoes and padded barefoot towards his office, a glass cube situated in the corner of the building.

Jack said hello as his other colleagues gradually took their seats, nursing steaming mugs or holding bowls of cereal or pieces of fruit. Breakfast was provided for free at Green Genie. Jack usually had Coco Pops, but this morning he felt too nervous to eat.

Finally, Deepti arrived. Cody waddled behind her on his leash. Today he wore a thin jumper with a polka-dot print. Flora brought up the rear, laughing at something Deepti must have just said.

Jack gulped.

They had stopped near the door. Cody was taking an

interest in one of Bryan's strange running shoes, the type that was the shape of a foot, with a strange, spongy sole.

'No, Cody,' Deepti was saying. 'Don't eat the boss's shoe or he'll have you fired.' She tugged on his leash.

Flora was crouched, trying to wrestle the shoe out of the dog's small jaws. He was surprisingly tenacious, but she managed. Deepti led him to his bed under her desk, where he curled up around one of the small cuddly Green Genie carrots that they gave to customers who took out a new vegetable-box subscription. Flora went to the kitchen to pour herself a bowl of muesli.

Jack watched both of them, while trying to pretend that he wasn't. He felt shy. But while he was pretending not to watch, Deepti looked straight at him and pointed.

'Here he is!' She walked towards him. 'Viral star Jack Barnes!'

Deepti had a very loud voice, and Jack's face went beet-root. A few of his colleagues watched as she walked from her desk to his, hands on her hips. Today she was wearing a pair of leggings with a banana pattern on them. When she reached his desk she seemed to tower over him. On cue, Flora arrived at her shoulder.

'Well?' Deepti smiled at him. 'Sounds like someone had an eventful weekend.'

'Saw you on the news, Jacko,' Flora piped up.

Jack was aware that a few of his other colleagues were staring, heads cocked in interest. He swallowed, then laughed, nervously. 'Yeah,' he managed, finally.

Deepti and Flora were still smiling at him. Flora had put her cereal bowl on Jack's desk and also had her hands on her hips now.

'Well?' Deepti said again. 'Tell us what happened!' She was balanced on the corner of Jack's desk now.

Flora picked up her cereal bowl and started eating slowly, watching him, as though the muesli was popcorn and Jack was a film.

'Well,' he started. He still felt like there was a sea of eyes watching him, although he wasn't sure anyone else was really listening properly. Many people were already plugged in, no longer interested in Deepti and Jack and Flora's conversation. So, emboldened by Deepti's murmurs of encouragement, Jack tried again. He explained it all in a bit of a rush, and a few of the details came out in the wrong order, but all in all, he was pretty pleased with it. He glanced between Flora and Deepti. He felt a little breathless.

'I couldn't believe it when I saw you on the news,' Flora said in wonder. 'It was just on in the background while I was having a glass of wine with my mum and then I saw you and I screamed, "Oh my God, it's Jack!!" and she jumped a foot in the air. Then we unmuted it to listen to you.' She cocked an eyebrow. 'She said you were "very charming".'

Jack's face felt warm.

'I was just sat on the Overground, with Cody, on my way to Hackney Marshes,' Deepti said. 'So, obviously, I was on Twitter. And then suddenly all these people I knew were retweeting you. At first I couldn't believe it was the same person.'

'Wait, so how did you end up on the telly, though?' Flora was watching him carefully.

'Well, the BBC producer guy DM'd me on Twitter and then asked if he could interview me –'

'Wait – I'm so confused about your housemates, though,' Deepti interjected. 'So they all knew each other? Or they didn't?' Cody had come in search of Deepti and was now circling her left foot, nose to the floor. She leaned down to ruffle his ears, still watching Jack.

'Well, two of them are best friends,' Jack said. 'Ellen and Alexa. They went to university together. But Ben –'

'The Hinge date,' supplied Flora.

'Yes, Ben was Alexa's date,' Jack explained. 'But Ellen thinks she went out with him at school, but then he broke up with her. On MSN. But he doesn't remember.' The radio started playing from one of the small speakers in the corner of the office. 'So then they had a big argument. Which was really awkward.'

'Sounds messy,' Deepti agreed. She reached down to pick Cody up. She flipped him on to his back so that she could cradle him like a baby.

'Super-messy,' Flora agreed.

'Yes,' Jack said, simply.

'Well, anyway,' Deepti said. She stood up, and put Cody back down on the floor. He walked towards his basket. 'Now you're a viral star, you should join us on social.'

'Green Genie needs you,' Flora said. She was grinning.

Jack held his breath. He couldn't tell if they were joking. They were always teasing him, which he mostly didn't mind. But this time he really hoped they weren't. Except it couldn't be as simple as all that, could it? They'd have to ask Bryan. And Bryan probably didn't know anything about it, and probably didn't really care that much. He opened his mouth and then closed it again.

Flora picked up her cereal bowl. 'We should get down to some work, I suppose,' she said, with a sigh. 'Before the all-hands.'

'Ditto,' Deepti said. 'Let's all have lunch today, yes?'

'Yes, please,' Flora said.

Jack smiled shyly, but his heart sank. He'd missed his moment to say that, actually, what he wanted more than anything was to join them on social. Maybe it had been a joke. But he still should have said something.

Flora was at her desk now, but Deepti was only a few paces away.

'Wait, Deepti?' Jack said, quietly, but not so quietly she wouldn't hear him.

She turned round.

He cleared his throat. 'Did you mean it – about the social team?'

She looked surprised.

'Because' – Jack decided he had to say it all quickly, before he lost his nerve – 'because, well, I would actually . . . well, I would like that. To join the social team, I mean,' he finished, in a rush.

She stared at him, which Jack found rather unnerving, and then spoke gently. 'OK, Jacko. Let's try and make it happen. I'll talk to Bry, OK?'

Bryan liked Deepti. They'd worked together previously at a company that sold subscriptions for coffee, which had given Bryan the idea for Green Genie, and when he'd set it up, he'd asked her to come work for him. Still, Jack wasn't sure if Deepti was just saying that.

'OK,' Jack said. He smiled. 'Thanks, Deepti.'

'Any time, buster,' she replied.

On Tuesday, Annie found out. She WhatsApped him.

Jacko!!! What are you doing all over the internet??

She sent a link to an article from a website that published lots of quizzes that helped you find out which type of cinema snack you were most similar to. Jack couldn't believe that his tweets were such a big deal. He felt bashful.

Yeah lol!!
Bit of a weird weekend
I was on the news!

After a few seconds he tapped out another WhatsApp.

Lol

She didn't reply, and the rest of the week passed slowly. Jack felt tired a lot, because he wasn't sleeping well on Maisie's couch. And one day he missed his interchange on the Tube and was late for work.

On Thursday, he was copied in on an email from Alexa.

From: alexa_ingram@gmail.com
To: elias@southeast_homes.com
CC: jackbarnes@greengenie.london; ellenfisher@gmail.com
Subject: Re: Re: 49 Rokeby Close

Dear Elias,

I am emailing to confirm in writing what you discussed with my lawyer on the phone this afternoon.

As agreed, you will pay for the kitchen to be fixed and for the carpets to be vacuum cleaned. This will be done ASAP. One of us can be available to let the handymen into the house and to supervise the work.

When this is complete, we will confirm a date for us to move back into 49 Rokeby Close.

Very best,
Alexa

Jack read the email a couple of times and felt awed by Alexa. On his third rereading, there was a message from Alexa to their WhatsApp group.

Hi guys! You may have spotted my email – I wussed out and let my dad (or rather 'my lawyer') deal with everything. Will keep you posted on any more news – one of us will have to go and actually let the plumber etc in, but hopefully we can move back home soon! X

Jack replied with a thumbs-up emoji. Ellen replied with a fire emoji and a couple of messages.

Yessssss Marcus!

Thanks Lex

Obv more than happy to wait for the handymen as I have the new keys

Let us know xxx

Jack was very relieved that it looked like things might be working out. He missed his space and 49 Rokeby Close. He missed Ellen and Alexa too. He didn't much like being back at Maisie's. He also knew that Rich wasn't delighted to have him back.

On Friday morning, Jack overheard them arguing in the kitchen very early. It woke him up half an hour before his alarm went off. Theirs was a small flat, and the kitchen was right next to the living room, with an arch rather than a door to divide them.

'I know it's not ideal but he doesn't have anywhere else to go,' Maisie hissed.

Jack heard the high, clear jangling of a spoon hitting the inside of a mug a few times.

'I don't see why he can't stay with a mate, or something,' Rich replied.

'I don't know – maybe none of them has the space,'

Maisie said then. 'You know what it's like at that age, all hutched up together in those dreadful tiny hovels.'

Rich said something indistinguishable back, and Maisie hushed him then, and started talking about the recycling.

He turned over and hoped he wouldn't hear any more. It was thirty minutes before his alarm was supposed to go off, and he hoped he'd get a little more sleep, though the couch was very uncomfortable – even if Maisie had got a new cushion since Jack last slept on it. In fact, he wondered if the cushion was the problem. It was square and its padding rather insubstantial. It was blank on one side and decorated with a beaded pattern on the other. It did not match the fold-out green sofa. The morning after the first night he'd stayed, Jack had left the cushion on the floor when he'd reassembled the sofa into sofa form. Maisie had pointedly fluffed it and returned the cushion to pride of place when he'd gone to make a cup of tea.

On Friday afternoon, Flora and the other intern, Kamal – who was working on the marketing team – were sent to Tesco with the company card to buy beers. There was a sense of celebration in the air. Green Genie had launched its first television advertisement: a ninety-second spot that had aired last night and had gone – very modestly – viral on Twitter straight afterwards. (Though Jack noted that he hadn't seen any reality-television stars tweeting about the advert.) As a result of this success, Bryan had mandated that they all 'down tools' early that afternoon and have drinks to celebrate.

There was a general hubbub of conversation, although Jack didn't really have anyone to talk to, because Flora was out and he didn't know where Deepti was, but he could see

Cody, asleep in his bed under her desk, wrapped around the carrot. So Jack just kept his headphones on and continued going through the customer-service inbox, answering queries methodically.

He was lost in some query about a box that had arrived containing four butternut squashes but not a single apple ('What am I supposed to do with four butternut squashes in the course of a week?' the customer had asked, and Jack didn't really have an answer to that), when Deepti came and tapped him on the shoulder, making him jump. She was saying something to him, except he still had his headphones on so he couldn't hear her.

She stretched out her hands and removed them for him. 'Let's start that again, shall we?' Deepti said, rolling her eyes. She lowered her voice and leaned in towards him. 'Bryan. Wants to see you.' She winked.

He stared at her, stricken.

'Now,' she added.

'Me? Now?' Jack looked towards Bryan's glass cube. His boss was leaning back on his chair, hands behind his back, feet on the table. Jack could see his eyes were closed.

'Yes. You. Now,' Deepti replied. She slapped him on the back. 'Go on, it'll be drinks time soon.'

Jack stood up. His heart pounded as though he was about to sit an exam. He walked towards the glass cube. He was conscious that Deepti was watching and was worried he'd trip over one of his feet. He arrived at Bryan's office and rapped, quietly, on the door. Bryan didn't seem to hear him the first time; he remained in the same pose. Jack looked back at Deepti, who gave him an encouraging grin. He turned and rapped again, a little louder this time.

Bryan opened his eyes and put his feet under the desk. 'Ah, Jack, come on in,' he boomed.

Jack swallowed and opened the door. Jack had never been in Bryan's office before. It smelled nice in there: like soap, or oranges. Jack wondered if it was the candle on Bryan's desk that was responsible for the smell. There was a bookshelf behind his desk, but it only had three books on it. Bryan's laptop was very new and very slim, and sitting beside it he had a notebook and four pens. The pens were all lined up in height order.

Bryan smiled at Jack and gestured to a second seat in front of the desk. Jack sat down. The chair made a small squeak. Bryan was very tall, and very broad. He had close-cropped fair hair and a deep, nutty tan. He was the only person at Green Genie who wore a suit at work, after he'd showered and changed out of his strange shoes and his running clothes. He leaned forward on his desk and concentrated on Jack.

'So, Jack, how are you doing?' Bryan had placed his palms together and was staring right at Jack. He looked a bit like he was praying.

'I'm . . . I'm very good,' Jack replied, surprised. 'Thank you.'

'Good, good,' Bryan replied. He smiled at Jack with big, straight teeth. 'And are you enjoying your work here at Green Genie? How long have you been here – a few months?'

'Since September,' Jack replied.

'Since September!' Bryan clapped his large palms together. 'And are you enjoying being a Human Bean?' Bryan's face was solemn now, searching.

'Oh yes, it's really interesting,' Jack said, hurriedly. He

was starting to worry now. He hoped someone hadn't said something to Bryan about him not liking his job.

'Great, great,' Bryan replied. 'I've always thought it's a great place for our talent to start. Really teaches you the ropes of the business. Get to know the customer.' He leaned back on his chair again. It was richly padded and looked a lot comfier than the one that Jack was sitting in. Bryan glanced at his laptop screen, frowned for a second, and then rearranged his face again. 'Well, look, Jack, I'm going to cut to the chase –'

Wildly, Jack interrupted. 'I do really like my job, it's just that sometimes I'm bad on the phone, but I'm getting a lot better –'

'Deepti mentions you'd be interested in moving over to the social team,' Bryan said, as though he hadn't heard anything. 'She said you've got a good knack for it, and you'd be a really good fit for that team.'

Jack opened his mouth and tried to swallow at the same time.

Bryan smiled indulgently. 'So, what do you say to that? Ready for the challenge?'

There was a roaring in Jack's ears, but he managed to say something. 'I'd really love that.' He swallowed properly this time. 'To join the social team.' His voice strengthened. He repeated it. 'I'd love to join the social team.'

'Great,' said Bryan. He clapped his hands together. 'I think it's a really exciting growth space for this business – now that we've moved into television marketing too, I think there's a lot more we could be doing with social.'

Jack was nodding, really fast, to show he was keeping up. He wondered if his head would fly off his neck.

'We'll need to hire a new Human Bean to replace you before we can move you over, so I'm going to get Kaspar on that ASAP' – Bryan said it strangely, like 'ae-sap' – 'and then once we do, we can get you sitting with Deepti and the rest of the gang on social. So, sound good?' He was prodding at his Apple Watch with his forefinger, squinting at the small screen.

'Yes,' Jack managed. 'That sounds great.'

'Ace,' said Bryan, looking up. 'Glad to have that sorted.' He looked through the glass at the rest of the Green Genie team, who were milling around the kitchen.

Flora and Kamal had returned with the drinks.

'Shall we go get a beer, then?' Bryan asked, gesturing towards the door, though not standing up.

'Great,' Jack said, quietly. 'Yes. A beer.'

'I'll follow – just need to do a few emails,' Bryan said, looking at his laptop. 'But you go get stuck in.'

Jack stood up. 'Thank you, Bryan,' he said, shyly.

'No worries.' Bryan was tapping at his keyboard. 'I think it's a great move for you.'

After an awkward pause in which Jack wasn't quite sure what to do with his face, he realized he was supposed to leave the office now. He did so, his hand slightly sweaty on the stainless-steel door handle.

He started to walk, slightly dazed, back to his desk. He noticed Deepti was still sitting there. She did a thumbs-up with both thumbs. Jack did one back. He smiled, unable to help himself.

'Beer?' Deepti asked.

'Beer,' he said, decisively.

*

And that was why Jack felt so hungover today. Plus, it turned out that Bryan had offered Flora a job too, so now they'd be a team. So they'd really had something to celebrate. When Jack thought about this, it almost made his hangover better. Almost, but not quite.

There was, Jack decided, nothing he wanted to watch on the massive television. He turned it off and put the remote on the coffee table in front of him, then pulled his laptop on to his lap and made his pilgrimage to all the usual sites: Reddit, Twitter (he was still getting notifications, even now, a week later) and Facebook. A few friends from university had seen the clip of him from BBC London and had messaged him over the last week, saying they couldn't believe it was him, and that they should meet up for a pint.

No one had suggested a drink today, but there was a single red bubble on his Facebook account: a friend request. Jack clicked on it and saw that Benjamin Kenny had sent him a friend request. For a second, Jack drew a blank. Finally, he got there: Ben! From the attic. He had not expected Ben to send him a friend request.

Jack clicked on Ben's profile. It was fairly blank – his profile picture was of him with several friends. But it was discernibly him: the same dark hair, blue eyes, the quirky grin, slightly lopsided. He returned to the friend request page and clicked accept, before going to his own profile. Jack's profile saw sporadic activity: the odd post from his Aunt Nancy, who composed her wall posts like they were texts she was sending only to Jack; the odd photograph from a day festival, or a birthday party. There were a few tagged photos from his graduation last year.

As Jack was looking over his own Facebook page, a

flashing toolbar appeared: Benjamin Kenny had messaged him. Jack clicked on the red flashing icon.

hey jack!

how's it going?

hope you've found somewhere to stay while the house is sorted out

He was pleased that Ben had messaged, actually, because it meant that he couldn't be all that cross about the Twitter business. Jack started typing quickly.

hi ben!

not bad, how are you?

yeah i'm staying at my sisters in earlsfield

hopefully not for too much longer tho

i think alexa has sorted it out :)

The three dots indicated that Ben was typing. Jack watched them rise and fall like a heartbeat.

ah nice

yeah, she mentioned that she'd managed to read elias the riot act by getting her dad involved

So they definitely were in touch, Jack thought. He replied, uncertain what to say next.

yeah

Ben did not start typing quite yet. Jack stared at the message box for a minute or so. He tapped the side of his laptop and continued to watch.

so I have a bit of a favour to ask

Jack frowned.

ok

He considered adding a smiley, but refrained. Ben's response came back instantly.

i was wondering if you could help me get ellen to a pub in new x next week

This was not what Jack had been expecting.

i'd ask alexa but i sort of think it might be better coming from you

trying not to make things awkward between them

bit of a long story, anyway, do you think you could help?

Jack stared blankly at this message for a few seconds, before another appeared.

obv you should come too!!

sorry, feel like i've made this quite weird

It was – a little. Jack wondered whether Alexa was coming too, or if it was some sort of trick. Ben was typing again.

look – long story short i've managed to sort of work out what happened over the msn messages

so i need to explain a few things to her

Ben was still typing.

it's more complicated than it sounds

but i owe her an apology anyway

so any chance you could help out?

This sounded like a good thing. Ellen would definitely want an apology from Ben. Maybe it would be good to get them all together in the pub, to clear the air before they returned to 49 Rokeby Close.

Jack stroked the keys of his laptop absent-mindedly for a few seconds, chewing hard on his lip.

ok i will ask her

He worried that this sounded a bit short.

i will let you know when she replies :)

Ben was already typing.

ah thanks mate!

iou a pint for sure

just message me on here when you've spoken to her?

Jack replied.

yes will do bye :)

Jack reread the message thread a few times. He wondered what to say to Ellen. He felt uncomfortable lying to her again. Perhaps he should just be open with her, and say that Ben wanted to meet. Surely she'd want to know if he'd found out what had happened with the MSN stuff. And Ben had specifically said that he wanted to apologize.

He closed the laptop lid. Abruptly, it was at peace; the whirring engine paused like a sharp intake of breath. Jack noticed that Trixie the cat was chewing the beads on the ugly new cushion.

He hoped Rich didn't like the cushion.

30. Ellen

The pub smelled like a pub: rich, woody, beery and a little damp, like standing in a forest after it had rained. Ellen breathed in the smell while cutting a hasty beeline for the bar.

She had arrived early – unlike her – in order to call the shots on where they sat. She had imagined the scene: arriving five minutes late, a little out of breath from her trot from New Cross Gate station. She'd have to squeeze into a booth fitted around a sticky table, the cushion making a squeal as the backs of her bare thighs rubbed against it (it was warm, and she had dared a skirt, prompting her boss, Felicia, to make a schoolmarmish comment about the length of the hem). No, she needed to be there first. She ordered a large glass of house white, and then cast her gaze around the fairly empty pub, selecting the best place.

It was a pub near 49 Rokeby Close – one that she, Alexa and Sophie used to come to fairly often, back in the day. It was the type that appeared to be undergoing some sort of identity crisis. It had the exposed piping, the bookshelf of obscure books about Victorian London, and the moss-green paint job of something in the gastro tier. But its clientele – Goldsmiths students, plus the likes of Ellen, Alexa and Sophie – dragged the place down a peg or four. And that was not to mention the loos, which were stone cold, whatever the season, and smelled, always, of manure.

(Not even human; it was a farmyard smell.) Ellen was enormously fond of the place.

She selected a booth by the window, assuming the window seat with the panoramic view of the entrance, though the early May evening sunlight poured through the glass in the doors, making Ellen squint. Still, she'd see the door opening, which was a start.

She took out her phone, partly as a prop and partly because she wondered if Lee had texted. He had not, and she was surprised at how disappointed she was.

Much to her enormous surprise, their relationship had stepped up a gear since the day of her imprisonment in the attic. One afternoon last week, she'd bumped into him in the entrance hall of their shared office building. She'd been on the way back from a meeting with a freelance social media manager called Piper, who wore a watch on a pendant around her neck and overused the expression 'actionable insights'. Lee had been carrying a large box.

She'd appraised him, smirking. 'Big box you got there.' This came out more suggestively than she'd intended it to.

'Yeah. New toaster. For the office . . .' A pause. 'I mean, I don't think the toaster is the size of the box. That would make it a very big toaster. So, actually, it's a bit of a waste of cardboard, really.'

Ellen winced but tried to pass it off as a winning smile. 'Make sure you recycle it, I guess?'

'Yeah.' Lee shifted the box on his hip.

She gestured towards the stairs. 'I'd better be getting back.'

'Of course,' Lee said. He'd met Felicia.

'You coming?'

'Ah, right. In fact, I think I might take the lift.' He pointed, unnecessarily, at the lift. 'Because of the box.'

'Right. Well. See you around, then.'

'Yes.'

Once inside the stairwell, she had put her face in her hands.

But an hour later, he'd WhatsApped her.

Sorry for box/recycling chat

Flustered by prospect of new office toaster

Then, a short while later, another message.

Do you fancy a drink on Sat?

Her breath had caught slightly as she'd read the last message. She'd replied on the way back to Kayleigh's.

How many loaves have you toasted so far?

Yes, drink on Sat sounds good

They'd met at a pub on Columbia Road. He had been earnest and nervous, and at first Ellen had been a little arch. But they'd both relaxed into the situation and they'd stayed at a corner table until the closing bell and then got an Uber back to his small house share in Clapton. He'd even kissed her in the taxi. Ellen wouldn't have thought he had it in him.

She'd had to leave early on Sunday morning, as Lee was cycling to Canterbury with a group called The Wheely Good Guys. As she climbed over his bike in the hallway, he'd legged it down the stairs in a Lycra all-in-one and said, slightly out of breath, that he wouldn't have his phone all day, but promised he'd text her when he got home.

She'd smirked, rolled her eyes, and hoped that he would.

It was on the walk to the Overground that she'd opened Jack's messages.

Hey ellen hope alls good with you :)
ben has messaged me on FaceBook
he wants to meet in a pub near rokeby close next week
says he has found some information about the MSN messages
he wants to apologies to you

The first thing she'd noticed at the time – blanking on the main issue – was that he'd misspelt 'apologize'. She checked herself, feeling mean, and reread the text. Feeling slightly dazed by the bright sunshine and families trooping off to Hackney Marshes, she'd dashed off a response.

Hey jack, am well ta – how's earlsfield?
Um yeah of course, weird that he messaged you, but sounds intriguing I suppose
Let me know details when you have them x

And then, all week, she'd allowed herself to consider what the message really meant. It was strange that it had come from Ben, via Jack: why not from Ben, via Alexa? Ellen missed her. They weren't used to this extended separation.

Not to mention that she had spent ten days now feeling increasingly ashamed about the way she had interrogated Ben, recalling snatches of that day: pointing an accusatory finger at him; flouncing off into the corner of the attic; then calling him out for the way he'd played it hot and cold with Alexa. On Sunday evening, miserable at the thought of the impending week ahead, she'd started obsessing about the box of her urine, and had had to order a pizza and a side of potato wedges in order to forget about it. She had made the mistake of setting the scene for Kayleigh, who teased her mercilessly.

And yet, after all that, Ellen did also want an explanation.

Of course she did: it was a mystery that had lurked in the background for a decade. Plus, she knew it would make Alexa feel better, which seemed the most important of all. And maybe it would make her feel better too, and she'd stop descending into hungover shame spirals in which she relived the whole day in vivid detail.

Not to mention, they were moving back to Rokeby Close soon. Harmony needed to be restored. Elias had responded to Alexa's curt email with a characteristically emphatic message.

From: elias@southeast_homes.com
To: alexa_ingram@gmail.com
CC: jackbarnes@greengenie.london; ellenfisher@gmail.com
Subject: HI ALEXANDRA

The carpets are CLEANED NOW AND DRYING OUT and the PIPES are SORTED BY MY PLUMBER so you can MOVE BACK INTO 48 ROKEBY CLOSE please INFORM ME the date that you will go back there.

I will meet you all at the house TO GO THROUGH SOME GROUNDRULES.

Elias

Noting that Elias had got their address wrong, the housemates agreed they would all move back in this Saturday. The thought of seeing Elias was making Ellen feel sweaty and unprepared.

Ellen took a huge gulp of wine, the acid warmth filling her throat. She took another – no one needed to know it had been a large glass to begin with – and busied herself playing with a cardboard beer mat, folding it until its surface broke, and then tearing it into small pieces and piling it on the table in front of her, while half watching the door, waiting for the others to appear.

Yet still she jumped when Jack appeared. Recovering, she sat up straight and pushed the bits of beer mat to the side of the table. He glanced around, looking a little lost, until he saw her, gave a trade-mark half-wave and sidled up to the table where she sat.

'Hello,' he said, clearing his throat at the same time. He stood at the side of the table, arms by his side, as if he was unsure what to do with them.

'Hi, Jack.' Ellen dislodged a piece of soggy beer mat that had become attached to the pad of her right index finger. 'I'm relieved to see you – I was worried it was just going to be me and Ben.'

Jack looked around, as if expecting Ben to materialize at any second.

'How are you?' she added.

'Yeah, um, good?' Jack shuffled.

'How's Earlsfield?'

'Yeah, it's OK,' he shrugged, a little downcast. 'How is – where are you staying?'

'My work friend Kayleigh's. It's fine. Miss my own bed, though.'

He straightened up a little.

'Are you going to get a drink?'

'Right, yeah.' He half-turned and then halted, turning back towards her, shoes squeaking on the stripped wooden floor. 'Um. Would you like one?'

Ellen looked at her half-full glass of wine. 'Go on, then.

House white.' Pre-empting a question that might send Jack into a tailspin, she added, 'A small's fine. Thanks.'

He padded towards the bar. It was a Wednesday evening, and the premises were lightly populated with student punters – one table was playing a board game – though there was no one else at the long wooden bar. Jack was served straight away. Ellen returned to the remnants of the beer mat. In the corner, one of the staff fiddled with the remote that controlled the speaker; for a second, a snatch of a forgettable indie song blared, before the speaker was quietened again.

Then – call it instinct – she glanced up and caught them: Alexa and Ben were walking through the front door. Ben pulled it open and gestured to Alexa to go in front of him. It was a casual but intimate gesture, and Ellen saw the way that Alexa lit up. They were together properly now, that private glance confirmed it. Ellen took a deep breath, just as Ben raised a palm in greeting. He looked a little reticent, but Ellen was more interested in Alexa, who was crossing the pub floor at a gallop. Ellen stood up, hearing her thighs squeak on the banquette, just in time to meet Alexa's hug.

They both yelped hello at the same time. Alexa looked precise and perfect, in a white sleeveless button-down shirt and cropped navy trousers and sandals, toenails painted scarlet. Her jacket was slung over one arm. In the kerfuffle of embrace, she dropped it on the pub floor and Ellen bent at the same time as her to pick it up, and then they both laughed. At which point Ben appeared and, after a fractional pause, Ellen reached for him too.

'Hi, Ben*jamin*,' she said, after they'd pulled apart, the hug short and functional.

He laughed nervously, and looked like he was about to say something. Except at this point, Jack appeared, holding his and Ellen's drinks. He placed them on the table.

'Hi, mate,' Ben said, deciding to give Jack a hug, which was more of a tap on the shoulder than a hug, but surely marked the closest they'd ever been to each other.

'Shall we?' Ellen said, gesturing towards the table.

'Wait, does anyone want a drink?' Ben asked.

'All good, thanks,' Ellen replied. She tipped her small glass into the rest of her large glass of wine.

'I'm good too, mate,' Jack said. He lifted his pint aloft for Ben to see.

'I'd love a glass of red, please?' Alexa asked.

Briefly, it was just the three of them. Alexa had taken a seat next to Ellen on the padded banquette, and Jack sat on one of the wooden chairs.

'I haven't been to this place in for ever,' Alexa said, arranging her jacket beside her.

'Not since Soph moved out, I think,' Ellen said, watching Ben at the bar.

'We should come all the time when we're back,' Jack said, hopefully. He was yet to take a sip from his pint.

'Yeah, for sure,' Alexa said, after a pause. 'It's really nice sitting outside here in the summer.'

Just then, Ben returned with their drinks. He placed them carefully on the table in front of him and lowered himself into the other wooden chair, next to Jack. He slapped Jack on the back again.

Jack had just taken the first sip of his pint and choked slightly.

'Oh, sorry!'

'No worries,' Jack managed, weakly, examining how much beer he'd dribbled down his front.

There was a pause as they all took a sip or two of their drinks, doing an exaggerated lipsmack of a noise to indicate that they were having a good time. Someone was going to have to talk. Ellen decided it wouldn't be her, at the same time that Ben decided it would be him.

'So, um,' Ben started, flashing a glance at Alexa, 'well, this is a bit weird, isn't it?'

Alexa smiled, encouragingly.

Ellen felt a little left out. 'It's less weird than the time we were all in an attic together,' she pointed out. She stared straight at Ben, a slight challenge in her glance.

'Well, yes. Agreed.' Ben swallowed. 'OK, well, I guess since I gathered us all here, it's sort of my' – he looked at Alexa – 'well, it's sort of my job to tell you why.'

Jack was staring at Ben, holding his pint halfway between his chin and the table.

'OK, well,' Ben started again. He looked at Ellen. 'Firstly, I owe you an apology.'

It was as solemn as she'd feared it would be. Ellen felt herself flush immediately. She could feel everyone watching her. She was about to say something, but Ben was still going.

'But it's not quite the apology you . . . it's not quite what you'd expect, you see.'

Ellen felt her stomach contract.

'It's not bad,' Ben said, quickly. 'No one died.' He stopped again, as if summoning up the courage to continue.

'Ben,' Alexa said, reproachfully.

She knows everything already, Ellen thought, with a prickle of hurt. She took an exaggerated slug of wine.

'OK,' she wiped her hand across her mouth, 'look, Ben, I'm going to need you to cut to the chase now.' She put her elbows on the table. 'I've been waiting since 2009 for this.'

He laughed, grateful that she'd broken the tension, before regaining his focus.

She tried to remember to breathe, and concentrated on a bit of torn beer mat. Frowning, he began again.

'OK, so basically you were right. About rainham_romeo1991. In a manner of speaking. Which is to say that, technically, it *was* me.'

Ellen looked up sharply, but Ben avoided her gaze. She found Alexa's instead, earning a cautious smile.

Ben continued. 'Well, maybe it's more accurate to say that, technically, it was my *account*. In that I set it up and everything. And I definitely used it. To speak to girls . . .' Ben paused. 'But the thing is, so did my younger brother. Oli.'

She froze.

'Yes.' Ben took a deep breath. 'So . . . well, I felt weird after that weekend, because . . .' He was struggling with his words, and then became unstuck. 'Well, didn't we all?'

Jack made a nod of vigorous agreement.

Ben was continuing, his voice low and just audible. Ellen felt a little light-headed.

'And I thought about it a lot,' he said. 'And I worried because you were so sure, and I couldn't remember any of it –' He broke off, looking anguished, fixating on the pile of torn, damp beer mat. 'So I messaged my sister, Ava. She couldn't remember anything about it but pointed out that Oli, my brother, was more into MSN than me. So I spoke to Oli. And I didn't think I was going to get very far with him. Oli was a sort of boy genius – man genius, now, he's at Oxford doing a PhD – but anyway, at school he was more fussed about books than anything else that was going on, bit intense, really.'

Ben looked at Ellen now, and she felt a sick horror.

He continued. 'And well, anyway, I spoke to Oli – on Thursday, I think – and it turned out . . .' Ben paused to take a sip of beer and looked at Ellen, Alexa and Jack in turn. 'Well, it turned out that Ol used to go on my MSN. Back in the day. He's four years younger, so he'd have been fourteen or so in 2009 –'

'Oh my God,' Ellen interrupted, still hoping, somehow, that what was coming next was not, in fact, coming next.

Ben squirmed. 'It was Ol, you see.' He looked as uncomfortable as Ellen felt. 'It turns out that he sort of hijacked my account and used it to, well, I suppose you could say he used it to impersonate me.'

Ellen covered her face with her hands.

Ben was, unfortunately, still talking. 'So, together, we worked it out. He remembers the day that you added him, you see.'

Ellen lowered her palms and peered at him. Alexa wrapped her arm around Ellen and squeezed her hand in hers. Ellen could not summon the strength to squeeze it back. There was a pause as Ben tried to work out whether it was OK to continue.

Having decided it was, he spoke quietly. 'He says he'd been using my account, off and on, because I always used the family computer – the one in the living room – and I always left it signed in.'

Ellen's scalp prickled like she'd been out in the sun too long.

'But then you added him, and so he decided to properly – well, *pursue* you. And I guess by that point in sixth form, I wasn't going online as much anyway – I was getting together with Imogen –'

She moaned by way of interruption. Mercifully, Ben sounded like he was winding down. He waited.

'But what exactly did he say?' Ellen asked, finally finding her voice, though it was rather hoarse. 'To you, I mean. What did he say about it all?'

'Oh, he remembers it all,' Ben replied, quickly. 'Starting talking to you. He doesn't remember every message, obviously, but he remembers the letters and –'

'But didn't you go on MSN once, in that entire time?' Ellen interrupted. Her voice still sounded rusty. 'Even just to chat to your mates, or something? Wouldn't you have seen the messages? Or wouldn't I have started chatting to you, and you'd have been, like, "Who the hell are you?"'

Ben shrugged. 'I don't remember. Maybe. I dunno.' He took another sip of his pint. 'But I mainly remember it being something I used for talking to girls. Not my mates. And I got a bit wrapped up in Imogen.' He made a face. 'First love and all that.'

Ellen thought about this. To be fair, she wasn't sure if she had ever spoken to Kate on MSN. 'This is even worse than when I thought it was you.' She put her head on her forearms, which rested on the sticky table. 'I got ghosted by a fourteen-year old,' she whispered.

'He was a very clever fourteen-year-old,' Ben pointed out. 'Basically, a full-on genius. Good at everything.'

Alexa squeezed her friend's hand again. 'It could have happened to anyone,' she tried.

Ellen looked at her. 'No, it could only have happened to me.' She ran her hands through her hair, massaging her temples. A mirthless laugh. 'My parents always warned me that you never knew who you might be talking to online.'

To everyone's surprise – particularly his own – Jack started laughing. Quietly at first, but then louder and louder, until he couldn't stop.

Ellen, Ben and Alexa all regarded him with no little concern.

'Sorry,' Jack said, after twenty seconds or so. He sounded very contrite.

'Don't you dare bloody tweet this, Jack,' Ellen said, sharply. She rolled her eyes. 'God, I'm so embarrassed. But wait –' Unfortunately, she needed to submit herself to the humiliation of a few more details. 'Did he at least say why he ghosted me? How on earth did I wrong my fourteen-year-old virtual boyfriend?'

Ben gave her a solemn smile. 'I think he really started to like you. That's why he sent the letter and everything. He was besotted, I reckon.'

Ellen winced. Alexa tucked a strand of hair behind her ears. She definitely knew the whole story.

Ben continued. 'But then, well, I think he freaked out a bit, basically. Because you had both started talking about meeting up and he realized it couldn't go on much longer. If you met him, you would know he'd been lying all along. And that he was actually fourteen years old.' Ben smiled sympathetically. 'Also, I think he thought that Ava had twigged, or something. My sister. That's what he said.' Ben gave a rueful smile. 'He couldn't believe I'd met you so many years later, you know. Got very excited about the odds of it all.' He added, 'Oli's a mathematician.'

'You said,' Ellen replied, huffily.

'Oh, Ellen.' Alexa made an amused grimace.

Ellen moaned. 'God. I know I was a sad virgin in 2009, but this was next level.'

Ben laughed, at least. 'Sorry. If it's any consolation, Ol does feel really, *really* bad about it. Once he'd got over the extraordinary coincidence of it all, he did feel really awful to know how much it had upset you.' Ben looked like he was about to try and reach out and take Ellen's hand, but thought better of it. 'He asked me to tell you that he was sorry, but he was fourteen and it all got out of hand and he didn't really know what he was doing.'

'That made two of us, then,' Ellen said, dully. She found that she could no longer look at Ben. 'I'm glad that your fantasist brother feels bad about the humiliation he caused me, though.'

'Can I get you another drink?' Alexa tried.

Ellen could tell she was still fighting back amusement. 'Yes.'

Alexa shuffled out of the booth and padded towards the bar.

'I guess at least it proves that it wasn't Ben,' Jack said, cautiously. 'Who ghosted you, I mean.' He added, brightly, smiling at Ben, 'So now you guys can be friends.'

'Yes,' Ellen growled. 'I suppose it does mean that.' She gave Ben a haughty look. 'But I never want to see or speak of your delusional sociopath of a younger brother again. Ever.' She drained her wine glass. 'If you and Alexa get married, it's me or him coming to the ceremony . . .' A pause, for her words to sink in. 'And it better be me.'

Ben was grinning now. 'Gotcha.' He glanced at the bar quickly. 'And look, I'm sorry . . . I'm sorry for the way I reacted. In the attic. Obviously, it *was* me, in a way. It just also wasn't. So. I'm sorry.'

'It's fine.' Ellen could see Alexa tapping her debit card on the reader at the bar. 'I owe you an apology too. I'm not sure the attic was my finest hour. Or several hours. All things considered.'

Ben looked like he was going to say something, but Jack got there first.

'I'm sorry too.' He sounded solemn and rehearsed. 'For the tweets.' He looked at the table. 'I shouldn't have put your personal lives on the internet.'

Ben and Ellen exchanged an amused glance.

'All's well that ends well.' Ben nudged Jack in the side. 'You did get us rescued. If you hadn't tweeted all about our teenage drama to the whole entire world, then the fire brigade never would have seen anything and wouldn't have driven to our rescue. Hey, just think, we might still be stuck up there now.'

Jack looked at him. 'I suppose so,' he said, quietly. He continued, 'And also, they gave me a promotion at work. Because of the thread, and it going viral and everything. I now work on the social media team.' He looked at Ellen.

'Wow. Nice one, Jack.' Ellen reached out and grabbed his shoulder to give it a squeeze. Everything she heard about Jack's company baffled her.

Alexa returned to the table just in time to stop anything becoming awkward and placed a large glass of white wine in front of Ellen.

'Get that down you,' Ben said, pointing to the wine.

Dutifully, Ellen took a generous swig. Alexa, detecting the shift in atmosphere, gave Ben a kiss on the cheek. Ellen cocked an eyebrow at them both.

'So, what time is everyone going to arrive at the house on Saturday?' Alexa asked, taking charge. 'Maybe we could all have dinner together in the evening, or something?'

'I could bring some spare vegetables from the office,' Jack offered, eagerly.

'Sounds good.' Ellen felt a rush of warmth which could only be attributed in part to the wine. 'I'll be there about lunchtime, I reckon.'

'OK, great – same,' Jack said, quickly.

'Me too,' said Alexa.

Ellen looked at Ben. 'I suppose you can come too.'

Alexa smiled at her.

She added, 'But you aren't allowed to touch any door handles.'

They stayed until 10.30 p.m. – even Alexa. Admittedly, she was crashing at Ben's nearby, which gave her some licence to stay out later than usual. Unlike Jack, who was definitely a little bit drunk, and had to make it halfway across London, back to Maisie's.

Jack and Ellen walked to the station together. They were quiet for a little while, unused to being alone with one another again. Ellen's mouth tasted a little metallic. She wished she had a cigarette. Jack walked a little faster than she did, and she had to trot, ever so slightly, in order to keep up.

'Are you sure you're OK?' Jack asked, out of the blue. Or at least, she was fairly certain that's what he'd asked, except that at the exact moment he spoke, a fire engine bombed past them on the New Cross Road, siren shrilling. Ellen wondered if any of their three handsome rescuers were aboard.

'Sorry, what was that, Jack?' she asked, not looking at him.

'Are you OK?' He didn't slur, exactly, but he sounded looser than he usually did, less halting and uncertain.

'Oh, I'm fine, really,' Ellen replied, surprised to learn that she meant it. She continued. 'I mean, I'm humiliated, obviously. And it feels icky to learn that I was exchanging, albeit very chaste, pretentious messages with a fourteen-year-old boy for months when I was seventeen.' She laughed, dismally. 'And that constituted the sum total of my teenage romances.' She sighed. 'But I'm fine, really. And I suppose it was nice of Ben to put me out of my misery.'

'Yeah,' Jack replied. 'He's not so bad, really.'

'No. Not at all.' Ellen elbowed Jack in the ribs. 'Plus, we'll need to get used to him now. He's going to be around the house all the time.'

Jack stared at her. 'Oh, yes,' he said, after a beat. 'Of course. With Alexa.'

Ellen thought about them all, reunited in Rokeby Close under one roof, Ben too. In time this would no longer seem weird, or even especially remarkable. Perhaps some mornings, while Alexa was showering, she and Ben would do a post-match analysis of whatever night out she'd returned from only a few hours previously. He'd be genuinely amused by her stories, now they could be friends (really) and could laugh (properly).

'I hope we do all have dinner together on Saturday,' Jack added, quietly.

'I'm certain that dream can be realized, Jack.'

They'd reached New Cross Gate station now. Ellen tapped her debit card on the reader and looked up at the board. Her Overground train was going in three minutes. Jack was still fumbling with his backpack, on the wrong side of the gates.

'Hey, Jack, I've got to go.'

He looked up.

'But look, I'll see you at the weekend. On Saturday. Home at last.'

He waved, still trying to get his debit card out of the front pocket of his bag.

Ellen did an awkward half-wave, realizing that she was a little drunker than she thought, and then ran up the stairs to the platforms. Just as she boarded her train, she saw Jack walk on to the other platform. He didn't see her, but she waved nonetheless.

31. Jack

Elias's bulk took up the whole doorstep of 49 Rokeby Close. He wore a shiny grey suit with brown shoes, and his long hair was slicked back behind his ears. His face was flushed, which might have been the heat, but might also have been because he was yelling. He seemed to have recovered since Alexa's dad's email.

'. . . and you're meant to TELL ME when you change the locks.' Elias paused here, to draw breath for his next explosion. 'And in fact, I don't understand why you've CHANGED THEM without my say-so, what was wrong with the existing locks? They were TOP-OF-THE-RANGE locks – and I'm supposed to be allowed to let myself into the property whenever I wish to –' Jack heard Alexa try to interrupt, but Elias did not notice. 'And so you have to provide me with one of the new keys, DO YOU HEAR ME? And from what I could see through the front-door window here it doesn't look like you've been hoovering the stairs AT ALL and you know that's in the tenancy agreement, I checked it myself this morning.'

Elias paused to gulp a breath again, and Jack noticed there was white spit in the corners of his mouth. He returned to staring very hard at his shoes, in case Elias made eye contact with him. Cynthia stood on the path, tapping at her smartphone with long, blue nails.

Alexa's voice sounded small and far away, although she was standing beside Jack. 'Sorry, yes, we'll make sure to hoover the stairs this afternoon –'

'It's just not good enough!' Elias was bellowing now, arms waving, spittle in the corner of his mouth. 'I go to all this trouble to make this house PERFECT for you, charge you barely ANYTHING, considering what it's worth, and this is how you repay me – by not hoovering the stairs. Those carpets are CUSTOM MADE and you've already ruined. Most. Of. Them.' With each word, he punched his left fist into his right palm.

In silence, they cowered. Jack could hear Cynthia's nails tapping on the phone screen, and felt Ellen shuffle from foot to foot.

'So that's ground rule number one,' Elias panted. 'Hoovering. Twice a week. And secondly, make sure you are doing. The. Grass. Every. SINGLE. WEEK. Because I'll find out if you don't.' He said this with delighted menace, and continued, 'And rule three is weekly house visits. I will visit this property EVERY WEEK to confirm that you are keeping it IN A FIT STATE and, to be honest, I don't trust you so I might do the odd surprise visit too –'

Here, Alexa made another sound as if to interrupt, but again thought better of it.

'And if anything happens with those pipes again, then it'll be YOU who pays, not me' – Elias looked at Alexa here – 'whatever your fancy lawyer says. I'll get my own and we'll take you to court for that.' He crossed his arms again. 'WELL? Understood?'

Jack and Ellen cowered.

Alexa managed a weak, 'Yes, Elias.'

He eyed them all beadily for a few moments. Then he cleared his throat and clapped both hands together again.

The noise made Jack jump.

'Right, Cynth?'

She did not look up.

'Let's go, shall we? We've got to be in West Norwood in twenty minutes.' Wordlessly and, indeed, without looking up from her phone, Cynthia walked down the path towards the street, still tapping at her phone with those long nails.

Elias stepped down from the doorstep and jabbed a finger right under Jack's nose.

Jack felt his heart pounding in his ears. He stared at the stubby, fleshy finger.

'I'm watching you lot,' Elias said. He waggled the finger once, for good measure, then strode off down the path after his wife.

In unison, the three of them watched as Cynthia climbed into the wrong seat – the driver's – which inspired a roar of frustration from Elias. Once she had moved – again, without saying a word or looking up from her phone screen – he swung himself into the car and slammed the door so loudly that Jack winced. He pulled out of his parking space at speed, narrowly avoiding a woman who was cycling down the road. Elias stuck a fist out of the window, then put his foot on the accelerator and tore off down the road.

'Jesus.' Ellen exhaled, loudly.

They all turned together to look at the front door. In spite of everything, Jack smiled at the familiar scene.

'Thank God he couldn't get in to see the damage the firemen did to the attic door,' Alexa said, with a shudder. 'We'll need to get that sorted too.'

'One thing at a time,' Ellen said, grimly. 'On which note' – Ellen put a finger in the air and then dived into the zip pocket of her cross-body bag, emerging with three silver keys – 'before I forget.' She passed one each to Alexa and Jack.

'Hero.' Alexa put hers straight on to a keyring.

'Yes, thank you.' Jack dropped his straight into his jeans pocket.

'I decided there was no point bringing up the security deposit.' Ellen shrugged. 'Leave that misery for another day.'

'I'll get my dad on it,' Alexa sighed. 'Most of those "ground rules" he was offering up were clearly illegal.'

'He won't really come round once a week, will he?' Jack glanced down the road, as if expecting Elias to reappear.

Ellen moaned.

Alexa smiled. 'He can't. He doesn't have a key.'

Ellen clamped a hand over her mouth, eyes wide.

Jack felt simultaneously terrified and dizzy with excitement, which wasn't a bad feeling.

'He doesn't have a key,' Ellen repeated, from behind her palms. 'Because we changed the locks.' She breathed out. 'We're geniuses.'

'So, I say we all agree not to let him in the first few times.' Alexa sounded pleased with herself. 'He'll soon get bored of weekly house inspections, anyway. And by that time, maybe I can get my dad to write another strongly worded email.'

'I love Marcus,' Ellen said, with feeling.

'He has his uses. Right.' Alexa jangled her keys. 'Shall we go inside?'

Jack swung his backpack on to his back. He couldn't wait to see his bedroom, which wasn't a sofa at Maisie's, and where he would not be woken by Trixie standing on his face.

Alexa was struggling a little with the stiff, unfamiliar key.

'You have to wiggle it a bit,' Ellen said, authoritatively.

Alexa stepped back. 'You do it.'

Ellen unlocked the door with a flourish and stepped into the hall. Everything looked the same, as though there had never been a flood in the first place, though it smelled a little funny, like shoe polish and air freshener.

Jack wrinkled his nose.

'Much better,' Alexa said, with feeling.

Ellen stepped over the post on the mat, and headed straight to her room.

Picking up the post, Alexa announced, 'Ben's coming over in twenty minutes. I think we're going to sit in the garden.'

'I'd be up for that,' Ellen called from her bedroom.

The door was open and Jack could see her lying on her bed, holding her phone with two hands above her head.

'Jack?' Alexa asked warmly, putting the post on the small table in the hall.

'Sounds good.' He tried not to seem too thrilled to have been included.

After he'd poured the contents of his bag on to his bedroom floor, Jack decided that was more than enough unpacking for the afternoon. He lay back on his bed for a while, relishing the presence of a real mattress, and feeling immensely comforted by the sounds of Rokeby Close: the odd creaking floorboard and ticking pipe, and Alexa and

Ellen's voices calling out to one another from the ground floor. He closed his eyes for a minute or so.

Eventually, the doorbell roused him from his stupor and he swung his legs round to sit on the edge of his bed. The door was opened, and Jack heard Ben's voice and the cheerful clinking sound of bottles. A little cautious, Jack tiptoed into the hall, and bumped into Ellen exiting the bathroom.

'Oh, hi, Jack.' Her hands were wet and she was wiping them on her jeans. 'Coming to the garden? Sounds like Ben's just arrived, and Lex said he was bringing loads of wanky beers from some shop in Peckham.'

Jack knew that shop: it would be Phil's. Johnny often went there with Annie to get craft beers and ales and talk to the owner – a man with a long beard and a pronounced paunch – about hops.

'Phil's!' Jack said.

'Probably.' Ellen sounded disinterested.

Jack followed her downstairs. From the kitchen he could hear Ben and Alexa chattering. He felt a little shy. Last time he'd seen Ben, he'd been rather drunk by the end. He hoped that he hadn't said or done anything embarrassing. 'Hi,' he said, standing in the door frame. He raised a palm and did a diffident wave.

Ben was putting bottles in the fridge, while Alexa perused the newspaper, arms stretched wide. Ellen had walked to the table to sift through the discarded supplements. The back door to the garden was open, and in the distance Jack could hear a lawnmower revving.

'Jack!' Ben offered a sort of mix between a high five and an arm wrestle, which Jack thought he'd just about pulled off. 'How you doing?'

'Good.' Jack was so reassured by Ben's reception that it took him a second to notice the kitchen was no longer ruined.

'Nice to be back, eh?'

'Definitely.' Still awed, Jack attempted to appear relaxed by crossing his arms.

'I was just saying we could do with some snacks.' Alexa was squinting at something on the page in front of her.

Jack saw his opportunity. 'I'll get them,' he offered. 'I'll pop to the shop at the end of the road.'

Ellen dropped the magazine she was holding. 'I'll come.' She patted her jeans pocket. 'Let me just get my card.' She sprang out of the kitchen in the direction of her bedroom.

Jack followed her towards the front door.

'Thanks, guys,' Alexa called out to their retreating backs. 'Just some crisps and things.'

Ellen appeared as Jack had finished lacing his trainers. She stepped out of the front door and he made a hasty pursuit. Ellen slammed the door behind them, and trotted down the path. Her phone was poking out of her back pocket.

'We should get something for the guy across the road.' Ellen pointed at the neighbour's house.

'Yeah, definitely.'

They walked to the shop in companionable silence. It was approximately a three-minute round-trip, although Jack and Ellen made it last longer by spending some time arguing over which specific flavour of Kettle Chips to bring home. Kettle Chips were what Flora would get on a Friday afternoon for the Green Genie drinks, so Jack knew they must be good. In the end, he picked sweet chilli and

Ellen salt and balsamic vinegar. Jack was taken aback when the cashier rang up the amount. It seemed that Kettle Chips were expensive.

'Oh, I'll get it,' Ellen said, moving to the card machine.

'Thanks. I'll pay you back.'

'It's just some crisps, Jack.'

They stepped back out into the sunshine of the May day.

Ellen took her sunglasses from her head and put them back on her eyes.

Jack squinted. Rokeby Close stretched out in front of them.

Ellen opened one of the bags of Kettle Chips and started eating. 'The sweet chilli ones are quite nice, actually,' she said, looking surprised. 'I stand corrected.'

'I have them at work,' Jack said, pleased.

'How's your new job?' Ellen popped another crisp into her mouth and Jack heard the crunch as her jaws closed.

'Oh, I don't start until June.' Bryan was making him train up the new recruit, who was called Niamh, and was Irish and very enthusiastic. 'But that's not long.'

'That's cool.'

'Yeah. I can't believe it.'

'Well, you are a viral star.'

He squirmed, but she smiled warmly.

They'd reached the door of 49 Rokeby Close now. Ellen handed Jack the open bag of crisps and pulled the key from her back pocket. There was a crunch as she unlocked it.

'Hi!' Ellen called out.

Jack followed her into the kitchen. He could see Ben and Alexa were curled up on a picnic blanket in the garden, Ben's arm snaked around Alexa's back, his other hand on her thigh. She was gazing at him. He watched Ellen sit down a respectful distance from them, and tear the bags of crisps in half. And then felt his phone buzz in his pocket: Johnny.

Hi mate

Fancy a beer?

Jack quickly tapped out a reply.

Maybe later!!

Hanging with my housemates at the moment!!

Shyly, not sure what to do with his hands, he joined the others outside.

Ben nudged a beer towards Jack with his foot and threw a bottle opener after it. Jack picked it out of the long grass, and popped the top in one fluent motion, managing to kick over the bottle. He looked up. No one had seemed to notice.

'What do you reckon Elias and Cynthia are off to do now?' Alexa asked, after they'd all taken a satisfied slurp.

'Rob some blind children?' Ellen tipped the bottle into her mouth again. She missed, and beer dribbled down her face, which she wiped with the back of her palm.

Dutifully, Ben laughed. He had shuffled down, and he and Alexa were lying on the picnic blanket now, his arm resting beneath her head.

Jack decided to try it too. He stretched out and stared into the sky. In the distance, a fire engine trilled. There was a contented pause, though he didn't feel very comfortable.

'So,' Ellen said, thickly, through a mouthful of crisps. 'Anyone for Risk?'

Ellen

Dating me is like
Taking part in The Hunger Games

My most controversial opinion is
Loving outdoor swimming is not
a personality

We're the same type of weird if
You also follow several hairless
cat accounts on Instagram

**The one thing you should know
about me is**
I work for an organic CBD tampon
company, and WILL talk about it

Worst idea I've ever had
Tbf it would be easier to list
the best ones

Ben

Believe it or not I
Lived in Berlin. I almost never
mention it

A random fact I love is
A baby puffin is called a 'puffling'!

**Fact about me that
surprises people**
I once won a 'cutest baby'
competition.
It's been downhill from there

I'm weirdly attracted to
Marge Simpson

Jack

One thing I'll never do again
A salsa dancing class

I recently discovered that
The Tube and the Underground
are the same thing

Let's debate this topic
Favourite vegetable. I like carrots

My biggest date fail
I turned up a day early

Alexa

All I ask is that you
Don't throw me a surprise
birthday party

My most irrational fear
That my father's cat is trying
to usurp me

The way to win me over is
Beat me at Scrabble

The key to my heart is
Never, ever using the crying
laughing emoji

Acknowledgements

Firstly, thank you to Hannah Weatherill, my agent, who read one of my mad *Evening Standard* columns and sent a lovely email enquiring as to whether I'd ever thought about writing a novel. Yes – but I definitely wouldn't have done it without you. Thank you for your wise notes, unwavering support and endless patience. (Oh, and for advising I fixed the ending before submission . . .)

Thank you also to Diane Banks and all the others at Northbank for all of your support. The pandemic owes us another lunch in Soho.

I struck gold with the team at Penguin Michael Joseph: I feel so lucky to have worked with such bright, brilliant and engaged women who love talking about books.

Firstly, my editor Rebecca Hilsdon, who has been a champion of *The Lock In* from the beginning. As soon as we met (on Zoom, natch) I knew I wanted to work with you. Thank you for polishing my rough cut, getting my (weird) jokes, and for all of your brilliant ideas, enthusiasm and kindness throughout. Thank you to Zana Chaka for your quiet insight and very hard work, and to Clare Bowron for being a brilliant and patient editor, not to mention for making sure I removed my approximately 14,000 uses of the word 'nodded' from the first few drafts. Thank you also to Shan Morley Jones and Emma Henderson, both of whom were kind and friendly voices at the end of an email, and demystified the (daunting!) process of copy-editing.

Sriya Varadharajan, brainstorming with you has been joyous and I hope by the time you read this we have actually met in person, and Lucy Hall, thank you for devising such a brilliant and fun marketing campaign.

As with almost everything in my entire life (apart from the two years before any of them were born), I relied on three people while writing *The Lock In*. Thank you to my brother, Toby, for all the Lockdown 1.0 walks during which you helped me to untangle all the inconsistencies in my plot, and to my sister Georgia for being my first, enthusiastic reader. Last in birth order but never least, Molly, you were a cheerleader at the end of the phone/WhatsApp group/Zoom call. Mum and Dad, thank you for buying me all those books and telling the whole family to buy this one.

Karen, Lucy and Emma (aka, The Heritage WAGs), thank you for your endless support (but, mainly, the lols). I so hope we get to work together again. (First, wine in Kaz's garden.)

I definitely also owe a debt to many housemates for inspiring several of the anecdotes in here, and – strictly speaking – a few landlords, but most of them still owe me part of a security deposit, so let's call it quits. A special declaration of love to Matt and Emma: the years we lived together were some of my favourites of our twenties, even if I did a really good impression of someone having A Personal Crisis a lot of the time. (Sorry I was so messy.)

And, lastly, thank you to Samuel – who makes everything shinier. I couldn't have done this last mad year without you.

To celebrate the publication of *The Lock In*, we've teamed up with Travelzoo to offer one person and their best friend a 2-night stay in a 4-star London hotel, with an afternoon tea!

TRAVELZOO®

To enter the draw go to
www.travelzoo.wyng.com/thelockin